SHUN THE HEAVEN

AN ANTEBELLUM MYSTERY

DAVE HOING &
ROGER HILEMAN

Black Rose Writing | Texas

ISBN: 978-1-68513-589-8
PUBLISHED BY BLACK ROSE WRITING
www.blackrosewriting.com

Printed in the United States of America
Suggested Retail Price (SRP) $22.95

Shun the Heaven is printed in Minion Pro

PRAISE FOR
DAVE HOING &
ROGER HILEMAN

Hammon Falls

"*Hammon Falls* takes its readers on a journey through multiple settings, points of view, and time periods, with every scene, every emotion, and every action described in beautiful prose that sparkles but is never overwrought."
–**Melissa Studdard, author of *Six Weeks to Yehida***

"There is something really beautiful about combining true-to-life stories with an openly-imaginative storyteller in order to pull out the delicate patterns of family and locale history. Hammon Falls is a great piece of work that has endeared me … to an entire genre that I don't often read: historical fiction."
–**Jen Knox, author of *We Arrive Uninvited, After the Gazebo,* and *The Glass City and Other Stories***

A Killing Snow

"The authors take the reader back 130 years, there to see characters facing a set of circumstances and challenges radically different from those of our digital age. As a reader of biographies, histories, and many sorts of novels, I found quite a bit to enjoy in *A Killing Snow.*"
–**William Tate, author of *Dark Strides***

"Hoing and Hileman do a great job of defining and elaborating the context of the times: a couple of decades after the Civil War, the height of immigration, the beginnings of modern technology (the post office gets a telephone but it is useless for the time being because no one else has one.) A wonderful and enjoyable read."
–**Karen Nortman, author of *The Time Travel Trailer***

In the Blood

This is a thoroughly researched, nuanced, well-written novel, packed full of meaning and metaphor and themes that could occupy a classroom of students for hours.

–Carol Kean, author of *Ironwolf* and reviewer for *Perihelion*

"*In the Blood* is a tour de force that cries out to be translated into a feature film ... I unreservedly recommend it as compelling period reading that explores a society of the not too distant past but seems so alien to many of us living today..."

–Donald Schnieder, Midwest Book Review

SONNET 129

The expense of spirit in a waste of shame
Is lust in action; and till action, lust
Is perjured, murderous, bloody, full of blame,
Savage, extreme, rude, cruel, not to trust,
Enjoy'd no sooner but despised straight,
Past reason hunted, and no sooner had
Past reason hated, as a swallow'd bait
On purpose laid to make the taker mad;
Mad in pursuit and in possession so;
Had, having, and in quest to have, extreme;
A bliss in proof, and proved, a very woe;
Before, a joy proposed; behind, a dream.
All this the world well knows; yet none knows well
To shun the heaven that leads men to this hell.

—William Shakespeare

SHUN THE HEAVEN

AN IMMODEST PROPOSAL, DECEMBER 1845

CHAPTER 1: MILES
"A charm of powerful trouble"

Undertaker Miles Kelley opened the door to his visitor. Before entering, the woman stamped snow from her boots. She wore a bonnet but no scarf.

"Mrs. Hinman?" he said.

"In the flesh, Mr. Kelley." She appeared to be about thirty-five, with a lovely face reddened by cold. Her kid gloves were stiff as she clasped his fingers in a delicate handshake.

"I was taken aback by your letter," Miles said, adding quickly, "Not offended, mind you, but, well, your request *was* rather unconventional. Families usually wait until afterwards to come to me."

"One never knows what the future holds, Mr. Kelley."

"Except, of course, in my profession."

"Of course. As Mr. Shakespeare said, 'The readiness is all.'"

"Please, be seated. I'll just add more wood to the stove."

It was only early December, yet already Arctic winds plagued Detroit. The upcoming winter was going to be a harsh one. He should have stoked the fire properly before her arrival, but he'd been uncertain of the exact timing of her visit, and the price of kindling soared this time of year.

"May I offer you tea?" he said once the wood had ignited.

"Yes, thank you, tea would be lovely," Mrs. Hinman said. She was bundled in an expensive leather overcoat made bulky by a thick astrakhan lining. "Your sign says Kelley and Sons. How many boys do you have?"

"I am one of the sons, madam," Miles said. He didn't care to engage in small talk, but recognized it as a necessary evil. "My father and brother relocated to Alabama some years past. On days like this I wish I'd gone with them. As many folks die in Tuscaloosa as Detroit, but the weather is more agreeable and the ground isn't frozen five months out of twelve. Digging graves is near impossible in earth hard as stone, and half again as expensive." He warmed his hands over the teapot before pouring them each a cup. "I apologize for your discomfort."

"Weather is God's work, Mr. Kelley."

"But buildings are man's, and this one provides little resistance to the cold, I'm afraid."

Miles sat down and slid a cup toward her. He rarely extended credit, and certainly had never done so for a woman. He'd been wrestling with misgivings about the arrangement since receiving her letter, yet he was impressed by the sheer audacity of the request. The woman spoke well and appeared to be cultured. People of culture tended to come from money, which didn't hurt her cause. "Do I understand you mean to pay one quarter now and the balance after services are rendered?" She nodded. He paused to consider the proper wording to his next question. "Forgive my indelicacy, but do you have an indication when the event will occur?"

She sipped her tea, once, twice, three times. "My compliments. This is excellent."

The shrieking wind rattled the door in its frame. Miles shivered. "Thank you, Mrs. Hinman, but…?"

"Please, call me Joanna." She smiled. "We should like a mahogany coffin."

"That does not come cheaply."

"Cost is not a concern."

She definitely had money, then. Miles suppressed a smile. "Size?"

"Made to fit an adult."

"Not a child, then. Good." Miles removed a quill, ink bottle, and his account book from the top desk drawer. The ink was nearly frozen. Leaving the stopper on it, he held the bottle above his teacup to heat its contents. The woman seemed to find that amusing, or perhaps resourceful. "And the trimmings?"

"Red velvet cushions," she said.

"You're sparing no expense."

"It does happen but once in a lifetime, after all."

"True, of course," Miles said. "Church plot or cemetery?"

"Russell Street Cemetery, please."

"Catholic or Protestant side?"

She glared at him as if he had just spoken blasphemy. "Protestant."

"You have your own minister, then?"

"*Mon dieu*, sir, we are not savages. The Reverend George Smith will perform the ceremony. He's Presbyterian."

Miles disliked the French language, mostly because he detested Canadians. Windsor was distressingly close to Detroit. "Do you reside across the border?" he said.

"Oh, no, Mr. Kelley. This is merely a consequence of educating females. Sometimes we find ourselves speaking French for no reason whatever."

And then she winked at him.

Miles looked away, straightened his ascot and coughed into his hand. "The cemetery charges five dollars for a half plot, ten for a full one. In addition, there's a small surcharge for our commission."

She shrugged. "Full."

"We can offer the finest marble monuments—"

"Yes, but it mustn't be too gaudy. Something pretty, yet tasteful. A small angel, perhaps, with name, dates, and some term of endearment."

"And whose name will we be etching on this angel?"

"Claire Hinman, date of birth November 3, 1818."

"So young. Pity. A sister?"

"In-law."

"I see." Miles tested the ink. Finding it had liquefied, he added a column of figures and showed them to her.

"Yes, that is satisfactory," she said.

"You are aware," Miles said, knowing what he was about to tell her should have invalidated her proposal before it began, "that under Michigan law a woman may not enter into a legal contract without her husband's consent."

Mrs. Hinman smiled and withdrew a bank draft from her coat. "You will note the name on the draft. You may rest easy, Mr. Kelley. No law has been violated. And now your contract?"

Miles gave her his quill. She scratched imaginary calculations in the air, then wrote a number above a masculine signature, already present on the paper. "One quarter of the sum," she said.

"Why does he not come in person?"

"He is engaged in other matters. I'm afraid he couldn't get away. He hopes you will find me an acceptable substitute."

Miles retrieved the form. Since he rarely operated on credit, he'd never bothered to have contracts printed. He had written this one out by hand after receiving her letter, unsure until now that he could or would agree to the arrangement. "The balance must be satisfied within two weeks of the funeral. Is that understood?"

"Perfectly," the woman said. "You may write in the date when the time comes, or deposit it immediately, if that suits you better."

She scribbled a man's name on the bottom of the contract, the same name that appeared on the draft, and added her signature as well. Then she returned his quill with the draft and the contract.

When she stood up, Miles also rose in deference to her sex. "Thank you, Mrs. Hinman."

"Joanna."

"Joanna. This looks to be in order," he said, examining the draft. "You are confident the remainder will be paid after our fulfillment of the contract? In other words, to be blunt, how may I be assured someone will return?"

Again the woman smiled, a dazzling sight. "Sir," she said, "if no one returns, then my dear sister-in-law will have made a miraculous recovery, and there will be no funeral and thus no contract to fulfill. I will have paid you for the pleasure of these few minutes of your company."

"Our business is concluded, then?" he said.

"It is," she said. "*Bonjour, Monsieur* Kelley."

"Good morning to you, Joanna."

"Indeed it has been, sir." She crossed the room, opened the door, and stepped out into a windy, frigid day.

PROLOGUE
1818-1846

CHAPTER 2: NOAH, 1818
"One foot in sea and one on shore"

Noah Blackbourne loaded the day's last wagon with the charred remnants of the Boston Exchange Coffee House. The Exchange had gone up in flames a week ago, on November 3. His daughter Claire had been born that same night. He'd spent much of the time since either at the docks or here, helping to cart away the ruins of the building's collapse. For most of the men who came every day, it was dirty, backbreaking work. For Noah, it was no different than hoisting barrels of blubber. Wood cinders and blackened stone, or barrels of whale fat, tea and whisky, everything was just a matter of chains and pulleys, balance and sweat.

His wife Jane didn't know he'd offered his services at the coffeehouse. Although he still spent his days at the harbor unloading ships, when there was a lull in arrivals he went into the city for the extra work. Dock work provided him enough income to support Jane and Claire, but the Exchange cleanup provided an excuse to avoid returning home any earlier than necessary.

Claire was dear to him, but Jane was frightening in her volatility. She could burst with amusement, like the wild woman who'd danced with him that first night and stolen his heart. But she was also susceptible to fits of rage, during which she was apt to throw a plate of food at his head. He was never certain which woman he would get, one or the other, and often both, with little warning between changes.

The sun had set for the day. Light rain, mixed with a few snowflakes, slickened the cobblestones. A cold north wind flowed over the sweat of his labors, deepening his chill. He walked to the harbor to one of the many mariners' taverns occupying that part of Boston. There he could swap gossip with sailors and recollect the old days—which, only a few months' past, weren't all that old.

Noah paused outside the *Scythe of Kronos*, a place fancier in name than in reality. It was the same as any other alehouse, dark and rundown, damp even when the nights were dry, except that it was at the *Scythe* where he'd met Jane. Fresh off the *Susannah's* successful whaling venture, he'd been in high spirits. Too much coin in his purse and grog in his gut loosened his usual reticence with women.

His dalliance with her had left her pregnant, and followed by a marriage proposal. One time. He was with her one time. Lean, with dark eyes and a handsome visage, he'd gotten amorous proposals in dozens of harbors, but an unimpressive prick made him too bashful to follow through. While he was a man of the sea, he was still a bumbling boy of the land.

Jane had changed that, in spectacular fashion, although he'd had no one else to compare her with. Being a serving wench, she likely had had many lovers. If he failed to measure up, she'd been too polite to say it.

Noah had been proud to have finally moistened his oar, as the lads called it, but thought nothing further of the milestone after he sailed out of port a week later. Returning in September from a short voyage to the West Indies, however, it had been his misfortune to find Jane great-bellied and in need of a husband.

Throughout his youth, his father had beaten morality into him. One of the many lessons he learned was that if a man impregnated a woman, he must marry her if he wished to avoid the torments of Hell.

And so he'd done right by Jane in the eyes of God and his father—who, in Noah's mind, were one and the same.

His mates aboard the *Susannah* had called him daft. Abandon the sea for *this* woman? They regularly took advantage of any female who offered herself to them—and some who did not—leaving bastards in their wake all along the eastern seaboard. Not one of them had ever evinced concern about the wellbeing of mother or child, and some even boasted of their conquests.

If they do not wish to be stung by eels, they'd laugh, *they should not go where eels congregate.*

Noah was not so cavalier. He was, for good or bad, the man his father made him.

***

He bypassed the *Scythe of Kronos* and chose the *Sea Dog Inn*, where he found a group of sailors from the whaleship *Titus* occupying three tables toward the front. The *Titus* had docked yesterday morning. Noah had helped them unload their cargo, and had learned a few names. Of those he remembered, the only one in the *Sea Dog* tonight was a lanky fellow named William Short. Everyone called him Short Bill as a joke, since he was actually quite tall. Since Bill was the only face he recognized, he asked him if he could join them.

"Buy a round and it can be arranged," one of the men said before Bill could answer. A serving wench sat on his knee.

Noah counted seventeen sailors and two women, many more drinks than he could afford, even for a single round. "Do any of you have a deck of cards?" he said.

"Are we not sailors?" the man said. "What do you propose?"

"A game. You choose a card, and without seeing it, I'll be able to reveal which it is. If I succeed, you allow me to join you without funding your drunkenness."

"If you fail?"

"I'll go away, with no one the worse for it."

"We've all seen the trick," the same man said. "Nothing is at stake. If you succeed, we gain your company, the desirability of which has not been established. If you fail, we gain nothing but your absence, which we already had until now. I make a counter-proposal. If you correctly pick the card, you may join us. We'll keep you in drink all night, and these ladies will dance with you."

"If I do not?"

"Then some of the lads will make sport of you."

"By that you mean?"

"You know what I mean. Navigate the windward passage, lad. Are you agreeable?"

"I am not. I've no need of that kind of sport."

"Then you have not spent endless months at sea, with nary a woman for a thousand leagues."

"Your assumption insults me," Noah said. "I was three years aboard the *Susannah*. I never resorted to such an abomination, nor saw it done. In any event, you do not need a man for sport. There are women here."

The wench on the man's lap smiled wickedly and nuzzled his cheek.

"Now, Evans," Bill said, holding his hands in a placating gesture, "he has done us no harm."

Evans ignored Bill and continued to address Noah. "And yet here you are, a pier monkey, unloading ships you dare not sail. Lost your legs, eh? Go away, boy."

Some of the other men nodded their assent.

"Perhaps it is for the best. I do not care to associate with sodomites."

It was a stupid thing to say. He was outnumbered seventeen to one. Bill remained seated, but the other sixteen jumped to their feet, Evans and one other pushing the women from their laps. They surrounded Noah. Aware this wouldn't end well for him, he nevertheless wasn't averse to a good free-for-all on occasion. His father had certainly taught him how to weather a blow.

He took the first swing, relocating Evans's nose a couple of inches to port, but thereafter his senses became a blur. Sailors from the *Titus* weren't the only ones in the tavern. The others had no stake in this conflict, but they willingly joined in, and a brawl erupted. Chairs flew, tables broke, spatters of blood and spittle rose like mists and settled down to speckle combatants, floorboards, and furniture alike in red and foam.

In an instant, Noah was no longer the focus of the melee, as it became each man for himself. Even the women took turns jumping on men's backs, pulling their hair, gouging their eyes, and inserting fingers into their nostrils, trying to jerk their heads this way or that.

It was a time-honored way to release frustrations. In the morning everyone would be friends again. This night, though, Noah was in misery. He had no idea how many of his punches had connected, but he got many more than he gave. Although he was staggered, it wasn't fisticuffs that brought him down. A small man hurled by a larger one crashed into his left knee, wrenching it into an unnatural position. As the joint collapsed sideways, he felt the sinews within pop and tear. He fell writhing to the floor, out of the game. If the knee injury wasn't enough, he was stepped on, kicked, and landed upon for several agonizing minutes until the sailors' energy waned and the fight fizzled to a close.

When it was over, the barkeep used two flintlocks to encourage the sailors' departure. Those that couldn't walk were dragged. Nearly senseless from head blows, Noah felt someone grasp his arms and pull him toward the door. His left knee bumped against the floor, each little jolt igniting like gunpowder in his bones.

"For the love of God," he croaked, "stop."

Bill helped him to his feet. "Are you all right? Can you walk?"

Noah tried putting weight on the leg, but was the pain was debilitating. This must be how whales felt when harpoons pierced them repeatedly, or perhaps a deer gutted before it was dead. "I cannot," he gasped.

Bill half carried him to one of the few chairs in the tavern that remained upright. Sitting was no better, for the joint would not bend.

"It's already swelling," Bill said. "The kneecap is dislodged. Our ship's surgeon is at hand somewhere."

"No," Noah panted. His stomach lurched when he saw the lump of bone on the side of his knee, and he vomited. The ramifications were obvious: He wouldn't be able to work for weeks or months, denying him a source of income. "You do it. Now."

The barkeep was still busy emptying the tavern of sailors. He had no pity for Noah. Only a few men remained. The surgeon was probably already on the street.

"I lack the necessary tools," Bill said. "It will only take a moment for me to find the doctor."

"Do it. *Please.*"

Bill picked up a sturdy wooden mug from the floor. "I am not qualified," he said, but before Noah could respond, he slammed the mug against the lump, forcing the bone back into place atop the knee joint with such searing pain that Noah nearly fainted.

"Am I whole?" he said when he regained the strength to speak.

Bill touched the kneecap. "It is in the proper position, but I fear it may be broken. Where do you live?"

"North of the city, on the coast."

"Have you a way home?"

"My feet."

Bill shook his head. "Not tonight, mate. You may share my room at the *Wayfarers.*"

"You needn't go to the trouble. Just find me a horse to rent."

"It's no trouble. The livery stables are closed until morning."

"This is not a ruse to seek 'sport?'"

"I am not Evans," Bill said.

CHAPTER 3: JANE, 1819
"There is no evil angel but love"

The following April, five months after Noah's injury, an unusually fierce late season nor'easter had chased a large number of ships into the Boston harbor. Sailors were thick as mosquitoes in alehouses all along the waterfront, which was good for Jane. With Noah incapacitated, and against his vigorous objections, she had returned to the *Scythe of Kronos*. They needed the money, and she lacked the skills for anything else. The tavern was all she knew.

It hadn't been an easy decision. The rewards of motherhood were many, but the needs of her offspring went beyond nursing and nurturing. Since Noah could do nothing else, he would have to care for Claire while she was away. The insult to his manliness was unfortunate but unavoidable. Mrs. Carmody, their neighbor and frequent nursemaid, was always nearby if he encountered difficulties.

Although Jane never admitted it out loud, the prospect of being housebound with her husband and child for long months had terrified her. She welcomed the nightly escape. She'd missed the dancing, the lewd suggestions, even the occasional grope. Sailors were bawdy, dirty, and foulmouthed creatures who stank of fish, but by God they were *alive*, and they were fun. She could depend on hours of laughter and tall tales, arguments and physical confrontations, and, not least, men willing to lay down good money for the pleasure of her companionship.

The Scythe had not changed since she'd left employment there to accept Noah's marriage proposal. The barkeep, Frederickson, was a red- and gray-haired fellow twenty years Jane's senior, although his face was still pocked with the scars of adolescent skin eruptions. Not many people liked him, but Jane did, after a fashion. He allowed her to return to work, didn't ask about her personal affairs, and paid wages in a timely manner so long as she performed her duties.

The storm clawed at the walls and ceiling rafters of the tavern. The sound was loud enough to compete with the din of drunken lime suckers. Jane stood at the door and watched the heavens rage. It was majestic, not unlike the night she met Noah, although that was wind and snow, with no thunder. But how they had danced, how they had danced!

Jane heard her name being called. She looked up to see Frederickson motioning to her. When she responded, he pointed to a middle-aged man who had a table all to himself in the back.

"What of him?" Jane said.

"He's been there all night."

"He looks lonely."

"I don't care if he cries himself to sleep every night. He's ordered but a single mug of ale since he arrived. No one seems inclined to join him, so he's occupying an entire table that could be filled with paying customers."

"What do you expect me to do about him?"

"Engage him, either with drink or favor, but see to it he parts with his money, or departs the premises."

"You cannot expel him into this storm."

Frederickson glared down his spectacles at her. "Define 'cannot.'"

"*Would* not?"

"Would. Go."

She went, wending through clouds of pipe smoke, through dancing sailors and serving girls, past card games, dice games, and drinking games. When she arrived at the man's table, he scarcely noticed her. He sat staring at his hands, which he had folded in his lap as if in prayer.

When she didn't go away, though, he said, "I'm not looking for a whore."

Jane felt her blood rising, as her blood often did, and she was tempted to rake her nails across his face. But she withheld her comments and the blow. Before her marriage "whore" was not entirely inaccurate. "That is fortunate," she said, "for you have not found one."

"What do you want?"

"What do *you* want? Another drink? A dance?"

He finally looked up. His was the face of a common laborer, careworn, dark and weathered. Beneath his shirt she could see he was heavily muscled. His hands were thick with calluses, his nails chipped. A blacksmith, perhaps. "To be left alone," he said.

"I fear I cannot do that, sir. My employer insists that I pry more coins from you."

The man nodded. "At least you're honest about it. I would rather stay."

"Then may I bring you another mug?"

"I'm not thirsty. Tell your employer I will pay him a half dollar an hour for every empty chair at this table, and a dollar for the one I occupy."

"You're offering to *lease* this space? He may have a room upstairs for less than that."

An argument broke out between several sailors at the next table. It escalated to insults and threats but no punches were thrown.

The man glanced at them and sighed. "I'll not be here all night." He removed several paper bills from a pouch inside his shirt. "Will ten dollars buy me solitude?"

Jane eyed the bills. Banks were printing too much paper money these days, and the country was in trouble because of it. "Frederickson does not accept paper," she said. "Coin only."

"Might as well use this shit as kindling," the man said. "No one will take it."

He was so alone, so despondent…. Furious with him only moments ago, Jane now felt pity. "What's your name?" she said.

He fished out a few coins and didn't answer. Without counting, he said, "These are the last of them. There are at least ten dollars here."

Jane scooped the coins into her apron, then took a chance and sat in the chair next to his. She had the urge to embrace him, to vanquish whatever demons were burdening his soul. "Frederickson said I may engage you with drink or favor. If not drink, would you favor conversation?"

"Of what use are words?" he said, but then shook his head as if ashamed. "Forgive me. My melancholy inspires a sympathy I neither want nor deserve."

Jane placed her hand on his shoulder. "Your name?" she asked again.

"Horace," he said. "Horace Hinman."

"Are you married?"

"My Lizbeth is dead."

Jane had never known the proper words for another person's grief, so she didn't try. "How long has she been gone?"

"Three years."

"Why do you mourn tonight? Is this the anniversary of her passing?"

"Every night is the anniversary of her passing. They're all the same."

"Have I seen you in the *Scythe* before?"

"I'm newly returned to Boston."

"From where?"

Horace waved his hand in the air as if to indicate everywhere.

"Have you any children?" Jane said.

"A son. Carl. Her life for his."

"The birthing fever?"

Horace nodded.

"I've a daughter," Jane said. "That sickness almost claimed me, as well."

"I'll have that drink now," he said glumly, "to toast your good fortune."

"It is not fair, is it, that one mother should live while another does not? And yet I cannot be ungrateful, for I am that one."

"The fever took me as surely as it did Lizbeth. You are gazing upon a dead man."

Jane clasped his hand in hers. "But what of your son? Do you not see your wife's likeness in his face?"

Horace lifted his eyes to hers, and they were cold as the nor'easter howling outside. "Every day, more's the pity. Would that he were never born. It is not the *likeness* of her that I desire."

CHAPTER 4: NOAH, 1820
"And oftentimes, to win us to our harm"

It had been nearly a year before Noah could return to the docks. Lack of exertion had caused him to grow stout around the middle. Nothing alarming, but he was no longer the spare youth he'd been before his injury. Even the long days of demanding physical labor since had not melted away the extra pounds. If anything, he continued to gain, but then he came by it honestly. His father had been a large man.

In the early mornings before work or late afternoons afterward, he had taken to strolling the rise above the beach two hundred yards outside their door. Jane seldom accompanied him, as she did not care for the sea, but he brought Claire when the weather was fair. Mrs. Carmody claimed fresh air and sun was good for the toddler.

On this spring morning Noah sat on one of the many flat rocks that jutted through the grass on the bluff, his little girl on his lap. She was walking now, so he kept hold of her to prevent her from wandering off into trouble.

He watched the swells of the Atlantic, the sun wavering above its surface. The day would be hot but for a sea breeze that brought with it the salty tang he so loved. Gulls floated in graceful circles above the water, bickering with their ungraceful squawks. The sails of distant ships sometimes appeared just above the horizon, parallel to shore, bound for other ports. He imagined—remembered—the excitement of whale blow as the beasts broke the surface.

Noah combed through Claire's fine black hair with his fingers, which made her giggle. She had a sweet disposition. Her laugh was the happiest sound in the world.

How could he not be in awe of this tiny miracle? He reveled in her, in the realization that at this moment he alone was responsible for her life and well-being. A father with his daughter: a wonderful thing, almost holy.

He gazed at her tenderly.

Then, because he could not *not* look, he again lifted his eyes to the slow rolling of the waves.

Noah, they whispered to him.

Noah.

Come.

Claire, he thought, loving her without restraint—loving her, and knowing that someday the call of the sea would overcome his resolve, and he would have to leave her.

***

Later that day at the docks he joined in the bustle of sailors and merchants, inhaling the brine, the sweat, and the stink of blubber, delighting in the spray that swept in on the easterly breeze. As always, his knee ailed him—he feared it would never fully heal—but it was functional so long as he was selective in his activities. Sometimes it buckled, sometimes it locked in place, but the rest was just pain, and pain could be tolerated.

He had sworn off taverns after Jane's return to the *Scythe of Kronos*. In all of them drunken men pinched and groped the serving wenches, a nightly reminder of what was being done to Jane. He couldn't bear the thought of that—and worse, knowing she enjoyed it. Instead, he frequented coffeehouses, where quasi-philosophical discussions were preferred to carousing.

Eventually Noah would have to dislodge his wife from the *Scythe*, since she'd no excuse to remain there once he could support them again. But making the woman see reason would be no easy task, and he hadn't the heart for that fight yet.

This night he bypassed the coffeehouses after he'd finished his labors. It was on this walk that he felt the most acute distress, a disquiet having nothing to do with his knee or Jane. The journey wasn't far, perhaps an hour, but every minute leaving the harbor was a minute farther from the ships. Yes, they lived next to the sea. He could see and hear it from their house. He could visit the beaches. He could wade and he could swim. Yet it was one thing to be *in* the Atlantic, bound to the shallows, and another to be *on* it. For that he needed a boat, and boats did not come to his house. They sailed in to the Boston harbor without him, and they sailed out of the harbor without him.

But they would not do so forever.

In the meantime, he had Claire, with whom he was well pleased, and Jane, for whom his feelings ebbed and flowed according to her mood.

Mrs. Carmody emerged from the house as Noah approached.

"Is all well?" he said.

"Yes," she said in her thick Scottish brogue. "The wee one is bringing forth more teeth. She fussed a bit, so I came by to rub laudanum on her gums."

Mrs. Carmody and her husband Erasmus had no children of their own, a fact Noah found curious, considering her profession as nursemaid and sometimes midwife. But then, didn't Catholic priests preach the evils of copulation, without ever having experienced the act they railed against?

"Thank you, that was considerate," he said.

"Be warned, young sir, your wife has a temper upon her."

Noah sighed. The sun was just now dipping below the landward horizon. Too late to return to the city. "What vexes her?"

"She is a young woman in an old woman's life."

"What would she have me do, foster the child and annul our union?" With the call of the sea in his ears, the idea was not without its appeal.

Mrs. Carmody touched his arm. "Kindness, young sir. Treat her with kindness. In you and Claire she has the best she can hope for in this world, but what gain has ever come without cost?"

A seagull winged by overhead. "I am well aware of costs, madam. I am twenty and she twenty-two. I too have given much to be here, at this time, with a wife and daughter, the sea within sight but not within reach. Neither of us may indulge our yearnings."

"Indeed. I wed several years before I was her age. I am happy enough with my husband, but there are nights even I lament the passing of my youth."

Noah nodded, although he did not lament his youth, wherein resided only bitterness and pain: his mother's early death, his father's frequent beatings. He'd willingly left it behind when he first set foot upon the gangplank to the *Susannah* at age fifteen. "Thank you again, Mrs. Carmody. You need not remain tonight. God grant you a pleasant evening. I fear mine will not be."

As she scuttled down the path, Noah went inside to find Claire asleep in her crib. Jane was staring out the window.

He embraced her from behind, one arm above her breasts, the other beneath. "What is of interest out there?" he said, resting his chin on her shoulder.

"Nothing," she said.

"Mrs. Carmody tells me you're troubled."

She unfurled his arms from around her and turned to face him. "I want to go to Ohio."

"Ohio? Where did that notion come from?"

"I haven't seen Alice since before Claire was born."

"Your sister would not come for the birth, so why should you go to her now?"

"She is a woman without a husband. She could not bear the expense."

Noah recognized the look in her eyes. She was gathering herself for an argument. He moved out of arm's reach, should her ire escalate to blows. "And how will we?"

"I knew you would say that. I've been saving my wages from the *Scythe*."

Noah sat on the bed. "Enough to pay for our transportation and food, and compensate for lost wages? I must work now that I'm able. We can't simply scurry off to Ohio for a visit. And then there's the child to consider. She's too young for such a journey. Ohio is a great distance, most of it over untamed lands."

Jane's face reddened and her eyes smoldered, a sight as frightening as a gathering gale at sea. "I didn't say *we*, and I didn't say *visit*."

"No." Noah rose from the bed. "That will not do. You would leave me after all I've sacrificed for you?"

"This doesn't concern you."

"Absconding with my child to Ohio doesn't concern me? Absolutely not. I forbid it."

"I'm not asking your permission."

"I am your husband."

"For the moment."

"No! You'll not risk my daughter's life for such a foolish venture."

Jane rushed at him, her fingers curled like talons.

He had endured his father's beatings without resistance because he was too small to fight back. He was a grown man now. Although he would never raise his hand against Jane, he wouldn't allow himself to be pummeled by her, either. He lunged at her, met her in the middle, and took her to the floor. He sat on her chest, pinning her arms to her side.

"I'll bite your bollocks off," she hissed.

Her voice startled Claire out of her slumber, and the little girl wailed.

"Now look what you've done," Noah said.

"You have done it. You are vile. I loathe you."

She didn't loathe him. He knew that. But despite her twenty-two years, when she was angry she reverted to pubescence, an age at which "I hate you" was the most powerful insult.

"If I let you up, will you promise not to strike me?"

"I promise you nothing but hell and damnation."

Noah sighed. "That," he said, "is not yours to decide."

He rose and helped her to her feet. She promptly boxed his ear. "Claire and I are going to Ohio. I'll brook no debate."

"Jane, even if you disregard my feelings, you will not take our daughter to Ohio alone."

"We won't be alone," Jane said. "I've met a man."

He should have anticipated this, but he hadn't. The sudden hollowness in his heart and stomach were worse than any physical blow she could have struck him. He'd always felt inadequate, unable to compete with the prowess of other men she'd been with in her life. After a long pause, he gathered himself and said, "I daresay you've met many men. Another who groped you in the *Scythe*, I assume?"

"He did no such thing."

Noah asked the question he already knew the answer to. "Have you bedded him?"

Jane was aware of his insecurity. "It has nothing to do with that," she said. "I have never been displeased with you in that regard."

"Then what?"

"You are a sailor. You *will* return to the sea. You know it and I know it. I'm simply leaving first to spare myself the pain of abandonment."

Struggling to maintain his calm, Noah said, "By giving my child to another man?"

"She is an inconvenience to you."

"I adore her."

Jane nodded. She picked up Claire and cuddled her. The girl immediately settled down. "I know. But we cannot go to sea with you. My mind is set. In the end you will be happier with harpoons, whale blubber, and your mates."

She was right, of course.

Noah, the waves whispered.

Noah, they said.

Noah, they shrieked.

Come.

"What is the bastard's name?" Noah said.

"Does it matter?"

"It does if he's to be father to my daughter."

"Horace Hinman."

Fury building, Noah didn't trust himself not to strike her. Instead, he plopped down at the table, put his head in his hands, and wept. Horace Hinman. He would not forget that name.

Jane, reverting to her gentle state, handed Claire to him. "*You* are her father. You always will be, for I will remember you to her with kindness. She will know of you. When she's old enough, she'll learn her letters. I'll see to it she writes to you."

"I don't know what to do," Noah said, but he did.

Noah.

Noah.

Noah.

Come.

CHAPTER 5: JANE, 1832
"As black as hell, as dark as night"

It was the summer of 1832, Horace was four years dead, the victim of a bad heart, and Noah had returned to the sea, so far as Jane knew. She hadn't seen him since Claire was a toddler. She writhed in bed in her own sweat and stink, her legs cramping, her bowels leaking watery, foul-smelling waste. She'd become so weak she needed her sister Alice's assistance to reach the shit pot. Unable to keep food or drink down, she was mystified how she could still have anything left inside her to expel.

The cholera ravaging the country was ravaging her. It was clear her time was at hand, if not today, tomorrow or the next day. Her family gathered round: Alice; Carl, Horace's son with Lizbeth; Claire; and Joanna and Meggie, her girls with Horace. Carl was seventeen, old enough to comprehend what was happening. Claire, too. She'd be fourteen in November. But Joanna at seven and Meggie at six were too young to grasp the death of a person. They'd seen Horace slaughter pigs and cattle, but those animals were always replaced by others that looked just like them. No human was ever born into the world twice. When their mother left them, she wouldn't be coming back.

While Alice fretted and placed wet rags on her forehead, the older children brooded, helpless to do anything. The younger girls just appeared bewildered.

"Mama," Meggie said, "your eyes are black."

"Mama," Joanna said, "why do you not get better? You have grown old."

Jane was not old. She was thirty-four. She refused to look in the mirror after Alice or one of the girls brushed her hair. But she could not avoid seeing her hands. Her skin was the color of rotting fruit, slick with perspiration. Her body was on fire, not from fever but from the exertion of trying to live.

And this only a few days after the onset of symptoms.

Never a large woman, she now felt desiccated as a long-dead mouse, without substance, as if the slightest breeze could carry her away.

Whenever she opened her mouth, her cheeks sagged onto her teeth. She resisted, to no avail, Alice's efforts to coax broth down her throat.

"You must have fluids, my dear," her sister said.

"I will only vomit it back up," she croaked. The effort to speak exhausted her. "Let me be."

Unbeknownst to Noah, she and Claire had returned to Boston shortly after the Ohio visit, moving into Horace's home with his five-year-old son Carl. Daughters Joanna and Meggie were born in '25 and '26, respectively. Alice joined them after Horace's death.

Jane loved Boston, but even in a different house she was still within the smells of the Atlantic, which she did not love. The devil take the sea, she thought, and the devil laughed.

I'm coming for you.

She looked past Alice to Claire, her pretty face somber with a grief she was trying to hide. Jane had followed through on her promise to Noah that Claire would learn to read and write. The girl had taken to schooling eagerly. Jane had done many things to make that possible, not all of which had met with her sister's approval. Alice's objections be damned. Jane was proud of Claire's intelligence. Here, at the end, she could tell herself at least she'd done that much right.

But to what avail was that education now? What was to become of Claire, to all of her darlings? Carl could take care of himself, but her girls, her beautiful girls….

Jane coughed, heard the death rattle in her lungs.

She sensed the breeze rising. It was to be today, perhaps this very hour. She flailed her hand, reaching for Claire. The girl's fingers trembled, soft and warm.

I will see you in heaven, Jane thought.

No, you won't, the devil laughed again.

CHAPTER 6: NOAH, 1832
"Spirits from the vasty deep"

For the first few years Noah dreaded docking in Boston, but now, twelve years after his return to the sea, he suffered only occasional pangs of regret that he had missed Claire's childhood. This time, however, those feelings quickly resurfaced when Frederickson, still the barkeep at the *Scythe of Kronos*, informed him that Jane lay stricken with cholera with little chance of survival.

He was surprised to learn she had returned from Ohio, but whatever her reason was, it certainly wasn't to see Noah, as she'd made no effort to contact him. But then, how would she? He was at sea for months at a time, with Boston only an occasional docking point.

Apparently the man she'd left him for, Hinman, had died a few years ago. That news didn't moisten Noah's eyes, but Jane's impending death did, despite her betrayal.

He didn't even have time to seek her out before word arrived that she had passed.

He attended the funeral service, sitting quietly at the back of the church. The coffin was open, but he didn't step forward for a last look at his wife. He didn't want to see the effects disease had had on her body. He needed her to remain the fiery young woman who had danced with and then bedded him that first night in the *Scythe*, back in '18 when he was fresh off the *Susannah*. And she was, of course, the mother of his child, which surely deserved fond reminiscence.

The mourners included Jane's older sister Alice, a youth approaching manhood, two younger girls, and his beautiful Claire, a blossoming flower of nearly fourteen years. Until recently she had written him letters—at least Jane had followed through on that promise—but the correspondence had slowed and eventually stopped altogether as she approached adolescence. Not surprising. A girl on the cusp of womanhood had better things to do than write to a man who was a stranger to her.

They hadn't seen each other since she was two. He hadn't expected her to recognize him, and she didn't. Alice did, but looked away quickly. Mrs. Carmody, had she been in attendance, would have had the decency to reintroduce him to his daughter. She cared very much for Jane, so her absence probably meant she was also dead.

He ached at the sight of Claire, and a little for the memory of Jane in her less tempestuous moods. But neither nostalgia nor the love for his child could root him to the land again.

He slipped out of the church before the final amen and returned to the docks.

∗∗∗

By early winter the *Titus* was a hundred leagues north of Venezuela. That was farther south than they usually ventured, but the northern waters had been overfished for the past two years, forcing the captain to seek better prospects elsewhere.

The first whale spotted was a young one, too small to bother with. It wouldn't bring enough return to justify the effort. But a baby of this age could not survive on its own. The crew manned the life boats and rowed out to where experience suggested its mother would breach.

When she did they launched their harpoons, burying the forked points deep into her flesh. Ribbons of red gushed into the sea as the beast thrashed beneath the water. The men needed only to secure the ropes that were tied to the spears and wait for the spermer to exhaust herself through effort and blood loss.

Noah never tired of the excitement of the hunt, and now he could enjoy it fully, as it was no longer his task to climb into the stinking cavities to carve out the blubber. That was left for the younger lads and the apprentices.

The *Titus* remained well back while the whaleboats formed a semicircle around the whale as it dived and surfaced, dived and surfaced. Even the mother was not particularly large. Her struggle should be brief. If she was the best they could do, it would take several her size to fill the hold with blubber. That meant many more months at sea.

Noah didn't mind. He was where his heart called him to be, where he intended to live out his years.

The men cheered as the whale came up for the last time, listing to one side. It expelled a final feeble blast from its blowhole and rolled belly up.

The boys would gut the thing, and then there'd be cracklings and rum for all.

Noah tugged on the oars of his whaleboat along with his mates, towing the corpse back to the *Titus*.

His blood was high from the kill, and yet a part of his mind dwelled on Claire, and the young woman she was becoming.

He did not expect to see her again.

CHAPTER 7: CARL, 1838
"Prodigious birth of love"

Carl Hinman's job today was scudding the hides, scraping the leftover fat and hairs from the skins of recently slaughtered cattle. He was twenty-three, just starting his second year at Koerselman & Ralston Tannery in Detroit. Scudding had been unpleasant when he began his employment here, but he thought nothing of it now. It was a more agreeable task than other aspects of tanning: soaking the leather in human piss and softening it with dog shit, for instance. That took a little more getting used to.

He'd learned the rudiments of blacksmithing from his father Horace, but the man had had no patience with him, and the lessons hadn't lasted long enough for him to make a viable trade of it. He'd spent time in various mills. He'd built furniture. He'd mined iron in northern Michigan. Nothing had lasted more than a few months until now. Tanning was dependable work, not subject to the vagaries of the seasons. Even last year's recession, already being called the Panic of '37, had not brought the tannery down. It had put tens of thousands of people in the poorhouse, but not Carl or his fellows. He'd been lucky enough to have been hired before the collapse. The tannery survived, but times promised to be tough for years to come.

He dragged his dulled blade across the skin, then deposited the fat in a small vat. It would later be collected from all the scudders to be made into glue.

Outside it was a rainy and cool May morning, but in the confines of the tannery the temperature was always hot, the air thick with humidity and every stink imaginable to mankind. Carl paused to rub his aching right arm. He'd been at it all morning, and still the pile of hides he'd scraped was not half the size of those yet to do. Workers were expected to finish every assigned hide by day's end or face a dock in pay. Too many days of failing to meet the quota meant discharge.

He drew in a deep breath and resumed his labors. His wife Claire was heavy with their first child, the blessed event due at any moment. Carl would like to have been there with her, but every penny counted now. He'd had to choose between a day's lost wages or retaining the services of a midwife. He couldn't afford both. Since he would be useless in assisting with a birth, he opted for the midwife, a reliable woman named Mrs. Hampton.

Like most men, he hoped for a boy, if for no other reason than to raise him with the love that his own father had denied him. But a girl would be precious, too. A little angel. Claire and he had discussed names. They were still negotiating about the boy, but they both agreed that a girl would be called Mariel. They just liked the sound of it.

CHAPTER 8: JUBAL, 1846
"Purpose is but the slave to memory"

Jubal Lawson stood in the darkness at the back of the hall. "Stood," most people would smirk, was a misleading term with him, as he was a full-grown man who measured three inches short of four-and-a-half feet tall—fifty-one inches, to be exact. It was Wednesday, January 1, 1846, the first night of a new year. It had been the same as every night for the past five, and would likely be the same as every night for the foreseeable future.

Jubal was the star attraction in Kürten's Kabinet of Kuriosities, a sleazy combination of bad singing, bad dancing, and embarrassing "exhibits." Tonight's show was over. The audience had gone home into a cold blast of snow, no doubt wondering why they'd come out in miserable weather to spend their money on such paltry entertainment.

Jubal kicked off his shoes and guzzled whisky from a bottle, as he did after each performance. He hated being gawked at on stage, he hated his employer, Henri Kürten, and he hated Detroit. Drinking was the only way to shut off his brain long enough to fall asleep.

Kürten sat with his feet hanging over the edge of the stage in front, reading a single sheet of paper by candlelight. He seemed not to believe his eyes and turned the paper over to see if there was anything written on the back.

"What in blazes?" he said, his German accent rendering his question as "Vut'n blayssuz?" His bald head was a crescent of orange in the candlelight, his beard a tangle of shadows. His cane lay across his lap. "What in *blazes*?"

Jubal assumed it was another bill from a creditor. Kürten rarely drew large crowds. Lack of income and poorly managed expenses mired him in a state of near poverty. Seemed like two or three times a week he received legal notices demanding satisfaction for unpaid obligations.

Jubal was good with numbers, payrolls and supplies, and he understood ledgers. His father, a man of normal height, kept the accounts for a law firm in Boston. He'd passed his knowledge onto his son and went so far as to write a letter of recommendation in hopes of securing respectable employment for him.

The letter had gained him nothing. No legitimate business would hire a man of his stature for serious work. He offered his financial acumen across the ever-expanding country, but it was always the same, an incredulous smile and amused rejection. Setting his goals ever lower, Jubal drifted down and down into society until he hit bottom with Kürten.

Even Kürten, a scoundrel of the worst kind, bristled at Jubal's offer of proper bookkeeping. "I go to debtor's prison first," he'd said. "Nein, there's only eine Sache you can do for me."

Desperate for income and with nowhere else to turn, Jubal did what the world expected of people like him. He put on pantaloons, a funny hat, a vest, and oversized shoes. He danced like a trained monkey before drunken crowds, enduring their laughter, scorn and ridicule for the sake of a livelihood. He pranced out from behind the curtain every night of the week, grinning and pretending to enjoy his humiliation.

"What in blazes?" Kürten said for the third time, still perusing the letter.

"What in blazes, what?" Jubal said. He was already lightheaded from drink. "Who's suing you this time? I'm telling you, I could prevent all that."

Kürten squinted toward the back, but apparently couldn't see him in the darkness. "Do not start that nonsense again, you ungrateful kleiner Arsch. Anyways, this nicht über meine Gelprobleme. Es geht um dich. "

"Just speak English."

Kürten sighed irritably. "This is not about my money problems. It is about you."

"Me?" Jubal walked up the aisle toward the stage. "What about me?"

"Some Bauernfänger aus dem Süden wishes to buy you from me."

Kürten called everybody a bauernfänger, so Jubal knew it meant a flimflam man. A charlatan from the South wanted to buy him? "I can't be *bought*."

"You signed a contract. I own you. So, ja, you can."

"What would anyone want with me?"

"I do not know. Perhaps he wants his own Tom Thumb."

Jubal scowled. P.T. Barnum was parading around a dwarf child, claiming he was an adult. "I'm nobody's Tom Thumb. Tom Thumb isn't even Tom Thumb. I don't know what his real name is."

Kürten waived him off. "Du bist für mich so gut wie wertlos, aber immer noch besser als alles andere was ich habe."

"Goddammit, Kürten, you're trying to annoy me again with that gibberish, and you're succeeding. Who sent the letter?"

"It is signed by a Major Marcus T. LaVoie of Franklin, Tennessee."

"Never heard of him."

"It does not matter. I will not sell you for the amount he is suggesting. Ich werde verhandeln."

"You're going to *negotiate*? I'm not a commodity, you son-of-a-bachelor."

"You are what I say you are." Kürten said, his English quite plain now.

"Piss off."

Kürten pounded his cane on the stage. "You know I am not afraid to use this."

Jubal swallowed the last of the whisky. "And you know that doesn't scare me. Do what you want, but get it over with. I'm going to bed."

FATHER AND DAUGHTER, WHALERS, SHOWMEN AND THE SLAVE, MAY-JULY 1847

CHAPTER 9: MARIEL
"More things in heaven and earth"

Mariel Hinman breathed on the telescope's brass eyepiece, then polished it with the hem of her dress, trying to wipe away the black smudges of long storage. Today, May 12, 1847, was her ninth birthday. "Daddy, there's some writing carved here," she said. She squinted to see, but the sun was already below the horizon, its light nearly gone. She traced the grooves of the letters with her fingertips.

"Careful with that," her father said. "Your Granddad Horace got it for his birthday back when it was new. Don't need no clumsy little girl busting it now."

"I am *not* clumsy," Mariel said. *And not little, either. Nine isn't little.*

He knelt next to her, his knee protruding through a hole in his wool trousers. Even in the near darkness he looked filthy. It had been another long and fruitless day in the fields, fields scoured by weeks of drought and wind. There hadn't been a significant rainfall since late March. Seeds were withering in the ground. Mariel had heard her father tell Harm Jensen that it'd be a miracle if they pulled out any crops at all come autumn.

The air was almost still tonight, with only an occasional breeze swirling up puffs of dust. Crickets sang from their secret hiding places, but the toads and frogs were silent, probably withered and dead in dry creek beds.

Her father adjusted his spectacles and scratched the small bald spot on the top of his head. He couldn't read, but he pretended to study the words on the eyepiece. "'Ramsden, London, 1789,'" he said. He was probably reciting words her Grandad had taught him, although she never met her father's father and didn't know if he could read, either. She knew her grandmother Jane couldn't, nor could her aunts Joanna and Meggie. Only her mother Claire had had any schooling. According to Mariel's father, Jane had had to make many sacrifices for her eldest daughter's education, although he never said what those sacrifices had been.

"What's a Ramsden?" Mariel said.

Her father pointed the spyglass toward the southern sky, checked the angle, and tightened the knob on the tripod. "Name of the fella that made it, I 'spect."

"London's in England," Mariel said proudly. She attended Miss Krause's class when chores and weather permitted.

"So it is," her father said.

Minutes later the last of the day's light was gone, and bright little dollops of light popped into the sky. Mariel had seen the stars on hundreds of nights, but their sudden appearance always seemed like magic, a shimmer of silent majesty that came out only when the world was asleep. She lay on her back and looked up. This part of Ohio was flat and dull during the day, but at night it became a panorama of mystery and wonder. The milky swath that stretched across the heavens only added to the riddle. There were times she missed Detroit, but not at night. In the city, smoke from coal stoves and gas lamps blotted out the lovely view, noises disturbed the peace, and the air was heavy like sickness and death. There were stars in Detroit, but not like this, not like this.

"Don't you fall asleep," her father said. "I got something to show you like you've never seen before. It's a lot prettier than just gawking up at the sky."

Mariel had never looked through a spyglass before, never even known they owned one until he brought it out from the barn this evening. To celebrate her birthday he'd given her a new dress for her dolly, probably sewn by Harm Jensen's wife Kristin, but the twinkle in his eye told her there was more.

"What's prettier than this?" she said as a falling star streaked and fizzled.

Her father smiled. He looked into the eyepiece for what seemed like a long time, making tiny adjustments in the telescope's position until he found what he was seeking. "Yup," he said.

Mariel rolled to her stomach and pushed herself to her feet. At the angle her father had placed the telescope, she was too short to see from her knees and too tall when she was standing, so she had to stoop awkwardly. "What is it?" she said.

"Look," her father said. "Just look."

The brass felt cool against her skin. The view through the lens was a blur. "I can't see—"

"Close your other eye."

As soon as she did, the stars came into focus. She gasped. They were so big—big and round and a million times more sparkly. And so colorful. She'd always thought stars were just yellow or white.

"Oh," she said.

"Go on," her father said, "you ain't seen it yet."

Seen what? But then there was something, something funny about one of the stars. It was no larger or brighter than the others, but it had a circle around it, almost like a handle on a teacup. Except that the handle glowed as if fashioned from rings of light, and it went all the way around the star without actually touching it. It was the most breathtaking thing she'd ever seen.

"Daddy," she said, and again, "Daddy."

"I know," he said.

"This is the best birthday present ever. You gave me my own star!"

"Ain't a star," her father said, "'cause it moves. It's called Saturn, and it's a planet like Earth."

The overwhelming beauty of this planet, this *Saturn*, brought tears to Mariel's eyes. She had to look away. "How'd you find it?" she said.

He put his left hand on her shoulder and wiped the moisture from her cheeks with the index finger of his right. "It's always been there, honey. Harm Jensen told me about it. I didn't believe him neither till he showed me with his own spyglass."

"Who could know the sky holds such a miracle?"

"God don't always tell us the answers," her father said, sounding pleased, "but sometimes He gives us real dandy questions."

CHAPTER 10: NOAH
"Everyone can master a grief but he that has it"

The news took fifteen months to find Noah. He had recently returned from a long whaling voyage aboard the *Titus*, and he had a pocketful of coins. He and several of his mates were swilling ale and swapping lies in the *Anchor & Dolphin*, a mariners' tavern in Portsmouth, New Hampshire.

"When I was an apprentice on the *Susannah*," Noah said, "we harpooned a blue of such size that it dragged the boat halfway across the Atlantic. Through waves and storms it carried us, and I swear the bastard *walked* across reefs trying to scrape us off. By God, we fought it for three days and nights before we finished it, but by then it'd lost so much weight that it was thinner than an eel. I fried it like a herring and ate it with eggs and butter."

The sailors laughed and pounded their wooden cups on the table. The smells of fish and salt water flowed in through an open door. The tavern was always dark, and now rain and dusk had taken what little light remained of the day. Noah bowed his head theatrically.

"I can do better than that," said Short Bill as he lit the lantern above their table. Bill was the *Titus's* botsteer. "I once carved up a whale that had more blubber in its belly than Blackbourne has in his arse."

The seamen cheered. Of all the whoppers told that night, Short Bill's was the most popular.

"Aye," Noah growled in an imitation pirate voice, "but when you scurvy dogs are becalmed in the Sargasso Sea with yer ribs kissing yer spines and yer backsides shriveled like raisins for want of food, I'll be living off the bounties of me own girth."

"Comes to that, mate," Short Bill said, appraising Noah as if he were a filet of tuna, "*we'll* be living off the bounties of your own girth."

Noah was trying to think of a clever response when a stranger walked up to the table and said, "Blackbourne?"

The man was dressed in a uniform, but not the uniform of a ship's officer. Whoever he was, he wasn't anyone Noah wanted to meet.

"Nobody by that name here," Short Bill said.

"That so? I got a letter here for a Noah Blackbourne." The man jerked his thumb toward the barkeep. "Lowe says it's the fleshy one."

All the sailors glared at Lowe, who just shrugged.

The man looked at Noah.

"Who's it from?" Noah said.

"How the devil would I know? I'm just the courier. Came to my office from Detroit by way of everywhere else."

"Well, you can keep it. Nobody in Detroit I want to hear from. Anyway, why would I pay for a letter I didn't ask for?"

"The sender paid." The courier dropped the paper on the table. "Tear it up or wipe your arse with it, I don't care. My duty has been met."

He strode out the door without asking for a tip. Noah picked up the letter. Although it was battered and dirty from its long journey, the stationary was of the finest quality, folded over upon itself to form an envelope and sealed with wax.

"Open it," Short Bill said.

"Why?" Noah said. "What but bad news ever comes on paper like this?"

"Give me that," said Samuels, the *Titus's* bosun. He snatched the envelope from Noah, pried the wax loose, and unfolded the letter.

"Says, 'Bancroft, Leytem and Slade, Solicitors, 2401 Holmes Street, Detroit, Michigan.' It's signed by someone called Jacob Leytem."

"Who'd you knock up this time?" Short Bill said.

"Me?" Noah said. He patted himself on the belly. "Can't even reach the little beggar for my own amusements anymore, let alone for pleasuring a lady."

Everyone laughed, but Samuels held up a finger to silence them. "Listen," he said. "'Our firm has been retained by Mr. Miles Kelley, Undertaker, of Detroit. The final expenses of decedent Claire Hinman were ordered on credit, to be paid by Carl Hinman on or before Friday 27 February 1846. This obligation has not been discharged. Although Mr. Hinman was contacted via courier, he did not respond. All subsequent attempts at communication have been unsuccessful. He has apparently vacated the city. We are appealing to you for information—'"

"Enough," Noah said with a hollow feeling in his stomach. He looked past his friends, trying to grasp the implications of those two words: final expenses. All the voices in the tavern seemed to fall away to silence, although the talking did not stop. The only sounds he allowed himself to hear were distant ones, seagulls on the pier pecking for morsels of food in the cracks. Peck, peck, squawk, peck peck peck.

"Who's Claire Hinman?" Samuels said.

His voice broke the spell and the tavern came alive again. "My daughter," Noah said. "Claire was my daughter. What happened?"

Samuels turned the paper over, and over again. "Don't say."

"Let me see," Noah said, and Samuels handed him the letter. There was nothing, no clue how she died. "February 1846? I was at sea all the while, not knowing."

"Sorry, mate," Short Bill said, and the rest of Noah's friends chimed in with words of sympathy.

"Final expenses," Noah said, although that's not what he wanted to say. He didn't know what he wanted to say.

He stood and limped to the barkeep for another mug of ale. Lowe was a homely man with a cauliflower nose that looked as if it had been chewed on by angry crabs. He had a well-deserved reputation for hostile indifference, but when Noah slid a coin across the counter, Lowe pushed it back. "On the house," he said. "No easy thing, losing a child."

Noah nodded his thanks and hobbled outside door onto the pier. Gulls scattered as he approached, then landed again after he passed. The night spit cold drizzle on a northeast wind. Waves splashed against unseen surfaces in the dark. He sat down at the end of the dock and listened as the ships creaked against their moorings.

Dampness soaked through his clothes, through his skin, and settled in his guts. He sipped his drink without tasting it, then took out his dagger and carved her name into the wood.

Claire.

Noah and Claire had lived apart for most of her life, he a creature of the sea and she of the shore. He'd seen her once since 1820, at Jane's funeral in '32. He'd been besotted with her when she was an infant, but time and distance had blunted that loss. The real breaking point came when she sent him her final letter after many years of silence, informing him of her impending wedding to Carl Hinman, son of Horace, the man who had stolen Noah's wife. From that point on, Claire had essentially been dead to him, ten years before her actual death. He'd fired off a letter declaring his outrage, and had had no contact since.

Yet, how could he dismiss the memory of that little girl on the beach?

And where *was* Hinman? Why hadn't he paid her final expenses?

CHAPTER 11: MARCUS
"Let them tell thee tall tales"

Marc Kane of Ebytown, Canada West—or, as he fashioned himself, Major Marcus T. LaVoie of Franklin, Tennessee—perched on the front of the platform and surveyed his audience. The crowd looked agreeable on this sunny and hot day. He raised a bottle over his head for all to see. "This nostrum is a curative for all ailments of the liver, bowel, and gut," he said, removing his Grandee hat and jabbing it toward the crowd to emphasize his points. "It cleanses the blood and purifies the kidneys. A mere tablespoon taken daily will prevent biliousness, yellow fever, jaundice, dysentery, dropsy, worms, and all female complaints. The cure may take a day or two, but you'll feel its effects instantly." LaVoie produced an exaggerated hiccough. "If you catch my meaning…."

The audience laughed.

A curly-haired, bearded man with muscles too big for his shirt stepped out from among the growing band of spectators. He shouted in a Slavic accent, "I can testify to the power of the Major's elixir. Just last week I was sickly and thin as a rail. Look what it did for me."

Flexing his biceps brought a gasp of appreciation from the crowd.

LaVoie allowed himself a small grin. The so-called beneficiary of his liniment was actually his strongman Otto wearing a wig and false whiskers. When the audience returned its attention to LaVoie, Otto would slip into his wagon, change clothes, and remove the disguise. In truth he didn't have a hair on his body, and his real accent was an uneasy blend of Norwegian and Virginia backwoods.

"One quarter dollar, friends," LaVoie called. He put his hat back on, adjusted his cravat, and hooked his thumbs inside his vest pockets. "Two bits will buy you the health that nature denies you. Let me assure you, this patent took exhaustive research and testing. In my many travels I acquired the ancient ingredients of Oriental alchemists. I combined these with the secret herbs and roots of the Seminoles, the knowledge of which I received from the lips of an injured warrior in the Battle of Wahoo Swamp back in thirty-six, as recompense for sparing his life. I experimented on myself until the perfect dosage was achieved. This elixir will cure you or your money will be cheerfully refunded."

He had them right where he wanted them. His medicine show had grown in popularity in one-horse towns throughout Indiana. The economic difficulties of the past decade were lifting, and anxiety about the war with Mexico had created a desire for entertaining diversions. The two events together made folks more willing than ever to part with their money.

But it was difficult to work a crowd in a city, regardless of the circumstances. Folks there were more worldly, a naturally cynical lot who'd seen every flimflam flummery east of the Mississippi. Dearbornville, near Detroit, had been a sticky disaster. He was glad to get away from there and find people less likely to paint their displeasure with tar and feathers.

Out here, the border ruffians had never experienced anything quite like his Ten Wonders of the Universe. The show wasn't the biggest on the circuit—four prairie schooners and a chuckwagon, a caravan into which he had to stuff ten people, food, lumber, costumes, oats and hay for the horses, bags of sawdust, and an enormous big top for the performances—but it was, in his opinion, the best. His impressive Phantasmagoria display alone was worth many times the price of admission.

LaVoie cut off sales of his liniment when it was time to begin the first act, the mind projection trick. He nodded to Jubal inside the tent. Jubal was a midget—*not* a dwarf, he was quick to insist. His services had been acquired from a cabinet of curiosities show over a year ago. LaVoie was a grifter, to be sure, but he'd never had or wanted a midget as one of his "dancing bears." He drew the line there. He didn't know why he had a soft spot for little people, since he had no such scruples about exhibiting André or Manfred, who had unusual physical characteristics of their own. Perhaps he simply needed to convince himself that he still possessed a modicum of humanity.

He'd hired Jubal as his accountant, but he was also perfect as a barker when LaVoie himself wasn't working the crowd. Jubal's deep voice was more effective than the nasally whine of his predecessor in that function, Leopold, the so-called Leopard Man.

Still, people snickered when Jubal emerged from the tent's opening carrying a step stool and pushing a podium with an advertisement plastered on the front. He was wearing clean but informal Sunday-goin'-to meeting clothes with a white straw hat but no tie.

INSIDE!
MAJOR MARCUS T. LaVOIE'S
TEN WONDERS OF THE UNIVERSE!
ONLY 25¢.
SEE:
AMAZING FEATS OF LEGERDEMAIN!
OTTO, THE WORLD'S STRONGEST MAN!
OPHELIA, THE BEARDED LADY!
ARTEST, THE BULLWHIP ARTISTE!
LEOPOLD, THE LEOPARD MAN!
HERMAN/HERMIONE, HALF-MAN, HALF-WOMAN!
GIOVANNI, THE SWORD SWALLOWER!
ANDRÉ, THE BONELESS MAN!
THE INCREDIBLE FLYING HUMAN!
AND THE MAIN ATTRACTION:
ALL THE WAY FROM PARIS, FRANCE
THE WORLD FAMOUS
<u>PHANTASMAGORIA</u>

From atop the step stool behind the podium, Jubal waved a cane toward the entrance as LaVoie stepped into the crowd to collect coins for admission. "Come inside and enjoy our Ten Wonders of the Universe, everyone," Jubal cried. "You'll have another chance to buy the Major's curative during the intermission and after the show."

***

"First on our bill," LaVoie called out to the crowd, "I'll need a volunteer to help me with an amazing demonstration of the power of the mind."

He always whetted the audience's appetite with some sleight-of-hand before he brought out the performers. Of course, the *coup de grâce* was the magic lantern show, his so-called Phantasmagoria. If nothing else left them awestruck, that would.

Several people raised their hands. LaVoie chose a farmer in the front row. "How about you, sir?"

The man's friends applauded and clapped him on the back. He stepped forward. "What now?"

"Sir, do we know each other?" LaVoie said.

"Nope, never met. You're a stranger to me, that's for sure."

"Good, good. What is your name?"

"Bob Hymes. Friends call me Hy."

No doubt because "Bob" had too many letters for them to remember, LaVoie chuckled to himself. He winked at the crowd. "Well, Hy, here is what I am going to do: By sheer concentration, I will place the image of a number into your mind. I will do this without any secret signal between us. And as proof that there's no tomfoolery involved, I will write the number down *before* you reveal it."

"Ain't nobody can do that."

"Kindly close your eyes, Hy, and turn away from me so these fine people will have no doubt that you cannot see what I am about to write."

Hymes grinned, shut his eyes, and covered them with his hands. Obviously new to the stage, he showed off by doing a little jig as he faced the spectators. When they laughed and applauded again, LaVoie knew he had them. They were practically begging to be bamboozled.

He produced a pencil and a sheet of paper. With a great flourishing stroke he wrote a number, then folded the paper and held it up to prove that the number was not visible to the farmer. "I will now call on Mr. Lawson to assist us. Jubal?"

Jubal emerged from behind the stage. He had changed into a white suit and black bowtie. "At your service, Major," he said. The audience didn't laugh this time, as they'd already seen him.

LaVoie handed him the paper. "Will you sign this document and keep it safe?"

Jubal printed his name in red chalk on the blank side, showed it to the audience, and placed the folded paper in his vest. He and LaVoie raised their hands, palms facing outward.

"You will note," LaVoie said, "that our hands will remain in plain sight at all times. Neither of us may alter the paper in any way." He addressed Hymes. "You may open your eyes, Hy, and turn to face us."

The farmer did as instructed. "Where's the trick?"

"Oh, this is no trick, I assure you, sir. I will need complete silence from the audience as I concentrate on a number."

The crowd hushed.

"Whadda I have to do?" the farmer said.

"You need only think. Momentarily a number between one and ten will appear as if by magic in your mind. When you're very sure of that number, please reveal it to all present here tonight."

"Between one and ten, you say?"

"One and ten, yes."

LaVoie now closed his eyes and touched his index fingers to each temple. He distorted his face into an exaggerated grimace to demonstrate that he was indeed concentrating very hard.

"I got it," Hymes cried.

"Please, sir, share that number with all of us."

"Eight. The number is eight."

LaVoie raised his voice to the crowd. "Did you all hear this gentleman say 'eight?'"

There was a chorus of "yesses" and "you bets" and "sure dids."

"Again," LaVoie said, "neither my hands nor those of my assistant have left your sight. Mr. Lawson, will you produce the document?"

Jubal removed the paper from his vest and held it up so the audience could see his signature in red chalk.

"And now, sir," LaVoie said, "will you be so kind as to unfold the paper?"

Jubal did so. LaVoie took it from him and handed it to the farmer. "Can you confirm the number recorded hereupon?"

Hymes examined it. Written large with curlicues and flourishes was a large number eight. "Well, I'll be," he declared, "it *is* an eight! How in hell'd you do that?"

"Please show it to our friends here."

When he did, the audience exploded in applause. LaVoie looked out over their eager, uneducated, wonderful faces. This is too easy, he thought. They were lucky he charged only two bits for admission. These mudsills would pay twice that, and more.

Hymes shook hands with LaVoie and Jubal, then returned to the crowd.

"This little demonstration," LaVoie said, "is a mere trifle compared to the acts to follow. And to top it off, the grand finale, my stupendous, incomparable Phantasmagoria."

***

After the show LaVoie went over the ledger. Although Jubal took care of the bookkeeping and never embezzled, LaVoie liked to see where the finances stood after the first night in a new location.

He was not normally a night owl. The sun rose early this time of year, and he rose with it. It was rare that he was still awake after midnight. But on those occasions, when his mind kept him up gnawing on this problem or that, he liked to go fishing. Give him a pole, a bit of salt pork for bait, and an hour of solitude, and he could calm his nerves. Give him the moon and the stars, and fishing became a redemptive act, absolving him, for the duration of the event, of his worries and indiscretions.

He sat on the bank of a nameless pond and watched the moon on the water. Drought had reduced the pond to a series of shallow puddles. The heat of the day had raised the water temperature too high to reasonably expect the fish, if any were left alive, to bite. They tended to be hungrier when water was deep and cold.

He'd brought salt pork, but didn't bother to drop his line. The moon was near full, obscuring some of the stars in its aura and reflecting light bright enough to cast shadows. The silver-gray hues transformed Indiana's bland landscape into a vision, almost, of snow-covered fields.

A breeze from the southwest tousled his hair. There was an odd duality about it, pleasantly cool yet somehow menacing. Usually in such a place, at this time of year, he'd expect wind to bring with it the scent of growing things, newly emerging crops, wildflowers and lush green pastures. But tonight it carried only the smell of barren dirt and grass burnt brown by the sun.

Rain was no friend to him, as it kept the crowds away, but if it didn't come soon, before long the farmers would start hoarding their coins against a poor harvest, and that would also keep the crowds away. Then, improving economy or not, he'd be out of work.

Still, the lack of rain was not the source of LaVoie's disquiet tonight. The show was doing well enough, sales were good and, at least on this night, the law hadn't come sniffing around. He wasn't aware of any discontent or egregious mischief among his performers. Well, Artest the Bullwhip Artiste was drunk again when he did his act tonight, but that was nothing out of the ordinary. It was a rare night indeed when that man was not drunk.

Something was missing. A few years back, that master trickster P.T. Barnum unveiled, or so he claimed, the mummified remains of a real mermaid. The Feejee Mermaid, he called it. Not Fiji, Feejee. LaVoie knew it was hokum—damn near *everybody* knew it was hokum—yet spectators by the thousands put their money down to see the thing. If LaVoie could come up with something like that to supplement the acts in his ten-in-one, his would be not only the best but the most popular medicine show this side of New York City.

What he had in mind would require cobbling together the body parts of different animals, but not a monkey and fish, as Barnum had probably done. Combining a badger with an octopus, perhaps, or a bobcat with a hawk. Ah, but where could he find a taxidermist skilled enough to create such a creature and make it look real?

Then there was the child dwarf, Tom Thumb. Barnum had made enough to tour Europe with the boy. LaVoie would not do that to Jubal for any money.

And even if he did get his own monstrosity or, heaven forbid, display Jubal as a freak, did he really want to be known as the Barnum of the West? Imitation could be profitable, but innovation was where reputations were made. His Phantasmagoria was the best he'd ever seen, maybe the best that ever was, but he didn't invent magic lantern shows. *Camera obscura* had been around for centuries, and really, the Phantasmagoria was simply a variation of that.

Damn it.

What he needed was an *idea*.

He sat and thought for the better part of an hour, but nothing came to him. His pocket watch read nearly two in the morning. Perhaps the magic of fishing worked only if he actually fished. Just sitting under God's great canopy wasn't enough.

As he rose to return to his wagon he noticed movement in a puddle a few yards to the west. It was more a thrashing in mud, as the water was nearly gone. He half-walked, half slid down the bank to investigate. A small catfish was wriggling and gasping, its gills just barely beneath the surface. LaVoie stooped to pick it up. It flopped weakly in his fingers.

"Ah, poor fellow," he said. There was a deeper pool nearby. LaVoie considered releasing the fish there, but to what end? The sun would rise in a few hours, the heat would return, and that water would evaporate as well, if not tomorrow, then the next day. The creature was doomed to suffocate in air and baked mud.

LaVoie unsheathed a knife from his belt, climbed the bank, and placed the fish on a flat stone. "My friend, you look nothing like a Feejee Mermaid," he said, "so you're of no use to me in that regard. Nevertheless, you'll not die in vain. Breakfast is not an ignoble fate."

If the catfish was grateful for its quick and easy death, it didn't show. As LaVoie cut its head off, one of its barbs pierced his thumb, drawing blood.

CHAPTER 12: CARL
"Such stuff as dreams are made on"

Carl held the bucket between his knees as he squeezed and pulled the cow's teats alternately in a steady rhythm. Ropes of milk splashed into the bucket and steamed in the early morning cool. Some people named their dairy cattle Bessie or Bossie or some fool thing, but Carl didn't. If weather conditions didn't improve, he'd have to butcher the animals for their meat. Much easier to put a bullet into the brain of an anonymous cow than into sweet old Bessie or Bossie.

It wasn't sunrise yet, but the wind had already come up, a wind from the southwest that would overwhelm the spring chill before breakfast. It whisked in through cracks in the wall planks, which popped and groaned like old bones. Carl's lantern swung from the rafter, spewing shadows and light unevenly throughout the barn. The door, which faced west, banged against the frame. At least the wind carried away the kerosene vapors and straw dust. But it also brought with it the stink of the chicken coop. To his mind chicken drips produced the most diabolical vapors in the world. By comparison cattle manure was like a whiff of French perfume.

"Mariel," he called. The girl had a good heart, but she was lazy. She'd sleep until the sun was full up if he'd let her. Last he saw she was huddled on the porch complaining about the cold.

"I'm getting the eggs," she said, her voice sweet as distant wind chimes. "Looks like a fox ate part of a hen."

Damn it. Foxes had to eat, too, but he didn't see why he ought to provide their meals. Best get out the gun and collect more pelts. Could never have too many come winter.

Mariel appeared in the open door, silhouetted against the last stars of morning, her dress rippling. Even in the lantern's dim light he could see her pail wasn't half full. "Again?" he said.

"Sorry, Daddy."

"Nothing you can do," he said. "They don't lay, they don't lay."

"Can I go to school today?"

Carl saw no good purpose for education, boys or girls. All it did was clutter up perfectly fine minds with nonsense that didn't mean a thing to anybody but the teachers. Just last week Miss Krause had made her students read a dreadful poem by Mr. Poe about a woman who died young. The last thing Mariel needed was to be reminded of the loss of her mother.

But Claire, God rest her soul, had wanted schooling for their daughter, so Mariel would have schooling.

"If we get chores finished in time," he said. "Help me with the manure, then wash up and fry them eggs. I'll feed the animals after I finish the milking. I 'spect Harm and me can do the rest."

"Thank you, Daddy."

Mariel skipped away to the house. Truth was, there wasn't much else to do. The fields were plowed, the seeds cast. Didn't matter how often he fertilized the soil, without rain the crops wouldn't grow. He'd need to borrow Harm's bull for another breeding attempt, but Mariel didn't need to see that.

Carl paused for a moment. Like so many in polite society, Claire had found the word "bull" vulgar. She would have preferred the silly term people slapped on the poor fellow these days—gentleman cow. He smiled, sniffled, and smiled again. His cattle were definitely ladies, no doubt about that, and it was time to fatten them up with more than feed. Might as well plan as if there was going to be a future.

Mariel returned a few minutes later with two buckets and a pitchfork. By that time the cow had given up as much milk as she was going to. Carl hadn't even washed and warmed the udders of the other three yet, so they could wait until the manure had been collected. He rose from his stool and stretched his back. He was only thirty-two, yet it seemed his joints ached more every year, every season, every day.

Mariel set the buckets behind two of the cows and scooped up a pile of their droppings. Carl got his own pitchfork and joined her. For a spell they worked in silence, side by side like he might've done with boys, if he'd had boys. When they'd filled the two buckets, they went out and loaded the contents into the wagon, then came back for more. The wind still blew, and the chickens still stank, but he felt at peace here in the dawning light, alone with his daughter, not saying words that didn't need saying, and knowing without speaking the things that mattered.

"Not much here," Mariel said when they finished.

"You know it's bad when there ain't even enough shit to go 'round."

"Daddy!"

Claire never took to cussing, and had apparently passed her distaste on to Mariel. "Manure," he said, smiling the sheepish mixture of repentance and mischief that had always melted Claire's heart after she'd scolded him.

Mariel wrinkled up her face and tried to look stern. "Just don't do it again, mister."

They took the last load to the wagon. The morning chill was gone. The sun had cleared the horizon now, its light rolling across the Ohio flatlands, brightening nothing, illuminating nothing. From here to the horizon in every direction the fields were parched and bleak, brown, useless, as if a wildfire had scoured the earth to its foundation. But there'd been no fire, only weeks of unrelenting heat. It felt more like July or August than May. Already the air above the ground wavered, distorting light itself.

He'd never had to endure weather like this as a child when he lived out east with his father Horace, stepmother Jane, and the girls. That close to the ocean, it seemed as if it did nothing *but* rain.

Carl emptied his bucket and then Mariel's. He looked at the sun and sighed. With Harm's help, he'd paid the government five dollars an acre for the land. This farm was to be his escape, his dream after Claire. This.

"But it sure was pretty last night," Mariel said. "Will we have to go back to Detroit if it doesn't rain?"

He squeezed her hand. "We ain't never going back to Detroit," he said. "Now get to frying them eggs."

CHAPTER 13: BILL
"The way to dusty death"

"Doesn't it seem likely that after fifteen months the matter has already been resolved?" Bill said.

"Nothing is resolved," Noah snapped.

"You don't know that."

"You're right, I don't. But resolved or not, Hinman will answer to me. How did Claire die? Why did he not notify me? Why did he not pay her expenses when they were demanded? I have to go."

Bill sighed. Noah's stubbornness was legendary onboard the *Titus*. "If your mind is fixed upon this journey," he said, stowing his clothes in a rucksack, "you'll not make it alone. Not with you in such a state."

The day had dawned lovely in Portsmouth, fair, crisp and cool. All over town church bells rang out the hour, seven chimes, a reminder that Sunday morning services had begun.

"Whaling's all you know," Noah said.

"A man grows weary of the sea, mate. Been there so long I got more brine than piss in my piss. Dry land'll do me good."

"You've no land legs. You'll only slow me down."

Bill smiled at Noah's girth. "How could anything slow you down? But what's the hurry? Pardon my saying so, but your girl's been dead some months now. She'll still be dead when we get to Detroit."

"She was alive when I last boarded the *Titus*," Noah said, his expression grim and determined. "And I'll know why she's not now."

"Could've been consumption," Bill said, "or cholera."

"Cholera took her mother. If God visited that pestilence upon Claire as well, then I will shake my fist at the sky and demand an answer. But I've a feeling my quarrel is not with the Almighty."

Bill glanced out the window of their room in the *Anchor & Dolphin*. The harbor was calm, the sea bluer than the eyes of the women sailors dreamed of. The sun rose through mist on the water. There was no activity around the ships. The only folk on the streets were the stragglers to church. "Given any thought to how we'll get there?"

"We'll have to rent horses and buy supplies," Noah said. "Still time for you to change your mind."

Bill clapped him on the ear. "Shut your pan, mate. I travel where I will, and that's the end of it. You mean to go overland?"

"Most direct route."

"Through the woods of New Hampshire and Vermont? No roads worthy of the name there. Never mind the Indians."

"Only thing I know about Detroit," Noah said, "is that it's west. What's your idea?"

"Any fool knows it's easier by water. Up around Nova Scotia, then book passage on a laker. After all these years at sea, that ought to be easy as skimming on ice. Or we could take the railway to Albany and sail up the canal to Lake Erie. That'd be quicker still. I've always had a mind to see the Canal."

Noah looked surprised. "Never been on a train."

"Nothing to worry about, long as the engine don't blow up. Or the tracks don't buckle. But we've ridden the backs of angry spermers and weathered the worst storms this side of perdition, so what's one little iron horse? It'll be a new adventure."

Bill sounded considerably more enthusiastic than he felt. He'd never been on a train, either.

"How much will it cost?" Noah said.

"No idea. But we just got our wages from the *Titus*, eh?"

"Don't recall any rail lines out of Portsmouth," Noah said.

"We'll take a freighter down the coast to Boston."

Noah tied shut his own rucksack and slung it over his back. "Well, the train it is, then. Think Lowe can spare a few supplies?"

"For the right price he could spare his own liver."

Noah walked out of the room, the floor creaking under his weight. He limped noticeably, favoring the left leg, the one he injured in a tavern brawl nearly thirty years ago. Bill watched him negotiate the stairs one step at a time. Left foot down, then right on the same step, left, then right, until he reached the bottom. He was heaving for breath by then, his neck wet with sweat.

Bill had been there the night of the brawl. He knew then Noah's knee would always trouble him, yet his friend seemed to do all right at sea. "How'd you ever get hired on as sailor?" he said.

"I'm smarter than the whales," Noah said, "unlike someone who shall remain nameless. It's worse in the morning. Once I'm limbered up, I can dance on the yardarms."

"I hope to live out the rest of my days without seeing that," Bill said.

Noah shifted his rucksack to his other shoulder and pounded on the counter for Lowe. He kept his weight mostly on the right leg. "It'll be a long way to Detroit," he said, "if I have to listen to your blather the entire journey."

CHAPTER 14: JUBAL
"Of hindering knot-grass made"

Jubal's tastes were simple. A good cigar, a clean shirt, and maybe, just once, a beautiful woman to tell him he was something more than cute. That's all. Since leaving Kürten's humiliating employment and joining up with LaVoie, it'd been a string of towns, one after another, learning a new trick here, selling a horse there, and always staying one step ahead of the local marshals. In this business there was little time for the niceties of life, but he had no reason to complain. In two weeks he'd gone from Kürten's freak show midget to LaVoie's barker, assistant, and financial manager. This opportunity had been years in coming. When the Major took him on, he expected to be prancing about on stage for drunken sodbusters, just like he had for Kürten. He'd shovel shit in Vicksburg before he'd ever do that again. Now he didn't have to, because for all of LaVoie's bluster, he had a humane soul.

From outside his wagon, he heard LaVoie playing the crowd. Although the show was over, the Major never missed a chance to sell one last bottle of his nostrum before everyone went home. Jubal enjoyed listening to him work. LaVoie had dressed tonight in his resplendent double-breasted tailcoat and Grandee hat, an impressive sight to any mudsill wearing dropfall trousers and a dirty wool shirt. With his neatly trimmed mustache and chin whiskers, his clean-shaven cheeks and practiced accent, he looked and sounded every bit the southern gentleman.

This added credence when he boasted of his war record in the '30s, fighting the Seminoles in Florida. In reality he was farming half a continent away in Canada West at the time. In his spiels to the crowd, he was usually content to take credit for capturing Osceola, but sometimes varied the story to claim he had personally killed the great Seminole in hand-to-hand combat. Never mind that Osceola didn't die from wounds inflicted on the battlefield, but in captivity from an abscess in his tonsils. LaVoie's gullible clodcrushers didn't care. To them he was a war hero clad in finery, and they couldn't buy his potion fast enough. How could such a magnificent specimen of manliness lie to them?

"You won't be sorry," Jubal heard LaVoie cry to a final willing victim.

Billy Powell, he thought with a smile. Anytime the Major got too full of himself, Jubal had but to mention the name to bring him down a few pegs and remind him what a fraud he was. Osceola, with both white and Indian blood, was born Billy Powell among whites, and had only changed his name after joining the Seminoles.

Voices gradually faded as the crowd shuffled away.

A few moments later LaVoie poked his head in the open canopy at the front of the wagon. He tossed Jubal a bagful of coins he'd just collected.

"Good show tonight," he said. "Bring me the books when you've got the final tallies." LaVoie chuckled. "They certainly were amused by Ophelia. If they only knew."

Ophelia was their bearded lady, although, truth to be told, Ophelia's real name was Manfred, and he had very real breasts the size of cantaloupes. Public decency prevented them from billing him as the double breasted man, so he grew long hair and a beard, put on a dress, and became Ophelia.

"He stirs my blood," Jubal joked. "Give me thirty minutes for the numbers."

"He stirs my bottom line." LaVoie waved and walked away.

Manny's bosom, Otto's muscles, André's apparent lack of bones, Giovanni's amazing gullet, or Leopold's ferocity—one could never tell which of them the audience would take a fancy to on a given night. Of course, LaVoie's Phantasmagoria was always the highlight of the show.

Jubal flipped the money bag from hand to hand, enjoying the weight. Combined with admissions, it would be a good night indeed.

As he opened the bag, he heard Petey call his name. Petey was a clever half-breed they'd picked up in Terre Haute several weeks back. At first Jubal resented having to share his wagon with him, but he'd always had a soft spot for children and had quickly become fond of the boy.

Petey climbed into the wagon. "We're running low on sawdust, Mr. Lawson."

He was barely a third Jubal's age but a foot and a half taller. Not for the first time, Jubal wondered what the lad thought when he looked down at him. Unlike most other small folk, Jubal was proportioned normally, lacking the barrel chest, short limbs, and stubby fingers of the sideshow dwarfs he knew. In fact, he had the angelic look of an ordinary six-year-old child—a six-year-old with a bass voice who shaved twice a day and smoked cigars when he could get them. If Petey was like everyone else, regardless how respectful he was now, he'd end up treating Jubal as if he *were* a child. They just couldn't help themselves.

"Make it stretch as long as you can," Jubal said. "There's a mill in Jeffersonville."

"All right, Mr. Lawson, but there ain't much left."

Petey's features could almost pass for white, but for the high cheekbones and dark hair. Osceola had been born with a white man's name and took an Indian one later. Petey had been born among Indians and then went to live with whites after the Trail of Death in '38. "I've never thought to ask you your Indian name," Jubal said. "Surely Petey isn't a Potawatomi name."

"*Bodéwadmi.*"

"That was your Indian name?"

"That was the name of my tribe. Only white folks call us Potawatomi. If I had an Injun name, I don't remember it no more. Mind if I go have a look around, see what they got for fun in these parts?"

Like many teenaged boys, Petey liked to explore, and had done so on the first night of every new stop the show had made since Terre Haute.

"All right," Jubal said, "but you better not wake me when you get back. And don't go chasing any girls."

Petey smiled. "I won't, Mr. Lawson. I might catch one, and then what would I do?" He went back to the opening, hopped down, and ran off.

Jubal lifted his table desk and set it on his lap. Flipping open the lid, he took out a quill, bottle of ink, and a ledger, then poured the contents of LaVoie's money bag out. Catching up the balance sheet wasn't bad when the crowds were large. The devil was in the little expenses, and out here in the sticks even the cost of sawdust was dear.

He'd already done the admission receipts earlier in the evening. After counting the liniment take, recounting, and recounting again, he brought down the totals in the book. They were well in the black, so he added sawdust to the supply list. Salt pork. Jerky. Pins. Kerosene. A new rim for one of the wagon wheels. The list went on and on.

The sun had dropped below the horizon now, leaving only the lamps to illuminate the inside of the wagon. He closed the table desk and rose to take the ledger to LaVoie. Then he thought better of it and sat back down. LaVoie could wait a few minutes. He pulled out a fresh piece of parchment and wrote:

My Dearest Annalee.

CHAPTER 15: MARIEL
"Because you are virtuous"

Mariel folded her hands in her lap as her father had instructed, kept her eyes focused on the table and remained silent unless spoken to. They were at Harm Jensen's home. Harm's wife had prepared them a dinner her father couldn't begin to repay in kind or courtesy, so he warned Mariel to be on her best behavior. If the Jensens were going to lay out the expense for such a fine meal, the least she could do was be respectful.

Not that she was ever anything but.

After saying grace, Mrs. Jensen scooped some mashed potatoes onto Mariel's plate and slathered them with chicken gravy so thick it quivered. The aroma alone was enough to make Mariel's stomach growl. "Eat, girl," the woman said.

"Thank you, ma'am."

Mrs. Jensen was stout as a grain silo, of the same solid Prussian stock as most of the second- and third-generation homesteaders in this part of Ohio. She always appeared jovial, but Mariel's father said she had a temper to her. *Ever noticed that scar on Harm's forehead?* he'd once said, nodding knowingly.

"This weather's got to break sometime," Harm said. He wouldn't let anybody call him Mr. Jensen, not even Mariel. His accent still bore a vestige of the old country, with elongated o's and u's. He bit into a chicken breast, right down to the wishbone. "Been here ten years and never saw a drought like this."

"I never would've come, I'd've known farming was this hard," Mariel's father said.

"City boy," Harm said, laughing and slapping his wife on the rump. She gave him a stern glare but then smiled at Mariel. "Never done a day of hard labor in his life," Harm said.

"Try tanning leather," her father said.

"I have. Stinks, don't it? Never get used to the smell of piss."

Mariel knew urine was somehow used to tan leather, but her mother would never have approved of the word *piss*. She frowned at Harm, who playfully held his hand to his mouth as if to say, *Ach, I've been a bad boy.*

"Anyway," her father said, "I don't mean hard like in hard work, I mean hard like in *hard*. Like in, can't make a living at it."

Mariel looked around the home. It was a log cabin like theirs, but so much bigger. Instead of dried mud between the planks to keep the wind out, there was something white like the stuff between the stones in Detroit's government buildings. Their own house had one room, with a half wall partition her father had put up where Mariel could sleep and change clothes. They had two windows, which were sealed by waxed cloth. But the Jensens had three real rooms with doors between them, a kitchen, a living space, and a bedroom, plus a loft above for storage. They had glass in their windows, wood on their floors, and brass on their fixtures. Harm even owned a bear rug, though God only knew where he'd found a bear to shoot in these parts. It was the kind of luxury Mariel hadn't seen since… well, ever. They never had it this good even when Momma was alive and Daddy worked at the tannery.

"Making a living just means planning ahead," Harm said, removing the wishbone from the chicken breast. He closed his eyes as if making a wish, broke the bone, then looked at it and shrugged. "I cut ice from the river in the winter and put it in the cellar to keep meat fresh in the summer. Kris cans everything she can fit into a jar—"

"Kristin," Mrs. Jensen said.

Mariel's father had once told her that Mrs. Jensen's German parents had called her Kirstyn, which was a common name in the Old Country. But Mrs. Jensen wanted something less foreign-sounding, so after she left to get married she switched the "r" and "i" around and changed the "y" to "i" to become Kristin. Having given herself a new name, she insisted everyone use it in full. Kris, according to her father, was too informal for her, even with Harm. Mariel thought Kristin was a pretty name. So was Kirstyn. But it wasn't her concern. She only called her Mrs. Jensen anyway.

Harm sighed and went on. "Then when the bad times come, we never go hungry. You and me both made it through the Panic of '37, Carl. Things don't get worse than that."

Mariel hadn't been born yet when the economy collapsed in 1837, but her family had felt its effects for years. The tannery only just made it, and there were lots of hungry people in Detroit well into the early '40s.

"We lost 'most everything we had," her father said.

"And yet you survived. You can do it again."

"Livestock still needs to eat. And I don't have a cellar for ice or a wife for canning."

"Plenty of ladies looking for husbands around here," Mrs. Jensen said. "Ladies from good families. Ladies with fine, wide hips, if you get my meaning. A man needs a wife." She looked at Mariel. "A girl needs a mother."

Don't want one, Mariel almost cried out. Nobody could take the place of her Momma, nobody.

"Ain't looking for a new wife," her father said quietly, and Mariel wanted to hug him. "Not just yet, anyhow. You knew my mother, didn't you, Harm? Got the puerperal fever after birthing me."

"Lizbeth was a fine woman, by all accounts. I only met her once, but I know Horace was never the same after she passed."

"*He* never married again," her father said.

"Well, not in God's house anyway," Harm said. "Should we be discussing this in front of the child?"

"I'm only saying he couldn't bear to take another wife, neither."

"Do you hear from your sisters anymore?"

"Half-sisters. You know Claire and them was also—"

"Shhh!" Harm said, indicating Mariel with his eyes, which she noticed. She didn't understand what Harm didn't want her father to say, but she knew he was treating her as a child, and she didn't like it, not one little bit.

Her father nodded. "They went to live with Jane's sister Alice here in Ohio after Jane died. Joanna married a fella named Bemis some years back. She didn't invite me to the wedding. Turned Hebrew, I think."

"Married to a Christ-killer?"

"I guess so. Don't matter much to me, I never met him."

"And Meggie?"

"She's out east again. Not married, last I knew. Truth is, I ain't heard from either of them since me and Claire's wedding."

"What's past is past," Mrs. Jensen said. "People die, families drift. It's a shame, but there's nothing can be done about it. No reason to curl up and die yourself, I say."

"Kristin," Harm said, hushing her. "Carl, you know I'll be glad to help you dig that cellar. As for canning, any reason your youngster can't learn how?"

"No reason at all," her father said, and Mariel didn't want to hug him anymore.

"I'll teach you," Mrs. Jensen said, pinching Mariel's cheek. The Jensens had no children of their own. "What do you say, little one? Would you like that?"

Mariel didn't think she would, but better that than a new mother. She looked at her father for permission to speak. He nodded.

"I like learning new things," Mariel said.

"Clever child," Mrs. Jensen said. "Won't do for a girl to get too many ideas in her head, but long as she's willing to work hard in the home...."

"I get the eggs," Mariel said, then without pause blurted, "Did you know Daddy has a spyglass that was made in 1789? That's almost sixty *years* ago. It was my grandfather Horace's. Daddy showed me a planet called Saturn, and it has a shiny ring all the way around it."

"Oh, I never heard of such a silly thing," Mrs. Jensen laughed, winking at Harm.

CHAPTER 16: NOAH
"Clothed in sorrow's dark array"

Noah sat on the pier as Short Bill negotiated with Lowe for the supplies. The *Titus* and other merchant ships lolled against their moorings, the wood groaning just enough to remind him who he was, to call him back, to make him question his decision.

The air was cool, but the sun warmed his face. Seagulls and terns swooped and squawked. The sails, furled on their yardarms, hung motionless. A crewman snored on the deck of one of the ships, but otherwise Noah had Portsmouth to himself this morning. Everyone was at church or occupied elsewhere. There were no swells, only a gentle wash of water against the pier's foundation posts, a *shhhh*, a caress, a whisper saying, *Noah, Noah, don't go.*

The water's movement was slight, but with no wind, he wondered where the energy came from to stir it at all. It was as if the sea were a living thing that breathed and moved on its own. A living thing, filled with living things, holding living things on its surface in the form of sailors on their ships. He always loved the sea and sometimes hated it. But for the brief adventure on land going on thirty years ago, it had been his home since he was fifteen. He stopped in port only long enough to squander his earnings on ale and, once, on a woman. It was that liaison that had kept him drydocked for two years, and led him, ultimately, to this day.

To Claire, to his dead Claire.

Footsteps approached from behind, Short Bill's familiar gait.

As Noah looked out over the ocean, he was seized by a foreboding thought: after their short jaunt down the coast to Boston, he would never see the Atlantic again, at least not from a whaler. It left him feeling melancholy.

Maybe his disquiet was grief for the daughter who had, as a tot, shown him the blessedness of fatherhood. Or maybe it was anger that, later, that same love had driven him to the gates of Hell. He had been absent from her life for all but two of her twenty-seven years. Though it was never likely they would meet again to make amends in this world, it would have been possible.

Now it wasn't.

The square sail of a distant ship broke the horizon. He couldn't see them yet, but seagulls would be circling the mast, their bodies white in the morning sun.

He was seeing this sight for the last time.

The *last* time.

Noah, Noah....

"Need help lifting that lazy arse off the pier?" Short Bill said.

"What did Lowe charge us?"

"A dollar seventy-three-and-half cents. I bought just enough to get us there."

"For that kind of money, he better have thrown in his liver."

His friend smiled. "Miserly bastard said he was using it."

Noah grunted to his feet. "Now what?"

Short Bill picked up Noah's rucksack and handed it to him. "The iron horse."

Noah glanced back at the light of the sun on the Atlantic. By all accounts, the Great Lakes were like inland seas. Maybe they wouldn't be so different. "Let's be at it, then."

Noah, Noah.... Goodbye.

CHAPTER 17: MARCUS
"Our doubts are traitors"

The first stars emerged as the medicine show closed for the night. A westerly breeze swept through camp. It should cool down nicely, LaVoie thought. Good sleeping weather. He took his meal in the chuckwagon, one of Otto's finest stews, then settled down under a tree to enjoy the evening with Jubal's accounting book. He had dozens of small problems to solve, mostly involving finances—what they needed as opposed to what he was willing to spend.

Tonight's show had drawn fewer spectators than usual, but a higher percentage of them bought liniment, so he'd broken even there. He'd had better days, he'd had worse. Although his Phantasmagoria was as popular as ever, his crew's timing with the images was off. With Jeffersonville looming, they'd need to do better. It was their biggest town since Terre Haute, and the more he could terrify, excite, and befuddle the yokels, the more often they'd come back. And when they did, they'd bring their friends, who would then bring *their* friends. Repeat business and word-of-mouth were the secrets to making real money.

It was too clear and glorious a night for work, but with the drought, every night lately had been clear and glorious, so the weather was no excuse for procrastination. He lit his small lantern, opened the book, and took a pencil from his vest pocket. The first thing he noticed was an X next to the name of Artest. That was curious. No one else had been singled out. Perhaps Artest had asked for a raise. LaVoie made a mental note to talk to him.

As he turned to the next page he heard the sound of voices, followed by footsteps. A few seconds later Petey and Manfred emerged from behind a wagon. Petey pinched one of Manfred's impressive breasts. "How does a man grow bosoms?" he said.

Manfred laughed, a deep, hearty rumble that belied his claim to be a bearded lady. "I'll thank you to keep your hands to yourself, young sir," he said. "Didn't your Injun momma teach you manners?"

"Momma was white," Petey said. "My father was Bodéwadmi."

"Well, one of them should've explained how you gotta marry a girl before you can touch her unmentionables."

"They never saw bosoms like *that*," Petey giggled. "I bet your momma was a cow."

Manfred saw LaVoie, winked, and said to Petey, "That was my daddy."

"Gentlemen," LaVoie said, "have you seen our good Artest?"

"Good and drunk, you mean," Petey said.

"Having one on in his wagon, last I saw," Manfred added. "And why not? Jubal discharged him."

Jubal did *what*? LaVoie prided himself on having control of his emotions, yet he felt his nostrils flaring and his cheeks reddening. *He* made personnel decisions, nobody else. Artest the Bullwhip Artiste was one of the first acts he had hired. The man was a drunkard with a taste for strumpets and a case of the French pox to prove it, but a decent enough fellow for all that. No one could wield a whip like him. When sober, he could cowhide a wing off a sleeping fly at twenty paces without waking the fly.

"I see," LaVoie said, and then again, "I see. You two should call it a night. By the by, Manfred, you didn't show enough cleavage today. They need to see you're a real lady."

"This pipsqueak's chub is already too piss-proud," Manfred said. "Don't want to get him any more riled up." He tousled Petey's hair, and they went on their way.

So much for his pleasant mood. LaVoie closed the book, rose, and grabbed his cane. He crossed camp with short, trembling strides, his fury growing by the moment.

Jubal was just closing his lap desk as LaVoie pushed open his tent's flap. He loomed over his assistant, raising his cane as if it were a sword. "How dare you, sir!" he bellowed in his artificial Tennessee accent.

Jubal folded the letter he'd been writing, then looked up and smiled calmly. "Artest?"

"Why was I not consulted?"

"He's been in his cups ever since we left Detroit. We can't have a drunken bullwhipper on stage. He'll kill somebody."

"We need him. He's the best."

"When he's not pickled. Which is never."

"You don't seem to understand, Mr. Lawson. I *must* bill a full show. We guarantee a ten-in-one. I assume you do not intend to put on Kürten's 'monkey suit' again and dance for the crowds…?"

"You assume correctly."

"Perhaps you've found a taxidermist to stitch together a new attraction?"

"Out here in the sticks? Besides, we don't need a fraudulent mermaid."

"It seems, sir, that because of you, we now need *something* else. The decision to discharge Artest was not yours to make."

Jubal sighed. "I'm not one of your mudsills, Marc. Drop the accent. It's just me."

"Yes, it is. And may I remind you that you are also on my payroll?"

Jubal touched his fingers to his brow as if saluting. "I apologize if I overstepped my authority. I thought you would have done the same. It was time."

LaVoie approved of apologies—receiving, not offering. He lowered his cane. True, Artest *had* nearly burnt the tent to the ground last week when his lash overturned a lantern. "So the question remains, what about a replacement?" This time when he spoke, it was in his native Canadian accent. He pronounced "about" as "a boat."

"We can gaff something. How about we move Leopold's Leopard Man act to the front end, then bring him back just before the Phantasmagoria as the New Guinea Wild Man? People won't recognize him as the same person. Or we could dust off the disappearing act."

"Have I told you about Dearbornville? That was just before you joined us. What a fiasco."

"André claimed it was an honest mistake. He said he tried to get the trap door to work, but the hinge was bent."

"I'm the one who got tarred and feathered for that honest mistake. Then they shattered my mirrors. Mirrors of that size are costly."

"It was just an idea. It's a great trick when it done properly. People love it."

"Therein lies the problem, Mr. Lawson. But the idea about Leopold isn't bad."

"I'll talk to him and see if he's willing. He might welcome the change."

"And Artest? Do we just abandon him in the wilderness?"

Jubal hopped down from his chair. He grinned and said, "I took away his whip and gave him his severance, along with four bottles of brandy. That'll keep him tight until we get to Jeffersonville. Garrett says we need to blow down and jump in four days' time. We can cut Artest loose there. He'll be so drunk he won't know we've gone."

Salmon J. Garrett was their advance agent, advising them not only where to go next, but when. He was a consumptive man, reeking of the sputum and blood he coughed up. He had been at death's door for years, hacking, sweating, and shivering incessantly. Every time he rode on ahead, they all expected that was the last they'd see of him. Yet he always returned. He had an uncanny nose for both avoiding trouble and finding profits. LaVoie swore the man could decipher a sheriff's mood before the sheriff himself did. That quality had helped them escape more than one potentially uncomfortable encounters.

"Sal's in camp?" LaVoie said to Jubal.

"He's still off scouting the next town after Jeffersonville. He sent us a letter. Manfred collected the mail in town. You owe him two cents for the fare."

"So you read my mail, too?"

"It was addressed to 'Marcus T. LaVoie or his minions.'"

LaVoie smiled. Minions. He liked the sound of that. His outrage salved, he said, "Sal is a peculiar man. I hope the brandy you gave Artest was from your personal stock."

The people here had been generous and relatively free of hostility, but movement was in LaVoie's blood. He bowed and gestured toward the open flap. Reverting to his southern patter, he said, "Have you had dinner yet, Mr. Lawson? Otto's stew is an exceptional repast. Some of the finest cuisine this side of the Appalachians."

"Please," Jubal replied. "Save it for the show, Billy Powell. Your accent is almost as grating as Kürten's, and his was real."

LaVoie tipped his hat. "Point taken, sir."

CHAPTER 18: CARL
"Boldly, but not wrathfully"

Elizabeth DeVilbiss Hinman, Lizbeth to friends and family, died a day after giving birth to Carl, her second son, due to that dreaded killer of young mothers, puerperal fever. She was buried next to her first son. His tombstone read simply: John Hinman, born 1812, died 1813, implying the child had lived a year. In fact, he survived his birth by a scant two hours. His delivery was breech, and the midwife had nearly had to amputate a leg to get him out. As it was, she very likely broke one or more of his tiny bones in pulling him from the womb. That was a few minutes before eleven on the night of Thursday, December 31, 1812. Little John expired just after one in the morning on Friday, January 1, 1813.

Two hours, two months, a year, Carl's father Horace used to observe bitterly, what did it matter?

When Carl came along in the spring of 1815, his mother wanted to call him John, too, but Horace was opposed to naming children after dead siblings. Thus, Carl was named for Horace's uncle, who had been wounded in the Seven Years' War and remained an invalid the rest of his days.

Carl was the child who, through no fault of his own, had killed Lizbeth. Horace never forgave him. "You don't deserve to be named after a war hero," his father often raged at him, especially when melancholy and the effects of whisky overcame his restraint. "You don't deserve to *live*."

At least Horace had known her as a living, breathing woman. Carl knew her only as a painted face in a cameo on the inside an inherited pocket watch.

***

He was thinking about his mother as he walked Mariel to the outhouse, which he did whenever she needed to use it after dark. There was no one here to harm her, nor any animal larger than a fox or stray dog. But he felt better if she wasn't alone, and so did she. He heard the wooden latch settle into place, then moved away a few paces.

There was no moon tonight, making stars shine the brighter. Damn it, where were the clouds, where was the rain? Going on two months and barely a drop.

Two hours, two months, a year. What did it matter?

It does matter, Carl thought. The rains'll come. They have to.

A flutter of wings near the barn was followed by a screech of pain and then an acrid stench. An owl had probably swooped down and nabbed a skunk kitten. A tasty meal for the owl meant several smelly days for Carl and Mariel, as the skunk would have released its displeasure the instant the bird's talons sank in. Harm told him once that nothing could kill a skunk fast enough to prevent it spraying, and nothing but time could get the stink out. If the thing had sprayed the hay, his cows wouldn't eat it. That was an aggravation he didn't need.

He went back to the house and sat on the porch with a handkerchief over his nose. Even so, his eyes watered at the odor. The creature's death reinforced the dark thoughts plaguing him about his mother, which inevitably made him think of Claire. Everything made him think of Claire. At least she'd had a photograph of herself made, done at considerable expense in happier times. Mariel would always have an image of her mother to remember her by, not some tiny painted likeness tucked inside the cover of a watch.

Somebody hit her in the head with a club, Constable Nortman from Detroit had said, *then stabbed her in the back when she was down. Any idea who'd want to do that?* He hadn't even given Carl time to let the news sink in. His tone of voice indicated he'd already decided who he thought did it.

Claire? Carl had sputtered. *Where?*

In a field outside the city. She was found earlier tonight, face down in the snow. Carl could almost hear Nortman thinking: *But you knew that, didn't you?*

You couldn't've made a mistake? She was at dinner with a friend. How'd she end up in a field? You're sure it was her?

She was known to the person who reported the crime.

Who was that? Carl started to say, but no words would come, because as the syllables formed on his lips, he knew the answer. He knew who was responsible. But Nortman would never believe him. Nobody would.

There were footprints, Nortman added, looking at Carl's shoes. *About your size, I'd reckon.*

The outhouse door opened and Mariel emerged. She pinched her nostrils shut. "Oh, Daddy, did you annoy a skunk?"

He walked over to escort her to the house. "A blasted barn owl got one. Don't know how they can eat them things."

When they got inside Mariel touched the tears on his cheek. "Thinking about Momma again?"

Carl looked at the framed photograph of Claire that hung above her beloved highboy. He tried to laugh off Mariel's question. "No, sweet girl, it's just skunk stink in my eyes."

Mariel squeezed his hand. "It's all right, Daddy. I think about her all the time, too. It makes me want to cry, but remember how Reverend Rodgers promised me she's in heaven? She can see us now, and someday we'll see her, too."

Carl believed that was true. Surely he did. He had to believe it, that or go mad. To see her again, to talk to her, to tell her all he wanted her to know....

Claire, my Claire.

"Go on, get into your night clothes now. You got school in the morning."

"Thank you!" Mariel scurried behind her privacy partition. "Do I really have to can pickles?"

"And pears and potatoes and beets and anything else we can fit into a jar." Carl sat in his rocker. "The crops'll grow soon as we get rain, but nothing grows in the winter. We gotta eat, 'less you want me to shoot skunks for supper."

Mariel didn't answer until she was finished changing. When she came out her hair was down and she had a comb in her hand. She climbed into Carl's lap. "I'll learn how to do it, Daddy. I will. I don't want another momma."

"Would that be so bad?" Carl said, taking the comb and gently brushing her hair.

"Momma would be sad if you found someone new."

"No, she wouldn't, darling. She don't want us to be lonely. She wants us to be happy."

"I'm happy, long as I'm with you."

Carl kissed her on the top of the head. "Read to me from one of her books tonight?"

"Mr. Keats?"

"Anything but Shakespeare," he said. Poetry was useless to him, but he especially detested Shakespeare. However, Claire had loved it all. She was always quoting this poet or that, and seemed to have a verse for every occasion. She even won a quotation competition with their minister in Detroit one time. It used to irritate Carl. Now the memory of her voice reciting those rhymes had the power to make him weep.

Mariel fetched a leather-bound volume from Claire's trunk. As she opened it and began to read, Carl felt a familiar trembling. He bit his lip.

Mariel sounded so much like her mother.

CHAPTER 19: BILL
"Days of absence, I am weary"

Bill and Noah had hopped aboard a freighter. Bill worked off their passage by helping the crew, but Noah stayed below deck the entire journey from Portsmouth to Boston, refusing to come up and breathe the sea air. He was burdened with a melancholy Bill had never seen in him before. Certainly the loss of his daughter could explain his mood, except that he'd rarely mentioned her during the nearly thirty years they'd known each other. They'd had few secrets between them in that time, but Noah was close-lipped about that part of his life, and Bill had never pressed him. He hadn't even known Claire's last name was Hinman until the letter from the solicitors came.

Hinman was also the name of the man Jane had run off with.

Had Claire married his son? Surely that had been a point of contention and a valid reason for Noah's estrangement from her.

This only made his obsession to investigate her death all the stranger. It *was* curious why Claire's husband would refuse to pay the funeral expenses, but how was that enough to justify Noah's behavior? Claire's family could have had financial difficulties, or the husband could be incapacitated, or dead, or any number of other innocent possibilities. There needn't be anything sinister in the whole affair. Nothing in the letter indicated the manner of Claire's passing. Most likely, natural disease had taken her.

Yet Noah was convinced it was something else.

At the Port of Boston Bill was able to dislodge him from his quarters. Even so, the man moved like the "zombies" they'd both laughed about in the voodoo dens of Haiti. His gait was slow and lumbering as always, with a limp favoring the left leg, but he walked without purpose, allowing Bill to guide him from the ship to the buckboard he'd hired to take them to the railway agent. Noah never looked back at the sea, never lifted his eyes from the ground. The soothing sounds of waves that were already calling Bill home might as well have been echoes in an empty galley to Noah.

Bill helped him onto the buckboard, shoving his shoulder into his friend's backside and pushing him up. Then he climbed in beside him and nodded to the driver. The wheels creaked as the buckboard clattered into the bustling traffic of the harbor's cobblestone lanes.

"Is this the way it's going to be?" Bill said.

"I said you didn't have to come," Noah said. "If I'm a burden, don't. Take the boat back to Portsmouth or hire on here. There are whale ships aplenty in Boston."

"Stop this nonsense. You don't have to go, either, but here we are. You are not the only one who has left everything behind."

Noah looked up. "Who's the greater fool, the man who charges into perdition, or the one who follows him?"

"What's wrong with you?"

Noah finally glanced back at the Atlantic. "Godspeed," he whispered, smiling grimly.

"Beg pardon?"

***

They booked passage on the Boston & Worcester Railway. The cars appeared sturdy enough, but Noah clearly viewed the steel tracks with suspicion. "How does a contraption this wide balance on those thin rails?" he said. Now that they were out of sight of the sea, his spirits were improving.

"They must know what they're doing," Bill said, not at all confident that was true.

"You put a lot of faith in 'they,' mate."

"What is life without faith?" Bill clapped Noah on the shoulder with false bravado. He'd been born into a Christian household in which one did not say the name of God without trembling. He had slipped in that observance during his long years of whaling, but not entirely. One could not gaze upon the great blue sea without feeling the presence of God. However, this contrivance, this train, was something else entirely.

They settled onto benches, their seats separated by narrow wooden partitions. The entire train vibrated, like an animal ready to pounce— and it hadn't yet started to move forward. The engine roared and coughed steam as hot and foul as the breath of Satan himself.

Who *is* the bigger fool? Bill thought.

He watched the other passengers as they entered the car. Most of them seemed unconcerned. Some were even accompanied by children. Nobody else showed the same nervousness and dread he felt. Travel by rail was hardly new. Trains had been primarily used to carry passengers for twenty years—in fact, they were only now being allowed to haul freight in competition with the Erie Canal—but Bill was a man of the sea, and he was terrified.

He clenched his hands together to prevent their shaking. Trains on short jaunts could reportedly attain the inconceivable speed of fifty miles per hour. He'd heard of some professor who had predicted that such a speed would cause men to lose consciousness and induce miscarriages in pregnant women.

He didn't know about that, but he did know that they'd have to endure two separate train rides before they could find haven in the safety of a boat. The Boston Line ended at Worcester, where they'd switch to the Western Line for Albany. From Albany they planned to book a steamer to Buffalo on the Canal, although the ticket clerk had warned them they should go on to Schenectady before taking to the water. Apparently an endless succession of locks between Albany and Schenectady made that stretch of canal tedious and difficult. But the distance between the two cities was only sixteen miles. What was sixteen miles of aggravation after the long journey by train from Boston to Albany? Bill and Noah were in agreement: they'd not travel one mile more by rail than was necessary. They decided to brave the locks between Albany and Schenectady, sail west to Buffalo, then take the palace steamer *Hercules* across Lake Erie to Detroit.

Bill looked out the window of the car. The Lakes would be a relief after this great clacking monstrosity of iron and wood, smoke and steam. The ground itself quaked.

"This was your idea," Noah said.

"We'd be fending off Indians in the woods of Vermont if we'd done it your way."

"And died brave men instead of cowering inside this infernal contraption."

"Don't have a conniption fit," Bill said, wanting to have one himself. Imagine, here he was, a grown man ready to piss himself over a mode of transportation that was so routine that most people weren't afraid to bring their children aboard. "We're doing this for Claire."

"Feels like the thing's about to explode," Noah grumbled.

"Nothing compared to being caught at sea in a nor'easter," Bill said. His voice sounded strained even to himself. "And we survived those, eh?"

With a piercing metallic screech and a rumble like thunder, the train lurched forward. "I'd crawl up the maw of a waterspout before I'd do this again," Noah said.

CHAPTER 20: JUBAL
"Fair fruit in an unwholesome dish"

The device was a modified lantern with a convex mirror behind it. A tube mounted on the front had an aperture with a lens at the end and a slot in the middle into which Jubal inserted glass slides. Horrific images had been painted on the slides. As the slides were placed into the slot, images would be projected from behind onto a gauze screen.

Jubal nudged André the Boneless Man, who whispered from behind the curtain. "Tell Marc we're ready."

LaVoie was on stage. Using a sinister deep voice, he said, "And now, ladies and gentlemen, all the way from Paris, France … the Phantasmagoria!"

On cue, the crew covered the lanterns circling the stage area, casting the tent in darkness. LaVoie pulled back the curtain, revealing a shimmering, ghostly pool of light on the screen. The standing room-only audience gasped in astonishment.

These clod-crushers had never seen such a thing as a limelight. Jubal was sure of that. Due to his stature, he was given the task of hiding behind the screen and operating the magic lantern. Covered in a black hooded robe, he stood next to Manfred, crouching uncomfortably and similarly dressed, unseen by the spectators. Jubal adjusted the heat to the gas burner and the quicklime brightened. The glowing apparition on the screen intensified.

"Friends," LaVoie drawled, "there was a time before natural philosophy, before the advance of modern medicine, when people lived their lives in terror of the unknown."

Jubal set the first slide into the lantern. The image of a wretched woman in a coffin was projected onto the screen. The people inhaled sharply.

"Pestilence devastated the land," LaVoie said.

Jubal slid in the next slide, the woman's soul leaving her body.

"Ghosts, demons, and devils ruled the earth."

Jubal pushed out more slides depicting creatures of horror, each more terrifying than the last. The magic lantern was fitted with wheels on a metal track. As he rolled it toward and away from the limelight's flame, the images on the screen alternately grew and shrank. At times monsters seemed to fly straight into the crowd, as if to rend their souls. Jubal couldn't see the audience, but by now they must be shuddering and covering their eyes.

Time for the big payoff. He tapped Manfred on the shoulder. The bearded "lady" reached down and pulled a heavy chain across a metal toolbox, then added a ghostly moan to accompany the clanking. Jubal put in a slide with a dancing skeleton and a glowing skull. Women shrieked. Men coughed nervously into their hands. When he thought they couldn't bear another minute, Jubal placed a second slide painted with a pair of eyes in front of the skull, wiggling it back and forth. The eyes appeared in the skull's empty sockets and moved as if surveying the crowd. The yokels were so frenzied, Jubal thought they might trample each other trying to escape.

"Friends," LaVoie said, "calm yourselves. There is no need to fear. What you have just witnessed is simple trickery. Modern science will triumph!" That was his cue. Jubal removed the frightening images and replaced them with a slide depicting a peaceful scene of trees and a sun-dappled brook. After the audience had caught their breath, he extinguished the limelight, the forest disappeared, and the crew uncovered the lanterns around the tent.

As the lights came back up, he and Manfred peeled off their robes and slipped out the back, then headed toward the front entrance. The crowd was shoulder-to-shoulder, clapping wildly now that the terror was over. They made it impossible for Jubal to see the rest of LaVoie's act. "Hey, Manny, I hate to ask, but...." he said, gesturing upward. Manfred smiled and pulled him onto his shoulder.

When all was calm, LaVoie asked for a volunteer for the levitation trick, which he'd decided to perform after the Phantasmagoria tonight in order to end the show on a more frivolous note. "Female, if you please," he said.

A covered table was behind him. Several white ladies raised their hands, and one small black woman, who cried with excitement, "Me, me!"

"I hope you weren't supposed to be working the stick," Jubal whispered.

Manfred smiled. "LaVoie gave that job to Otto. He didn't want me to damage my girlish proportions. Say, you turned off the burner, didn't you?"

"Of course I did. I think."

On stage, LaVoie was extending his hand toward a middle-aged housewife wearing a calico dress, when the black woman jumped between them and clasped his wrist. "Me!" she said with a jubilant smile.

Jubal knew LaVoie was startled, perhaps annoyed, but he was too much the consummate showman to betray his emotions. "It seems we have an eager volunteer, a lovely young Negro woman."

"Don't call me Negro," she said. "I know it's more polite than nigger, but they got signs down South saying 'Negroes for sale,' and I won't be called nothing that gets sold like a sack of oats. I ain't no slave and I ain't as young as you think, neither."

"What would you like to be called?"

"By my name, if it's all the same to you."

"And that is?"

"Cuff."

"Cuff?"

"That's the name Old Man Beddow gave me when I was just born. Well, that's all right. 'Course, it don't mean nothing now, 'cause I'm free. I just got used to the name."

Jubal's mother's family in Georgia had owned slaves. That was before she'd met his father and moved to Boston. He did his best to feel guilty about that, although it happened long before he was born and was therefore beyond his control or responsibility. He'd never met "the family property," as his mother called their slaves, but he had seen hundreds, maybe thousands, of colored women before, free ones in Detroit and shackled ones in the South. None of them had been as handsome as Cuff. She stood upright and tall—by Jubal's standards, anyway—and her face was untouched by scars. If she'd been someone's property, she must have been well cared for.

LaVoie smiled and turned to the crowd. "This woman will now assist me by defying Mr. Newton's laws of gravity." He placed her on the table and covered her with a sheet. "Just relax, my dear. This won't hurt a bit."

As she lay under the sheet, the crowd oohed their excitement. LaVoie pulled the table out from underneath her, and she appeared to be floating freely. "Well, looky me, Momma," she giggled.

From his vantage point above everyone's heads, Jubal noticed a puff of smoke drifting over the curtain. He grabbed Manfred's chin and jerked his face toward the smoke.

"Damnation," they both cried together.

It took them only a few seconds to run back, but it was too late. They could only watch the disaster unfold. From behind the scenes, Otto was running the rope and pulley that kept Cuff afloat. Jubal saw him sniff the air, then glance toward a small glow emanating from under the gauze screen. The screen burst into flame.

Otto faced a dilemma. He needed to douse the fire before it got out of control, but if he released the rope, Cuff would fall to the floor. Either way, the trick was ruined. His solution was to take the rope with him as he lumbered to the screen to stomp out the flame. Jubal could only imagine what was happening on the other end of that rope. Poor Cuff must be jerking in midair like a drunken marionette.

The audience obviously didn't realize the flames and smoke weren't part of the act, because they cheered enthusiastically as Cuff hollered, "Lord Almighty, I am flying like a bird."

***

Jubal handed Cuff a glass of hard cider. She sat on his folding chair in the vacated tent, wrapped in LaVoie's levitation sheet.

LaVoie stood behind her and patted her shoulder. "We have given you a dreadful fright, my dear. Are you all right?" He shot Jubal a look that said, *We'll discuss your situation later, sir.*

"I'm just fine," she said, talking to LaVoie but smiling at Jubal. "That was more fun than a Sunday morning revival meeting. When's your next show?"

"Not until we fix some of the apparatuses. Otto's feet are even bigger than his muscles. He knocked over a few things." Again Jubal noticed Cuff's delicate, unspoiled features. Her skin was a lovely shade of brown, lighter than most Negroes he'd encountered, but not so light that she could be mistaken for white or even mulatto.

"I'd think you was a child if you didn't need a shave," she said to Jubal. Her voice was captivating. "You're the littlest man I ever did see."

"Second tallest in my family," Jubal quipped. "Are you a slave?"

"Well, now, your hearing ain't no better than this gentleman's pretend accent. Didn't I say I wasn't one no more? No, sir, me and my girl took our freedom and made it north on the Railroad."

"Good for you," Jubal said. "Where's your daughter?"

"She went on ahead."

"I commend you, Miss Cuff," LaVoie said. "That was courageous. But what are you doing this close to the line? Slave hunters are thick as gallnippers down here."

Cuff leaned back and crossed her arms. "I got me some business needs tending to. That's all I got to say about that. But I was just thinking while I was sitting here. I do a lot of thinking these days. Momma always said I was a schemer. I need to keep moving 'round, you know, to keep myself scarce. Seeing as how I could use a little money for expenses, ever think of putting on a singing act in your show? I can play banjo, too."

LaVoie laughed as if he didn't think she was serious. "What do you sing?"

"What d'you like? Spirituals, 'course. Slave songs. 'Yankee Doodle,' if you want. I can read, too. Old Beddow kept me in the house to put his children to bed. I'd read 'em some Coleridge and such, maybe slip in a little Jupiter Hammon or Phillis Wheatley when Beddow wasn't listening. But they liked my singing best. Lord, I do miss those children."

"Beddow was your master?"

"Ain't no one my master," Cuff said, "except me."

"Wouldn't being on my stage call attention to yourself?" LaVoie said.

"Beg pardon, sir, but white folk can't tell one of us from another. There's so many minstrel shows nowadays, nobody's gonna think nothing about a colored gal singing. Make you feel better, I could put white shoe polish 'round my mouth and be a black woman pretending to be a white woman pretending to be a black woman. I'm ready to go. Got my banjo and a trunk with my things back in town. Just need someone to take me in and get 'em. I even got me a name I used when crossing the Ohio: Guinevere Brewer."

"How… Arthurian," LaVoie said.

"Who's Arthur Ian?" Cuff said.

"Never mind. Maybe I should have called myself Merlin. Well, too late now."

"I don't know what you're talking about."

"Neither does he, half the time," Jubal said. He turned to LaVoie. "Where will she sleep? Our wagons are full as it is."

"You got one for supplies?" she said. "I don't take up much room."

"What do you think, Jubal? Could she round out our ten-in-one?"

"Let's have a listen," Jubal said.

Cuff stood up. "Right here?"

"Good a place as any."

"Well, all right, then."

Before she started, LaVoie lowered his eyes and said, in his natural voice, "Is my accent really that bad?"

"Sure is," Cuff said.

CHAPTER 21: MARIEL
"And gave me up to tears"

The chalk clicked against her slate as Mariel wrote over and over *I will pay attention in class, I will pay attention in class*. Her classmates had gone home for the day. Her teacher, Miss Krause, read at her desk at the front of the schoolhouse, spectacles worn low on her nose. As always, the woman's expression was grim.

"That lady's got all the humor of a Millerite the day after the world didn't end," Mariel had once heard Harm Jensen say. She didn't know what a Millerite was, but she guessed they didn't laugh much. That was certainly true of Miss Krause.

Mariel's chalk was worn to a nub. She raised her hand and cleared her throat.

"One hundred times," the teacher said without looking up.

Given the large size of her handwriting, Mariel's slate could only hold three sentences, so she had to write and erase, write and erase, keeping track of the number of sentences on a separate slate. She was up to fifty-seven.

"I need another stick of chalk," she said, "please."

Miss Krause took a piece from her desk drawer and approached the dunce chair in the corner of the room. Her boots thudded on the wooden floor. She checked both slates, then examined Mariel's chalk. "Wasteful," she said. "You could fill your slate two or three more times with this piece."

"Sorry, ma'am."

"*Miss*, not ma'am. 'Madam' is a term for a married woman. I am not married." Her voice was calm, but Mariel thought, or imagined, she heard an underlying melancholy.

"I'm sorry, Miss Krause. The chalk is so short my fingers are getting cramps."

Giving her a new stick, the woman said, "You're usually such a good girl."

"I *am* a good girl," Mariel said aloud without meaning to. She clapped her hand over her mouth, but it was too late. The damage was done. Miss Krause did not tolerate backtalk, not ever, nor the slightest hint of contrariness. Already in trouble, Mariel made it worse by blurting, "Daddy's mighty sore with you for making us read Mr. Poe."

"I see. Would your father like to teach my class, then?"

"He said you don't know what it's like. And you don't. You don't!"

Miss Krause retrieved a ruler from the nearest student desk. "You will not speak to me in that manner, young lady," she said. "Hold out your hand."

Mariel did as instructed, and the teacher rapped her knuckles once, hard. Mariel didn't want to give her the satisfaction of tears, but she couldn't stop herself.

When her sobs had run their course, Miss Krause turned a student desk around and sat down facing her. "Tell me, Miss Hinman," she said, "what is *it* and what *is* it like?"

Mariel sniffled. "I don't know," she lied, and Miss Krause knew she was lying.

She counted the tally marks on Mariel's other slate. "You still have forty-three sentences to write. Or you can go home now. Tell me."

"It's Momma," Mariel said.

Miss Krause's expression softened. "Your mother has been gone some time now, has she not? Why were you so distracted today?"

"Because last night Daddy was sad. Mrs. Jensen wants him to get a new wife. He asked me to read Mr. Keats' poems to him, which makes him even sadder, because those poems were Momma's favorites."

Miss Krause sighed and almost smiled. It was a sad almost-smile. "I never heard how she died."

"Daddy said it was an accident. She fell down and hit her head."

"In Detroit, wasn't it?"

"Near there," Mariel said.

"I take no pleasure in disciplining a student," Miss Krause said. "Let me see your hand." When Mariel raised it from her lap, the woman tenderly took it in hers, barely touching, fingertips brushing fingertips, and blew on her reddening knuckles. She looked as if she was about to kiss them to make them better. Instead, she said, "The world is a difficult place, Miss Hinman. God does what He does, and there's a reason, even if we don't understand it. I can't tell you why He took your mother from you, but He knows. He knows. It must be for the best."

Mariel let Miss Krause continue touching her hand. Like the Jensens, she didn't have any children. Unlike Mrs. Jensen, she didn't have a husband, either. "If God took Momma away," Mariel said, "can He bring her back?"

Astonishingly, Miss Krause's eyes filled with tears. "Oh, child," she said, and it suddenly dawned on Mariel that other people suffered losses in their lives as well. "You may go home now."

CHAPTER 22: CARL
"Nothing is but what is not"

There was no reason today's arid weather should remind Carl of a cold, foggy spring night in Detroit three years ago, but as he watched Harm ride toward his house to help him dig the root cellar, a memory kept nagging at him, like a tune stuck in his head. It was a memory he didn't want or need, yet there it was.

Claire had cajoled him into attending a performance of Shakespeare with her. After all, she said, it wouldn't be proper for a married woman to go unaccompanied into a theatre. He couldn't recall the name of the playhouse, let alone the play. The plot involved some nonsense about a wedding, and fairies, and a play within a play. Most folks in the audience laughed throughout, but Carl didn't see one thing funny about it. All he knew was that the actors talked too damn fast and said words that didn't make a whole lot of sense.

They sat next to a woman of obvious refinement and her escort, a man who looked as bored with the whole thing as Carl was. But Claire and the woman were enthralled. After the performance, they struck up a conversation and an immediate friendship. The woman offered to accompany Claire to plays in the future. That pleased Carl very much, because society didn't frown on two respectable ladies attending the theatre together, and it relieved him of the burden of listening to actors in funny clothes spouting poetry. He was so grateful.

His emotions would change many times in the next few months after that night, and none of them involved gratitude.

***

As they worked, Harm reminisced about his days as an apprentice with Carl's father Horace. Horace liked to tell young Harm ribald jokes. The older Harm certainly enjoyed retelling them to Carl. Out of respect for Claire, Carl felt he shouldn't laugh, but he laughed anyway. Good thing Mariel wasn't here.

"Of course, he never talked like that around ladies," Harm said.

"What did you know of my mother?"

"Not much. I only met her the one time," he said. He had stripped to the waist in the hot spring air. A stout man around the middle, Harm needed suspenders to hold his trousers up. But he was impressively solid in the chest and arms. Carl watched his friend's muscles flex as he heaved shovelfuls of earth aside. The sweat and sun on his skin made him gleam like polished brass—and he seemed almost like a machine sometimes, working tirelessly, refusing to stop even to quench his thirst. "Your dad wasn't married yet when I apprenticed with him. And after he married Lizbeth in '09, he got the wanderlust. He was always moving the two of them around, out east, down south, I lost track. I was just a boy then. When he came back to Michigan, Lizbeth was dead and he had you and his new woman. Can't say as I cared much for Jane. Don't recall where he said he met her. Massachusetts?"

Thanks to Harm, the root cellar was already half finished.

Carl, fifteen years his junior, was having trouble keeping up. "My real mother died of fever just after my birth," he panted.

"I wish I would've known Lizbeth better," Harm said. "She was young. I thought there'd be time."

"So did they, I reckon."

"But if we knew the future, we'd tell all our old-men tales when we're young, and then what would we talk about later? Besides, what use is getting old if you got no regrets? Your dad told me once that a life without regrets ain't much of a life at all."

Carl smiled. His father had surely had quite a life, then. "I think I sunburned the top of my head. Let's rest a spell. Come in, have some lemonade."

Harm rolled his eyes and said, "City boys," but climbed out of the hole and followed Carl into the house.

They sat at the kitchen table, which was little more than a flat surface to pile things on: pots, buckets, scraps of leather and cloth, yarn, tools, and Mariel's schoolbooks. The Lost Tribe of Israel was probably marching around somewhere in all that clutter. There was just enough space for two people to eat if they squeezed in close.

The lemonade was warm and sour and just what Carl needed. Harm, too, apparently, as he gulped down three glasses in succession. Even machines needed oiling sometimes.

"This tastes like horse piss," Harm said, and poured himself a fourth.

"Drink a lot of that, do you?"

"Only when I come here."

Carl couldn't keep up with Harm's banter, and they both knew it. He got up and opened a drawer on the highboy Claire had inherited from her aunt Alice. It was the nicest piece of furniture he owned, and she had cherished it, so he kept it polished and shiny. Her photograph hung on the wall above it, always looking down over him and Mariel. Photography was new, and therefore expensive. Cost him half a week's wages to have it made, but now that Claire was gone, he blessed every penny he'd spent on it.

He took out two cigars, one half-smoked and the other still wrapped in paper. He put the stub in his mouth and offered the whole one to Harm.

"You gonna light these," Harm said, "or do you just gnaw on them till they're gone?"

Carl struck a match and lit both cigars. He puffed twice and said, "Claire didn't approve of smoking. Or drinking or cussing, come to think of it."

"Yet well worth the trouble, eh?" He gazed her photograph. "She was a mighty handsome woman, Carl. Never could figure why she settled for you."

"Well, it wasn't my brains."

Harm looked him over with amusement. "Unless you got some *real* big secret hidden away, wasn't your looks, either. I thought maybe you won her in a poker game from one of her other suitors."

"Sure do miss her."

Harm nodded. "You should listen to Kris. Find yourself another wife."

"Mariel will learn to can the fruits and vegetables. If we ever have any fruits and vegetables."

"It'll rain sooner rather than later," Harm said. "Mariel is a fine child, but she can't be a wife. Not a *wife*."

"Don't miss that as much as you'd think."

"Then I *really* don't see why Claire married you."

Carl was hurt more by the jest than he cared to show. He stubbed out his cigar on the sole of his boot and returned it to the highboy. When he sat down again, he said, "Got something on my mind."

"That would be a pleasant change."

"I mean it."

"Let's have it, then."

"Some solicitors wrote to me. Back in Detroit. I found the letter under my door just before I left Michigan."

"And?"

"Mariel tried to read it to me. But she didn't know what the words meant. It's here somewhere."

"You never asked anyone else?"

"Guess I put it away and didn't think about it, till now. Things got strange in Detroit there at the end."

"Show me."

Carl had an inkling what the letter said, but not exactly. Maybe he was foolish to mention it to Harm. Maybe he was foolish to mention it to anyone. Harm had gone from his father's apprentice in the smithing trade to a dear family friend, but if the letter said what Carl feared it might, things could change between them. "Never mind," he said. "Come on, daylight's wasting."

"You brought it up. I want to know."

"Just some leftover business of Claire's."

Harm looked at him suspiciously, shrugged, and stood up. "In other words, not my concern?" he said, draining the last drop of lemonade from his glass. "Try whisky next time. Tastes just as bad but makes you feel a whole lot better."

"Mariel should be home from school soon. Don't need her seeing you prancing 'round half naked. Let's finish that cellar."

Harm's joints crackled as he stretched his muscles. "Getting soft," he said. Carl turned toward the door, but Harm put his hand on his shoulder to stop him. "I'll have that letter."

"Don't remember where I put it."

"Yes, you do. I'll wager it's in Claire's trunk. I'm not the best reader in Ohio, but I can do better than your child. Go on."

Carl bent over his wife's trunk and moved her precious poetry books aside. Most were leather-bound, but the letter was in the one with the newer cloth binding, a bible she had received as a gift from Reverend Smith shortly before her death. He handed it to Harm.

Harm looked at the letterhead on the front. "Bancroft, Leytem and Slade?" he said as he unfolded the paper. The more he read, the grimmer his expression became. "The undertaker retained a law firm? You didn't pay for her funeral?"

Ashamed, Carl stared at his feet. How could he tell the whole story to Harm? He remembered his last sight of Claire, weeping over her as she lay in her coffin at the undertaker's. Her face was still pink, her hair still lustrous. His love, his only love, had been made to appear as beautiful as a sleeping angel, despite her battered skull.

Carl couldn't have prettied her up better had he made the arrangements for her himself. But he hadn't, yet he was expected to pay for them. He'd answered Kelley's summons to discuss the matter, but once he learned the of the arrangement made with his "sister Joanna," he had suddenly bolted from the establishment, crying, *God in Heaven, what have I done?*

With that information he knew instantly who was responsible for Claire's death. It wasn't him, although he'd been made to look guilty. And it certainly hadn't been Joanna. She'd recently married a man named Bemis and had been nowhere near Detroit at the time. Kelley had prepared the body and reported the manner of death to the police. When constable Nortman closed in on him, he'd been forced to make a choice. Michigan had abolished the death penalty. It didn't matter. Life imprisonment would have made Mariel an orphan as surely as a hanging.

The letter demanding payment had arrived a day before he'd fled with her to Ohio.

"You don't understand," Carl said.

"No, I don't," Harm said. "Did you even *go* to her funeral?"

Carl didn't answer, and that was answer enough.

CHAPTER 23: NOAH
"Praising what is lost makes the remembrance dear"

"Her name was Jane," Noah said to no one, shifting his weight on the train's bench to try to get comfortable, "Jane Olive." It was the middle of the night, and most of the passengers were asleep. Short Bill had wedged himself into the corner where the bench met the car's wall. His head flopped back and his Adam's apple bobbed as he snored. The train's wheels went clack-a-clack-a-clack, incessantly chugging, yet somehow the sound of Short Bill's snoring rose above the din. His friend's exhalations were uneven, coming in gasps, as if he were having trouble breathing and sleeping at the same time.

Noah yawned. "I met her in Boston when I was apprenticing on the *Susannah*. We'd pulled in to harbor with the finest catch I'd ever seen. 'Course, I was only a pup then, so I hadn't seen much yet. It was at a mariners' tavern that night—oh, I remember it well, the *Scythe of Kronos*—and all the mates were dancing in a circle. 'Round and 'round we went, laughing, singing, grabbing anyone foolish enough to come into our orbit. We all had money, and were determined to squander every last penny of it before the sun rose. There was no music playing but the song of a storm outside. Thunder and rain, lightning and wind, that was our music. What a glorious night! And then there she was, with a face like a goddess and a shape like damnation calling."

Short Bill groaned, lolled his head to the side, stopped snoring for a moment, then started again with a furious choking sound. Noah wasn't concerned. Short Bill always slept like that.

"I know what you're thinking," Noah said. "How could such a temptress hold the likes of me in her gaze? How could she not turn away? Well, I wasn't always flesh and lard, mate. You saw how thin I was at the *Sea Dog*. I cut a fine figure in those days, let me tell you. I was a lad, strong and lean, not so in love with a well-set table as I am now. She was a serving wench, and as she passed I pulled her in. She didn't complain, no, not her. She smiled and laughed and had a dance with the lot of us, and afterward she sat at my table and, breathing hard, said, 'I'm Jane.'"

Clack-a-clack-a-clack, and the train jerked from side to side as it crossed over a rough patch of track. Not unlike the swell of a wave, Noah thought. The "infernal contraption" from Boston to Worcester hadn't blown up, fallen over, or collided with anything, and so far there'd been no trouble with this one, either. Nevertheless, he was anxious to get to Albany and board the steamer for Buffalo. It would be good to feel water beneath his feet again. He nudged Short Bill. "I haven't always been so gloomy," he said. "I was happy once. Are you listening?"

"Huh?" Short Bill mumbled. He opened his eyes, blinked, and went back to sleep. He'd heard this story before anyway, but Noah still needed to tell it.

"We were young, Short Bill. Our blood was high. We didn't know it yet, but by morning we had given spark to our child. Our daughter Claire."

Noah felt the train's vibrations pass upward from the wheels, through the car and bench, and into his legs and backside. He both marveled and recoiled at the sheer power of the contraption.

Short Bill shifted positions and ended up with his face buried in Noah's shoulder, warming his neck with hot breath and wetting his shirt with drool.

"You probably wonder," Noah said, "if I did right by her. By God I did. I loved her, and we were married within the week after I learned of her condition. But she didn't do right by me. She met a man called Horace Hinman, and that was all for us. We'd had our rows, and she'd threatened to leave me before, but I never believed it, right up until the day she did."

***

In Albany they spent a night in a boarding house before booking passage on the steamer *SS Empire.*

They were exhausted but relieved to be rid of the iron horses. "Never again," Noah said. He sat on the edge of the bed and took his boots off.

"Or until we return from Detroit," Short Bill said, "whichever comes first. Shall we away to the tavern?"

"These landlubbers don't know how to drink," Noah said. "Go if you must, but I'll just have a few winks."

Short Bill lay back on the other side of the bed. Soon he was snoring in short gasps again, perhaps dreaming of the tavern he wasn't in and the drinks he wasn't drinking.

When Noah slept he dreamt of women in general and Jane in particular. He knew Short Bill didn't dream of women at all, nor of men, but that was all right with him.

Noah lifted his feet onto the mattress and plumped the straw pillow under his head. There was only one bed in the room, and it wasn't big enough for the two of them to fit comfortably. Noah folded his hands across his belly and tried to remember when everything in his body didn't hurt.

He closed his eyes.

In the morning he was awakened when Short Bill kicked him in the backside. "You crushed me against the wall, you great whale," his friend said. "I had to sleep on the floor."

"You should choose your sleeping partners more wisely. What's the time?"

"Morning, what do you think?"

Noah rolled to his side and sat up. "Food," he said.

"I had a biscuit at the tavern next door, but you've no time. The *Empire* leaves in an hour."

"I can't last the morning without eating."

"You can last until the Second Coming without eating. Quick now, up with you. I don't intend for us to miss that boat."

Noah grunted as he pulled his boots back on. "You might have woken me sooner."

Short Bill smiled irritably. "There's many things my life that I might have done, mate. What I did do was sleep on the floor in a boarding house in Albany, New York. And, I know, I know, I didn't have to come with you. But here I am and here we are. Now shut your pan and move."

***

Albany was a river town, but a river town was not a harbor town. Near as Noah could tell, the only thing they had in common was seagulls. Seagulls were the same everywhere: swooping, squawking, scavenging for food, and shitting on everything that didn't move, and some that did.

The town was orderly. The dock was orderly. The steamer was orderly. The passengers, what few there were, were orderly as they boarded the steamer. That was another difference. Chaos reigned around the whaling ships whenever they were in port, crewmen loading and unloading, jostling with the crowd at the fish markets, and everyone shouting at everyone. There were always fights and occasionally fatalities.

Even the smell was different. On the coast it was coal, salt, fish, and dampness. Here it was coal, trees, dirt, and river scum. Noah had been insulated from dry land by the train cars while enroute to Albany, but now he wondered how strange the view of it would be, with only forests, fields, houses, and fences, and no water save for rivers and rain.

Land. He'd had a life there when he was a child, before his apprenticeship onboard the *Susannah*, but that had been in Boston, always in view of the sea, not in the vast green spaces of New York State. Whatever memories remained of those years had been distorted to a grotesque purgatory, although surely there must have been some happy times. Running, playing with friends…. His mother had been a kind woman, but every thought of her was accompanied by one of his father, who must have considered kindness a sign of weakness. Certainly he'd never displayed anything like it to Noah, much less affection. The beatings had become more frequent after his mother's early death, so that the apprenticeship, when it came, had been a godsend.

Then there'd been those two years with Jane and Claire. In the beginning everything had been wonderful, but the disaster at the end forever jaded his opinion of land (and of women). After Jane's betrayal, he'd returned to whaling with no intention of ever coming farther inland than a seaside pub. Yet here he was again, old pain flowing to new.

He and Short Bill stood on the pier, prior to boarding the *Empire*. A few people patiently waited their turn ahead of them, a few behind. Many were dressed in clothing several stations up the social order from theirs. If anyone commented on their vulgar appearance, Noah didn't notice. His eyes, and Short Bill's, were fixed on the gigantic paddlewheel on the boat's port side.

Both astonished and wary, Noah said, "What in blazes is *that*?"

CHAPTER 24: MARCUS
"My words fly up,
my thoughts remain below"

Rosie lay on her side, her great flanks heaving, white showing all around her pupils. She snorted and whinnied in fear or pain.

Petey tugged on LaVoie's arm. "She's dying, Major!"

LaVoie had seen this many times. "She's all right, Petey. Let nature take its course."

Cuff laughed at them both. "Begging pardon, but sometimes nature's way is to let 'em die. Just needs a little help, is all."

She knelt next to the panting mare, stroking her bulging abdomen. Then she rolled up her sleeves.

"What're you doing?" Petey said.

"The foal's in sidewise. Needs straightening out."

"You've done this before?" LaVoie said.

Cuff looked at him like he was the stupidest man on the planet. "Where d'you think I come from, Mr. LaVoie? Ever live on a plantation?"

"Call me Major," LaVoie said.

"And I'm Queen Vicky of England." Cuff looked at Petey. "This old girl's fixing to go. I'll do all the work, but you be ready when I tell you."

"Ready for what?" Petey said, and his eyes were wider than Rosie's.

"I got to reach up inside her and help her."

"*Inside* her?"

"She's birthing, boy. That's where the foal's at, so that's where I got to go to fetch it."

"I'm going to puke."

Cuff laughed again. "What kinda Injun are you, never seen a horse get itself born?"

"I was four when the soldiers came," Petey said. "Went to Terre Haute after that, where all the horses I saw was already born."

"Oh, you think the foal is bad? Just you wait till you see what comes out *after*. Now, stop all this foolishness. Put your arms 'round my middle, and when I say pull, pull."

Even LaVoie felt a little queasy as Cuff inserted her arms up to the elbow in Rosie's birth canal. Little rivulets of blood and other fluids dripped out. Petey knelt down behind Cuff and embraced her as she'd instructed.

"Where're your hooves, little one?" she said. "Ah. You got yourself all tangled up. Come on now." She braced a foot against Rosie's backside. "Three, two, one, pull!"

Rosie neighed loudly as Cuff and Petey jerked backwards. It only took a few seconds before two hooves appeared, and then two spindly legs. Cuff released her grip and reached back in to clasp the foal's flanks. "Let go, Petey. I can finish it alone. Babe'll come out easy now."

Petey stood up and backed away. He stared as if in awe of the miracle he had helped bring about.

One more tug and the foal was free. "You big strong men might want to look away," Cuff said. "Now comes the messy part."

LaVoie heard the high-pitched whinny of the foal's first breath, all the while Cuff cooing at it as if she herself were the mother.

"Mr. Major LaVoie, sir," she said, "you got yourself a colt. And a fine boy he is."

Petey smiled, clapped his hands, and then suddenly gasped in disgust as the "messy part" oozed out. "I really am going to puke," Petey said, and did.

Cuff stood up. "You best not ever get married, child," she said. "Find me some rags to clean up with."

"Chuckwagon," LaVoie said.

"Will she be all right?" Petey said.

"Old Rosie, she'll be fine," Cuff said. She lifted the foal up next to Rosie's head. "Her babe, too."

"What'll we call him?" Petey said.

"You can name him some other time," LaVoie said. "Give him a Potawatomi name if you'd like."

"Bodéwadmi."

LaVoie acknowledged the correction with a tip of his hat.

"Thank you, Major," Petey said. "We had quite a time getting her born, didn't we?"

"What d'you mean, *we*?" Cuff said. "Come with me. Babe's like to be hungry. Let him be now."

As Cuff and Petey left the enclosure, LaVoie straightened Rosie's blanket, lifted a brush, and stroked her mane. Next to her, the newborn colt whinnied and tossed his head. Rosie nuzzled him in return.

A slow breeze cooled the night. The stars were lovely. LaVoie was experiencing a rare moment of clarity and peace. It was nearing dawn, all was quiet, but soon the sun would break over the Ohio River, just east of camp, and a new day would begin. Birthing a foal was a common enough event for the medicine show, what with five teams of horses to contend with, although none had ever needed help with the process.

Probably most thought that horses were merely transportation, but when a man witnessed one coming into the world, he got attached. That was simple human nature.

He felt rather the same about Petey. In Terre Haute, the boy had begged to come along, promising to do anything. The romance of the road and the spectacle of the show had seduced many a dreamy-eyed lad. Never mind the dust and rain and endless pocked roads, if there were roads at all. The heat and stink and hard work. The unruly crowds and local constables and hasty escapes in the night. None of that mattered at first, it was the idea of the show that lured them. Most didn't last a week when reality overran the mystique.

Petey was different. Part of that was because the people who raised him had treated him so badly that the harsh conditions of a ten-in-one were an improvement. But part of it was the innate nature of the boy himself. True, LaVoie had found him to be an undisciplined nuisance at first, always under foot, but he'd matured a great deal in the weeks since Terre Haute, and had become a real asset.

He'd grown to like the young fellow. Perhaps he might even make it in the trade himself someday. He was especially good with Chelsea, the pony LaVoie had bought for children to ride while their parents were occupied with the show. Petey's skills were meant for greater things than leading children around in a circle for a halfpenny per ride. The boy had quickly caught on to the tricks, the gaffed wheel, the three-card monte, the shell game, the razzle-dazzle.

Why shouldn't Petey make a living this way? Why shouldn't LaVoie? It was all entertainment. It was theatre for the vulgar, the common, the gullible. The yokels longed for wonder and excitement, and that's what LaVoie gave them. Of course they knew they were being bamboozled, but that was the charm of the performance. It's why they came the first time and then came back for more.

Surveying the row of darkened prairie schooners, LaVoie realized that men like him had the power of possibility. Since leaving Ebytown, he'd discovered his gift with the crowds, the power to suspend their disbelief and change their notions of the world. The best audiences were those who would willingly trade common sense for distortion. It was good if they'd encountered science at some time, though briefly, just enough to spark their imagination. People yearning for new visions sought him out as eagerly as he sought them. These were the half-educated souls who needed to know that the universe was truly a wondrous place, and that each of them occupied a prominent seat in the scheme of things. *I am the counterfeiter of knowledge,* LaVoie thought, *serving up a rehash of science in a form that suited their appetites.*

This was what he was teaching to Petey, to all his acts: Feed their imaginations with stories of faraway places. Bring magic into their ordinary lives. Make them feel special. If you can't give them what they need, then give them what they want. Give them theatre.

***

"Belgrade, Michigan?" LaVoie said. "Isn't that by Detroit?"

Salmon Garrett coughed into his kerchief, examined the sputum for blood, and finding none, said, "Yup."

LaVoie was seated at a small table in his wagon, playing whist with Cuff, who had learned it on the plantation. He noted that her breathing quickened at the word *Belgrade*. "Correct me if I'm wrong, Salmon, but wasn't that where we were when—?"

"That was Dearbornville."

"You remember how that turned out. Tar and feathers aren't my favorite apparel."

"You don't look so good," Cuff said to Garrett.

The advance scout glared disdainfully at her. He smoothed both ends of his drooping mustache. The thing was the color of a dead mouse and extended below his chin. The remnants of the eggs and lard he'd eaten for breakfast were still visible. "Where did you pick up a servant, Marc?" he said.

LaVoie put his hand on top of Cuff's, which she had balled into a fist. She was trembling, and not with cold. "Miss Cuff is nobody's servant, Sal. Sings like an angel. She's my new act. And my friend."

Garrett raised an eyebrow. LaVoie, and probably Cuff, too, could hear him thinking, *Friends with a colored woman?*—although it was unlikely his terminology was quite so polite. What he said, though, was, "Will you pour me a drink, or do I have to get it myself?"

LaVoie laid his cards face down, rose, and retrieved a bottle locked in a drawer of his personal trunk. As soon as he left the table, he noticed Cuff sneaking a peek at his cards, and she saw that he saw. He smiled.

She shrugged and smiled back. It was well after sunset, and the air was chilly. He lit a second lantern. "Warm enough?"

"Never," Garrett said. "Except when the fever's on me. Is that whisky?"

"And a damn fine one. Too good for you, which is why you're only getting one." LaVoie filled a mug, corked the bottle, and locked it in the drawer again.

"You ever going to settle on an accent, Marc? You got a little Canada West here, a little Indiana there, a little N'Orleans—"

"It's Franklin, Tennessee," LaVoie said, sitting down at the table.

"Ain't nothing of the kind," Cuff said.

LaVoie ignored their jibes. "Jubal won't want to go back there. Kürten's still in Detroit, last I heard. He thinks I owe him for 'his' midget."

"Did he have a contract?"

"Jubal's been vague about that. We slipped out of town without satisfying Kürten's price."

Garrett endured a lengthy coughing fit, after which he wiped his mouth and nose and said, "You mean you absconded with Mr. Lawson?"

"We were in the process of negotiation when Jubal and I, uh, left."

"We won't be in Detroit. Kürten can go to hell."

"Belgrade is how far from there?"

"You've stared down the barrels of how many angry sheriffs, yet now you're frightened of one man because of a dispute over Lawson?"

"I've run away from those barrels, if you recall."

"Even if Kürten sends the law to get him back, what's the problem? Sideshow dwarfs are common as air. Just get a new one."

Cuff stomped her foot and said, "I'm starting to get a strong feeling against you, Mr. Garrett. Maybe Jubal ain't as big as us, but he's as much a person as anybody, and more man than you."

"Cuff, shhh," LaVoie said. "Sal, you know that Jubal is my business manager. He's not an act, nor a commodity that can simply be replaced. And, as he'll be happy to explain, he is most certainly not a dwarf."

Garrett shook his head. "Keep him, then. But you're missing a chance, Marc. If you have a dwarf—sorry, a small person—use him. Barnum's making a killing with Tom Thumb."

"The matter isn't open for debate."

"You've formed some strange bonds, but do what you want. You will anyway."

"Now, about Detroit?"

"*Belgrade.*"

Outside a horse whinnied. LaVoie swore he could recognize Rosie's voice. He wondered how the colt was doing. "Why Belgrade?"

"Wages are up, and people are spending money again. Belgrade is a growing town, but its population is still mostly border ruffians, as you like to call them. Perfect for your particular talents."

"That describes a number of places not nearly as close to Detroit."

Garrett looked at Cuff. "What kind of name is Cuff, if I may ask?"

"What kind of name is Salmon? You a fish or something?"

"Fair enough." Garrett turned to LaVoie. "I've been talking up your magic lantern show in Belgrade, Marc, and I met a man who—"

"Phantasmagoria."

"Whatever you call it, I met a man, name of Zug, who saw your performance in Detroit, and he says he's interested in sponsoring you. Fella's made a fortune in the furniture business. If you can be in Belgrade for the Independence Day celebration, he can assure you of the largest crowd you have ever known."

"Zug? Never heard of him. Why would he want to sponsor me? What's in it for him?"

"I didn't ask, but he must smell a profit."

"And just what does this sponsorship entail?"

"He'll pay your expenses and supplies, guarantee a two-hundred dollar gate and another fifty just for making the trip. Plus whatever you take in selling that potion that doesn't cure anything."

"Don't you speak scornfully of my liniment. It's a scientifically proven medicine."

"It's a villainous brew. And it may well be poisonous."

LaVoie smiled. "No one's died yet."

"High praise indeed."

"So: Expenses, supplies, two hundred fifty dollars—in exchange for what?"

Garrett coughed again, this time bringing up blood. "God damn you, sir," he said, apparently addressing his illness. "Begging your pardon for my language, Miss Cuff."

"You gonna die, or what?"

"That is not my intention, but I don't suppose I get a vote in the matter." He cleared his throat. "I don't know what Zug wants, Marc. All he said was he was impressed with your show and will pay you cash money to return."

"Sounds suspicious."

"Not to agree with this cottonmouth," Cuff said, "but I heard of Belgrade. They say it's nice. We gotta go, Mr. Major LaVoie."

LaVoie smiled at her use of *we*. Although she'd only been with them a short while, she'd become as much a part of the show as Manfred or Otto. She seemed a little too eager to go to Belgrade. On the other hand, why wouldn't a former slave want to get as far away from the South as possible?

"It's the country's birthday," Garrett said. "The fireworks will draw a great number of people. There'll already be an audience in place for you."

"Other towns have fireworks," LaVoie said. "I don't know, Sal, something doesn't feel right. And being that close to Dearbornville makes me nervous. I appreciate your efforts on my behalf, and do thank my benefactor if you see him, but I'm afraid I must decline."

Cuff kicked him under the table.

"Ouch. What's it to you?" LaVoie said, allowing his annoyance to show.

Cuff took a deep breath before speaking. "'Cause Belgrade's right across from Canada. That's where my girl lives. Evelyn. Surely would like to see her again."

"Ah. That makes sense. Nobody wants to visit Belgrade, Michigan, just to visit Belgrade, Michigan."

"See?" Garrett said. "Your friend has a perfectly good motive. If not for the money, go for her sake." He smiled. His teeth were brown, with a smudge of exhaled blood on the front two. "How often have I been wrong about business matters, Marc? You'll have the crowds of a large city with the gullibility of small town sodkickers."

"There'll be advance promotions, I assume."

"Of course."

"Then it's likely people in Detroit will hear of it. Kürten knows my name. He is a vile and violent man who has it in for me."

"Did I mention two hundred fifty dollars? That's pure profit, Marc. How long would it take you to earn that kind of money down here?"

Garret was certainly correct about that. It might be worth risking Kürten's ire. And Cuff could see her daughter.

Yet LaVoie still hesitated. Garrett had obviously anticipated this. He saved the *coup de grâce* for last. "If not for her sake and not for the money, I have one more consideration that may intrigue you."

"Which is?"

"I know of a taxidermist there who can make anything he's got a mind to. *Anything*. Like a Feejee Mermaid, for instance."

Now *that* was something the show could really use—not a mermaid, of course, because Barnum already had one—but some kind of unnatural creature that would awe the masses. "What's his name? What kind of work does he do?"

"Charles Forrest-Hosier. Best I've ever met. He's not inexpensive, but with the money you'll make, you can afford him."

Forrest-Hosier. Sounded British. No matter. Two hundred fifty dollars *and* his own special monster?

"You've convinced me," he said.

"Good," Cuff said, clapping her hands. "Jubal's gonna throw a fit, but we'll make him see the light."

"I'll let you break the news to him," LaVoie said. "I believe the lad is sweet on you."

"How'd that little man get a fool notion like that in his head?" She turned over LaVoie's cards and lay them face up. "Good thing these ain't Tarots, that's all I got to say."

CHAPTER 25: CARL
"For I can raise no money by vile means"

Carl hammered a shoe onto the right front hoof of Ben Gorman's second-best appaloosa. Carl wasn't the area's most skilled blacksmith, but he'd gotten some experience before his father gave up on him. More importantly, he worked fast and cheap. Until the rains came, this was how he paid for their meals. It was hot, sweaty labor, but after ten years at the Koerselman & Ralston Tannery in Detroit, hot and sweaty was not a problem.

But that was a different time, a different life.

As soon as he finished, the horse tested the shoe by stomping her foot. Then she whinnied and unloaded her bowels onto the hay where Carl knelt. Nothing he hadn't stood knee-deep in before.

"Come along, you cantankerous beast," he said. He saddled his own bay, mounted, and led Gorman's appaloosa behind on a tether. The two horses kicked up enough dust that they might well be riding through smoke. Within minutes he met Mariel on the road as she walked home from school. Just last week her teacher had sat her in the dunce chair and rapped her knuckles for some insolence on Mariel's part. Carl didn't like anyone striking his child, but he left teaching matters to the teacher, and in the end the two seemed to have worked out their dispute. "Hello, sweet girl," he said.

"May I ride with you?" she said.

"No, I'm just going to the Gormans'. Miss Krause give you schoolwork tonight?"

"Not much," Mariel said. "What shall I cook for supper?"

"I'll stop at Schmidts for supplies after I deliver Ben's horse. Anything I should buy?"

"They brought chocolate bars back from their journey to England."

"Don't sound like a very hearty supper." Truth was, he didn't know what it sounded like. He'd tasted chocolate beans crushed and mixed with sugar and milk to make cocoa, but in a solid bar? He wasn't even sure what that meant. Like a bar of gold? A jail bar?

"Don't you fret about supper, Daddy," she said. "I'll cook whatever you buy. Just remember that chocolate bar. Ple-e-e-ease?"

"We'll see," he said.

Mariel clapped her hands and skipped off toward home. To her "We'll see" meant yes. And it almost always did.

Carl smiled. By all that was holy, he loved his little girl—*Oh, Daddy, nine isn't little*, she frequently scolded him. He didn't know how he would have survived Claire's death without her.

He plodded to the end of his lane and turned left. The Gorman plot was a mile and a quarter down the road. Just west of them were the Jensens, and past them, in the small village of Eagle, the Schmidt's general store. He and Harm hadn't spoken since the day they'd dug his root cellar. He was tempted to stop by to say hello, but decided against it.

Ben wasn't home when he arrived at the Gormans', but his wife was. Mrs. Gorman bore the unusual first name, at least to Carl, of Ciara. He'd been told it was spelled differently than it sounded, which was "Sierra," but spelling didn't matter to a man who couldn't read.

"What did you and Ben agree to?" she said.

"A dollar."

She scuttled into the house while he waited at the door. He was surprised she didn't invite him in, but apparently courtesy didn't mean as much to the Gormans as it did to most folks. She returned and dropped a silver coin into his palm.

"Why so little?" she said. Her hair was greasy and she smelled of skillet lard. "You do bad work?"

"Not on purpose, ma'am. Had no complaints so far." Eight bits surely wasn't much for the amount of labor he'd done, but then, what did he expect? Ben would entrust him only with his second-best appaloosa. He sent his best animals over to Eagle for their care, or so Harm had claimed once. Didn't make sense.

"Obliged," Ciara said. "Remember me to that girl of yours, won't you?"

She closed the door before Carl could answer.

He took the appaloosa to her stall in the barn, gave her a forkful of hay, and rode off on his bay. As he passed Harm and Kristin's place he thought, Hmmm, a chocolate bar, all the way from England.

***

Eagle was a small settlement in the west central part of Hancock County, Ohio. Its one street was dirt solid as stone and pocked with ruts. Carl passed the bank, the assayer's office, and saloon before coming to the Schmidt's general store. A group of elderly men were sitting in rocking chairs around a cracker barrel on the planks that formed the sidewalk outside Schmidt's. One of them was Ezra Brumm, but Carl didn't recognize the others. Ezra was too old to remember his own name, let alone Carl's. The men were bragging about their exploits in some battle. Must be the War of 1812, Carl thought, although these graybeards looked old enough to have been in the Revolutionary War. Ezra certainly was. Hell, he looked like he could have come over on the *Mayflower*.

Carl dismounted next to a parked stagecoach, threw an empty saddlebag over his shoulder, and tied his horse to the post.

Ezra looked directly at Carl and said, "Lafayette?" as if he were addressing him. The man didn't have a tooth in his mouth or a hair on his head, but his beard hung down below his chest.

Carl couldn't think of anything to say, so he just nodded and went inside.

He was greeted by the pleasant smells of coffee, tobacco, and leather. The only other customers in the store were a family of five: a man, woman, and three young girls, all dressed in black finery, plus another man, presumably the stagecoach driver. Although he knew many of the people in Eagle, this family was unfamiliar to him.

Abner Schmidt was behind the counter. Carl overheard the father tell him that his wife had lost her brother, and they were on the way to the funeral. They had stopped to buy some confectionary to calm the children.

As Carl gathered the supplies he needed, the little girls peered up at him with the sweetest sad eyes, and he was reminded of Jane's funeral in Boston in '32. Since his father's death four years earlier he'd been the man of the family, looking after Claire and their mutual half-sisters, Joanna and Meggie, while Jane was out doing whatever she needed to do to make ends meet and to pay for Claire's schooling. Then the cholera had come and everything changed.

Carl had been seventeen then, Claire going on fourteen. The girls were six and seven. He remembered sitting in the pew with them while the minister had spoken with passion about Satan and redemption, and of the life awaiting those of faith. Like the children in the store today, everyone had been dressed in black. Claire had wept, but Joanna and Meggie were too young to grasp what was happening. The reverend had praised the blessedness and necessity of morality. He'd often glanced with sympathy toward a portly fellow seated a few rows back. Carl had never met him, but was told later that the man was Noah Blackbourne, Claire's father. When Carl and Claire had wed a few years later, she'd told him Blackbourne didn't approve of their match, to the point of developing a hatred for Carl, and perhaps for Claire, too.

Though it had been Jane's funeral, the minister rarely mentioned her name, and Horace's not at all, because the two had never married. Even then, Carl recalled thinking that the reverend's rebuke-byomission was in poor taste. Both were dead, after all. Whatever reward or punishment they were due had already happened.

After the funeral Claire, Joanna, and Meggie had been taken to live with Jane's sister Alice in Ohio, an invitation that was not extended to Carl. He'd been separated from Claire then, but he came back for her three years later. Damn right he did.

Memories of death spurred more memories of death, this one more recent. He recalled that cold and foggy night in Detroit again, when Claire had dragged him to a Shakespeare comedy—a night with tragic consequences that made Job's troubles look like mere annoyance.

"What can I get for you, Hinman?" Abner Schmidt said from behind the counter. Abner had never been an overly friendly man, but today his tone was harsher than usual.

The family had bought what they'd come for. The stagecoach driver held the door open for them. As they filed out, the smallest of the girls took her thumb out of her mouth and smiled at Carl. He smiled back at her. Mariel used to suck her thumb at that age, too.

He placed his supplies on the counter, a bag of sugar, a bag of flour, some salted pork. He couldn't read, but flour was finer than sugar, and meat was, well, meat. "Mariel says you brought chocolate bars back with you from England. I ain't even sure I know what those are. They any good?"

Abner reached under the counter and produced a small rectangular object wrapped in paper. "Wife likes 'em. Looks like mud hardened in the sun, but tastes something like cocoa, or so she says. Never tried 'em myself. They ain't cheap, two bits apiece."

"Hell, Abner, two bits for that?"

"Money ain't just for the bars themselves, it's for the going to England to get 'em."

"Makes sense, I guess." Carl heard the stagecoach pull away outside. He loaded his supplies into his saddlebag and said, "I gotta know. Give me two."

"Keep 'em out of the sun," Abner said. "They melt easy."

"Obliged. What do I owe you?"

Schmidt added the total in his head. "With the chocolate, eleven bits twenty."

Carl knew the coin denominations by their size. Abner counted it twice anyway and dropped it in his till.

Both bars were for Mariel, but he tore the paper off one end and took a small bite as he stepped out onto the planks. The old men were still regaling each other.

Carl grimaced at the taste of the chocolate. It was too bitter for his tastes, but Mariel might like it.

"Lafayette?" Ezra said.

"Lafayette," Carl said.

CHAPTER 26: BILL
"Ships are but boards, sailors but men"

There were five locks in the sixteen miles between Albany and Schenectady, five interminable locks in which the SS *Empire* simply floated between flanking wooden walls and fore and aft gates. But for the slow rising of the water as the lock filled, the boat might be resting in dry dock.

The *Empire* was a remarkable vessel, unlike any Bill had seen before. Its keel was nearly flat and seemed to skim the surface of the Canal without sinking in more than a few feet. The hull was short and compact, with three decks, all painted white, rising above the waterline like a multi-story building. Two funnels on top belched out coal smoke. Bill thought the vessel looked dangerously top-heavy. A strong crosswind ought to capsize it. He wondered what kind of ballast was used to keep it upright.

The most startling difference, though, was the paddlewheel that propelled it. No sails were needed, no tacking, no favorable winds or currents. Noah stood on the port side of the ship where the wheel was mounted, apparently fascinated with the thing, though at the moment it wasn't spinning. More likely, it was just an excuse for him to collect his thoughts in the warm New York sunshine.

Bill grew bored with the motionless wheel and returned to their berth. Their accommodations were little better than steerage on a big liner, but that wasn't a problem. Even the rankest, filthiest steerage compartments were a world above the belly of the whalers he'd spent most of his life in. By comparison, their living space here seemed luxurious.

He wondered, for the thousandth time, what motivated Noah to make this journey. It was a mystery his friend would either reveal to him, or he wouldn't. Perhaps Noah himself didn't know for certain. Bill had no stake in Claire's death, but he'd accepted some kind of unspoken responsibility for Noah since that long-ago night in the *Sea Dog Inn*, when Noah's knee had been so badly damaged. They hadn't met again for over two years after that incident, but the bond remained.

Too much thinking. If he spent one more minute in contemplation, he'd go barking mad. He tried reading a discarded Albany newspaper, but that made him sleepy. He tried sleeping, but that made him restless. He tried pacing, but that made him thirsty, so he walked up two flights of stairs to the second-class passenger lounge and ordered a whisky.

Next to the bar several well-dressed men were playing blackjack and smoking cigars, with a group of ladies, presumably their wives, seated behind them. While the women chattered about the latest fashions from Europe, the men discussed someone named General Scott taking the Mexican city of Veracruz. Bill had seen something about that in the newspaper, but hadn't read the story. When he stopped to listen in on their conversation, the men made no attempt to hide their disdain.

"You've no business here," a man said. "Be on your way."

"Sea rat," a woman said.

Bill looked them over. Here they were in all their finery, putting on an air of beauty and sophistication, culture and superiority. He smiled. He'd gutted whales prettier than they were. But the men were wearing sidearms, so he chose prudence over taking offense. Instead he tipped his cap and said, "Beg pardon ladies, gentlemen."

He finished his whisky and ordered another. The card players resumed their game. "There must be a war on...?" Bill said to the barkeep.

The barkeep rolled his eyes. "You been on the moon, mister? Mexico, Santa Anna? Sound familiar?"

Bill shrugged. "Been out to sea too long. Do you serve food here?"

"Fish," the barkeep said. "Got fresh beefsteak, too, but by the looks of you I'm thinking it's beyond your means."

"My means are just fine," Bill said. He still had nearly two thirds of his wages from the *Titus*, which wasn't bad but was something short of "fine." He'd been eating fish his entire adult life, fish and salted pork. He remembered trying beefsteak once before, in some inn in North Carolina. He found its red color revolting and its flavor greasy. But he wasn't going to let a stranger decide what he could afford. He slapped two nickels onto the counter. "Will this buy me that beefsteak?"

"It'll buy you the fat off a beefsteak."

Bill put two more coins down. "Bring me the whole cow."

The barkeep slid one of the coins back to him. "Sit somewhere. I'll bring it out."

Bill looked toward the tables across the room. The people there were more to his liking. The men were probably laborers or farmers, folks in higher standing than a whaler's botsteer, but not in the same class as the card players. The women? Well, by the way they were dressed, they might be "adventuresses," as polite society called whores. Of course there'd be whores here, even on the steamer *Empire* bound for Buffalo. Bill had put in to port in coastal towns and great cities on every continent save one, and there was not an alley, gutter, or corner that didn't have them. If there was a chance of money changing hands, there'd be whores.

The men were shooting street craps. They had no open chairs. The ladies did and beckoned him to their table. He nodded to them and sat down.

"Oh, you're a ripe one," one of the women said, wrinkling her nose. The powder on her face made her look like a ghost. Her perfume was strong enough to wilt a flower.

"Means he's a working man," said another. "I like working men."

Bill concentrated on the dice game. The wagers were small, and the men didn't have any organized way to keep track of who bet what, but no one seemed to care. They were having fun.

The woman on Bill's left put her hand on his thigh. "These bastards don't know how to treat a lady," she said. "Plenty of money for dice but not a penny for us. Who're you?"

"Everyone calls me Short Bill."

The women giggled. "Good heavens, *that* don't sound promising," said the one fondling his leg.

Bill felt his face flush. "No, my last name is Short. But since I'm tall, the lads turn my names around. Bill Short, Short Bill. It's something of a joke. Never mind."

"Well, the lads call me Paige," she said, "'cause for the right price, this Paige can be turned. If you get my meaning."

Turning Paige was the last thing on Bill's mind. He'd never been comfortable in the company of women, never been alone with one and never wanted to. He gently removed the lady's hand from his leg. If she so much as breathed hard her bosoms would pop right out of the bodice of the dress she was wearing. He looked at her, at her quivering breasts, and marveled at how Noah could have held such love for Jane. It was a feeling he couldn't fathom. "Sorry, madam. I'm only a sailor. I've money for naught but food and drink."

Paige put on a show of outrage. "A sailor, is it? On ships with all those *boys*? Oh, I see how things are."

"I didn't say that—"

She crooned a ditty Bill hadn't heard in years. He was surprised anyone this far inland would know it. "'*Oh, give me the bum of a boy on a boat. It's the tenderest morsel that makes my boat float.*'" She shoved Bill's shoulder. "Help me out, missus, I've forgot the next line."

One of the men looked up from the dice game. "Give it a rest, slut. Don't mean nothing just 'cause he won't pay for the likes of you. I ever get lonely, I'd rather have a go with a boy, or a dog, or a tree stump than you."

"Well," Paige cried, but no tears streaked her powdery cheeks. Bill suspected she'd been insulted before.

The other men laughed and went back to their game.

The ladies scooted their chairs around to the other side of the table from Bill. They pretended to comfort their friend but glared at Bill in earnest. He didn't know what to say or do. He had no love for women— nor men, nor boys, nor dogs or tree stumps—but he didn't go out of his way to hurt anybody's feelings.

His awkwardness was short-lived, as the barkeep soon brought him his beefsteak. He was no longer hungry. The meat was not to his liking anyway. He'd only bought it to make a point. "Ladies," he said, "may I offer you supper?"

The women stopped their commiserating and looked lustfully at the meat. "Is that beefsteak?" Paige said.

"Enjoy," Bill said, then excused himself and returned to his berth below.

Noah was still not back.

CHAPTER 27: JUBAL
"Therefore let him pass for a man"

Jubal dug through his travel trunk, looking for the last letter Annalee had written him. He had no idea how many letters she had actually sent, since he was always on the move, but he savored the ones that did find him. Whenever the show arrived in a new town, the first thing he did was check the local post office, hotel, or general store for mail. He always kept her apprised of their next destination, at least when he knew far enough in advance that he might reasonably expect a letter from her to be waiting for him.

Jubal enjoyed corresponding with his cousin, but too often he'd get only as far as "Dearest Annalee" before some other task demanded his attention. Not tonight. Tonight he had news for her, including LaVoie's decision to return the show to Belgrade, a village uncomfortably close to Detroit. That town represented a time in his life he'd rather forget, the dreadful memories and the endless supply of cruel people who gawked and laughed, as if his capacity for hurt feelings were as small as his frame. The best he could ever expect of them was to be treated as a child, and the worst....

Well, aren't you cute.

It made him shudder.

Buried at the bottom of the trunk he found the costume he'd been wearing when LaVoie had freed him from Kürten's Kabinet of

Kuriosities in '46: the silken blouse with lace cuffs, the waistcoat, the round cap, the funny pantaloons, the shoes made for a normal man but ridiculously oversized for Jubal. Kürten might as well have played a hand organ and made Jubal dance and chitter like a monkey.

LaVoie had never saddled him with the outfit when Jubal joined the ten-in-one, for which he was eternally grateful. He was allowed to dress as a man. How the Major had heard of him and his accounting skills was a bit of a mystery, but Jubal had learned never to question good fortune when it came his way.

He probably should have burned the clothes from his Detroit nightmare, but he kept them around as a reminder: *Never again.*

All of Annalee's letters had been bundled together in a stack and tied with string, but Petey was constantly digging through Jubal's trunk, looking for this or that. The lad was goodhearted, but he'd never been taught respect for personal privacy.

Jubal found the letters by the lingering scent of hyacinth and jasmine perfume Annalee always applied to the wax that had sealed the envelopes. The aroma brought back visions of her lovely face and perfect skin, her dark auburn hair, her laughter that twinkled and danced like a spring brook, her beguiling ways.

Jubal breathed in the smell of her perfumes, of *her*, and the memories came flowing back, good and bad. He reread her most recent letter, then sat down with quill and ink to share his news with her. Thoughts of Detroit was churning him up inside, but writing to Annalee always calmed him.

***

Dearest Annalee,

How sweet my Summer has been! Living and roaming the country has restored to me strength of Body and Spirit. Remember how we danced and played when I came to you from Boston? And the swimming! It was joyous. My thoughts now likewise ring.

My days are full here, my duties many. I have acquired a young friend, a boy named Petey. He's a fine fellow with a sad tale. His white Mother was kidnapped by Indians in the early 30s. Back in 38, when Petey was four, his Indian Father was killed when the government sent troops to force his tribe out of Indiana. Remember the Trail of Death? He and his Mother were rescued by the soldiers, but I believe she has since died. In any case, she was at that time unable to care for him alone in white society, so she sent him to live with relatives in Terre Haute. Petey tells me these people hated his Indian blood and beat him daily, so when our ten-in-one came to town, he ran away to join us. I have taken him under my wing, and think of him, almost, as a son.

I know what you're thinking: What is Jubal, an unmarried man, doing raising a boy? You know I've always loved children.

That brings me to my main reason in writing you, Cousin. I have discovered a treasure, a mate for my Soul. She radiates with Life and fills me with newfound vigor. We spend evenings talking about all those things young sweethearts do—and I a man of 39 years! Such foolishness, I know, but my heart sings. No, I do not share our secrets, which are yours and mine alone. Nor have I expressed to her my feelings; I cannot bear to tell her. She may suspect, but I am afraid to speak, lest her affections lie with another, or with no-one at all. She acknowledges my stature but does so without the slightest ridicule. I have respectable Employment, yet what have I to offer her beyond my small wages? She is so worldly, and I so naïve in these matters.

You know, Cousin, such things I only confide in you.

I have more news. It appears our journey will take us full circle. We shall be traveling toward Detroit for the Independence Day week-end. Our advance agent promises great crowds will be gathered in a little village called Belgrade. I am aware of the risks, but LaVoie insists that we go where the money is.

Therefore, I hope to see you again soon.

Has any handsome new Lothario captured your fancy? I am anxious to hear of your latest adventures!

Your adoring Cousin and obedient Servant,

Jubal

***

Normally Jubal shaved before he went out in public, but today he was tired and didn't bother. He still wore his suit, though, along with his fancy D'Orsay hat, because he liked the way he looked in good clothes. The suit was a little constricting, but the soft beaver pelt of the hat was both comfortable and practical. Besides, its high top made him appear taller.

He saddled the pony Chelsea and rode her into town, which was no more than a small clutter of buildings at a bend in the road. There wasn't even a livery stable. The lone hotel, Jubal learned, consisted of three rooms on the second floor of a saloon. He figured these were most likely let by the hour to folks whose need for a bed didn't include sleeping. If this town was like most of these little one-horse settlements, the saloon would also serve as the post office and probably general store, too.

There were only four people inside, a crooked old man behind the bar, a piano player with a cigar in one hand and a drink in the other, and two bearded farmers playing draughts at the table closest to the door.

"Dammit, ya gotta jump," one of them cried, startling Jubal, who at first thought the man was talking to him.

"Like hell," the other said.

"It's the rules, Clete."

"Since when?"

Jubal left them to their argument and approached the bar. The barkeep had thick spectacles balanced on the tip of his nose. His lips moved as he counted a stack of silver coins.

Peering up at the counter, Jubal removed his hat, cleared his throat, once, twice, a third time.

"We don't serve children," the old man said. "Get outta here."

"Who's a child?" Jubal said. His deep voice must have surprised the barkeep.

"What the hell?" he said. "You got whiskers like a full-growed man."

"Could be because I *am* a full-grown man," Jubal said. Lord knew he was used to that reaction. He introduced himself and asked if he had any mail waiting for him.

"Don't look like much growing was involved." The old man checked beneath the bar and said, "Nope, nothing for nobody named Lawson."

Not surprising, but disappointing nonetheless. Perhaps there'd be a letter from Annalee waiting in Jeffersonville. No matter. Jubal hadn't come to get mail, but to send. "Do you have a courier to Detroit?" he said.

The old man frowned. "It'll cost."

"How much?"

He checked a chart on the wall. "A letter to Detroit? Says here six bits."

"Seventy-five *cents*?" Jubal whistled.

"You could send it by coach. Got one coming through in a couple of days. Won't cost you nothing then."

If he did that, Annalee would have to pay for the letter when it arrived. The cost was nominal for someone who'd come into her parents' fortune, but Jubal didn't think anyone should have to pay to read his missives. "Don't want to put her out the money."

"Come July one, the government's issuing adhesive postage stamps. Put one on a envelope and drop the envelope in the mail sack. The sender'll always pay then, not the one receiving. I hear it'll only cost two cents, or maybe a nickel. Whole lot better than six bits."

"What's *adhesive*?" said one of the farmers. He was speaking to the barkeep but eyeing Jubal with suspicion.

"Means the stamp sticks to the envelope all by itself, Clete," the barkeep said. "Well, you gotta lick it first."

"Like revenue stamps?" said the farmer who wasn't Clete. He also glared at Jubal.

"I reckon, except it's not for taxes."

"What is it for, Ike?"

"Lets the government know you paid to send the letter."

"So it's really a tax, too," the second farmer said. "A tax on the mail. Well, what'll they tax us for next, breathing?"

Ike the barkeep shrugged. "Don't worry, Orry, being out in the middle of nowhere, we ain't likely to get ours till autumn anyhow."

Ike, Orry and Clete, and the anonymous piano player. Always good to know people's names.

Jubal was amused by the farmers' ignorance, but concerned by their interest in him. "I'll just have to go with the courier, then." He slapped the letter and a silver half-dollar onto the counter. "Looks like I'm a little short," he said with a smile and a wink.

Neither Ike nor the farmers laughed. The piano player was so pickled he probably hadn't noticed Jubal's arrival. That joke had always worked to defuse the tension he caused whenever he mixed with normal-sized folk. Apparently these men didn't have a sense of humor. He placed two dimes and a nickel on top of the silver piece. "Six bits," he said.

The farmers stood up, which seemed to make Ike nervous. "Might I interest you in a drink, too?" the barkeep said.

"Not today."

Clete moved in front of the door, blocking the only exit, while Orry approached the bar.

"Look at this here little feller, all dressed up in a highfaluting suit and hat," Orry said. "Me 'n' Clete been wondering, where'd a freak like you get them clothes?"

Jubal hated that word. He'd been saddled with it his whole life. But he wasn't among friends here, so it was best not to let his anger show. He grinned at the sodbusting bastard. Affecting a bluster that would make LaVoie proud, he said, "Good sir, standing before you is such a freak of nature as you have never before seen in all your days. A freak of astonishing fame and grandeur, celebrated in the greatest cities of Europe. I once dazzled the young Queen of England herself. She was so taken with me, she invited me to sit at her side beside the throne. Have you ever beheld such a sight as myself?"

He removed his hat and bowed theatrically.

"You Tom Thumb or something?" Clete said.

"Tom Thumb was my replacement when other engagements forced me to turn down Mr. Barnum's offer."

Orry's jaw clenched. "Whoever he is, he's got more fertilizer coming outta his mouth than the north end of a south-bound mule."

Jubal put his hat back on and tried to think of a way out of this impending pickle.

Clete stepped up beside him, then bent over and looked him in the face. "Listen here, Orry," he said. He picked Jubal up by the armpits and shook him. "I seen this little feller before. You hear them coins a-jingling in his pocket?"

Orry nodded. "I surely do."

"You know where he got them?" Clete's voice had an ominous tone Jubal had heard many times before.

Ike quickly gathered Jubal's letter and money and set everything beneath the counter. "Come on, Orry, Clete," he said, "you got a problem with him, take it outside." He turned to the piano player. "Lou, play something happy."

Lou gaped at him and belched. "I gotta piss," he said. He looked down. "Oops, too late."

"This don't concern you, Ike," Clete said. He put Jubal down. "Or maybe it does. You go see that medicine show the other night?"

"I didn't go in," Ike said. "I just went so my grandson could ride the pony. An Injun boy led kids 'round in a circle outside the big tent. Didn't look all that interesting to me, but my grandson liked it."

"I'd wager my farm this here's the little bugger who come out barking and drawing a crowd so's that flimflam scoundrel that calls himself a major could sell us his quack remedy."

"Reckon you're right," Orry said. He took hold of one of Jubal's arms, while Clete grabbed the other.

Jubal stiffened. "Unhand me, sirs."

"Like hell," Clete said. "I bought a bottle of your boss's potion. My wife's got a bad fever, so I give her some spoonfuls just like he said. She puked it back up, and next day's she's just as sick as before, maybe worse."

"I got some, too," Orry said. "When it spilled on the floor my dog licked it up. Damn near killed him."

Jubal drew a deep breath. This wasn't the first time he'd encountered unhappy victims of LaVoie's concoction. "Gentlemen," he said, "I sympathize. You see, when I was a lad just entering manhood, I attended a performance of the Major's show. After hearing his pitch, I convinced myself his elixir would cure me of my diminutive stature, although he had made no such claim. Imagine, friends, what it was like for me, a vigorous young man trapped in the body of a six-year-old child. So when the Major spoke of the wonders of his nostrum, I immediately bought a bottle and eagerly drank its contents."

Orry and Clete watched him intently. Ike did, too. He was now holding a shotgun. Jubal wasn't sure who it was intended for.

"Go on," Clete said.

"Well," Jubal continued, "as you can see, it did not bestow normal size upon me. Like you, I was incensed. I cursed the Major as a huckster in the employ of Satan himself." He paused for effect. "But bear with me, friends, for, believe me or not, the Major is the most honest of men. To that I can testify. Although he had never claimed his potion would end my affliction, he happily refunded my money. Being a medical doctor, he was able to explain to me that mine is an unnatural condition of the bones and sinews, while diseases are the result of a natural imbalance in the humors of the body. No medicine, not even his, can overcome an unnatural condition, but people who are merely sufferers of natural disease are susceptible to its curative properties. He not only returned my money, but he also gave me another bottle without charge and bade me use it should someone I love become incapacitated.

"As it happened, my own dear mother was a victim of the cholera outbreak of '32. Oh, my friends, have you ever seen the effects of the blue death on the human body? It is horrible, horrible. No Christian man or woman should have to endure such indignities. For two weeks I had watched her waste away, two weeks that felt like two years. Though she had survived longer than most, I despaired of ever witnessing her recovery. In desperation, I administered the Major's elixir. And slowly, slowly she improved. It did not occur overnight, my friends. Most assuredly not. But it *did* occur, and within another week's time she was fully restored to the loving woman who raised me. I can only ascribe the improvement to the Major's medicine. I was so delighted that I joined with him the next time his show came my way, and I have remained contentedly at his side from that day to this."

"How come it took so long?" Clete said.

Jubal was waiting for that. "The answer is simple, Clete—may I call you Clete?—although in telling you this I am revealing a great secret that most men of medicine will not admit. The secret is this: Not all people are the same. They are affected differently by similar conditions. Medical science will have you believe that for each affliction there exists a single solution that is the same for everyone. But I testify to you now that this is untrue. Have you not seen one man die from the tiniest of scrapes, while most shrug it off and heal within days? The same precept applies to medicine. What succeeds in minutes for some may not succeed for weeks or even months for others. And I must confess the sad fact that, for those few most unhappy of souls, medicine will not help at all.

"And that, sirs, is why the Major has his money-back guarantee. His potion helps a great majority of those to whom it is given, but he does not wish to take advantage of the small number who receive no benefit."

Orry and Clete sat back down at the table. "What about my wife?" Clete said. "She gonna get over this fever or not?"

"I grieve that she was not immediately healed," Jubal said. "I pray that she will be in time. But neither I nor the Major wish to be perceived as villains seeking to profit from the misfortune of others. Thus, although I am confident the bloom of health will be bestowed upon your beautiful bride again within the week, I will, in the Major's name, return your hard-earned money."

For the first time he saw the farmers grin. "Beautiful bride?" Clete said. "Ain't no concoction under God's blue sky can do *that!*"

Both men laughed.

Jubal reached into his pocket and produced two fifty-cent coins.

"It was only two bits apiece," Orry said.

"I appreciate your honesty, Orry, but let there be no taint of scandal upon us. I will double the price you paid."

He placed two coins on the table in front of them.

Orry raised a coin to his mouth to test the metal, but his teeth were rotten and he winced when he bit down. "Hellfire," he said. "I gotta stop doing that."

"And please," Jubal said, "buy your dog a bone at our expense."

"You ain't such a bad littler feller after all," Orry said.

Ike put the shotgun under the counter. Lou finally started to play the piano and sing. The lyrics were to "Adams and Liberty," but he played the tune, now better known as "The Star Spangled Banner," in a different key than he sang, mostly because he sang in no key known to man.

Jubal smiled. "Next time our show is in these parts, I hope you'll come again to see the greatest spectacle in the universe."

"Don't press your luck," Clete said.

"Indeed, sir."

"Say, do you play checkers?"

"I call it draughts, but yes, I enjoy a good game every now and again."

"Is it true you gotta jump when you can?" Clete said.

Orry glared at him, daring him to give the wrong answer.

Either way, Jubal was going to make one of them angry again. "I've played it both ways. I like them equally well."

He tipped his hat and strode out the door as quickly as his short legs would take him without appearing to be fleeing.

CHAPTER 28: MARIEL
"There is nothing either good or bad, but thinking makes it so"

It was raining. On Sunday, June 6, 1847, at last it was raining. The storm had blown in during the night, lighting the heavens and pounding the earth. Water dripped in through gaps in the roof, but Mariel didn't care. The rain made Daddy happy, and that made her happy.

To celebrate, her father had taken her to church himself this morning. He hadn't set foot in a church since Momma died. Usually he stayed home and she rode in with the Jensens, but today he said he wanted to give proper thanks.

Reverend Rodgers practically sang his sermon today, giving voice to the two dozen farm families who had been praying for rain since April. "You see," he bellowed, "God listens. He answers. May each of you find a bounteous harvest in the earth and glory in your soul."

The downpour continued throughout the service, a steady drumbeat on the windows. The entire congregation, dressed in their Sunday finest, was soaked to the skin from the trip in. No one complained. Even her father was wearing a white shirt and tie, though the shirt was smudged and the tie edge-worn. He grinned at Mariel and squeezed her hand.

Maybe everything would finally be all right. Mariel noticed, though, that Harm and Mrs. Jensen seemed distant today. Oh, they were laughing and singing like everyone else, but whenever Harm looked at her father, his smile disappeared.

She wondered what happened. Why would Harm be angry with Daddy?

After Reverend Rodgers stood at the door as people filed out. He nodded at the ladies and shook hands with the men, offering all a kind word. When Mariel and her father approached him, he got down on one knee and clasped Mariel's shoulders with hands big as feed sacks. "Little one, your mother is looking down on us this day, and she is smiling." Then he stood up and clapped her father on the back. "Good to see you, Carl. I hope you'll come again. Blessings upon you and your beautiful child."

"Thank you, Reverend. I enjoyed your sermon."

Mariel and her father stepped out into the rain. At the bottom of the church's steps he stopped and raised his face to the sky. It was as if he were trying to soak up all the water from the sky and save it for later.

"Daddy?" she said. "I'm getting cold."

He lifted her onto the buckboard. "All right, my angel," he said.

As he climbed up beside her, Mariel saw Harm and Mrs. Jensen whispering something to Reverend Rodgers while all three of them looked at her father.

Her father had noticed as well.

"What are they talking about, Daddy?" she said.

"It's nothing, darling. Grownup business."

He clacked his tongue at the horse and the buckboard pulled forward. He had to wait for the Schmidts' wagon to pass, though, and in those few moments Harm and Reverend Rodgers caught up with them.

"Carl," Harm said, "if you won't talk to me, will you talk to James? He's given counsel to many a troubled soul."

Her father looked at Reverend Rodgers, who nodded back at him.

"I got plenty to answer to the Lord for," her father said, "but ain't none of it what Harm thinks."

"What I'm thinking, Carl, is that you got yourself a heavy burden," Harm said.

"Let me help you bear it," Reverend Rodgers said. "It will be good for your soul."

"My soul's out of your reach," her father said, and pulled out behind the Schmidts.

CHAPTER 29: NOAH
"Thus conscience does make cowards of us all"

The steamer didn't speed up, it didn't slow down, it simply maintained the same monotonous pace, mile after mile after mile. The Canal was smooth as glass, except during an afternoon thunderstorm. Even then the waves were laughable compared with the monstrous walls of water pushed ahead of hurricanes and nor'easters. After an hour the clouds started to thin, allowing a few rays of sun through to light patches of the New York forests and farmlands. Noah and Short Bill stood on the top deck watching the hills crawl by.

"All that green," Noah said. He'd lived within sight of the sea as a child. In the ports he'd visited all down the Eastern Seaboard to South America since, he'd never ventured so far as the landward boundary of a town, even during those two years married to Jane. He was used to wood and stone and dark corners in the guts of a city, spires and slums, rats and stray dogs, never these queasy expanses of green. The Erie Canal was more than wide enough to accommodate the *Empire*, yet Noah felt as if the banks were pushing in on him. Green to the horizon, blue to the horizon, it shouldn't matter, but there was no sense of mystery on land, no sense of the infinite, no sense of the divine. A lonely lookout in a crow's nest during a gale knew God. An awestruck apprentice seeing Saint Elmo's fire blaze on the yardarms knew God. A drowning man certainly knew Him, but who, or what, could anyone feel here? "I can't breathe," Noah said. "There's no *space*. It's as if I'm waiting for the coffin lid to close."

Short Bill looked up as the sun passed behind a cloud, dropping a shadow over them. "Go below, then, mate, and dream we're sailing on a calm sea."

"At least there's water beneath our feet." Noah turned away from the scenery and limped toward the stairs leading down to their berth. His body hurt more each day.

Short Bill accompanied him. "Your melancholy seems worse than usual," he said. "I've got one for you: what's it called when the President eats bacon?"

"A pig in a Polk," Noah said.

"You've heard that one."

"No more than a hundred times."

"Did you know the country is at war?"

"With who?"

"Mexico, I think."

"What's our quarrel with Mexico?"

"I haven't a clue," Short Bill said. "There's a newspaper on the bed. Someone named General Scott took Veracruz."

"Scott's on our side?"

"It seems so, but I didn't read the story."

Noah stopped at the top of the stairs and looked down dolefully. Four flights. Descending steps was harder on his bad knee than climbing them. "I'm weary, mate," he said. "I'm worn out and tired of everything. I don't want to go down into the belly of this beast today."

"What do you want?" Short Bill said.

"I want to be young again with Jane and Claire in a house by the sea."

"Can't build a life on regrets. Have you been to the passengers' lounge? They've got food and whisky aplenty, and playing cards. What better to ease your yearnings?"

"You don't know what my yearnings are," Noah said.

"Do you?"

***

Later that afternoon, outside the lounge, they encountered an overdressed black man wearing a wool coat with astrakhan lining the bottom hem and cuffs. His hair and whiskers had gone white, and the lines in his face told his life's story. He didn't appear to be doing anything, just standing with his back to the wall and his eyes on his feet. Noah had worked with a few Negroes on whalers over the years, all of them free men born in the North. Of course he and Short Bill had mingled with many colored people in the Caribbean, and had once spent a memorable night in a voodoo den in Haiti. That was silly nonsense from which he'd emerged laughing, stumbling, and stinking drunk, but certainly not undead.

"What's your destination?" Short Bill said to the man.

The old fellow seemed surprised that a white man would engage him in conversation. "Me, sir?" Several of his teeth were missing, causing his cheeks to sink into his face. What teeth that remained were yellow.

"Well, I know where *we're* going," Short Bill said with an amiable smile.

"Of course, sir. Buffalo."

"You have family there?"

The man spoke slowly, almost warily, as if he expected the situation to go bad. His eyes never left his shoes. "No, sir. I don't have family. The man I'm traveling with has business there."

"He's in the lounge? Why aren't you with him?"

"I take my meals in my room below."

Noah understood immediately what the man was saying, and he could see that Short Bill did, too. "New York is a free state," Short Bill said. "Just walk away from him."

The old gentleman finally looked up. His white hair against black skin made him look so dignified, but his jaundiced eyes were fiery as a cat's and brimming with powerful emotions Noah couldn't begin to fathom. "And go where, sir?"

***

Noah forked a piece of cod into his mouth. "Three showing," he said. He turned up the card that was lying face down. It was a seven. He tapped it with the blunt end of his knife. "Another."

Short Bill had a ten, a six, and an ace showing. He dealt Noah a four.

"Fourteen," Noah said. "Can't stop with that." He tapped his cards again. Bill dealt him a nine. "Twenty-three. Story of my life."

The lounge was sparsely populated. Two couples and their children were eating just inside the entrance, and some laborers were playing cards at the next table over. Whoever the black man's companion was, he must have left shortly after they arrived. None of the laborers looked as if they could afford a slave.

"You owe me a halfpenny," Short Bill said.

"Put it on my tab."

"One more hand?"

Noah took another bite of cod. "Not my day," he said. He finished his meal in silence.

Short Bill went to the bar and got them each a glass of whisky.

Noah listened to the paddlewheel chugging and the seagulls squawking. A boat that didn't depend on sails or oars wasn't natural.

Short Bill sat down and pushed a glass across the table to him. He jerked his thumb toward the lounge door. "That old colored man out there. What are your thoughts on slavery?"

"Don't have any."

"You don't think it's wrong?"

"It's the way of things. Can't say as I like or don't like coloreds. Nothing specific, but I'm not comfortable around them."

"Except for Haiti," Short Bill said, raising his glass.

Noah managed a weak smile and clinked his glass against Short Bill's. "Except for Haiti."

They sipped their whisky and sat quietly for several moments. Short Bill stared at Noah throughout the silence, his expression growing more and more somber. Finally he said, "When was the last time you saw Claire?"

Noah twirled his glass, watching the amber liquid swirl around the bottom. "You know the story."

"Tell me again."

Noah sighed. "I raised her until she was two. That's when Jane left me. Only time I saw her since was at Jane's funeral in '32. She was thirteen or fourteen then. She'd grown into a fine young lady."

Both men gulped their whisky. Short Bill wiped his mouth on his sleeve and said, "Been meaning to ask—"

"Don't," Noah said. "Not your concern."

"It *is* my concern," Short Bill said. "I made this journey on faith because you're my friend. I've a right to know."

Noah rose and walked out of the lounge. He hauled himself up the stairs to the deck again and looked out at the identical New York scenery he'd seen an hour, and a day, and two days, ago.

Short Bill followed him.

Noah turned to face his friend. "There was no blood between Claire and Hinman, so there was nothing unholy in their marriage. And Jane never bothered herself with divorcing me, so the children were never even brother and sister by law. But for many years they had lived in the same house as if they were, or so I thought. It sickened me. It sickens me still."

"Then why make this journey?"

"Claire was my daughter, and I let her go. If I'd fought for her, none of this would have happened."

"Ifs and ifs and ifs, mate."

"I failed to do right by her during her life, but by God, I will now."

"And if the mystery turns out to be nothing?"

"I will have answered to myself."

CHAPTER 30: MARCUS
"And pluck my magic garment from me"

The show stopped outside of Jeffersonville in an open field LaVoie had rented from a local farmer. Although it was a prime location, straddling the main road into town, he resented the outrageous sum of four dollars a day, plus deposit, that the yokel was charging him. Garrett had negotiated two dollars a day, but that had changed when Jubal had insisted they move up the arrival date. When the company rolled in two days early, the farmer sensed he had LaVoie over a barrel and increased the price. And he was right, because it made no sense to set up in one location, then break camp and move to another two days later.

Jubal was directing the raising of the main tent while Cuff unbridled the team from the lead wagon. LaVoie watched the little man's eyes follow her as she and Petey fetched water for the horses. Petey must have said something clever, because Cuff smiled and touched him on the hand. Jubal frowned as if he were jealous of her attention to the boy. His adoration of her was unseemly. However, his attraction worked to LaVoie's advantage. Cuff had done an admirable job of softening his objection to Belgrade. Oh, he was still gnawing that bone, but he wasn't squawking as often or as loudly.

Today it wasn't just jealousy or Belgrade that had Jubal out of sorts. While buying supplies in Jeffersonville, he'd retrieved a long-awaited correspondence from his cousin. Her news had distressed him. Apparently the lady was having man troubles. She made a habit of encouraging the wrong type of suitor, and had found herself with another bad one. Jubal had seen her through many an awkward situation, or so he claimed, but as she was in Detroit and he in southern Indiana, there was nothing he could do to assist her at the moment. Then again, the show would be traveling to Michigan soon. The cousin's problem was another argument LaVoie could use to convince him of the desirability of Belgrade.

It was mid-afternoon under a blue sky. The day was warm but not hot, a pleasant surprise for this time of year in southern Indiana. The humidity was low, with just enough of a breeze to keep the workers from overheating. Underlying the smells of canvas and sweat were the sweet aromas of wildflowers and prairie grass.

As was his custom, LaVoie walked through the camp as it was being erected. Off to one side the performers had emerged from their wagons to begin the setup. Artest had left with the four bottles of brandy Jubal had given him on the night he was discharged, but the rest of the men were hard at it. André, Leopold, and Giovanni busied themselves with cutting paths into the tall grass and laying sawdust, while Otto, Manfred, and Herman strung rope fences from the road, leading to the tent. Herman made a snide comment about Manfred's breasts, to which Manfred replied, "Is that Hermione's envy or Herman's lust speaking?"

"Herman need never be lustful when Hermione is willing," Herman said. All three men laughed.

The acts were good about helping with mundane tasks, but Jubal engaged local rousters to do the heavy lifting. This time he'd hired men who seemed to enjoy the work, stout fellows who sang and roughhoused with one another as they toiled. The circle for the tent had been drawn, the stakes driven, the post holes dug, the canvas laid out. The men attached the block and tackle and slid the poles under the canvas.

LaVoie paused to admire the scene. No matter how many times he witnessed the tent's raising, it always gave him goose flesh. Once it reached its full height, the rousters went inside to set the center pole, stretching the tent to its full glory.

Satisfied, LaVoie went to his wagon and pulled the canvas flap down behind him. He opened his locker. Inside, among his other precious possessions, lay a tall bundle of paper bound with baling twine. He pulled it out and sat down. On the cover sheet, written by hand, was the title, *The Secret Book of Magick.*

***

LaVoie knew the fellow was trouble the instant he entered his wagon. He was dressed in torn and dirty clothing, but it was his feral, hungry look that gave him away. This was a man who tracked human beings for a living: a slave hunter.

LaVoie had been expecting a visit like this since Cuff joined the show.

"You LaVoie?" he said, and his Southern accent was genuine, vowels thick as custard in the back of his throat.

"I am."

"Name's Tom Villisca. I hear tell you got a nigga gal singing in your show."

"I have a *woman* singing in my show."

"I come up from Kentuck with a warrant for a slave that escaped from Mr. Julian Beddow. She's small, with skin a shade or two lighter than your everyday nigga. Goes by the name of Cuff."

LaVoie betrayed no reaction. "Cuff? Don't know her. My singer's name is Guinevere Brewer."

"Like hell."

"Are you saying every small, light-skinned colored woman is a slave named Cuff?"

"Naw, they ain't. But I got a reason to believe yours is." Villisca unfolded two sheets of paper and set them on the desk in front of LaVoie. "First is a likeness of her. Second is a legal warrant for the return of Mr. Beddow's property. If you got her, I'm taking her."

LaVoie didn't even glance at the papers. "Would I be stupid enough to employ an escaped slave in the border states?"

"Maybe you're counting on me thinking you ain't stupid enough to do that. I don't care. My job's to bring Cuff back."

"Excuse me one moment," LaVoie said. He went to the front of the wagon and lifted the flap. Petey was outside with the pony Chelsea. LaVoie beckoned to the boy and bade him to fetch Otto. Then he returned to his chair and studied the papers. "I understand your confusion, Mr. Villisca. The rendering does bear a slight resemblance. Yet need I remind you, sir, that Indiana is a free state?"

Villisca had obviously heard this argument before. "Fugitive Slave Act, 1793."

LaVoie shook his head. "Unenforceable. In any case, irrelevant. My 'nigga gal,' as you so charmingly refer to her, has been with me for some years, and in fact came with me from Canada West in the early '40s."

Otto poked his head inside the flap. "You sent for me, Major?"

LaVoie motioned him in.

"Is this ape intended to intimidate me?" Villisca said, tapping his gun in its holster, a Colt Paterson revolver. "If your colored songbird is Mr. Beddow's, ain't heaven or hell will stop me from taking her."

"I'm afraid," LaVoie said, "you will have to ply your trade elsewhere, Mr. Villisca. You have the wrong woman."

"I'll decide that when I see her."

"No, sir," LaVoie said, "you will not. You are vile. A slave hunter is the lowest form of vermin to crawl the earth. Otto, will you escort this gentleman off the grounds?"

Otto smiled. The strongman was six and a half feet tall and shirtless. "Glad to, Major."

"If he resists, you may use any means necessary to encourage his departure. If he returns for the performance tonight, you may indulge yourself."

Villisca's hand crept toward the revolver. "If I shot you, I'd be within my rights. Self-defense."

With a quickness that belied his size, Otto crossed the distance between them before Villisca could react further. He loomed over him and said, "You don't want to think about what'll happen to you if you touch that gun. In fact…" He reached down, took the Colt, emptied its bullets, and returned the weapon.

"I have a legal warrant," Villisca protested.

LaVoie shrugged. "I have Otto."

***

Cuff didn't seem worried. "Mr. Major LaVoie," she said, "I been dodging slave hunters longer than you been selling your moonshine. I don't soil my bloomers every time one comes sniffing 'round."

They were sitting alone at a table in the tent.

"This one called himself Tom Villisca."

Cuff shrugged. "Don't matter, they're all the same. I don't know why Beddow wants me back so bad. I read his children to sleep, is all. Maybe he can't find other slaves that can read." Her face tightened with disgust. "Ain't legal schooling us down there, you know."

"Is there anything I can do? Otto will be on the lookout for Villisca tonight, but if someone different comes, or he brings the law…."

"There's one thing," Cuff said. "Been meaning to talk to you. I was in Jeffersonville with Jubal today, and I met these two people looking for work, a man and his wife."

"I have all the help I need, Cuff."

"They can cook or wash our clothes, or even help us set up so's you don't have to hire so many rousters. Names are Destiny and Cyrus."

LaVoie rose and paced with his hand clasped behind his back. An inkling of a suspicion was entering his mind. "This Destiny and Cyrus wouldn't happen to be colored, would they?"

"What, you don't like colored folks? 'Cause, you know, I can leave—"

"You know better than that. Are they runaway slaves?"

"I didn't ask."

LaVoie paused by the table, looked down at her, and sighed. "I'm a showman," he said. "I provide a few moments of diversion from people's troubles, that's all." He sat down across from her and grasped her hands. "I like you a great deal, Cuff, and I admire you. I really do. But I've got no part in great causes."

"Maybe it's time you did."

"In any case, my expenses are spread thin as it is. We do our own cooking and laundering—"

Cuff stood up. "Mr. Major LaVoie, Indiana's a free state, but that don't mean they like us up here. Ain't easy for colored folk to find regular work. Cyrus and Destiny, they don't need much. They're young, strong folks. They'll work for less than what you pay the rousters."

"I'd have to feed them, and find a place for them to sleep, and—"

"I'll pay 'em outta what you pay me, if I got to. You could give 'em Artest's bed in that wagon to sleep in. But it don't matter, they'll sleep on the floor, they'll sleep under the wagons, they'll do whatever you want. Please, Mr. LaVoie. You know what masters do to slave wives down there?"

LaVoie nodded. "I can imagine."

"No, you can't. And then they sell 'em, and the next master does the same. Husbands and wives never see each other again, and if they got children, they don't see them, neither. Nobody sees nobody. Dying's a kinder fate than what happens to slaves."

LaVoie studied her. Her crow's feet were deep and narrow, her jaw clenched. Her pulse pounded visibly in her neck. Lord knew she was a strong woman, full of pride. She wouldn't lower herself to begging, but he saw in her eyes a look of such fierce desperation that he couldn't say no. "The one thing I do not need with slavers on the hunt is more colored people traveling with the show. But for you, Cuff, just this once. This one time."

A single tear slid down the right side of her nose and beaded on her lip. She leaned over and kissed his hand, and he could feel the coolness of the tear on his skin. "Underneath all your big talk and your pretend accent," she said, "you are a Godly man, Mr. Major LaVoie."

***

"Before the main event," LaVoie called out, "I'll need a volunteer to help me with an amazing demonstration of the power of the mind." He scanned the crowd and spotted a middle-aged woman with brown hair. "How about you, madam?"

She blushed and lowered her eyes. "Well, I don't know."

A man with a thick neck and a large hole in his hat, presumably her husband, moved between her and LaVoie. "She ain't going up there with the likes of you, mister. You just leave her brain be."

LaVoie smiled. "Very well then. How about you?" To the crowd he shouted, "What say you?"

They bellowed their approval.

"All right, but I'll be watching you."

"What is your name, sir?"

"Mangin."

As he introduced the trick, LaVoie sensed something different with Mangin. Instead of the usual attitude of embarrassment or exaggerated glee he received from most of his volunteers, Mangin seemed hostile. Yet he did as instructed and turned away as LaVoie marked his paper with his usual flourish. He folded it and showed it to the audience to demonstrate that the number was not visible. "I will now call forth my assistant. Mr. Lawson, will you join us?"

Jubal stepped onto the stage. "At your service, Major." He chalked his name on the paper as always, and slipped it into his vest.

"Our hands will remain in plain sight at all times. Neither of us can alter the paper in any way. Open your eyes, Mr. Mangin, and turn to face us." The man did so. "Now think. A number between one and ten will appear in your mind's eye. When you're certain of it, reveal it to us all."

"Four," he said.

"Mr. Lawson?"

Jubal's timing was usually impeccable, his performance flawless, but tonight his attention was elsewhere, and he made a mistake. As he pulled from his vest the paper bearing the number four, he also dislodged an identical sheet with the number three. It fluttered to the wooden floor, its writing invisible to the audience but its meaning unmistakable.

"What in hell?" Mangin said, pointing to the paper on the stage. He turned toward Jubal. "I knowed you was a villain. Little feller, you best open up that vest of yours, and I mean now."

Jubal's eyes held a look of panic LaVoie had not seen before. "Now, why would you want to undress my assistant in front of all these good people?" he said.

"I ain't undressing him, I'm exposing *you*," Mangin said. "'Cause the way I see it, he's got ten pockets in that vest, and every one of 'em's got his name on the back and a different number writ by you on the front. Ain't no 'power of the mind' to it."

"Are you calling me a fraud, Mr. Mangin?"

"All you got to do to prove you ain't is to tell the dwarf to open his vest."

"I am no *dwarf*, sir," Jubal said.

LaVoie nudged him with his foot. This was not the time to quibble over terminology. "I hardly think it is necessary."

"Open his vest," someone in the audience cried, and then another joined in, and soon the entire crowd was chanting.

LaVoie had seen how quickly an audience can turn from incredulous clod-crushers into a seething mob. This situation was about to explode. He raised his hands to try to quiet them, but among the calls of "Open his vest," he began to hear those most dreaded of words, "tar and feather." Just like Dearbornville.

Mangin abruptly reached down and pulled open one side of Jubal's vest, exposing the ten pockets. "See?" he yelled triumphantly. "This man's a cheat. He's stealing our hard-earned money!"

The crowd started to surge forward, and LaVoie felt his own panic rise. He could talk his way out of most situations, but charm, wit, and intelligence didn't work against brute strength and fury.

The commotion brought all the acts out of the tent. At the same time, two colored people, a man and a woman, stepped out of the audience to join the performers on stage. LaVoie had not met them yet, but they had to be Cuff's new friends Cyrus and Destiny. They formed a barrier between LaVoie and Jubal and the mob. LaVoie was never so pleased that Otto was six and a half feet of sculpted muscle, or that Ophelia the Bearded Lady now transformed into the much more imposing Manfred the Breasted Man, or that Giovanni, bless his heart, carried a sword.

"Stop," Otto snarled, and the crowd paused.

In that moment of silence LaVoie said, "If my harmless diversion has offended you, if my attempt to ease your cares on this night has failed, I will happily refund your money and still grant you admission to the main attraction, the Phantasmagoria. It is not a trick. There is no attempt to deceive. It is all done with the tried and true principles of science. If you'd like, I will demonstrate its inner workings after the show, for often there is more wonder in the knowing than in the not knowing."

"You'll give every nickel back?" Mangin said. "What about that potion you sold?"

LaVoie sighed. "For that, too."

Mangin's smiled smugly. "You might just get through this night alive, maybe even without feathers."

LaVoie couldn't afford the loss of income, but it was better than being torn to pieces. Or tarred and feathered. Or torn to pieces *and* tarred and feathered. He'd been tarred once, and that was an experience he never wanted again. The feathers had pulled out easily enough, but it had taken him over a week to wash, rub, and peel the tar off.

He nodded to Jubal, who went inside the tent to get the strong box.

"Form a line for your refund," he said wearily, forgetting to use his Tennessee accent. "Those with my liniment may keep the bottle and the refund."

Once the money changed hands, not a single person stayed for the Phantasmagoria.

***

After all the excitement, LaVoie and Jubal followed Cuff to the chuckwagon, where she'd carved a space for herself among their food, lumber, tents, and other supplies.

Lying out in the open were her performing dress, with its puffy sleeves and cotton cording, two petticoats, a chemise, and a corset. Her most personal garments seemed to make Jubal uncomfortable. She gathered them up and tossed them aside.

"Why so shy, little man? It's just my clothes without me in 'em."

"I'm not shy," Jubal said, his eyes never leaving his feet.

Cuff laughed. "Lord help you, you ever bust in here and find me in all my glory. Go on now, you gentlemen have a sit down."

LaVoie sat in the chair, Jubal on top of Cuff's trunk. Once the three had settled, Jubal said, "I'm sorry, Marc."

LaVoie shook his head wearily. "We certainly gave them a show, didn't we?"

Jubal sighed. "Not the kind we planned."

"Jubal's timing is usually impeccable with this trick," LaVoie said to Cuff. "There was one night, though, shortly after he joined the show…. Do you remember, Jubal?"

"How could I not? You reminded me about it for weeks."

"What happened?" Cuff said.

"A perfectly understandable mistake. He was new, and he simply drew the paper from the wrong pocket—which, I daresay, made me look foolish. But I talked my way out of it, convincing the yokel that it was he who had made the mistake by calling out the wrong number."

"You *are* a smooth-talking devil, Mr. Major LaVoie," Cuff said.

"On that occasion, there was no indication how the trick was done, so the audience didn't suspect they were being bamboozled. Everyone had a good laugh at me, and then at the yokel. After that the rest of the night went smoothly. I think that was the most liniment I ever sold." He turned toward Jubal. "Tonight, the cheating was apparent for all to see. Fortunately, we got through it without harm."

"Without a penny, either," Jubal said.

"Kindly do not repeat the error, sir."

"My mind was occupied with the letter from my cousin. Once again she's found herself with the wrong beau."

"Lemme tell you about that," Cuff said. "If a woman's got a man, she got man trouble. She don't have a man, she got man trouble. What

I'm saying is, all men're trouble. She best get used to it, 'cause that ain't never gonna change."

"Maybe if I'd been there—"

"You her daddy?"

"No."

"She a grown woman?"

"Yes."

"Then don't get yourself in a dither over something you can't do nothing about. She don't need you choosing her fellas for her."

"It's not the choosing that's trouble, it's the losing. But that's no excuse for letting it distract me. I ruined the night."

"Even I have a bad day every now and again," Cuff said with a grin.

"These things happen," LaVoie said, trying to view the situation philosophically. But he couldn't deny that the loss of income hurt. Hopefully this Zug fellow in Belgrade would come through with the big payday he promised. "Cuff, kindly extend my gratitude to Cyrus and Destiny for stepping in as they did. A bit foolhardy, but appreciated."

Jubal frowned at Cuff. "Those colored people are friends of yours?"

"What, you think all black people know each other?"

"I didn't say that."

Cuff smiled. "Aw, I'm just teasing. I met 'em in town today while you was off buying sawdust and boo-hooing over your cousin's letter."

"The meeting was fortuitous for us," LaVoie said.

"See, I told you they'd be good for the show, Mr. Major LaVoie."

Jubal shot a glance at LaVoie. "You hired them, Marc?"

He nodded.

"For what purpose?"

"Mr. Lawson," LaVoie said, his Tennessee accent in full force, "you discharged Artest without consulting me. Is it now your contention that I need to solicit your permission before making hiring decisions as well?"

"No, but—"

Cuff stood up. "Now look here, Jubal Lawson. We gonna need every hand we got if we mean to skedaddle in the morning."

Jubal's face reddened. "We're going to jump tomorrow? I told the rousters we wouldn't need them again for three days."

"Hence, Cyrus and Destiny," LaVoie said. "Due to your distraction this evening, I'm afraid Jeffersonville is a lost cause." He glanced at Cuff, who nodded almost imperceptibly. "From here, it's straight to Belgrade. That's a guaranteed pay day. We'll only stop overnight along the way, no setup. Cut costs to the bone."

"But the coloreds—," Jubal said.

"They got names," Cuff said.

"Did they not shield us from disaster tonight?" LaVoie said to Jubal. "We both owe them for our dignity at the very least, and perhaps for our lives."

"Where will they stay?" Jubal said. "With Petey and me? Two adults won't fit into Artest's bed. And they'll have their own possessions to bring, which will have to be stored somewhere. Then there's the extra food we'll need to buy—"

"Have I not made myself clear, sir?"

"You have." Jubal hopped down off Cuff's trunk. As he exited the chuckwagon, he paused to give them both a final suspicious glare.

"What's wrong with him?" Cuff said.

LaVoie shrugged and stood up. "He'll be all right. I'd best get ready, too."

"'Fore you run off, I wanna say something."

She didn't speak for a few moments, as if weighing her words.

"And?" LaVoie said. "Speak up, Cuff. It's not like you to hold back."

"All righty, then. I think you're gonna need a new magic trick."

"Oh, don't worry about Jubal. He won't make the same mistake again."

"I don't mean that, I mean put a new one in."

"Why do I suspect you already have this new trick in mind?"

Cuff smiled slyly. "You know me too well. How about a disappearing act?"

"Have you been talking to Jubal? He suggested that after we—he—discharged Artest."

"I knew he was a smart little man."

"We haven't attempted a disappearing act since one went horribly wrong in Dearbornville. Because of it we lost our mirrors and I acquired feathers."

"That would be something to see."

"Are you sure you're not in collusion with Jubal?"

"I don't know what collusion is. But I swear I never talked to him about this."

LaVoie scrutinized her. "Then one is tempted to ask why you're making this suggestion. Perhaps I don't want to know. This wouldn't concern Cyrus and Destiny, would it?"

Cuff radiated innocence at him. "What if it do?"

LaVoie didn't answer. He knew the pair must be runaway slaves, and that they were almost certainly using his caravan to get closer to Canada and freedom from their pursuers. But lots of former slaves escaped to Canada without the need for a disappearing act. Something, to paraphrase Mr. Shakespeare, was rotten in the state of Indiana. "To do it right," he said, "will require a bigger stage than we currently have the resources to build, not to mention replacing those two large mirrors. Neither is inexpensive."

"What're the mirrors for?"

"We need a way to keep the spectators from seeing the person dropping through the trap door."

"Still don't see why mirrors. Just put something in front of the stage so folks can't look under it. A curtain or frilly stuff."

"Would that fool you, Cuff? If somebody disappears from a stage enclosed on the bottom, it's obvious he's hiding under it. But if the audience can see the area beneath and nobody appears there, well, then, that's magic."

Cuff scratched her ear and shook her head. "If you say so."

"Listen, the mirrors are about three feet tall—the height of the space beneath the stage—by five feet long. We put them together, with the outside ends obscured by the tent flaps. The other ends will come together at a ninety-degree angle between the trap door and the audience. They'll form a V, but that junction will be hidden behind a support beam. The point of the V will protrude toward the audience and the mirrors will be tilted slightly downward. That way they'll reflect the ground on either side of the stage, making it look like there's nothing under it."

"Won't it reflect the audience, too?"

"That's why you tilt the mirrors. At that angle they reflect the grass but not the people. And since they'll be between whoever's disappearing and the audience, no one will see the escape, either."

Cuff nodded, but she probably didn't yet understand. "Get some mirrors, then, and wood for a bigger stage."

"With what? And put them where? We'll need a lot more lumber than we have room for now. Even if Jubal and Petey allow Cyrus and Destiny to take Artest's bed, where will we store the wood? I was hoping to move that bed out of there to open up more space."

"You gonna give Jubal and Petey a choice? I thought you was in charge here."

"That's not the point."

"'Course, you're in your wagon all by your own self."

LaVoie shot her a withering glare. "Surely you're not serious, madam."

"Well, maybe not, but you got yourself a good brain, Mr. Major LaVoie. I know you'll think of a way. Some things are worth doing, that's all."

LaVoie was suspicious. "Are you planning to use this act to disappear yourself?"

"You plan to take this show into the South?"

"Of course not."

"Then I'm already disappeared from the place I need to be disappeared from."

"Tonight was a financial disaster. We're still ahead this season, but Zug had better come through with his promised purse."

"Sometimes you got to have faith, Mr. Major LaVoie. You helped me, now I'll help you."

"I'm not sure how acquiring more expenses is helping me. Still, disappearing acts have always been popular…."

LaVoie did some calculations in his head. Jeffersonville was a big enough town that it would have a place that sold mirrors. He didn't know about Belgrade. Every town had lumber, though. Since it took up more room in the wagon than mirrors, they could buy the mirrors here and wait until Belgrade for the wood.

"I see your brain ciphering. Well?"

"You ask a lot, Cuff," he sighed. "With your 'Guinevere Brewer' act replacing Artest, I have my ten-in-one again. And I still have a taxidermy display I want to do."

"Well, I don't got to sing, if it comes to that. But nobody'll miss the floating-in-air trick, neither. I liked all that flying 'round, but you near killed me. I wasn't such a kind-hearted soul, I might've made a fuss about that."

"The audience loved it."

"What, you gonna set something else alight again? 'Cause that's what they liked. One of them white folks been up in the air instead of this here colored gal, maybe they're not so happy."

"I must admit I'm not as proficient at that trick as I might be." LaVoie sighed. "Let me think on it."

"You'll be a better man for it," she said.

LaVoie wasn't sure he wanted to be a better man. It was neither safe nor profitable. More to the point, of course, was that as a charlatan himself, he knew he when was being bamboozled.

CHAPTER 31: CARL
"In a false quarrel there is no true valour"

"Knickerbocker rules," Harm announced. "No plugging!"

The rains had lasted for a week, a boon for all, but they'd temporarily rendered the fields too muddy to work. It was not, however, too muddy for a base-ball match. Men and boys from the local farms, as well as several from Eagle, had gathered in a pasture. Carl and Mariel had come, too, uninvited. Carl would love to play, but he knew they wouldn't ask. Still, it was a glorious June day, and he enjoyed the excitement of a match, even if he was only a spectator. More importantly, Mariel had developed a cough and chill in the past few days, and the warm sunshine would do her good.

"No plugging?" Reverend Rodgers complained. Out here he preferred to be called James, or even Jim, but most people still addressed him as Reverend. "What fun is base-ball if you can't plug them?"

"Now, Jim," Harm said, "don't you do enough smiting on Sunday mornings?" The rest of the players laughed. Harm held up two balls. "The old one was soft as a pillow," he said of the one in his right hand, "but this is what they're using now."

Rodgers and Abner Schmidt examined the new ball. Everyone but Carl and Mariel gathered around.

"It's hard as stone," Reverend Rodgers said.

"Man could get killed if he got hit with this," Abner said.

"And that's why…," Harm began.

"No plugging," the entire group chimed in.

As the men chose sides, Carl and Mariel found a spot close enough to see and hear the action without being in the way. There were twenty-three players, leaving ten to a team, two nonparticipating captains, and an umpire. Harm appointed himself one captain and Reverend Rodgers volunteered to be the other. After selecting the order of the lineups, they marked off the bases with seed sacks half filled with sand, carefully counting out forty-two paces between first and third base and another forty-two between home and second.

"Twenty-one aces wins it," Carl said, "as long as each side has an equal number of hands."

"Hands?" Mariel said. She coughed and wiped her nose on her sleeve.

"A turn." Although they were well within earshot of the others, no one acknowledged their presence. "One team gets a turn at striking, then the other."

"Why don't you play, Daddy? I'll be all right here."

"Because, sweet girl, I'd a whole lot rather stand here with you than play with all those smelly fellas. Anyhow, I'm odd man out. They got just enough without me."

Abner Schmidt was chosen as pitcher for Reverend Rodgers' team. He positioned himself between first and third base, a few feet closer to second base than to home.

Joe Allen, from Eagle, was Harm's first striker. When the umpire, a man Carl didn't know, nodded for the match to begin, Abner lobbed the ball to Joe underhanded. Joe swung his bat and hit it straight toward Harm's man on second base, who caught it on the first bounce.

"Hand out," the umpire called, and Joe went to sit down at the end of the line behind his teammates.

"What happened?" Mariel asked.

"If the ball's caught in the air or on the first bounce, the striker's out."

"Out?" Mariel said.

"He has to sit down. Each side's got three outs per hand. Then the other team gets a chance at striking."

"It's confusing."

"Just watch."

The second striker was another Eagle resident, a boy of about fifteen. Although Abner's pitches seemed fat as muskmelons to Carl, the boy swung and missed three consecutive times.

"Hand out," the umpire said.

Mariel sniffled and leaned her head against Carl's shoulder. There was no feeling in the world as wonderful as having his little girl by his side. He smiled and tweaked her nose.

The third striker was Ben Gorman, a lefthander who'd been made to use his right in school, but reverted to his natural tendency when playing base-ball. He knocked Abner's first pitch outside the range of first base.

"Foul," the umpire said.

The second pitch followed an almost identical course, another foul. Ben waited on the third one. As the ball arced down he uncorked a solid hit, sending it over the second baseman's head. He dropped his bat and skedaddled toward first. The ground was still wet from the rains, though, causing him to slip as he rounded the base. By the time he'd regained his feet, the outfielder, Abe Trimble, had retrieved the ball. If Carl understood Knickerbocker rules, Abe was required to throw the ball to second base in order for the second baseman to touch Ben with it before he got there. But old habits died hard, because Abe took aim at Ben's midsection and plunked him right in the ribs. Ben crumpled to the ground, howling in pain.

"No plugging," Harm cried.

"Safe," the umpire shouted emphatically. "Striker, take your base." He shook a finger at the fielder. "Dammit, Abe, you can't *do* that anymore. You gotta tag them out now. Next time I'll disqualify you from the match."

"Sorry, Ben," Abe called. "You all right?"

Ben sat up, clutching his side. "I think a rib is busted."

His teammates rushed to help him up. He walked doubled over, gasping for breath. "I'm done," he said, glaring at Abe.

The umpire looked at Carl. "You," he said, but Harm shook his head. "Sides aren't even," the umpire protested.

"I'll be our tenth," Harm said.

"Captains ain't supposed to play," the umpire said.

"Why don't we let him in the game?" Reverend Rodgers said.

"No," Harm said.

"Why is Harm being mean, Daddy?" Mariel said.

"It's nothing, sweet girl. A silly quarrel."

Harm approached Carl. "Sorry, Carl," he said, "but you know why."

"Wish I never showed you that letter," Carl said.

Harm patted him on the shoulder. "I wish you hadn't, either."

Mariel coughed. "What letter?"

"Shhh. We should be on our way."

"Why'd you come?" Harm said.

"I like base-ball."

"Your father meant the world to me," Harm said. "So do you. People are suspicious, Carl. You can settle this with a few words."

"Maybe I could," Carl said. He looked Harm directly in the eye. "But that letter was between us. How come everyone knows about it?"

He turned his back on his former friend and led Mariel away from the base-ball match. She coughed and sniffled and shed a few tears.

"Daddy?" she said.

"Sweet girl." He kissed her on the forehead as he lifted her onto the buckboard.

CHAPTER 32: BILL
"Glory is like a circle in the water"

The tavern in Buffalo was packed with travelers journeying westward. The structure was a little ramshackle affair overlooking the docks and a wooden lighthouse, beyond which Lake Erie twinkled in the light of the stars and moon. Bill and Noah drank whisky while they waited for the palace steamer *PS Hercules* to pull into port. The *Hercules* would ferry the short distance from Buffalo to Presque Island in Erie, Pennsylvania, where it would drop off some passengers and pick up others before departing for the Detroit River and Lake St. Clair in Michigan.

"I fought with Commodore Perry back in the War," said the man sitting next to Bill. The fellow was as drunk as a person could be and still be upright.

"Who's Commodore Perry?" Bill joked.

"You some kind of limey lickspittle? I fought in the Battle of Put-in-Bay in '13. I was with Perry when we took back the Lake from the Brits."

While Bill was just getting used to the idea of a war with Mexico, he clearly remembered America's "second war of independence." His own father had been one of the American sailors seized and impressed into service by the British navy. Bill was fifteen and all set to join the fray when word came that the Treaty of Ghent had ended the war. Instead he'd signed on with a merchant fleet and, until now, hadn't left the sea since.

However, the man talking to Bill would have been in swaddling clothes when the war began in 1812. Bill, who'd had a few too many himself, said, "You are a scoundrel, sir, and a liar. I was a strong lad then, but you, villain, were still at your mother's breast."

"You question my honor?" the man cried out. "I challenge you to a duel. Who will be my second? Who will be my second?" He stood up, fumbling with a flintlock pistol. "I'll kill you on this very spot."

Bill belched, then calmly punched him in the face. The inebriate collapsed like a net of fish guts, unconscious before he hit the floor. That was more a result of the whisky than the force of Bill's blow.

Everybody in the tavern laughed at the man, who was already snoring. Bill held up his glass and toasted his fallen adversary. "Have a good sleep, mate," he said. He downed the last of his drink and signaled for another.

Noah picked up the man's pistol and handed it to the barkeep. "That went well," he said to Bill. "I believe you've had enough whisky."

"Would you have been my second?" Bill said. His tongue felt as if it had been nailed to the roof of his mouth, his head as if he were spinning into a whirlpool.

"In a duel? And watch you get yourself killed?"

"That scurvy jack-tar," Bill said, his mind as slurred as his speech, "couldn't find his own arse with both hands and a map."

"Well, then, he probably would have shot me instead."

Bill threw his arm around Noah's shoulder. He was suddenly blubbery. "I ever tell you you're my best mate? That's why I came with you on this foolhardy quest. I don't know what you want. You can't bring your girl back. But I accompanied you, didn't I? I gave up the sea, didn't I? For love of my best mate. And so, and so... What was I saying?"

"Would I have been your second."

"Well?"

"You're pickled, Short Bill. There isn't going to be a duel."

Bill took a step back from Noah and shoved him with both hands. "You ungrateful bastard, you wouldn't do that for me, after all I've done for you?"

The blast of the *Hercules'* horn rattled the walls and rafters of the tavern. "Time to go," Noah said. Then he embraced Bill and whispered in his ear, "You know I don't like fighting, mate. But of course I'd be your second. I'd take the bullet in your stead, if it came to that."

Bill sniffled and drooled. His anger drained away. "Oh, hell, Blackbourne, don't be such a popinjay. The man couldn't shoot straight anyway."

And then he giggled like an idiot.

"Come on," Noah said. "Our boat has arrived. Let's sail, you and I, on this inland sea. It'll be like old times, eh?"

"Old times," Bill said as he collapsed into Noah's arms.

CHAPTER 33: JUBAL
"A lover's pinch, which hurts and is desired"

On the first night out of Jeffersonville, Jubal lay on his bed, listening to a gentle rain on the canvas covering his wagon. LaVoie had his own schooner. Jubal shared his with Petey and, until now, Artest. Giovanni, Manfred, and Otto had the third. Herman, André, and Leopold the fourth. And Cuff the chuckwagon. LaVoie had moved Artest's bed in with her in the chuckwagon to make room for two large mirrors with Jubal and Petey. The chuckwagon had already been stuffed to capacity before Cuff arrived. Now this colored couple, Cyrus and Destiny, had squeezed in there with her, Artest's bed, and all the show's gear.

Jubal didn't know how they managed to fit everything in. He lit a cigar. He didn't like this situation. Even here in the North, it was no small thing LaVoie had done by giving Cyrus and his wife shelter and employment. This close to Kentucky, there was a constant threat of slavers—despicable men who would stop at nothing to capture their quarry. Although many local sheriffs refused to cooperate with them, southern sympathizers abounded in these parts, and they had no qualms about running ex-slaves to ground, especially if a bounty was involved.

Jubal got up and paced beside his bed, puffing out cigar smoke.

Despite LaVoie's dangerous altruism, Cyrus was confrontational. He behaved as if LaVoie owed him something. Yes, Jubal had noticed the scars on the man's back. Yes, he knew what those scars meant, and therefore where Cyrus and Destiny had come from, and why they wanted to go north. But LaVoie wasn't to blame for atrocities some other white man had inflicted on him.

The Major could employ whomever he chose without consulting the others. It was his show. But that gave him the most to lose. Why would he offer passage to two fleeing slaves—three, counting Cuff— even if it was a one-time good deed? Marcus T. LaVoie had a number of redeeming qualities, but nobility and bravery weren't among them. He had absconded ahead of half a dozen angry sheriffs rather than face jail or fines. Yet at great risk to everyone, he'd taken on these two strangers, apparently at Cuff's request. Cuff herself claimed she had just met them.

That was the worst thing of all. Jubal didn't consider himself a jealous man, but he could think of no other word to describe his feelings about Cuff's attention to the couple. She'd barely spoken to him since Cyrus and Destiny arrived.

Rain was no longer tapping on the canvas. Jubal dropped his cigar and crushed it underfoot. He decided to go check on Rosie's new colt. He knew the foal was all right, but it was an excuse to be out and about, and if he found himself heading in Cuff's direction, well, he wouldn't mind having a word with her.

Broken clouds raced past the moon as he scrambled out of his wagon. The breeze was fresh with the purifying smell of the recent shower.

Cuff's unmistakable voice came from the other side of the chuckwagon. Beneath its belly Jubal saw the flicker of fire. He couldn't make out her words yet, so he hurried toward her, then paused out of sight behind the wagon wheel.

Cyrus, Destiny, Petey, Manfred, Otto, and Herman sat in a circle around a small campfire, with Cuff standing in the middle, the flames at her back. Destiny was nestled in Cyrus's arms, her head on his shoulder. The rain hadn't been heavy enough to douse the fire, but everyone had been out in it long enough that they were soaked. Apparently they didn't mind. They'd been content to sit through the weather, come what may, to listen to Cuff speak. Jubal wondered what she had been saying that had kept them out in the elements.

As if in answer, Cuff said to them, "This here's a poem by Miss Phillis Wheatley." She had a book tucked under her arm to protect it from the rain, but now she took it out and opened it. "She's the first colored woman who ever got a book published in this whole country. This one's called 'Hymn to the Evening.' Listen.

"'Soon as the sun forsook the eastern main
The pealing thunder shook the heav'nly plain;
Majestic grandeur! From the zephyr's wing,
Exhales the incense of the blooming spring.
Soft purl the streams, the birds renew their notes,
And through the air their mingled music floats.
Through all the heav'ns what beauteous dies are spread!
But the west glories in the deepest red:
So may our breasts with ev'ry virtue glow,
The living temples of our God below!
Fill'd with the praise of him who gives the light,
And draws the sable curtains of the night,
Let placid slumbers sooth each weary mind,
At morn to wake more heav'nly, more refin'd;
So shall the labours of the day begin
More pure, more guarded from the snares of sin.
Night's leaden sceptre seals my drowsy eyes,
Then cease, my song, till fair *Aurora* rise.'"

Gone was the thick southern accent of an ex-slave and her usual crow-pitched twang, now replaced by the rich deep tones of a Baptist preacher, if a woman could be a preacher. Jubal was swept up by the rhythm of the words. He didn't know if it was the poem itself or the music in Cuff's voice, but whatever it was, he set aside his jealousy, his suspicions, his questions, and his concern about Annalee. No Guinevere of legend could be more stunning.

Manfred draped his arm over Petey's shoulder. Destiny turned her face up to Cyrus so he could kiss her. Jubal listened and fell in love with Cuff all over again as she finished that poem and went on to another.

***

The next night the medicine show camped somewhere in south central Indiana. The air was muggy, the moon dark. There were no bird songs, but crickets chirped from the underbrush and bullfrogs croaked from a nearby pond. The faint scents of Queen Ann's lace and wild chicory were in the air, but these were overpowered by sweet aroma of morning glories. Jubal knew there must be a town nearby, because morning glories weren't native to Indiana. They'd been brought here to help mask the stench of outhouses and brighten the unsightliness of tree stumps.

After the debacle at Jeffersonville, he had to admit it was good to be on the road again. Once making camp, Jubal and Cuff had gone on separate walks, coincidentally ending up under the same apple tree, or so Jubal told her. He'd actually followed her at a distance. When she lay on her back by the tree to gaze into the stars, he just "happened by."

She invited him to join her, and then they were both enjoying the night sky. "They spin 'round and 'round," she said. "Watch 'em long enough and you can see 'em move. They go by us every night but don't ever touch us."

"They do touch us, Cuff," Jubal said, hoping he sounded as poetic as Miss Wheatley. "With their beauty. They pull us around with them and draw us in. Someday there'll be a great convergence."

"Well, I don't know what that means. All I know is I like them. Makes me feel like God is truly looking down, saying 'Hush, child, everything's gon be all right.'"

Jubal sat up and leaned against the tree. A few of the small, unripe apples had fallen to the ground. He rather preferred looking at Cuff than the sky. By normal standards she was a small woman, under five feet tall, but of course she still towered over him by several inches. "I don't think much about God," he said.

"That 'cause you blame Him for making you so little?"

"I doubt He had anything to do with that."

"So why didn't you grow tall?"

"Why is your skin black?"

Cuff laughed. "'Cause my Momma and Papa's skin was black, that's why. Can't mix black with black and get white."

"My parents mixed tall with tall and got me."

"What else then but the hand of the Lord?"

Jubal shrugged. What purpose would God have in inflicting this miniature stature on a man of normal desires? If He did have a plan, Jubal would learn of it soon enough. Or he wouldn't. He changed the subject. "My father is a law clerk in Boston."

"What's a law clerk do?"

"Kept their books, for one, like I do here."

"Half a chip off the old block, eh?"

Her comment was meant as a jest, but it stung.

"It keeps the creditors away. One of the men my father worked with was Moses Kimball. Kimball owns the Feejee Mermaid. P.T. Barnum just leases it from him."

"God's truth? I don't care too much about mermaids or any of the Major's hair pulling and jumping about nonsense. Oh, I like him well enough, and you and Petey too, but singing 'Yankee Doodle' for white folks wasn't what I planned to do when I escaped."

"That was your idea."

"I know."

When she didn't elaborate, Jubal said, "Everyone in the show is a good fellow, in his own way. Except Herman slash Hermione. He's a good fellow *and* a fine lady."

"André makes my skin crawl. Sometimes I think he really don't have bones."

"His appearance is alarming. But if you can get by that...." Jubal paused. "And then there's Cyrus and Destiny. What's their story?"

"Don't you fret none about them, they're fine people. Just hitching a ride for a spell, is all. They needed to go north, and we're going north."

"Fortuitous you came upon them, as LaVoie would say."

"You talk real good. You go to school, or what?"

The bullfrogs raised their voices, hundreds of them singing for a mate. A breeze came up from the south, bringing with it a stronger aroma of wild chicory, the roots of which people in these parts ground up and used as a coffee substitute.

Jubal detested the taste of coffee, although the smell of it brewing was pleasant.

"I did," he said, "for as long as I could. But mostly it was my mother who taught me my letters, as well as proper etiquette and manners. That was important to her."

"What was your Momma like?"

"Is. She's still alive. Both parents are, or were, last I heard. She was a true Southern belle from Georgia."

Jubal felt Cuff's body stiffen. Her voice was tense as she said, "Southern belles from Georgia got themselves slaves."

"We never did. I don't know if Mother's family did or not," he lied. "That was before I was born, and she doesn't talk about those days anymore."

Cuff remained silent for a long time, and Jubal didn't push her. He'd never been a slave, but he had once been Kürten's "dancing monkey," and that, he imagined, was not much better. When she finally spoke, the tension was gone from her voice. "You heard of this Zug man in Detroit?"

"Not until LaVoie mentioned him."

A falling star blazed across the sky from left to right and melted above the western horizon. There'd been a lot of those this June.

"Well, me and my Evelyn know about him," Cuff said. "Makes furniture or something. She lives up there, you know. In Windsor, Canada."

"So why is Zug sponsoring LaVoie?"

"You got to ask him that."

Jubal thought he detected in Cuff's tone more than she was saying, but again didn't challenge her. "I'm sure LaVoie will."

"Why'd you stop going to school?"

Jubal sighed and lay back again. The stars truly were beautiful. "Because I stopped growing. The other children made it difficult. They were always laughing at me, when they weren't beating me. I learned to talk my way out of the beatings by making fun of myself, but I hated that. I *hated* it."

Cuff rolled over onto her stomach. She pulled up a clump of grass and held it to her nose. "Never get tired of this smell," she said. "You ever had a lady friend, Jubal?"

The question took him by surprise. "Women found me charming," he said, and it was true, "but they all tried to mother me. When they weren't treating me like a child, they said they wanted to arrange a suitable match for me, as long as it was with someone else's daughter. But it was never serious. What normal girl could look at me and say, 'Yes, he will be an acceptable husband?'"

"You ever, uh, *you-knowed* with a gal?"

"If you mean fornicated, no."

"So you never even seen one in all her glory, naked as the Lord made her?"

"Are you trying to humiliate me, Cuff?"

She sat up and took his hands in hers. "Oh, don't mind me. It surely ain't my business. We don't gotta talk about it, you don't want. It's just, there's something powerful when a man and a woman first behold one another. I never met no one like you before, so I was just wondering if you ever got to know that joy."

"No," he said, his second lie of the night. "Most adult women my size are dwarfs. Some of them were willing enough, I suppose." Jubal looked at his feet. "They were perfectly nice people, but I found the shape of their bodies repugnant. I wanted someone of normal proportions, like me."

"Well, everybody got to be vain about something."

Jubal rose, picked up one of the fallen apples, and offered it to her. "For milady."

"Milady?" Cuff seemed delighted by the sound of that. "Bible says the woman who give the apple to the man."

"André is the serpent, not me."

"You got *that* right." She rolled the small green apple around in her hand. "What kinda gift is this, anyhow? It ain't half the size it oughta be."

She looked at Jubal, and they both laughed.

"Like me," he said. "I like them this way, but they're sour."

"Like me," Cuff said, and they laughed again. She extended her hand for him to help her up. "C'mon now. Best be getting back to camp. Mr. Major LaVoie's gon wanna pull out early."

Jubal would have been perfectly happy staying here with her all night. He knew they couldn't, but as they walked she put her hand on his shoulder, and that was all right with him.

CHAPTER 34: MARIEL
"An untimely frost upon the sweetest flower"

Mariel lay in her bed behind the partition, shivering and sweating. She coughed constantly now, sometimes bringing up a thick green mucus. Mrs. Jensen placed a hot rag across her forehead, then went around the partition to speak with Mariel's father.

"Has there been any blood in her phlegm?" she heard Mrs. Jensen say.

"Not that I seen," her father said. "It ain't the cholera, is it? Claire lost her mother Jane in the plague of '32."

"Cholera?" Mrs. Jensen said. "No, there's been no diarrhea. But I fear it could be consumption."

Mariel heard a loud thump, as if someone had struck a wooden surface with a fist. "No," her father cried.

"I didn't say it *is* consumption," Mrs. Jensen said, "I said I fear it. Everybody's scared it's that at first, but that doesn't mean it is. Time will tell."

There was a long silence on the other side of the partition. Between her coughing and wheezing Mariel heard only shuffling feet, chairs being pulled out, pushed back, pacing. Outside the wind had come up, bringing another round of rain. She lay in the dark. The flickering of candles on the other side of the partition bathed the rest of the house in red and yellow.

Finally her father said, "Thanks for coming, Kristin, 'specially after all the talk."

"This is more important," Mrs. Jensen said. "But nothing has changed. After this is all over with Mariel, you'll still have to answer for yourself, Carl Hinman. People think—"

"Shhh," her father said. "She can hear us. I know what they think."

After another pause, Mrs. Jensen said, "Whatever Mariel has, she needs a doctor. This is beyond my skills."

"I don't know any doctors down here."

"There are only midwives in these parts. Harm speaks highly of a doctor he knew in Eagle, but he's since moved to Pontiac. Name's Clarence Finch."

"Ain't that right outside Detroit?"

"Is that a problem?"

Mariel moaned and shifted under her blankets. She knew her father never wanted to go back to Detroit. That was where Momma had died, and it made him sad to even talk about that town. But her father said, "Depends. Is this Finch fella any good? Can he help my girl?"

"Don't know the man myself," Mrs. Jensen said. "But he saw Harm through a rough patch before we met. He swears if it is consumption, Finch is the best man for the job. You won't find a better doctor outside of New York or Philadelphia. It's not that far to Pontiac, but you'll have to go through Detroit to get there. Are you sure you want to do that?"

"For Mariel I'd walk through hell doused in kerosene."

"I'll arrange it with Harm, then," Mrs. Jensen said. "He's already said he'll tend the farms. I'll go with you."

"You'd do that for me?"

"I'll do it for Mariel. A word of warning, Carl: We'll require a full accounting from you."

Mariel didn't hear what was said next. They might have been whispering something, or that might just be the wind and rain. Mariel coughed and rolled to her side.

They were going back to Detroit.

CHAPTER 35: NOAH
"If there were a sympathy in choice"

Although Lake Erie was a large expanse of water, it was nothing like the Atlantic Ocean. Noah was startled by how smooth its surface was. The small swells were lovely in the morning light, but they rolled past the hull of the *Hercules* without causing the slightest vibration. Indeed, the steamer's engine and screw propeller rattled the deck and overpowered any sensation of being on water. If he closed his eyes, the motion seemed more like that of those infernal trains than a ship.

Erie didn't feel like the sea and it didn't smell like the sea, its fresh air lacking the tang of salt. Yet its infinite blue, with no land in sight, brought the divine back to Noah, the peace, the freedom, the endless open spaces. Oh, yes, God was here, drawn to water, as He'd always been. He'd simply overstepped the land from ocean to lake.

Noah took comfort in that. He only hoped he could retain his faith once he was landbound again, in Detroit, pursuing the mystery of his daughter's death.

***

The *Hercules* was roughly twice the size of the *Empire* and had no paddlewheel. Shaped more like the whalers Noah was familiar with, it had two steam funnels in place of masts and sails, but at least it had a recognizable fo'c'sle for the crew and cabins, and storage compartments below the waterline where they belonged. He stood on deck with Short Bill, who was busy annoying the *Hercule's* second mate, keeping him from his duties with questions about the inner workings of steamships. Noah hoped he didn't get himself challenged to another duel. His friend was still suffering the consequences of last night's whisky.

"Tell me about this screw propeller," Short Bill said. "How does it work?"

The second mate sighed and began to explain, but Noah wasn't interested, so he hobbled toward the lounge. Passage across had cost them each five dollars, and that didn't include their cabin—another two dollars—or food. The supplies they'd bought from Lowe at the *Anchor & Dolphin* were gone, so they had to buy all their meals now. Noah had enough money left to get to Detroit, but no clue how, or with what, he'd return to the coast. But maybe he wasn't meant to.

On another day that thought might have triggered his melancholy, but today his mood was lightened by the sun and open water. Never one to willingly miss a meal, he went in search of breakfast. Despite his undiminished appetite, he had developed a gap of a finger span between his trousers and his waist. Only his suspenders were preventing them from falling down. The ordeal of trains and greenery had probably cost him a few pounds. That was a good thing, but not enough to take the strain off his ailing left knee.

The *Hercule's* lounge was half again as large as the *Empire's* and its menu more varied. With so much room, there were plenty of unoccupied tables. Noah ordered ham, sausages, eggs, potatoes, toasted bread with butter, flapjacks, and a flagon of beer, then chose a table and sat to await his food.

Many of the conversations of the people around him touched on the war, politics, and slavery, but some concerned the excitement of settlers headed west to find their fortunes in the bustle of boomtowns or the rich farmland of the country. These were the as-yet untainted dreams of new beginnings. A feeling of hope pervaded the place, which Noah found pleasant.

As his breakfast was delivered, he noticed an adolescent lad and a little girl sitting by themselves in a corner, with no sign of guardians. They stared longingly at him, or rather, at his food. He tried to ignore them, but he could feel their gaze as he ate. Finally, after disposing of the ham, he looked at them again. Their clothes were clean, but their bodies were thin as train rails. There was still a bit of fleshiness in their faces, especially the girl, but the skin of their arms looked like painted bone.

Noah motioned them to his table. They rushed over to him. Clearly they'd never been taught to be wary of strangers.

"Where are your parents?" he said.

The girl was wearing a blue sailor's cap that was too big for her, probably given to her by a crewman. It flopped down low enough to obscure her eyes. She kept her head down and didn't speak, but the boy said, "Ain't got none. Going to live with Auntie Sarah."

"Who paid your passage?"

"Granddad didn't want us no more."

"When did you last eat?" Noah said.

"Don't know. Utica?"

Noah pushed his plates across the table. "Sit down. What are your names?"

"I'm Zeke and this here's my sister Bella. Those're short for Ezekial and Isabella."

Ignoring table utensils, the children gulped down the rest of Noah's breakfast using their fingers.

"Your parents are dead, then?" Noah said.

"Guess so," Zeke said around a mouthful of eggs. "Never met 'em."

"Are you in steerage?"

Zeke nodded. "But it's too crowded, and the people are mean, so we slept out on deck last night. It's only two days to Detroit. One more night, and we'll be there."

"How old are you?"

"Can you just let us eat?"

Noah had been hungry before, but never like these children. The boy looked to be thirteen, the girl perhaps seven. He tried to picture Claire. Although he'd seen her once when she was a teenager, his best memories of her were when she was a toddler, sitting on his knee with those dazzling eyes, that heart-melting smile. She'd looked nothing like this fair-haired urchin. Even at two she'd borne a striking resemblance to Jane. She had her mother's dark hair, but not her dark disposition. In fact, Claire had been a surprisingly even-tempered child, not given to tantrums or idle chatter.

If only—

No. Jane had made her choices, Claire had made hers, and Noah had made his. Short Bill had been right, a man can't build a life on regrets. That was a certain path to madness, and worse.

"Can we have more?" Zeke said.

Bella smiled, and in that smile Noah saw the sum of all little girls everywhere. Framed by the sailor's cap, her face was so adorable that he wanted to sweep her into his arms.

Instead he raised the cap in front and gazed into her pretty blue eyes. "Your Aunt Sarah will meet you at the dock in Detroit?" he said.

She nodded.

Noah gave Zeke two dollars. "It's cold on the open water under the stars. Get a cabin tonight, just you two. There's plenty available. Take care of your sister."

Noah rose and lumbered toward the door. He had no illusions about the money. The children would either buy more food the instant he was out of sight or, more likely, they'd pocket the coins and ply their starving routine on other strangers.

That was all right. The giving of charity was its own reward, and he felt wonderful. If he never did another good thing in his life, at least he'd be able to stand before God and say he'd done this.

CHAPTER 36: BILL
"And rolls its awful burden on the wind"

Their second and last night aboard the *Hercules* started off warm and calm, with the moon in the east and clouds in the southwest. A light breeze hinted at rain. They were due to make the Detroit River at dawn and the eastern shore of Lake St. Clair by mid-morning. From there they'd rent horses to ride into Detroit proper.

Bill sat on the edge of the bed they shared while Noah lay behind him, trying to sleep. The keel cut through the water effortlessly, but this far below deck, he could hear every creak and groan the ship made. "These steamers are interesting," Bill said, "but give me a whaler any day. Modern ships are beyond me."

"Most things are beyond you, Short Bill."

Bill smiled. "Aye."

"I feel like I should be sharpening harpoons or raising sails," Noah said. "It doesn't seem right to remain idle on a boat voyage."

"I'm sure the captain won't mind if you want to swab the deck."

"I'm not that unhappy with idleness."

"What's your plan once we arrive in Detroit?"

"Tomorrow will take care of itself," Noah said. "My plan now is to sleep."

Before Bill could respond he noticed that the ship was rising and falling as if in choppy water. Until now the only sensation of motion had come from the engine's vibration. "Feel that?" he said.

Noah sat up next to Bill. "I did," he said. "Iceberg?"

Bill and Noah looked at each other and laughed. There were no icebergs in the Great Lakes, and no ice of any kind in June. "Wind's come up, I'll wager," Bill said. "Let's find out."

"You go," Noah said. "Leave me to my dreaming."

Bill left their cabin and climbed the steps to the deck, only to find the door blocked by a young ship's mate. "No one allowed on deck, sir," the boy said. He couldn't have been more than sixteen. "Stay below. Big storm's brewing."

Only moderate rain was falling, but the ship's company flag already rippled straight out toward the stern. Lightning flashed continuously in a line across the horizon, south to north, although the timing of thunder indicated that the brunt of the tempest was still some distance away. "Ever ridden out a hurricane on a whaler, lad?" Bill said.

"Can't say as I have, sir."

"After that, this little blow is like a spring breeze."

"That may be, but you're still not allowed on deck."

"Is there a guard at every door?" Bill said. He'd like to experience what these landlubbers considered a storm.

"I'm only assigned to this one, sir. I can't speak for the others. My duty is here, and you'll not pass beyond." The boy's words were resolute, but his voice quavered.

"There's nothing wrong with being scared, lad."

"I'm not scared, sir, I'm cold. It's going to get worse. Go below and warm yourself."

Bill saluted him. "Aye-aye, cap'n."

He decided not to try the other doors. No sense causing trouble with only a night left on their journey. By the time he'd reached his deck, the ship was heaving. He could hear the moans of passengers not used to floors that rollicked beneath their feet, but his sea legs took over and he made it to their cabin without incident.

The oil lamp's light jerked with the ship's motion. This was more like it. He'd had enough of calm water and smooth sailing.

Noah was snoring peacefully, oblivious to the storm. Bill noticed that at some point he had carved the name *Claire* into the bed's wooden frame.

Poor fellow, he thought. He picked up the Albany newspaper he'd saved and sat next to Noah to read the article about Veracruz.

General Winfield Scott had taken the city on March 29 after a three-week siege. The story still didn't explain the reason for a war with Mexico, but Bill didn't especially care. He wasn't in the war and didn't know anybody who was. Maybe it had something to do with the Alamo, although that battle had happened over a decade ago.

As he read on he learned that the state of Michigan had abolished the death penalty, a fact Noah might find interesting if it were true, as his friend suspected, that Hinman had had something to do with Claire's demise.

His lesson on current events was quickly curtailed when the *Hercules* rose on a swell and then dropped into a trough. In a matter of minutes the ship was no longer creaking and groaning, it was shrieking. Even in a cabin without a porthole Bill could hear the wind howling, lashing at the hull like, well, a hurricane. The ship was battered, racked by winds above and waves below. Bill and Noah's rucksacks flew across the cabin, along with chairs and anything else not nailed down. The oil lamp was secured in place, but its flame was extinguished, leaving them in darkness. Noah, however, was not secured by anything but his own weight, and that wasn't enough. His body slammed repeatedly against the wall and then back into Bill. A sailor could sleep through anything, but eventually even Noah was awakened by knocking his noggin against pine panels.

"What in blazes?" he said, struggling to sit. Bill helped him up. "Where's the light?"

"I think we're in the middle of a sou'wester," Bill said.

"Didn't know there was such a thing."

A tremendous crash somewhere above shook the ship so badly that Bill feared the hull might split. He knew whalers, what they could do and what they could withstand, but he had no idea how well a steamer was constructed. Presumably its makers understood Great Lakes weather and had planned accordingly. Yet the sound of metal grinding against metal didn't bode well.

Something, likely wood, shattered with terrible force.

"Believe I'll have a prayer now," Bill said.

He bowed his head and chanted a verse to St. Brendan, the patron saint of sailors. It never hurt to seek the intercession of higher powers.

The *Hercules* felt as if it were lifted completely out of the water and hurled back down. The timbers of the walls and floors expanded and contracted as if gasping for breath.

Bill shook Noah's hand. "Been good knowing you, mate."

Then something in their cabin broke loose, striking Bill in the face.

CHAPTER 37: MARCUS
"And rapt in secret studies"

The medicine show had been on the road for several days. A week before they were due in Belgrade a powerful thunderstorm overtook the caravan and churned northeast toward the Great Lakes. LaVoie ordered the wagons to hunker down and ride it out. It passed leaving no injuries and only minor damage, so they were able to continue on for another two hours before stopping for the night. Darkness brought the rumble of retreating thunder and a strong north wind.

LaVoie, Jubal, and Cuff sat around a small table. Jubal had had to stack the Major's thick dictionary and *Book of Magick* on his chair in order to speak to the others on their level. LaVoie had watched him clamber up the wooden leg supports to his perch of books. It must be demeaning for him. He was genuinely fond of the little man, but wouldn't trade places with him for any amount of money.

LaVoie puffed on a cigar, Cuff on a pipe. Although Jubal himself smoked, he'd frequently expressed his disapproval of women doing so. "Only if they're on fire," he once joked. Now, as the smoke encircled Cuff's dark face, LaVoie noticed he gazed at her as if she were Saint Teresa of Avila and the smoke a halo from heaven.

Of course he was being a romantic fool. Cuff was protective of him, a trait LaVoie knew Jubal interpreted to mean more than it did. Surely she could not take him seriously as a potential mate. More likely, she saw in him a kindred spirit, a fellow outcast in a world dominated by white, normal-sized people.

"What's the plan in Belgrade?" Jubal said.

"I've never had a sponsor before," LaVoie said. "I don't know what Zug's expectations might be. Until we get there and find out differently, let's assume we'll be setting up and performing as we ordinarily do."

"I talked to Garrett before he jumped camp," Jubal said. "Is this really about the money, or is it that taxidermist and your damned Feejee Mermaid?"

LaVoie sighed. He felt an uncharacteristic melancholy tonight. "I have no interest in imitating Mr. Barnum. I don't want a mermaid."

"But something of the sort."

"My plan is to do the show, sell my liniment, and collect Mr. Zug's money. And yes, I'll call on Mr. Forrest-Hosier to see if his work is of sufficient quality to enhance our acts."

"Whoo-ee," Cuff said, "listen to you, *sufficient quality to enhance our acts*. I told you that accent's no good."

"Perhaps not," LaVoie said. He didn't want to discuss business tonight. "So, Miss Cuff, tell me more about how you got your unusual name."

The lantern hanging from the wagon's curved frame swayed, throwing eerie shadows. When distant lightning flashed on the north side of the tent, the canvas seemed translucent, the unseen outer world revealed through its fabric.

"Same as everybody else," Cuff said. "I was born, and I got a name. Only wasn't my Momma that gave it to me. What about you?"

"What about me?"

"Well, beg pardon, Mr. Major Marcus T. LaVoie, but you ain't a major in no man's army, you ain't from Tennessee, and I got a dollar here says your name ain't even LaVoie."

LaVoie usually changed the subject when someone brought up his past, but every now and again he tired of the pretense.

He rose and went to the canvas flap that covered the gap at the front of the wagon. As he pushed it aside, wind rushed in, nearly extinguishing the lantern. The opening faced away from the departed storm, and the night sky was ablaze with stars. Peering outward, he sighed and said, "We're all friends here." He dropped the Southern accent. When he spoke, his pronunciation was pure north woods. "On the plantation, Miss Cuff, did you ever have occasion to raise chickens?"

"Can't live without eggs and meat, Mr. Major LaVoie. 'Course we had chickens. It was the only real work I did, 'cept reading the young ones to sleep."

"Marc will do." He bowed. "Marc Kane, at your service."

Jubal and Cuff smiled.

"Who'd buy moonshine from Marc Kane?" Cuff said.

"Exactly. LaVoie is French, two words, *la voie*. It means 'the way,' as in 'this is the way to Belgrade.'"

"So what's that got to do with chickens?" Cuff said. She blew a ring of pipe smoke in LaVoie's direction, but it was carried away from him by the wind.

"My parents were farmers outside a little town in Canada West. It was called Ebytown then, but it's Berlin now. Papa raised maize, soybeans, cows, hogs, and those infernal chickens. He and mother have passed now, but my younger brother Zachary is still at it, last I heard. I remember a time, I couldn't have been more than three or four, when I was chased across the barnyard by a chicken. Terrified me to such an extent that to this day I get anxious whenever I see one."

"A chicken?" Cuff said. "Bird the size of a jug of rye whisky, and you're scared of it? What, you think it gonna peck you to death?"

LaVoie closed the flap, returned to the table, and sat down. "The chicken was *dead*, Cuff. It was to be supper. My mother had chopped its head off, but it wouldn't lie down. Some demonic force animated its legs, and that headless monstrosity ran straight at me. Seemed like it chased me for hours, but of course it would only have been a few seconds until it fell over. I wept and wept, and although I did spend a number of years farming as a young man, I have detested the horrid things ever since. The next day I was so angry that I captured a live one and dropped it down the outhouse."

Cuff put her hand to her mouth and tried to stifle her laughter. "Well, hell, *Marc*, that wasn't nothing but twitching muscles that didn't know they was dead yet."

***

Yesterday's storm had eased the temperatures, but not the humidity. The day had dawned cool, with low-hanging clouds that obscured the sun.

LaVoie had given in to Cuff's request for a disappearing act, as she'd known he would.

"Hold still, Petey," LaVoie said. He unfurled the blanket over the boy's head, snapping it dramatically. Petey watched as it floated above him, then dropped to the ground when LaVoie called, "Now."

As the blanket fluttered down on him, LaVoie nodded with satisfaction.

"*Now* do I escape?" said Petey, peering from under the blanket. The boy was impatient, but eager. LaVoie had taken him into a nearby wood, away from camp, where they'd found a clearing. It had been a while since LaVoie had done this trick, and it was going to take practice getting the timing back, especially since Petey had not been with the show the last time they'd performed it

"Once we build a stage with a trap door."

"How come you always snap the blanket over my head?"

LaVoie smiled and pulled Petey to his feet. Excellent question, he thought. He had plans for this youngster, big plans. Someday, when he had had enough of the life, he could turn the medicine show over to Petey, confident he was leaving it in good hands. "It's a diversion, my boy. The sound makes the audience look up and away from the stage. That way if the timing isn't perfect and the trap door opens an instant too soon or late, their attention will be elsewhere."

"You mean they won't see the hole in the stage."

"Exactly."

"How you gonna stop the audience from seeing under the stage?" he said. "I mean, if I jump through the trap door, won't they see me?"

LaVoie explained the purpose of the mirrors.

"Well, ain't that something?" Petey said, beaming a toothy grin at him. Once he lost the baby fat in his face he'd be a lean and handsome fellow indeed. "You're the smartest man in the world."

LaVoie felt something that might be a blush. "Hardly, but thank you. Shall we go through it once more? Only this time you do the blanket."

When it came to stealth, Petey would be fine, but he wouldn't be the one escaping when they got to Belgrade. LaVoie was convinced that would be Cyrus and Destiny.

After another half hour of practice, the boy was panting. "Can we get some breakfast now?"

LaVoie nodded. "We need to be on the road soon anyway. Go on."

As Petey ran into the wood toward camp, he nearly collided with Cuff. They spoke briefly, then she sent him on his way. When she stepped into the clearing, she didn't seem pleased.

"This was supposed to be a secret rehearsal," LaVoie said.

"You call that a disappearing act? How you gonna make two people that don't know nothing about magic fall under a blanket and jump into a hole without nobody seeing 'em?"

"One at a time, Cuff, one at a time."

"Mr. Major LaVoie—"

"Marc."

"*Marc*, Cyrus and Destiny only got one chance to get it right."

LaVoie sighed. "I'm aware of that. Trust me, Cuff. If I can get Petey to do it, don't you think two adults whose lives depend upon it will make it work?"

"What you're asking them to do is taking an awful chance, is all."

LaVoie placed his hands on her shoulders. "I'm doing this at your request, Cuff. Wait till we're in Belgrade and the stage is built. It'll work, you'll see."

"Maybe I'm just getting nervous."

"Perfectly natural. But leave it to me. Tricks and illusions are my trade."

"You sure Cyrus and Destiny'll get away?"

"No. But if they don't, they won't be the only ones in danger. I have no doubt that slave hunter Villisca is still on our trail, and by now he may have reinforcements."

CHAPTER 38: CARL
"Past all comforts here but prayer"

As Carl, Mariel, and Kristin neared the Michigan border in the late afternoon, a ferocious thunderstorm blew in from the southwest, bringing with it surprisingly little rain, but winds more powerful than any nor'easter's he'd experienced on the coast and hail the size of baseballs. Carl had never seen anything like it, short of a twister. It overtook them so fast he barely had time to drive the two-horse team to shelter beneath a copse of trees. Even so, some of the hail made it through the limbs and leaves and struck the ground with frightening force. One of those stones could fracture a human skull.

The canvas canopy rippled like a sail. If the fabric remained intact, the gusts were strong enough to overturn the wagon. But it wouldn't. If the wind didn't shred it, the hail would.

"Get Mariel under the wagon," Carl cried to Kristin, his voice nearly lost in the wind.

He tethered the terrified horses while Kristin swaddled his daughter in layers of blankets. Then he joined them both under the wagon. Mariel was weeping, so he lifted her from Kristin's arms and stroked her hair.

"It'll be all right, sweet darling. Just a little blow." The thunder forced him to shout into her ear. Lightning hit the ground so close by he felt a tingle in his legs.

Kristin was a strong woman, not given to panic, but her eyes were round as flapjacks. Carl squeezed her hand for comfort.

***

The canopy sustained two large gashes, as well as dozens of punctures. Kristin, ever practical, had brought needle and thread. Carl and she spent much of the evening binding up the gashes and patching the holes. The canvas wouldn't survive another wind like that, but it would slow any further raindrops.

They decided not to move on until morning. Indians were no longer a threat in this part of the country and there were few wild animals that could harm them. Still, traveling by night wasn't safe. The horses could step in a rut and throw a shoe or, worse, break a leg. In any case, the beasts were weary and hungry. They needed rest, too.

Carl led them to a stream so they could drink and graze overnight.

Although he and Kristin had protected Mariel from the elements as well as they could during the storm, it was obvious she had taken a turn for the worse. In addition to green mucus, she was now coughing up small amounts of blood. Kristin fretted over her, covering her with blankets, only to have Mariel throw them off again.

"I'm on *fire*," she moaned.

"Shhh, child," Kristin whispered, "that's natural. You have a fever. It's your body trying to cast out your illness."

Streams of thin red clouds stretched across the darkening eastern sky as the first stars appeared. Carl paced beside the wagon, alternating between cursing and praying. Losing Claire had been unbearable. He couldn't lose his daughter, too. He *couldn't*.

His feeling of helplessness was maddening.

Of course, Carl didn't have his heart set on this Doctor Finch from Pontiac. Had there been a competent medical man in any of the small towns they'd passed along the way, he would have sought help for Mariel there. He'd do anything for her, yet truth was, he had no desire to pass through Detroit, even briefly, and wouldn't be disappointed if they could get her the help she needed elsewhere. But towns were few and far between, and most had no doctor at all. The only one that did employed a useless eighty-year-old quack who wanted to bleed her. Carl didn't care what science said, that just wasn't natural. Spilling blood made a body weaker, not stronger.

Kristin touched his arm to stop his pacing.

"She's sleeping now," she said. "You should build a fire to keep her warm. Then you must take your rest, too. You'll be of no use to her if your strength fails. I'll watch her."

"You can't stay awake all night."

"I can do whatever is necessary."

Mariel's chest rose and fell peacefully, but her breathing was raspy. Carl placed his hand on her brow. Her skin felt both hot and clammy, and she was slick with sweat. He wiped her face with his sleeve. As he did, he noticed Kristin gazing at him with tenderness, the first time since they left home that she'd regarded him with anything other than suspicion and wariness. He knew this wasn't the tenderness a woman felt for a man, but her appreciation for the love he had for his daughter—the love Kristin herself might have known had she and Harm been able to have children.

Carl took comfort in knowing she didn't consider him a complete fiend. He nodded his gratitude to her as he went to collect firewood.

***

Unable to sleep, he sat back against the wagon wheel and watched the flames stream upward. He folded his hands together and repeated, "Please, God. Please, God. Please."

A few moments later Kristin tapped him on the shoulder and knelt next to him. "God does not take innocents."

Carl knew she was trying to comfort him, but she chose the wrong words. "He took my brother John two hours after his birth. I never met him. He took my mother a day after she brought me into the world. She wasn't no more than twenty-five, I reckon. I never knew her, neither. Truth is, Kristin, God don't answer to us. He takes who He will."

"And yet you pray."

Carl nodded and balled his hands into fists. "What else is there? I see my angel laying there—*dying*, Kristin—and I wanna reach right into her and pull that sickness out, take it into myself. If God requires another death of my family, let it be me."

"Carl, I worry if it is for Mariel alone you should be praying. You know what I mean."

"Get some sleep, Kristin. I'm gonna be up all night anyway."

Kristin sat down and draped her arm over his shoulder. "Tell me, Carl. Just say it. You'll feel better. If you like, it'll be our secret. I promise I won't even tell Harm."

Carl rose and peered over the wagon to make sure Mariel was still asleep, then joined Kristin on the ground again. "Would Harm have let you come if he really thought I killed Claire?"

"I'm armed."

"Sweet Jesus."

"I don't know what to think, Carl. None of us do, not Harm, not Reverend Rodgers, no one. That letter said you didn't pay for her funeral, and Harm is convinced you didn't attend it, either. Why would a man…?"

There was no need for her to finish the sentence. Carl knew what she was asking. He folded his arms around his knees and lowered his face to his arms. Kristin gently rubbed his back, as she might do to comfort a distraught child.

"We had to leave town. Mariel didn't even get to see her dear mother into the everlasting," he said, and now he couldn't hold back the tears.

"Why, Carl?"

He looked up and sniffled. He saw the firelight in Kristin's eyes and realized it must be blazing in his own, too. "I didn't kill her, Kristin. But I'm the reason she's dead."

*****

In the morning they crossed into Michigan, and all the familiar emotions came flooding back: Claire's death, the mystery of her funeral, Constable Nortman's accusations, the flight from Detroit.

He hadn't requested her body be sent to the undertaker Kelley, nor had he arranged, let alone agreed to pay for, her funeral. He would have buried her properly, of course, if given the chance. He couldn't have afforded such a fancy coffin, but he would have found the money to do right by her.

There were footprints, Constable Nortman had said. *About your size, I'd reckon.*

Carl had been in shock. *What's my shoe size got to do with it?* he'd said when he found his voice. *Ain't nothing unusual about my shoes. Lots of fellas wear this size. And how'd you know the killer made them footprints, anyway?*

It was a fresh snowfall, two sets of prints going into that field, one coming out. A lady's and a man's. Only the man walked out.

Did she suffer?

You tell me.

I didn't do it.

We'll see about that.

In the first two days after the murder, Nortman had followed Carl whenever he left his home, to the tannery, to the undertaker—the one, final time he would ever see his beloved Claire, dead in a wood box— even, he suspected, to the outhouse. He'd been tempted to tell him what he knew, or at least suspected, but Nortman would never have believed him, or have acted on that belief if he had. The monster behind Claire's murder was from a family no law in Detroit could touch. With the truth so explosive and Carl's freedom so tenuous, he'd decided to flee Detroit before the funeral. With Claire gone, Carl couldn't risk leaving Mariel alone while he rotted in prison. She had nowhere else to go. Jane's sister Alice had followed her to the grave a few years after the cholera took

Jane. Joanna, Meggie and, as far as he knew, Claire's father were still alive, but they might as well have been dead for as much interest they'd shown in Carl's family since Jane's passing.

***

They came upon a flat stretch of open country. Despite yesterday's storm, there'd been little rain, so the ground was firm and the ride comfortable.

Today was cooler, the previous day's heat replaced by dreary, low-hanging clouds that occasionally spat drizzle. Usually a storm scrubbed away the humidity, but not this one. The air was heavy with dampness.

Mariel rested quietly in the back of the wagon. Kristin had done as much as she could for her, then come up to sit beside Carl as he held the reins. They spoke little. Carl had refused to say more about Claire's death, and Kristin was furious. "If that was your explanation," she grumbled, "you shouldn't have said anything at all."

"The devil's set aside a place in hell for me," Carl said. "Be satisfied."

After a few hours the terrain became rougher, less flat, and started to fill in with pin oaks, white spruce, elm, and maple trees. Soon dense woodlands loomed in front of them. Carl had come this way when leaving Michigan. They'd have to take the route around the trees, which was over a day's ride, or brave a gnarled, root-strewn path through them. Either way would be dangerous to Mariel.

"This Finch better be worth the trip," Carl said.

"Or what?" Kristin said.

Or else you and Harm'll answer for any misfortune that comes to my girl, he thought. What he said was, "Around or through?"

"What?"

"Long smooth ride around, or short bumpy one through?"

Kristin gazed with obvious discomfort at the woods. "You'd take your daughter in there, where there's no sunshine? Who knows what beasts we'll encounter?"

Carl looked up at the overcast sky and laughed. "You scared of tree spirits or something? This ain't the Old Country."

"Don't you make sport of me, Carl Hinman. Of course I don't believe in fairy stories. But there might be wolves or bears."

"Nothing in the woods today that couldn't've come out last night and ate us while we slept. Anyway, you're armed, remember? And I got my rifle. We'll get through the trees before nightfall with light to spare. Be after noon tomorrow if we go around."

As Kristin rose to return to Mariel, she squeezed his arm hard. "I know what you're thinking, Carl. I saw it in your eyes. I'll not be blamed if something happens to Mariel. We can only do what we can do, but God decides."

CHAPTER 39: NOAH
"Then burst his mighty heart"

The *Hercules* limped into dock on the Detroit River, but wouldn't be in service again anytime soon. One of the two steam funnels had toppled in the wind but, still secured at its base by cables, had flung back and forth, destroying everything it hit. The upper deck was a disaster, and many of the lower decks had sustained significant damage as well.

The number of casualties wasn't yet known, but Noah and Short Bill were not among them. Short Bill had survived with a black eye, a bump, and a nasty headache. Noah was uninjured.

"What hit me?" Short Bill said.

"A pipe, maybe," Noah said. He felt distracted, uneasy. "Your skull's so thick, you probably did more damage to the pipe."

They sat on a bench on the wharf as dazed passengers were led off the ship. They'd come a long way to learn what had happened to Claire, but she wasn't the one on Noah's mind at the moment. His gaze was fixed on the people disembarking the *Hercules*.

"Who are you looking for?" Short Bill said.

"There were two children. Zeke and Bella. They're orphans. I met them in the lounge. Have you seen them? They were both fair-haired and fair-skinned. Thin as ropes. The boy was about thirteen and the girl seven."

"I haven't, but I wasn't looking. Why?"

"They'd been sleeping on deck. I gave them food and money for a cabin, but I fear they pocketed the coins and stayed on deck anyway."

"Good Lord, mate, nobody could have survived up there. The storm would've swept them overboard. If they weren't crushed first."

Noah put his head in his hands. Despite frequent bouts of melancholy, he'd never wept in front of his friend before.

"They had guards at the doors," Short Bill said, "stopping anyone from coming up on deck."

"But did they look to see if anybody was already there?"

Short Bill put his arm around Noah's shoulder. "Let's hope so, mate."

Noah shrugged off the embrace and grunted to his feet. He took out the letter from Bancroft, Leytem and Slade, studied the address, then folded the paper and put it away again.

"I assume we'll start there?" Short Bill said.

"I'll not leave here until I find out what became of Zeke and Bella."

"If they're not onboard, how are we to know whether they went into the sea or simply walked off when we docked?"

"If they survived, someone will have seen them." Noah noted that the large bruise under Short Bill's right eye had blackened considerably since they'd left the ship. The bump on his forehead continued to swell. "You need a doctor."

"What can a doctor do but wrap my head in cloth? I've endured worse than this. Remember when I broke my shoulder in…. Where was that? The Canaries?"

"Antigua," Noah said.

"I knew it was somewhere in the Atlantic."

"Antigua is in the Caribbean."

"I knew that. If a broken shoulder didn't slow me down—"

"You had to put ashore for three weeks," Noah said.

Short Bill rose and took a few woozy steps toward Noah. He was clearly more injured than he claimed. Noah nudged him back onto the bench. "Aye, but I was drunk for two and a half of those."

"And useless for a month afterward. I had to do your job and mine."

"You couldn't steer a boat in a bathtub."

Word of the storm had spread quickly, and more and more people streamed in to the *Hercules* to assist with the cleanup. A crane normally used to load and unload cargo was now lifting the fallen funnel from the deck. Screeching metal created a pitch that sent shivers up Noah's spine. He'd always hated that sound.

If he and Short Bill didn't move soon, the children could be standing three feet from them, and never be seen for the crowd. "When you're ready, we'll start with the captain. He'll have a passenger manifest."

"We already know they were onboard," Short Bill said. "I thought we came here to learn how your daughter died."

"We did and we will. But if Zeke and Bella are still alive, perhaps a sailor directed them to the captain. That's what I would have done."

Short Bill leaned back against the wharf's railing and closed his eyes. "And what if they *are* alive? And what if they aren't?"

"Then I'll know."

"And how will the knowing benefit Claire?"

"Nothing will benefit Claire now. I've a suspicion it's myself in need of saving."

"A noble quest, then. I'll wait here while you make your enquiries."

***

The captain, a gruff old laker named McNamee, flipped through his manifest in his cabin. "Yes, they were here. Ezekial and Isabella Kendra. Brother and sister, both minors, traveling in steerage."

"Do you know what became of them?" Noah said, shifting his weight to his right leg. The bad left knee was giving him fits today.

McNamee looked down his spectacles at Noah. "Why would I? Are they your kin?"

"I just met them."

Throngs of people were congregating outside the captain's door, shouting for news of their relatives. To them McNamee called,

"Passengers have been asked to gather at the *Okseteka Inn* to meet with families. Officers are stationed around the wharf. Inquire with them if you don't know the way."

"Captain, I must insist," Noah said, but McNamee cut him off.

"Insist on *what*, sir? The children are not with me. If they aren't at the inn, I can be of no further assistance to you. Now be about your business, and leave me to mine." He slammed the manifest shut. "Can you not see what the storm has done to my ship? I've no time for this."

The desperate crowd was still barking questions at McNamee as Noah shoved through them and struggled up the stairs. The fallen funnel had been removed, but everything was still in shambles. The ship's crew and workers from shore swarmed the deck, adding to the chaos. He moved among them, looking in every nook, hoping that, miraculously, Zeke and Bella might be hiding somewhere. The men shouted at him to either work or get out of the way, and cursed at him when he did neither.

He didn't find the children, but he did find a blue sailor's cap impaled on a piece of debris against the ship's rail.

It could have belonged to anybody. Every crewman wore one.

But so did Bella.

Noah dislodged it from the rubble. It was still wet, with a large tear in the top. There didn't appear to be any blood, however. He ran a finger around the ragged edge of the hole, then folded the cap and tucked it inside his shirt.

***

He and Short Bill sat at a table in the *Okseteka Inn* until mid-afternoon. By that time all the families had been reunited with their loved ones among the passengers, or had gone away brokenhearted. There was no sign of the orphans. Noah knew their aunt's Christian name was Sarah, but he had no idea if she shared the same surname with them. He made a nuisance of himself approaching every woman who might be old enough to be their aunt. There were two other Sarahs, but neither of them knew anything about Zeke and Bella. One of them had slapped him for intruding on her own grief.

Noah absently stroked the sailor's cap and tried not to become emotional.

Short Bill sipped a whisky. "Anyone could have lost that cap."

"I know," Noah said.

"Even if it was hers, that doesn't mean she was swept overboard."

"I know."

Short Bill squeezed Noah's shoulder. "You can't save everyone, mate."

Noah sighed. "I know."

"You fed them and offered them shelter. If it pleased the Everlasting to bring them home to Him last night, the last thing they knew was your act of kindness."

"They last thing they knew was terror and pain." Noah folded his arms in front of him and put his head down. Short Bill left him to his thoughts.

Zeke and Bella.

Zeke and Bella and Claire.

Claire.

As the images of their faces rolled through his mind, he realized that Short Bill was right. He hadn't failed Zeke and Bella. He bore them no obligation, yet by offering them his small aid, he'd given them a chance. He was blameless for anything that happened afterward. No man could have held back the storm. Only God could do that, and He didn't reveal His plans. Short of kidnapping them into his own cabin, Noah had done as much as he could for them.

He knew, now, a deeper source of his distress. Zeke and Bella's parents probably didn't choose to make them orphans. But Claire was Noah's only child, the one decent legacy he'd left to the world, and he *had* chosen to make an orphan of her after Jane's death. By his obstinacy, neglect, and selfishness. He'd given her nothing after her second year, no financial support, no affection, not even forbearance of judgment. Because he didn't approve of her husband, he'd cast her out, not only of his life but out of his thoughts.

Her father's love had not been wrenched away by tragedy. It had been withheld out of spite.

Damn you, Noah Blackbourne. Your kindness to Zeke and Bella was an act of contrition but not of redemption. You can't save yourself through them. Only the blood of your blood can do that, and she is lost to you.

Because of Carl Hinman.

He lifted his head, pushed away from the table, and rose with grim determination. "Are you fit to travel?" he said to Short Bill, who had waited patiently, comforting and supporting him by his silent presence.

"Nothing the whisky didn't cure."

"Have you money left from the *Titus*?"

"Some. You?"

"The same. We'll need to rent horses. I saw a placard for a Barnes' Livery nearby."

"It's late," Short Bill said. "Shall we find lodging for the night and make a clean start of it in the morning?"

"Why do we place such high hopes on morning?" Noah said. "Yes, by all means, we should sleep first. What's another few hours? The dead aren't going anywhere."

"Do we seek the answer to Claire, or to the children?"

"My life is plagued by Hinmans."

"So, Claire." Short Bill stood up and looked at him. "Are you sure, mate, that Carl Hinman is the source of your anger, and not his father? You cast Claire out of your life. Was that because of what she did with Carl or what Jane did with Horace?"

Noah sighed. "I'm not sure of anything, except that this world is writ crueler than it's got any right to be, and I'm one of its authors."

CHAPTER 40: JUBAL
"For you are spell-stopp'd"

Jubal drove the caravan hard enough to make good time, but not so hard as to exhaust the horses. Rosie's little foal, which Petey still hadn't named, was having a difficult time keeping up as it was.

Sitting alone in the lead wagon, his thoughts led him down dark paths. Michigan loomed with every mile north: Detroit, Annalee and her entanglements, Kürten and his claim on Jubal's services, the mysterious Mr. Zug. He was anxious to get to Belgrade and let this thing play out, come what may. Afterward perhaps they could turn south again and resume a normal routine.

He'd always considered himself the heir apparent to run the show when LaVoie retired. He knew all the tricks, and he was the only other one in the troupe who could manage the finances.

Yet LaVoie had grown more distant from him the last few days. His preoccupation with the new disappearing act had become a thorny subject, primarily because he had chosen Petey as his assistant. Jubal's role? To operate the trap door beneath the stage. It was humiliating. The finances, the Phantasmagoria, the mindreading bit, all of those depended upon his talents, timing, and intelligence. But his value to the disappearing act consisted of being able to stand upright under the stage. After Kürten, he'd never intended to let anyone take advantage of his small stature again. LaVoie was the last person he would have expected to treat him that way. Given the Major's fair treatment of him otherwise, it was almost certainly more thoughtlessness than a deliberate insult, but how difficult would it have been to ask someone else to sit under the stage?

Petey, for instance. The boy had a bright future, but he wasn't yet ready to work at LaVoie's side. That was Jubal's place.

And what about LaVoie's secret meetings with Cuff, meetings that stretched late into the night, long after the Major's customary bedtime? Jubal wasn't stupid. He knew whatever they were plotting involved Cyrus and Destiny. No question that the two were escaped slaves, or that the disappearing act involved them.

Despite Cuff's powers of persuasion, LaVoie was no crusader. It was inconceivable that he would risk harboring runaways if he didn't expect a large profit. For the life of him, Jubal couldn't figure where that kind of money was to be found in Zug's offer. Two hundred and fifty dollars was generous enough, assuming it was legitimate, but even if it could sate LaVoie's greed, he couldn't spend it from the grave.

Jubal's reverie was interrupted when Petey called to him from behind. "Mr. Lawson, stop the wagon!"

He tugged on the reins. In a moment Petey, astride Chelsea, caught up with him. Both rider and pony were out of breath.

"What's the matter?"

"The chuckwagon's busted an axle clean in half."

Damn it. They'd used the reserve lumber a week ago, and didn't replenish it in order to make room for Cyrus and Destiny. Now they'd have to find the money and time for a wheelwright to install a new axle. According to Jubal's calculations, Monroe, Michigan, should be less than an hour's ride up the road, but even if a wright was available and willing to travel, it could take half a day to fix the wagon. Belgrade was another thirty miles past Monroe, at least two days' travel without the broken axle. Any delay would jeopardize their chances of getting there in time to set up for the Independence Day week-end.

"I assume the Major knows?"

"He's cussing up a storm. We called and called, but you didn't stop. He said to come right away."

Jubal looked back. The rest of the caravan was a good quarter mile behind. He'd been so preoccupied with his thoughts that he hadn't noticed they were no longer following him. "All right, Petey, I'm on my way."

Chelsea fought the bit as Petey tried to turn her. She'd spent most of her life clopping in circles with children on her back or making leisurely strolls into town. She wasn't used to being ridden hard, even for short distances. After making her point with a kick of protest, she gave in to Petey's heels.

Jubal maneuvered his wagon around. From here he could see LaVoie pacing furiously. The rest of the crew had come out of their schooners to see what was happening. The crippled chuckwagon sprawled in the middle of the road, blocking further passage. The front end had collapsed to the ground, the right wheel off completely and the left intact but resting at an impossible angle.

He urged the horses to a trot. LaVoie confronted him as soon as he arrived. "Have you lost your hearing, sir? The crack of the wood alone could raise the dead."

Jubal hopped down to inspect the damage. The axle had splintered and pushed through the right wheel, breaking several spokes.

Well, why not a ruined wheel, too? More expense, more time lost.

Kitchen implements, a trunk, clothing, and a number of tools lay scattered on the ground. Cyrus and Destiny, who'd been driving the chuckwagon, were dusty and disheveled. They stood next to Cuff, annoyed but unhurt.

"Do something," LaVoie yelled at Jubal.

What the hell? Jubal thought. "I'll just carry the front end on my shoulders, then, shall I?"

"I don't need this attitude from you."

"Then stop being an ass, Billy Powell."

The others gasped at his insolence. LaVoie glared at him. "Don't test me, Mr. Lawson. How far are we from Belgrade?"

Jubal examined one of the fractured spokes. "It might as well be on the moon."

"Don't recall us ever busting an axle before," Leopold said.

LaVoie kicked the side of the wagon, a rare display of violence from him. "Can it be repaired?"

"Not by us," Jubal said. "We don't have the supplies or the skill. As I recall, Monroe's a mile or two ahead."

"Then, sir, I suggest you go there and find us a wheelwright," LaVoie said. "Unhitch one of the horses and take Otto with you."

***

Monroe was a fair-sized town, its main street bustling with activity. Several people slowed to give Jubal and Otto an odd look. One woman started to speak, but scurried away when Jubal tipped his hat to her. Everyone else made a wide path around them.

"Apparently the locals don't take kindly to strangers," Jubal said. Who could blame them? What a pair he and Otto must appear, a six-foot-six, musclebound behemoth sharing a horse with a bewhiskered man more than two feet shorter.

"We'll tell 'em you're my father," Otto said with a wink.

The businesses gave way to residences as they crossed the center of town. A half block ahead Jubal spotted a thin blonde boy of about eight marching back and forth in front of one of the houses. He was dressed in a pretend military uniform with a toy rifle at his shoulder.

"Got guard duty?" Jubal said as they approached.

When the boy turned around, his eyes grew wide at the sight of the strange pair. "Well, knock me into a cocked hat," he said. "Never seen a kid with whiskers before. Them painted on?"

"Who you calling a kid?" Otto said.

"I meant him." He pointed at Jubal.

"I know you did, son," Otto said. "Just joshing you. This here fella's old enough to be your grandpappy."

"Huh," the boy said.

Jubal made a face. "Maybe not *that* old. We need a wheelwright."

"That'd be Mr. Dupree. You just missed the turn. Back two blocks, then three blocks west."

A woman appeared at the door to the house the boy was guarding. "Time for lunch, Autie," she called.

"Aw, Lydia," he complained, "I'm having fun."

"Nevertheless," she said, and closed the door.

As he unshouldered his weapon, he said, "Acts like she's my momma, but she's only my dumb sister. Well, so long."

He blew an imaginary bugle and led a charge toward the house.

Jubal and Otto followed his directions and soon came upon a collection of small buildings, including a dwelling house, a workshop, a timber shed, and what must have been the lathe house. Planks of oak, pine, and hickory were stacked just outside the workshop door, and a loaded wagon with a team was parked nearby. From inside the shop he could hear the sounds of sawing and hammering.

Otto reined in their horse next to the wagon.

A middle-aged man carrying a large toolbox emerged from the workshop. He had long gray hair, except in front, where a bald patch bore an ugly scar from above his eyebrow halfway up to the crown. After dropping the box into the wagon, he stepped over to greet them.

Otto dismounted, lifted Jubal from the horse, and deposited him on the ground.

"You Dupree?" Jubal said.

"That's me. Howdy, fellas. Ain't you two a sight? You from a circus?"

Jubal nodded. "Something like that. Our chuckwagon broke an axle a mile south."

"Love to help you boys," he said, "but I'm headed out to the St. James's. That big storm dropped a tree on their family wagon. Their place is a couple hours west. Time's a-wasting."

"Can anyone else from your crew help us?"

Dupree shook his head. "I got a couple sawyers, a lather, and a junior apprentice who doesn't know his ass from a hole in the ground. Nobody that can replace an axle in the field."

"This is an emergency," said Jubal. "We have to be in Belgrade by the week-end for an Independence Day show."

Otto stepped closer to Dupree. He didn't say anything, he just loomed.

"Well," Dupree said, "seeing how I'm already loaded for repairs, I guess I could be persuaded. Gonna cost you, though. Need wheels, too?"

Jubal nodded. "Just one."

"You'll take two. I buy 'em in pairs and that's how I sell 'em."

Jubal pulled out his coin purse. Zug had better be worth it. "Couldn't hurt to have a spare."

Otto pointed at the scar on Dupree' forehead. "Bet quite a story goes with that. What happened?"

"Injuns."

"You still got Indian problems up here?"

"Not no more. River Raisin Massacre back in '13. British sacked Frenchtown in the war, then Injuns come in after and killed a bunch of the survivors. I was near on twenty then, I reckon. You ever have to lay still and play dead while an Injun scalped you? It hurts a *lot*."

Otto ran his hand over his own bald head. "I shave mine myself."

"I hate the red butchers to this day."

Jubal made a note to himself: Keep Petey out of Dupree's sight. "Any objection if we stable our horse here and ride in your wagon with you?" he said. "We have to come back this way anyway, and he could use the rest."

"Suit yourselves. My apprentice'll take care of it. That shouldn't tax his birdbrain too hard." He called out to the lad, who answered immediately and did as instructed. Then Dupree turned back to Jubal and Otto. "Well, quit lollygagging, boys. Get in the wagon, and let's go. You ain't the only ones with a deadline. The St. Jameses are taking the family to some important get-together. There's a whole brood of them, so they need that wagon.

***

Once they arrived at the caravan, Dupree set to work, employing Manfred, Leopold, Herman, and Giovanni to unload the rest of the contents of the disabled chuckwagon to make it lighter, then to hold it level while he extracted the broken axle from the frame. Of the other men present, LaVoie supervised—meaning he stayed out of the way—Cyrus wasn't inclined to take orders from a white man, André had the muscle power of a nightcrawler, and Jubal hid Petey from Dupree for his own safety.

To everyone's relief, Dupree was a master craftsman, and was able to finish the job in less than an hour. He charged them for not only the labor and material, but for the St. James's inconvenience in having to wait. Considering the speed with which he accomplished the task, Jubal thought it a reasonable expenditure.

There was enough sunlight left to put in several miles today. LaVoie ordered the caravan to get moving. Cyrus, Destiny, and Cuff helped the others repack the supplies into the chuckwagon, and within minutes the show was enroute to Belgrade again.

Petey sat next to Jubal and prattled on and on about topics of concern to children his age. Jubal didn't pay much attention. To give the appearance that he was listening he nodded or muttered "I see" whenever the boy paused for a breath.

No need to hide Petey when they retrieved their horse, because Dupree wouldn't even have arrived at the St. James farm yet. At the wheelwright's shop they found the apprentice snoozing behind a stack of hickory planks. Jubal woke him and gave him a nickel to hitch the horse back in with the team. The kid acted like he'd been handed a bag of gold dust.

In five minutes they were back on the road. North of Monroe, Jubal handed Petey the reins. "You drive," he said.

"Thank you!"

Jubal watched Petey's face as the boy concentrated on the road. He was a good lad, a worthy lad, but too young to be working a crowd the way LaVoie would need for the disappearing act. Whatever was going on, it wasn't Petey's fault. As casually as he could, Jubal said, "How's the new trick going?"

"It'll be easy."

"It's for Cyrus and Destiny, isn't it?"

Petey peered at him from the corners of his eyes, looking nervous. "I didn't ask to be his partner, Mr. Lawson. He asked me, I swear."

"It's all right, Petey. If the boss tells you to do something, you have to do it."

It wasn't all right, not at all. He allowed himself a brief violent fantasy involving LaVoie, a knife, and the Major's favorite body parts, not only for bypassing him in favor of Petey, but for diverting Cuff's attention when Jubal thought he was making progress toward her affections.

He put the image out of his mind, though, and they spent the rest of the day traveling in the safety of more small talk and, finally, silence.

The caravan didn't stop for the night until two hours after sunset. It seemed like Jubal had just closed his eyes when LaVoie was barking orders to get started again. It was four-thirty a.m., and the first hints of the sun were tinting the eastern horizon.

By pushing the horses a little faster and longer than usual they pulled into the outskirts of Belgrade on time almost two days later. Zug had already rented land for them just off the main road, marking it with a huge banner announcing their coming. He'd already built them a stage, too, one large enough for a disappearing act.

Zug's odd offer. Cyrus and Destiny. Disappearing act.

And the proximity to Canada.

Jesus Christ, Billy Powell, Cuff's really got you all in on this, doesn't she?

The troupe was exhausted and in ill humor, but no one was allowed to sleep until the animals were tended to and the tents erected.

Rosie's colt was in such poor shape that Jubal was afraid they might lose him. Petey was frantic with worry, but Cuff calmed him. "We pulled this little fella into the world," she said, stroking the sobbing boy's hair, "and we ain't about to send him out of it so soon. You and me'll stay with him tonight. I'll show you how to nurse him right."

Jubal's heart swelled with love all over again, but the feeling quickly turned to something darker. LaVoie, intentionally or not, was stealing her away from him.

CHAPTER 41: MARIEL
"For some must watch,
while some must sleep"

Mariel remembered bits and pieces of the long and bumpy ride. She remembered hiding under the wagon with her father and Kristin Jensen until a terrible storm had passed. She remembered a dark passage through woods with her father cursing the bad road and Mrs. Jensen hugging her and muttering prayers. She remembered emerging from the trees into bright sunshine that hurt her eyes when she peered out the opening of the wagon's canopy. And she remembered the dirt path giving way to cobblestone streets, houses and buildings springing up to replace grass and trees, and her father saying to Mrs. Jensen, "I hoped to never see this town again."

But mostly she remembered coughing constantly and blowing her nose so often her nostrils were raw. She remembered the pain in her chest, the taste of blood in her mouth, the fire in her body, and the chill on her skin after night sweats. The days since they left home blurred into periods of fitful sleep and waking misery. Mrs. Jensen seemed to never leave her side, forcing her to eat and drink and watching over her while even when she relieved herself.

They'd stopped for supplies, followed by more cobblestone streets, more countryside, then more buildings and stone streets, and one more stop to ask directions. She heard the words "Pontiac" and "Doctor Finch."

And then she slept.

When she awoke she was naked in a bathtub, with no recollection of how she got there. Mrs. Jensen was washing her with a cloth that smelled of lye soap. The water was steaming hot. It felt wonderful.

"Ah, child," Mrs. Jensen said, "you're awake. It's been a long journey, and you had many days' worth of grime on that little body of yours. Doctor Finch suggested a bath before he examines you. When we're done, we'll dress you in clean bed clothes." She poured a hot liquid over Mariel's head. "The doctor had some borax and olive oil, so I was able to mix a nice hair wash for you."

Mariel had a question, which she may have asked out loud, but whether she did or didn't, she fell asleep again before hearing an answer.

***

"You ain't gonna bleed her?" she heard her father say.

"Good God, Hinman," an unfamiliar voice bellowed, "this isn't the Dark Ages."

Somebody's finger lifted Mariel's eyelid. A tall man with spectacles, a balding head and a wiry beard was leaning over her, staring into her opened eye. For some reason he lit a match and passed it back and forth in front of her face.

Startled, she gasped, but she felt Mrs. Jensen squeezing her right hand and her father squeezing her left. Her father said, "Shhh, it's all right."

"My name is Doctor Finch," the man said, blowing out the match.

"Am I going to die?" Mariel said.

"Pupil's not dilated," the doctor told her father. "Let's have a listen to those lungs."

The doctor produced a device with a small opening on one end, a bell-shaped wooden bowl on the other, and a brass tube in between. It looked something like her father's spy glass, without the lenses. He stuck the small end in his ear, rolled Mariel to her side, and placed the bowl against her back between her shoulder blade and spine.

"What is that?" her father said.

"Snake ear trumpet," the doctor said. "The French call it a stethoscope."

"What's it do?"

"Lets me hear what's going on inside her. Deep breath, little lady," he said.

She had no idea what he was doing, but she did as he ordered. Drawing in the breath brought on a coughing fit. He waited for it to pass, listened, then moved the bowl lower, over her ribs.

"Again," he said.

He did this two more times before returning her to her back.

"Well?" her father said.

"Patience." The doctor now placed the bowl of the device in the middle of Mariel's chest. "Another big breath, only hold it this time."

He listened intently for a few moments, then smiled and said, "You can breathe." To her father and Mrs. Jensen he said, "I don't think it's consumption."

"Praise God," Mrs. Jensen said.

Her father lowered his head and kissed Mariel's fingers.

"There's congestion in the upper lobes of her lungs, but not to the extent I typically hear with consumption. Most of the illness has settled in the lower lobes. Perhaps it's influenza, perhaps pneumonia. Either can be almost as bad as consumption. She needs complete bed rest until her symptoms improve. I can give her quinine powder for the cough and laudanum to help her sleep."

"Where shall we stay?" Mrs. Jensen said.

"You may stay here tonight. Afterward, the widow Winslow runs a boarding house down the street. Her rates are reasonable."

"Will my girl be all right?" her father said.

"She's got a strong heart. With a nod from the Almighty, you may expect a full recovery."

***

The next morning they rented two rooms with Mrs. Winslow, a rotund woman who made the stout Mrs. Jensen look bony. Mariel and Mrs. Jensen took one room, her father the other. The house had been built in the last century, Mrs. Winslow proudly proclaimed. Until coming here, the biggest home Mariel had ever been in was the one belonging to Harm and Kristin Jensen. This one dwarfed theirs. The wood floor was smooth and shiny, and the walls were adorned with pretty pink wallpaper decorated with flowers.

And the beds! Both the mattress and the pillows must've been stuffed with the softest eiderdown in the world. As Mariel lay down, the mattress felt as if it reached around her body and hugged her in its warmth.

The quinine powder Doctor Finch had prescribed tasted terrible, but her father made her take it anyway. Then he kissed her on the cheek and said, "Rest, sweet darling."

"Should we give her the laudanum now?" Mrs. Jensen said from the rocking chair across the room.

"If she can't fall asleep, we will."

That was the last thing Mariel remembered. When she awoke, it was dark outside and Mrs. Jensen was spooning hot beef broth into her mouth. It made her stomach churn, and she may have vomited.

And then it was morning. She opened her eyes to find her father, Mrs. Jensen, and Mrs. Winslow standing at her bedside.

"You're right, Carl, her color is better," Mrs. Jensen said. She placed her ear on Mariel's chest. "She doesn't sound as congested."

Her father knelt and took Mariel's hand. Great tears brimmed in his eyes. "You're gonna be all right. You're gonna be all right."

"You should eat," Mrs. Winslow said.

Maybe her color was better, but the thought of food repelled her.

"I'll get the food," Mrs. Jensen said.

"*I'll* get it," Mrs. Winslow said, and she scurried out of the room.

Mrs. Jensen glared at the door Mrs. Winslow had just exited, then sat back down in the rocking chair.

"I'm not hungry," Mariel whispered, but her voice was so soft she doubted anyone heard.

Her father stood up. "Kristin, I don't know how I'll ever pay you and Harm back for all this."

"Don't worry about that now, Carl. We can discuss it later."

"Sooner than later," her father said. "I know Mariel's in good hands with you two ladies, so I got one more favor to ask, though Lord knows you've done enough already. I need to borrow one of the horses and ride back to Detroit. Long as I gotta be here anyway, there's some business I oughta look into. When I get back maybe we'll talk."

Mrs. Jensen rocked furiously for a few moments without answering. Then she said, "No 'maybe' about it, Carl. Swear on it, and you can take the mare."

"Word of honor," he said.

Mariel turned to her side and looked at them. Her father leaned over and whispered something to Mrs. Jensen. She couldn't make out much, but some of the words might have been "if she's well enough" and "visit her Momma's grave."

CHAPTER 42: BILL
"He that dies pays all debts"

"February of last year, you say?" said Eli Bancroft. Bill thought the old solicitor seemed on the verge of nodding off. Or dying. It was past noon. After finding breakfast Bill and Noah had wasted the morning haggling with an unpleasant fellow named Barnes over the cost of a week's rental of two horses and saddles. "May I see the letter, Mr. Blackbourne?"

Noah produced the document.

Bancroft unfolded it and read it carefully. "Oh, yes, yes, the Hinman case. Jacob—Mr. Leytem—was handling that, but he retired some months back. We retained his name on the firm because it's good for business."

"Can you tell me anything about it?" Noah said.

"I don't recall many of the details, beyond what's written here. A woman presented a bank draft for down payment on a funeral for someone who wasn't dead yet. The person she expected to die did so, but no one ever returned to pay the balance. Jacob's client, the undertaker Mr. Miles Kelley, engaged our firm to locate the man whose name was on the down payment bank draft. Who are you to the decedent?"

"Her father," Noah said.

Bancroft nodded. "That would account for why Jacob contacted you when he failed to locate Hinman. My condolences for your loss."

"It was a woman who presented the draft?"

"Yes. Kelley informed her that under Michigan law a woman may not enter into a contract without her husband's consent, but she already knew that. Since she produced a bank draft signed by Hinman, Kelley naturally assumed the woman was his wife."

Bill looked at Noah, whose jaw was clenched. "Are you saying Claire made a down payment on her own funeral?"

"Let me think. Let me think. As I recall, the woman's last name was Hinman, but her first name wasn't Claire."

"That makes no sense," Bill said.

"Hinman had two half-sisters," Noah said. "If he sent one of them, that meant he knew Claire was going to die."

"Perhaps she was mortally ill," Bill suggested.

"Perhaps. But why didn't he go to the undertaker himself? And why didn't he then pay the balance?"

Bancroft removed his spectacles and pinched his nose. "I don't remember. I got this all secondhand from Jacob, of course. Here, allow me to consult our files."

He pushed himself from his chair with the aid of a cane and hobbled over to a wooden file cabinet. "Can't recall if Jacob filed the papers under Hinman or Kelley," he said. It took him several minutes to find what he was looking for.

In the meantime, the knot on Bill's forehead was throbbing. His right eye was nearly swollen shut. He felt nauseated. Noah was little better off. He kept shifting his weight from foot to foot. His bad knee must be acting up again.

"Do you mind if we sit?" Bill said.

Bancroft glanced over his shoulder at them. "Good Lord, forgive my manners, gentlemen. Please."

Noah sat in the chair on the other side of Bancroft's desk. Bill dragged one from the other side of the room.

"Ah, here they are," Bancroft said. He removed several sheets from the file and returned to his desk. "It was in our closed case file."

"Closed?" Bill said.

Bancroft skimmed the papers. "The woman identified herself to Kelley as Joanna Hinman, your daughter's sister-in-law."

"That was the name of one of Jane's girls with Hinman's father," Noah said. "She was Claire's half-sister."

"But also her sister-in-law," Bill pointed out. "So that much was true."

"I'm confused."

"Don't get him started on that subject," Bill said.

Bancroft spread his hands out in bewilderment. "Gentlemen, in retrospect Jacob was never certain of the woman's true identity. She used the name, but if you ask me Kelley was a fool to enter into such an arrangement. It stank to high heaven to begin with."

"You're sure it was Hinman who signed the draft for the down payment?"

"Kelley was satisfied that it was."

"It doesn't matter who delivered the draft if Hinman's name was on it," Noah said. "Why he didn't follow through?"

"That's what this firm was engaged to learn. Kelley wanted the obligation satisfied, of course, but there was something else. The death was not a natural one."

"I knew it," Noah cried.

"How did Kelley know her death was not natural?" Bill said.

"He prepared the body. Then when her husband abandoned his home, leaving most of his belongings behind… Well, fleeing seemed rather extreme for a simple unpaid debt. This was particularly true because we would have worked something out with him. We only resort to debtors' prison when all other efforts have failed."

Noah slammed his fist on the desk. "I knew it," he said again. "The bastard killed my daughter."

"How was she murdered?" Bill said.

Bancroft opened a box of snuff and stuffed some up his right nostril. He sneezed, then blew his nose with a kerchief monogrammed with the letters EB. "I wish I could tell you more."

"Kelley went through with the funeral?"

"He'd accepted a down payment and considered it his duty."

"Where may we find this undertaker?" Noah said.

"You can't," Bancroft said. He turned to Bill. "The case is closed because Miles Kelley is dead. Drowned while fishing nearly a year ago. Without a paying client, Jacob had no reason to pursue the matter further. Kelley's estate is still in probate until his father and brother decide what to do with it. Perhaps they'll seek to recover his losses, but I doubt it. As Jacob explained to Mr. Kelley, our services would cost as much as he could hope to obtain from Hinman."

"Where does Jacob Leytem live?" Bill said. "May we speak with him?"

"He retired for health reasons. I'm afraid he would be of little use to you. His mind has undergone an alarming decline. He doesn't know his own children anymore."

Noah's face paled and his mouth fell open. "We came all the way from New Hampshire," he said.

"I am sorry, sir," Bancroft said.

"Did Kelley have associates, assistants, people he worked with?" Bill said. "Anyone who might shed some light on this?"

"If he did, they didn't maintain the business. It's been boarded up since his death."

"What about the bank that issued the draft?" Noah said.

Bancroft riffled through the papers. He read for a moment, then shook his head. "I was afraid of this. The account was closed shortly after the draft was honored. They would not provide Jacob further details, citing confidentiality."

"Do the authorities know Hinman killed her?" Noah said.

"I believe Kelley notified the law."

Bill squeezed Noah's shoulder. His friend was trembling with rage or grief, or both. "Who headed the investigation?"

"I'm sorry, gentlemen, but I have no idea. If an officer ever called on us, he would've spoken to Jacob. As I've said, I wasn't involved with the case."

"So every door of inquiry is closed to us," Bill said.

"It isn't my intent to be an impediment. I simply don't know."

"Where is she?" Noah said.

"I beg your pardon?" Bancroft said.

"My daughter's grave. Where is she buried?"

This time the paper Bancroft needed was right on top. "Russell Street Cemetery, corner of Gratiot and Russell Street here in Detroit. Protestant section. Ah, here's something. The funeral was officiated by a Reverend George Smith. I believe he is still living."

"Do you have an address?" Noah said

"Only of his meetinghouse."

"Meetinghouse?"

Bancroft shrugged and rolled his eyes. "He's Presbyterian. That's their word for church." He removed a blank sheet of paper from his desk drawer, dipped his quill in ink, scribbled the address, and handed the paper to Noah. "Good luck to you, sir. I wish I could have been of more assistance."

He inserted more snuff into his nose.

CHAPTER 43: MARCUS
"Such as we are made of, such we be"

The sun had just cleared the horizon on what promised to be a hot day. LaVoie paced in front of his wagon, anxious to receive news before opening for business. He wasn't sure what he had expected. A welcoming committee? Zug himself? So far no one had presented himself. If Zug had special instructions, he'd better make them known soon, because LaVoie wanted to get started. They hadn't performed since the disaster in Jeffersonville, and with the latest expense of the broken axle and two new wheels, finances were running low. He risked, for the first time, being unable to pay the acts. They were good people, but their loyalty only went so far.

The outer tents were set up in a field adjoining the river, just to the south of a set of military earthworks. Zug had roped off the area for them, placing several large placards around the perimeter announcing the imminent arrival of Major Marcus T. LaVoie's Ten Wonders of the Universe. The stage their benefactor had built for them fit the specifications of their show tent perfectly. Garrett must have given Zug the measurements. Having a stage in place saved LaVoie the cost of buying the lumber and his crew the toil of building it.

Zug had thought of everything. To light the grounds at night at all his previous performances, LaVoie hung lanterns on widely-spaced poles. Zug had strung wires around the perimeter with dozens of lanterns hanging on them. That would look spectacular. Even the horses had been provided a lean-to shelter, complete with water trough, hay, and bags of oats.

The show's small circle of prairie schooners were dwarfed by the field. Located two hundred yards from Belgrade's main street, they were visible to anyone entering or leaving town. LaVoie worried that the crowd could get too big. It was a matter of security. With that many people, it would be impossible to keep an eye on all of them. The slaver Tom Villisca or his ilk may still be lurking about, waiting for the right moment to pounce on Cuff, Cyrus, and Destiny.

A dozen or more curious passersby had gathered outside the ropes, but for now Otto, Manfred, and Giovanni were able to keep them at bay. They only allowed one man to pass. LaVoie heard Garrett's consumptive cough before he saw him. He was on foot, leading his horse through the people. Unaware of his connection to the show, they were not happy that he was allowed in while they were not.

Garrett said something to them that made them step back from the ropes. Maybe he threatened to hack his bloody sputum on them.

A box wrapped in brown cloth was tied to his saddle. He frowned as he approached LaVoie's wagon, his mousy mustache as droopy as ever. "What the hell, Marc. Zug didn't know if you was gonna make it in time."

"Complications. But here we are."

Garrett gasped for breath. "Next time I'll just ride over the damn fools," he said, nodding back toward the crowd. "Walking's bad for the lungs."

"Take this in the spirit in which it's intended, but why aren't you dead yet?"

"Naturally contrary, I guess." He smiled, coughed, and spat. "Come on, let's go into your office. I got something for you."

"I hate it when you spit in my presesnce."

"I hate having consumption but what can I do?" He untied the box from his saddle and entered LaVoie's wagon. LaVoie followed him in, and they both sat at the table. Garrett set the package on the ground next to him.

"What's in it?" LaVoie said.

"Patience, Major. There's more." He removed a coin purse from his vest and placed it on the table. LaVoie could hear the money jingle.

"That's a good sign."

"Indeed it is, sir." Garrett loosened the purse's string and shook the coins out. "Two hundred fifty dollars, as promised. And you get to keep the gate, plus whatever you take in selling your poison."

LaVoie whistled as he examined a gold piece. "He's as good as his word."

"If you bite that to make sure it's real, I'm going to shoot you in the face."

LaVoie smiled. "What reason would I have to distrust Mr. Zug?"

Garrett lifted the package onto the table and removed the cloth. The box was a small wooden crate, nailed shut at the top. He unsheathed a knife and pried the lid off.

LaVoie jumped back at what he saw in the box. "For God's sake, Salmon. What on earth is *that*?"

"Your answer to Barnum's Feejee Mermaid. You said you wanted one. Ask, and ye shall receive." Garrett removed a glass case from the box. Inside was a hideous conglomeration of a beast floating in preserving fluid. About the size of a raccoon, it had the face of a skinned monkey, the wings, tail, and talons of a bird, and the hair and breasts of a woman. The entire body, except the head, was covered in fish scales. The eyes glowed like a wolf's in firelight. "It's a harpy."

"Come to steal the king's food?"

"Come to steal your audience's soul, by way of their purses."

"This is ghastly," LaVoie said with a grin. "I love it."

"I thought you would." Garrett set the case on the table. "I went to the man I told you about, Forrest-Hosier, but he wasn't interested in creating a 'fraudulent freak show chimera,' as he called it. 'I do honest work,' he said. By that he meant he mounts fish. I thought I knew him better than that. But he was good enough to refer me to a miller who does taxidermy on the side. Took it on as a challenge."

LaVoie peered through the glass, looking at the thing from different angles. "Good idea, pickling it. The distortion of the liquid makes it look even more grotesque. How much will this cost me?"

"Compliments of Mr. Samuel Zug."

***

They were saving the disappearing act for their final performance Saturday night, just before Belgrade's fireworks display for the Independence Day celebration began. LaVoie and Petey would practice it again late tonight to make sure the timing was perfect.

Between the first and second morning performances on Friday, LaVoie closed off the show tent to observers. He posted Otto out front to stand guard while he climbed the stage to check the trap door. As he approached the door, it suddenly dropped open and Cuff's head popped out.

LaVoie nearly screamed. "Damn it, Cuff, I could've fallen in on top of you."

"I might let some men on top of me. You ain't one of them."

"What are you doing?"

"Hinges were a little squeaky. A little whale oil fixed it up fine. Come on down here and see what else we got." When LaVoie hesitated as he peered into the hole, she frowned her impatience and said, "Oh, just jump. It's only four feet, it won't kill you."

Instead, he walked to the back of the stage and down the stairs. Jubal could almost stand upright in the space beneath, but normal-sized people would have to stoop or crawl. LaVoie was not going to crawl. He bent over and made his way to Cuff, his back bumping the stage floor above him with every step. The choice for escape was either stealth or speed, but not both. Destiny was fairly petite and would have no trouble, but Cyrus was a big man, and LaVoie wondered if he'd be able to get away quickly enough.

He checked the mirrors. They jutted out toward the audience, their junction hidden by two support columns and their ends by curtains overhanging the sides of the stage.

"Don't you worry about them mirrors," Cuff said. "Looky here, I got something else to show you." She reached down through loose dirt and pulled open a second trap door buried in the ground. "Surprise."

What in hell? he thought. "A tunnel? Where does it lead?"

Cuff smiled. "To them earthworks just north of us. Government's building a fort, and there're tunnels all under here. Easy to get lost if you don't know the way. I know the way."

"Surely the tunnels don't extend under the river?"

"What, you wanna drown someone? Nope, there's an old Irish ferryman'll take folks 'cross the Detroit River. Follow me, I'll show you."

"I believe you." LaVoie stood upright through the opening in the stage and hoisted himself so he was sitting on the edge. This was a development he didn't like, not one little bit. He offered his hands to Cuff. "Come up here, please."

"Don't need your help." She climbed through the hole and stood over him. "Something wrong?"

LaVoie clenched his jaw as he considered his words. "Cuff, what's going on? Clearly, this is why Zug built the stage here for the main tent. I thought it was little too convenient that he'd already have a stage with a trap door waiting for us. It doesn't make sense. If these tunnels are here, you don't need my disappearing act to help Cyrus and Destiny escape. Why expose them and the entire show to danger with such a public charade? Just send them through the tunnels tonight. Who'll know?"

She sat down next to him and put her hand on his shoulder, an act of familiarity that made him uncomfortable. "Marc," she said softly, "Cyrus and Destiny, they're already gone. Left this morning before the sun come up. Lord willing, they're sitting over in Windsor having a picnic with my girl Evelyn this very minute. Ain't nobody gonna go through that tunnel tomorrow night. Tomorrow night'll be just another act."

LaVoie got to his feet and paced in a circle around her. "Let me see if I understand this. I purchased those expensive mirrors for an act that was added for the express purpose of helping Cyrus and Destiny escape, and they're already gone? Damn you, Cuff, why do we need a disappearing act at all, then?"

"Ain't no call to cuss at me. I didn't know they was gonna leave early. The plan was to leave during the show. But you try telling Cyrus he got to stay put when freedom is right there, right now."

"So who's going to disappear, Cuff?"

"I don't know, Petey or Jubal, maybe. Me, if you want."

"Petey's my assistant on stage. Jubal will be working the trap door. I'm disappointed in you, Cuff. I've been lied to."

"I don't know if that slaver came all the way up here after us. Most times they don't, but sometimes they do. And even if they don't, most white people ain't as gracious as the ones who dug these tunnels. They don't care what happens to coloreds. They sure ain't gonna risk their lives to help us. A lot of 'em hate us as bad as the Southerners do. This stage was just built. Before that, anyone who saw coloreds going into the tunnels could've turned them in for two dollars and a slap on the back. What I'm saying is it ain't as easy as Cyrus and Destiny made it look. They was lucky." She took a deep breath. "But that don't matter."

LaVoie glared at her as the obvious dawned on him. "You're working for Zug. You have been all along."

"'Course I am. That wasn't no accident I just happened to be down there by the Kentucky border when you come by. Wasn't no accident I asked to do your floating-in-air trick. Mr. Zug saw your show last time you was here, and it got him to thinking."

"Why the subterfuge?"

"You use a lotta big words."

"Why the secrecy and lies?"

"Mr. Zug don't need you up here, not in Belgrade. If slavers are scratching 'round, how many times you think they gonna be fooled by you making colored folks disappear before they figure it out? Once? Twice?"

LaVoie had wondered about that. "Then why are we in Belgrade?"

Cuff rose and retreated to the far side of the stage. She seemed nervous. "Ever hear of the Underground Railroad? Now, don't gimme that look, 'cause I know you have. Lotsa good folks helping slaves cross the Ohio River. Zug works on this end, but he needs you down in the border states."

"Using the show as cover to move runaways."

"Marc, it's hard down there, real hard. Them plantation owners don't like losing their slaves. They pay good money to get them back, even if they get them back dead. They can't stand 'niggers' getting the best of them, but it's more than pride. It tells the other slaves: 'See what'll happen if you run?' So Mr. Zug, he'll pay you plenty to take your show wherever he needs you to be, and then when you jump, maybe you take on one or two extra people."

"Like Cyrus and Destiny."

"Like that, except you won't be coming up this far, just to the next stop on the Railroad."

"Why me? There must be dozens of other medicine shows he could have chosen."

"Your fish-name scout told him you worked the border states. Still don't like that Garrett, even so." Cuff crossed back to him. "Slavers know some of the routes, and they got regular patrols. Farmers down in Iowa put on a pretend funeral once just to move a slave from one town to the next. He was in the coffin." She shook her head. "Nobody'll suspect a medicine show."

"Villisca did."

"Slavers look into anyone employing colored folks in the border states. Nothing comes of it most the time. If I stay with you, folks'll get used to me and won't think nothing of it. It's the ones they don't see that you'll be moving."

LaVoie was angry. He was the trickster, the magician, the sleight-of-hand artist. He didn't like it when the fleecer got fleeced. "Zug decided to appeal to my greed with the promise of a big payday and the stuffed harpy? In essence, he thought he could bribe me. That's offensive. Couldn't he have just asked?"

"Wasn't your greed. Oh, you like your money all right, ain't no doubt 'bout that, but Garrett said you was a man who got a kindly heart that maybe you don't even know about yourself. You bamboozle people, but only to ease their cares for a spell. And look how you treat Jubal. Like a man, not a sideshow freak. Look what you did for Cyrus and Destiny. So Mr. Zug made Garrett an offer. He said plenty of men might take the money, but not many would risk their lives to carry runaway slaves. You could've told him, 'No, I ain't coming,' But you didn't. You came even knowing the danger. That's the kind of man Zug wants."

"So this was a test of sorts. Were Cyrus and Destiny part of it?"

Cuff shrugged. "Didn't know it'd be them, but somebody was gonna be waiting in Jeffersonville."

"What if I'd come without them and demanded the money?"

"He'd've paid you and wished you well. He wants you, but you gotta be all in. If not, he'll find other who'll to help him. I mean, he will anyway, but he wants you, too."

"Well, I'll be damned."

"You'll do it, then?"

"I can't decide that kind of thing for my crew."

"Mr. Zug figured you might say that. If they don't wanna be involved, he'll hire new acts who will."

"And my people will just be out of a job?"

"He's a big man up here. He'll find them work. But I seen how they love you. They'll go where you go."

"Will he reimburse me for the mirrors?"

"He'll buy you a hundred mirrors, you want him to." Cuff leaned in toward him. The top of her head barely reached his shoulders. "Please?"

LaVoie felt his anger drain away. Looking down at her hopeful face, he took her hands in his and said, "What about you, Cuff? Why don't you walk through that tunnel right now?"

Tears filled her eyes. "Don't you think I want to? Don't you think I'd a whole lot rather go to my Evelyn and leave all this behind? But how can I be free when so many others ain't?"

LaVoie sighed. Incredibly, almost in disbelief, he spoke the words that would change the course of his life forever. "All right, this chicken farmer's son is with you."

CHAPTER 44: CARL
"One man in his time plays many parts"

Carl had never been much of a drinker. He'd never gotten drunk, even after Claire's death, though Lord knew he had reason to. Now an occasional whisky or beer hit the spot, but only in small doses when the weather was hot or his spirits needed numbing. Claire had loved wine, and while he enjoyed the evenings they had shared a glass, he didn't really care for the stuff. Too sweet, too much of an unpleasant aftertaste.

He'd been sitting in a saloon on the outskirts of Detroit, swilling beer for two hours. A sensible man would've laid low at the widow Winslow's house in Pontiac until Mariel recovered, then hightailed it out of Michigan and gone home to the farm. He doubted that Constable Nortman was the kind of man to stop looking for him. Carl had never seen a likeness of himself on a wanted poster in any post office in Ohio, but that didn't mean Nortman had given up on him in Detroit.

Outside, signs of the recent storm were everywhere, houses without roofs and twisted tree branches, but except for a broken window, the saloon itself had been spared. The day was hot and humid, the wind dead calm, making the air inside so thick it was like breathing hot milk through a reed. The heaviness was accompanied by a familiar stink, as if the building sat on top of the pit of an old outhouse. The smell stirred memories of his years at the tannery, treating leather with human piss and dog shit. And going home every night to Claire. The woman who had loved him and smiled as she washed his reeking clothes and scraped his filthy boots. The woman who had borne him the most beautiful daughter in the world.

His wife.

Claire.

Who now lay dead in the ground because of him.

Carl gulped the last of his beer and tapped the glass on the counter to get the barkeep's attention. As he was the only customer here, that wasn't difficult.

"Why don't I just give you the whole keg?" the barkeep said.

"What's it to you?" Carl said. His clothes stuck to his skin and chafed his privates. Sweat trickled down his legs. He was slurring his words. The room was beginning to spin. Was this what *drunk* felt like?

The barkeep shrugged. He was a young fellow with a cleanshaven chin but a bushy mustache that swooped down and joined with his side whiskers. "So what's your story?"

"Do I got to have a story? Maybe I just want beer."

"Have it your way."

As the barkeep held his glass under the tap, Carl watched the amber liquid swirl from the spigot, splashing and raising a white foam. The motion made him queasy. He fumbled for a coin and slapped it onto the counter. As he did, another woman's name popped into his head. He stared quizzically at the barkeep, said, "Oh, hell," and fell off his stool.

∗∗∗

He didn't know if he was asleep and dreaming, awake with wishful thinking, or somewhere in between, but the woman's name grew in his brain, took shape, and became a face. So lovely, so lovely....

He rode Kristin's mare up a deeply rutted lane. At the end of the lane stood a magnificent colonial house, erected when England still ruled America. It was white with imposing turrets and a red gabled roof. Behind the house were untold acres of prime Michigan farmland, and beyond that, the city of Detroit. Here was the kind of wealth and culture he could never have aspired to because he could never have imagined it. Not before he'd seen it with his own eyes, anyway.

He approached the house and dismounted the horse. At the door he removed a calling card from his pocket, expecting a servant to answer when he knocked. He just wanted to leave a reminder of the past and perhaps a warning for the future: I was here. I'll be back. Neither statement was actually written on the card, only his name. It was his calling card, a hundred of which had been printed long ago for him should he ever need a means of formal introduction. He himself couldn't read, but he'd seen his name written often enough to recognize its form.

It wasn't a servant who answered, it was her. *She was as he remembered her, adorned in a flowing white gown of the latest fashion, the spaces behind her ears and between her breasts perfumed with a familiar flowery scent. Her hair had been curled like a China doll's, with auburn tresses draped over each shoulder. The woman was four years older than Carl, yet she still dressed like an adolescent at her coming-out ball.*

It took her a moment to recognize him, but then her eyes grew wide as two full moons and her face contorted into a grimace of fear.

"Carl Hinman," she whispered.

Carl smiled grimly. "God damn you," he said. "She was your friend.*" He clenched his hand into a fist and struck that lovely face with all his strength. The woman crumpled to the floor, her nose crushed, her lips split, blood gushing all over her pretty white bosom.*

***

The young man with muttonchops stared down at him. "You all right?"

"Maybe I don't like beer as much as I thought."

"You're not the first to fall in my saloon." The barkeep extended a hand to help Carl up.

"Obliged." Carl felt sick and lightheaded as he rose. The barkeep steadied him and led him to a chair. "Ain't never been drunk before. Can't say as I like it all that much."

"You a preacher or something?"

"About as far from a preacher as a fella can get, I reckon."

"Never heard of any man but a preacher who ain't been drunk. Your wife one of them teetotalers?"

Carl folded his arms on the table and put his head down. "How do I make it go away?"

"Wife or the effect of drink?"

"Drink."

"Stop drinking."

Carl belched. "I gotta get going. How soon'll I feel better?"

The barkeep smiled and pulled a pocket watch from his vest. "Three, four hours."

"Can't wait that long. There's a man I gotta see."

"You new to Detroit?"

"Nope. I know the way."

Carl tried to stand, failed, tried again. Rays slanting in through the saloon's swinging doors were like needles in his eyes. He wobbled in that direction. "Do me a favor," he said.

"What's that?"

"You see me in here again, have me arrested."

The barkeep gave him a friendly salute. "The sheriff's a friend of mine," he said.

Carl stumbled out the doors toward Kristin's mare. The animal wasn't amused by his clumsy attempts to mount from the right side. She shied away, then nudged back into him, knocking him over.

You always mount from the left side, his father had told him when he was a boy just learning to ride, although he had never learned why. How could a horse know left from right?

"Sorry, old girl," he said from the seat of his pants. He got up, dusted himself off, and went around to the left side.

He put his left foot in the stirrup and swung his right leg over the horse. The change in altitude made his head spin more. He vomited onto the wooden sidewalk, narrowly missing his trousers.

Shielding his eyes against the sun, Carl tapped his heels against the horse's flanks. When she lurched out into the street, the motion brought up the rest of the beer. This time he splattered the mare's mane.

His own stench repulsed him.

Determined to proceed, he urged the beast to a trot. The hot wind in his face steadied him somewhat.

In the outskirts of Detroit the streets were still narrow dirt lanes, the buildings mostly wood. Carl hadn't been out this way often, but as he entered the city proper, he began to recognize enough landmarks to get his bearings.

His hands were shaking, and it had nothing to do with the beer. It was time to bargain with an undertaker, although he had nothing to bargain with.

***

The building was boarded up. There was a sign on the door, but that did Carl no good. He tied Kristin's mare to the post and paced outside the door, not knowing what to do or where to go now. Finally a man and woman passed by pushing a pram with a squalling infant.

"'Scuse me, folks," Carl said, "but what happened to the undertaker who used to do business here?"

They looked at the sign and then at each other. Carl saw by the pity in their eyes that they realized he couldn't read. "Mr. Kelley died last year," the wife said.

"An accidental drowning," her husband said.

"Sign says that?"

"It says 'Building for Sale or Lease.' We knew Mr. Kelley. Not socially, of course. He was a fine gentleman."

"For an undertaker," the wife added.

"I have business with him," Carl said.

"Not anymore," the husband said.

"Well, goodbye," the wife said.

They started to walk away, but Carl remembered the letter in his pocket. Harm had read it to him, and Mariel had tried, but neither of them had mentioned an address. He took it out and looked at it. "One more thing?" he said. "What's the address on this letter?"

The baby was screaming.

The husband sighed and examined the letter. "'Bancroft, Leytem, and Slade, Solicitors, 2401 Holmes Street, Detroit Michigan.' Holmes Street is two miles from here."

Holmes Street was only a few blocks from Koerselman & Ralston Tannery. "Thanks, I know where that is."

***

"It seems I'll never be lonely," Eli Bancroft said, "as long as I've got this case in my files."

"What do you mean by that?" Carl said.

"You're the third person this week to inquire about it. Two fellows were here on … what day was it? Well, no matter."

Carl didn't like the sound of that. Perhaps Constable Nortman was indeed still poking around. "Who was it, can you tell me? Was it the law?"

"They weren't clients of mine, so I owe them no confidentiality." Bancroft opened a box of snuff, but it was empty. "Nasty habit, anyway," he said. "I don't know their professions, and I don't believe the one gentleman ever introduced himself. But the other called himself Blackbourne."

Carl felt he might vomit again. "Noah Blackbourne?"

"Why, yes, I believe that was it. Do you know him?"

"Noah Blackbourne," Carl said again.

"And you are?"

"Hinman. Carl Hinman."

"Oh, my."

CHAPTER 45: NOAH
"I think him so because I think him so"

"I've heard the name Blackbourne, of course," the Reverend George Smith said from the stage of the Presbyterian meetinghouse. "I never met Jane, but I knew of her through Claire. You're Claire's father?"

"Was."

"Of course. My condolences."

Noah and Short Bill sat in the front pew of the meetinghouse. The minister was a spindly fellow whose shiny bald head was in stark contrast to his beard, which hung down to his chest. He didn't wear a mustache. The wrinkles and liver spots on his face suggested he might be nearing eighty. He scuttled back and forth with a broom as he spoke, sweeping around the lectern and pushing dust into nooks where it wouldn't be seen.

"I would speak to you about Claire," Noah said, clutching the sailor's cap that might have been Bella's.

Smith stopped and gazed at him. By the movement of his eyes, Noah could see his mind was at work, putting pieces together. "Claire was a fine young woman. She walks with the Lord now." He looked at the injuries on Bill's face. "I hope you gave as good as you got, Mr. Short."

"A hard wind from the southwest gave me these marks. We were aboard the *Hercules* when the storm blew in."

"That was more than an ordinary gullywasher. It struck here before crossing over Erie. It destroyed many of the banners and decorations erected for the Independence Day parade on Saturday."

"The Fourth is on Sunday."

"We're a civilized nation, Mr. Short. We don't have parades on Sundays. You should see a doctor about those bruises."

Noah nudged his friend in the ribs. "I told him the same thing."

"Nonsense," Short Bill said. "What can you tell us of the circumstances of Claire's death? We've heard it was murder."

"I'm aware of the talk, but I'm a man of the Lord, gentlemen, not a doctor. I needn't tell you that I didn't examine her remains. Mr. Miles Kelley, God rest his soul, could have told you more, as it was he who prepared the body. A constable investigated the case. He spoke with me, but I don't recall his name. North, Norton, something like that. Odd fellow, persistent as a bulldog."

"And no wonder," Noah said. "I believe it was her husband, Carl Hinman, who murdered her."

Smith leaned the broom against the pulpit and joined them on the bench. "The constable had the same concerns. I'll ask you what I asked him: Did you witness the event?"

"We were at sea when Claire died."

The minister nodded toward the cap in Noah's hand. "That explains the sailor's hat."

"This one belonged to a friend."

"It's bad enough to pass judgment upon a man you know to be guilty," Smith said. "How much worse the sin, then, when you base that judgment on nothing more than innuendo?"

"Show him the letter, mate," Short Bill said.

Noah stuffed the hat into his rucksack and withdrew the paper.

Smith read it over, nodding the whole time. "I know this story. Many a time I endured Mr. Kelley's complaints that Carl had refused to pay the balance owed. And yes, it is true the man did not attend his own wife's funeral. I understand why that would raise concerns. I may also have been alarmed, had I not known the circumstances."

"The solicitor Bancroft spoke of the unusual funeral arrangements."

"Then you should realize, gentlemen, that this entire affair is preposterous."

"It surely is," Noah said. He had a pleasant vision of Hinman being keelhauled under the *Titus*.

"But not, perhaps, in the way you're thinking."

"It is our understanding," Short Bill said, "that someone who may have been Hinman's sister presented a bank draft to Mr. Kelley as a down payment for Claire's funeral, although she was not yet dead. The bank draft was signed by Carl Hinman."

"Was it?" The Reverend folded his hands together and cracked his knuckles. "Are you aware, Mr. Blackbourne, Mr. Short, that Carl Hinman can neither read nor write?"

Noah glared at him with suspicion.

"That's right, sir," Smith continued. "He couldn't have signed that bank draft with his name. He could only write an X. Somebody knew in advance that Claire was going to die, I'll grant you that, but it needn't have been Carl. And having known him for several years, I found him to be a decent, loving man whose only failing was that he didn't always walk with the Lord as closely as he should."

Noah stood up and paced in a circular orbit in front of the pulpit, limping heavily. His ailing left knee had not taken well to the horse today. It had rained during their journey, and his leather boots were still wet. They made squishing noises as he walked. "But he didn't attend the funeral. He fled."

Smith grabbed Noah's hand as he passed, pulled him in, and bade him sit. "Think, my son. Even if Carl could write, why would he make a down payment for the funeral of his wife, who he hadn't yet killed, then call further attention to himself by absconding to parts unknown without attending the funeral? Tongues were wagging here, sir, I daresay they were. Carl wasn't an educated man, but he wasn't stupid."

"This isn't a satisfactory answer, Reverend," Noah said. "We came all the way from New Hampshire—"

"And enroute convinced yourself of his guilt. Now you want me to confirm that suspicion for you. I won't do it, Mr. Blackbourne. I've never met a man as ferociously in love with his wife as Carl Hinman was. What possible motivation could he have had to murder her?"

"How would I know? All I know is my daughter lies murdered in her grave, and who but Hinman could have put her there?"

"Is this not more likely to have been an attempt to implicate Carl in a crime he didn't commit? And a clumsy one, at that."

"Then let me ask you," Noah said, "if Hinman was such a decent man, why would somebody go to all that trouble to make him look like a wife killer?"

The minister squeezed Noah's hand. "There is that," he acknowledged. "But I wasn't there. I can't tell you what I don't know. However, if Carl was being made to look the culprit, isn't it understandable that he'd flee before the funeral rather than face a lifetime in prison?"

"He'd also leave town if he was guilty," Short Bill said.

Noah smiled and patted his friend on the back.

"If you're determined to persist in this belief, gentlemen, I can't dissuade you. I bid you Godspeed. I've work to do cleaning the place. As you see, I'm not very good at it. Usually ladies from my congregation do this, but they're restoring the holiday decorations after the storm."

He rose and retrieved his broom.

Noah and Short Bill didn't move.

Smith made a few desultory sweeps, then turned to study them. He didn't speak for long enough that Noah began to feel uncomfortable. Clearly, they had worn out their welcome, but there was more Noah wanted to say.

"Reverend?"

"Shhh." Smith dropped the broom and approached them. His eyes gleamed with both kindness and accusation, as if a spark of understanding had come into his mind. "You didn't come here to establish Carl Hinman's guilt, did you, Mr. Blackbourne, but to be absolved of your own?"

The question took him by surprise. Unbidden, unwelcome, and utterly beyond his control, emotion welled up inside him, and he wept. "I'm a blubbering fool," he sobbed.

Short Bill put an arm around Noah's shoulder and said, "You're a wise man, Reverend."

The old minister knelt before them, his joints popping. "You're seeking redemption in the right place, Mr. Blackbourne, but asking it of the wrong person. Claire can't save you."

Noah rubbed his eyes with the balls of his fists and wiped his nose on his sleeve. "I was her father," he said. "I *should* have been her father."

"Both of you are careworn and weary," Smith said. "You've journeyed a long distance. Do you have accommodations in Detroit?"

"We've enough money for another few nights in a hotel."

"Then what?"

Noah and Short Bill both shook their heads. "We haven't thought that far ahead," Short Bill said. "Our purpose was to get here and learn what we can learn."

"You're welcome to remain in this house of the Lord, my sons. Will you take my hands and join me in prayer?"

***

The meetinghouse was small and simple, its square frame whitewashed on the outside and devoid of frills, icons, or images on the inside. The windows were stained by nothing but carelessness, where paint had dripped onto the glass. The pews, both benches and backing, were constructed of wooden planks that weren't entirely level. There were only two rooms, the larger one where services were held, and a smaller one that looked as though it served as kitchen, storage closet, and waiting room. Smith probably changed his clothes and practiced his sermons in the small room, as there was a large mirror on the inside of the door, before which he could hone his gestures and expressions to best effect.

Presbyterians were certainly an austere lot, Noah thought. He and Short Bill had been offered the smaller room as temporary sleeping quarters. Reverend Smith provided them with blankets and pillows. The floor was uncomfortable, but it was no worse than conditions they'd endured before, and had the virtue of costing nothing. Because of that, once their business here was concluded, they'd have enough money between them to buy passage for one person back to the coast. Noah planned to prevail upon Short Bill to go. He was a good man and a loyal friend, but the sea was where his heart lay, and always would.

Noah looked out the north window. The sky had cleared, the quarter moon waning, the stars and planets twinkling brightly. He could see no body of water of any kind, not Lake Erie, not Lake St. Clair, not a pond, not a river, not a stream, not even a rain barrel. He, too, longed for the sea, but he also despised the idea of returning to it. Whaling was for physically capable men. His middle years would soon be behind him, and he was of sufficient girth that his body could no longer withstand the rigors. Both knees ailed him, one from injury and both from encroaching age.

He would stay in Detroit, making a livelihood any way he could. He vowed to visit Claire's grave daily, and beg her forgiveness until he heard her voice ring out from heaven, "Father, come to me." And if the good Lord chose to reunite them in Paradise, he would sit at his daughter's feet until the end of time and love her, love her, love her.

***

Reverend Smith entered the meetinghouse in clothes and boots that smelled of hay and horse droppings. Despite his age, he seemed a spry old fellow.

"Perhaps you should go alone the first time," Short Bill said to Noah. He was on all fours with a bucket of water in front of him and a scrub brush in his hand. "I'd feel like an intruder."

"After all we've been through?" Noah said. He felt guilty about not helping with the work, but his entire body pained him today, not just his knees. He twisted this way and that in the pew, trying to stretch the ache out of his muscles. "After the trains and the boats and the storm? You've made the journey with me, mate. It isn't possible for you to intrude." He paused to look at the minister. "I don't know if I can face her by myself."

Short Bill slopped water onto the floor beside the pulpit. "Blackbourne, sometimes you are thick as a tree trunk. Go make your peace with her and leave me to my task."

Noah could see his friend was uneasy about going. Were the situation reversed, he would feel the same.

"I'll accompany you, Mr. Blackbourne," Smith said. "I often ride on fine mornings like this anyway. Exercise is good for the constitution. Mr. Short has insisted upon prettifying the meetinghouse floor to ceiling as payment for your lodging, although I assured him that was unnecessary."

"Reverend, your cleaning women are occupied elsewhere," Short Bill said. "I've swabbed many a deck in my time. This is small enough price to pay for your kindness."

"Kindness needs no repayment, Mr. Short." Smith started to say something else, appeared to lose his train of thought, then held up a finger until he remembered. "Ah, yes. How long did you let your horses and saddles for?"

"A week," Short Bill said. "Paid in advance."

"That's an expensive proposition for men watching their purses. Let's return the beasts and request a refund on the unused days. You may borrow our horses for the duration of your stay in Detroit. Some of my people shelter theirs in the stable out back."

Noah was humbled by the minister's generosity. "I don't know what to say."

Smith smiled and clapped him on the back. "'Thank you' is customary. Shall we? I saddled my favorite palomino when I mucked the stable. The cemetery isn't far."

Noah followed him to the stable, his knees screaming with every step. They strapped the rented saddles to the rented horses, then tethered the animals to the ones they were going to ride. Smith mounted the palomino while Noah grunted and puffed his way onto a fat little bay.

The cemetery was closer, but they went to the livery first to return the horses and try to get some of the money back. The proprietor Barnes put on a show of indignation. The right Reverend George Smith introduced himself and hinted that perhaps hellfire could be arranged should Barnes choose to be obstinate. As leverage the threat was only partly effective, and in the end they compromised and allowed him to keep the entire fee for the day, even though the horses were back before nine in the morning. Located as he was by the docks, Barnes would have no trouble renting them again, as passengers in need of land transportation would be disembarking from incoming ships throughout the day.

"Bless you, my son," Smith said as he and Noah turned to ride away.

Barnes mumbled something that wasn't, "Bless you."

For several minutes there was no sound but the beats of the horses' hooves and occasional barking of dogs. Finally Noah said, "My most striking memory of Claire was when she was two. We were on a rocky coast, and she was running in the water up to her waist and laughing. She'd just found a seashell with all the whorls on the back that seem to spin down into a single point. 'Look, Daddy,' she said. I told her to put the hollow side against her ear. 'Oh!' she cried when she heard the sea within. You should have seen her little face. It's as if she understood."

"Understood what, Mr. Blackbourne?"

Noah shrugged. "I don't know. Everything." He paused and pulled up on the reins. Smith stopped beside him. "Tell me, Reverend, you knew her. Did she speak of me?"

Smith hesitated long enough that the hesitation became the answer. He looked at Noah apologetically. "Mr. Blackbourne, the only man she remembered as her father was Horace Hinman, Jane's ... consort. Of course I knew he wasn't the father."

Horace Hinman, father of my daughter. "She knew of me, Reverend. She wrote me letters for a few years."

"*Of* you. She didn't know *you.*"

Noah wanted to curse the heavens. Instead, he tapped his heels into his horse's flanks and didn't say another word until they arrived at the Russell Street Cemetery. Smith left him to his silence. His hands shook on the reins. He expected to make a whimpering fool of himself at Claire's grave.

Instead, the simple headstone provoked more fury than sorrow.

Claire Hinman
Born the 3rd day of November in the Year of Our Lord 1818
Died the 10th day of February in the Year of Our Lord 1846
In the 28th Year of her Age.

They dismounted.

Smith stood over the grave, bowed his head, and folded his hands together. "Will you join me in a prayer for your daughter, Mr. Blackbourne?" he said.

"It says Hinman," Noah said. Of course he knew that was her name, but to see it like this, etched in stone.... Not even Blackbourne Hinman, just Hinman.

"What did you expect?"

"She was a *Blackbourne*. It was unnatural. She shouldn't bear his name. They lived in the same house as brother and sister."

Smith sighed. "Only God can judge that. Jane and Horace never married. Carl and Claire were not related, Noah."

Despite his raging knees, Noah knelt and ran his fingers over the letters *C-l-a-i-r-e* on the headstone. "Jane and Horace couldn't marry, Reverend. Jane was still my wife on the day she died."

Smith allowed surprise to register on his face, but recovered quickly. "Don't try to find your daughter in that stone, Mr. Blackbourne. She isn't there. You cast your eyes down, when you should be lifting them up. Let her see your face."

His knees no longer able bear his weight, Noah collapsed next to the grave. From the seat of his trousers he looked upward to watch the wisp of a cloud pass across the sun. Could that wisp be the wings of an angel, momentarily dimming the light, his daughter in flight, whispering *Hello, Daddy*?

Claire.

Claire.

"Claire," he said aloud.

Reverend Smith put his hand on Noah's shoulder. "You didn't know her at all?"

"Not since that time on the coast, really. I saw her at Jane's funeral. Our final communication was a letter I sent her expressing my outrage over for her engagement to Carl Hinman. I forbade the marriage. She married him anyway. That was ten years ago."

"Pity it was your anger that drove you apart."

"And her refusal to do her father's bidding."

"Old grudges," Smith said, shaking his head. "Even now, even here."

Even now. Even here. Noah lowered his eyes. "What was she like? Was she happy? Was she kind?"

"She was both, and more. What a remarkable woman. For a poor man's wife, she had exceptional intelligence and culture. She especially loved Shakespeare, and was so well-versed in his works that I once challenged her to a friendly contest of quotations. She won."

"She beat you in a contest of Shakespeare quotations?"

"Much more than that, Mr. Blackbourne. She quoted Shakespeare better than I quoted scripture."

"She didn't get that from me," Noah said. "What did you do when you lost?"

The old minister chuckled. "I gave her a Bible and told her she was committing the wrong books to memory."

"What did she do?"

"She gave me a copy of *Romeo and Juliet*. 'There's God's love,' she said, 'and there's human love, and truth in both.' As I said, remarkable."

Noah lowered his eyes. The cloud was just a cloud. He stared at the headstone. *Claire Hinman Born on the 3rd day November in the Year of Our Lord 1818 Died the 10th day of February in the Year of Our Lord*

1846 In the 28th Year of her Age. He pounded his fist on the ground. "And yet God allowed Carl Hinman to take that creature of light away."

"Show respect, Mr. Blackbourne. This isn't the place for your rage."

"Then tell me, Reverend, where is that place, if not over the corpse of my daughter?"

CHAPTER 46: JUBAL
"She makes hungry where most she satisfies"

In the summer of 1826 Jubal was eighteen, his cousin Annalee fifteen. Jubal had fled Boston to live with the family of his uncle near Detroit, hoping the change of scenery would improve his prospects. Sadly, there was nowhere outside the mythical land of Lilliput that held prospects for a young man who stood four feet, three inches tall. No university would accept him, no business would employ him, and no woman would look at him as anything more than a child. In the end, Detroit was no better than Boston: join a freak show or beg on the streets.

All was not dreary, though. It was during this time that he and Annalee developed a bond of friendship. Since Jubal was so small, her father did not see him as a threat, and once a week he let them take the buckboard into the country, where they spent many a summer day walking through fields and over hills, smelling the wildflowers and talking of their dreams. Jubal supposed it was normal for teenaged girls to be curious about boys, but even then Annalee's interest in them seemed unusually specific. She spoke of nothing else, often speculating about subjects not proper for grown women, let alone teenaged girls of fine breeding.

If her father had ever learned of their conversations, he would have whipped them both. If he'd learned what *else* Annalee did in the country, he probably would have locked her in a nunnery and shot Jubal.

In the valley between three hills a small pond had formed. After a good rain the water was deep enough for swimming, which was Annalee's second favorite pastime. When she swam, she swam naked. There were no trees, no shelter from passing eyes but the hills and nothing between her and Jubal but the buckboard.

They were cousins. She made him promise not to look as she disrobed. Only when she was submerged to the neck would she give him permission to turn around.

But Jubal always peeked, and she knew he peeked, and she laughed with a musical sound that was both innocent and lascivious. Jubal felt as if he were about to explode from the inside. He prayed that she would not walk out of that pond in full view, and he prayed that she would.

One day she did.

He felt his face burn with shame and desire as she stood before him, the sun glistening on her wet skin. His body was on fire. She lowered her eyes to his midsection and smiled coquettishly. "So it's true about that," she said. "Give me my corset, won't you?"

They were cousins. They didn't touch. They never touched, except when he offered his hand to help her onto the buckboard.

Nor did they speak of her swimming, or what he saw, or how he felt about what he saw. She continued to swim as opportunities allowed throughout the summer, and in their conversations she still babbled about boys, and babies, and the process by which one acquired both.

Jubal's longing grew until it was nearly unbearable, but he refused to cross that line. He told himself she would not have let him had he tried. Then in the autumn, when cooler weather curtailed their sojourns to the country and calmed his passions, he noticed a change in the way he thought about her. His lust became something else entirely: a transformative feeling of gratitude and a deep, *almost* pure love.

Annalee had given him a gift no other woman had, or may ever again, a glimpse at a great mystery he'd had no reasonable hope of experiencing until that day at the pond. In truth, she probably intended nothing profound by revealing herself to him. Yet there was an unwitting wisdom in her teasing. He vowed then he would never forget that summer with Annalee, and that, should she ask, he would walk through Hell for her.

***

Jubal lay back on the bed in his wagon. This close to Detroit, he couldn't help thinking about Annalee. Oh yes, the two of them had had some adventures, but the teenager of his fondest memories had grown into a woman, and now that he was here, he was having mixed emotions about seeing her again. No question, he loved her dearly. Beautiful, refined, and charming, Annalee was all the things he wasn't and would never be, but she was also spoiled, vindictive, and volatile. She was an only child, and her parents, his aunt and uncle, passed away in the '30s, leaving her their entire estate. Men who didn't find her personally irresistible, if such men existed, were certainly attracted to her fortune. Jubal preferred not to entangle himself in another one of her romantic pickles. Her last letter had mentioned beau troubles again, and he wasn't sure he could bear to be her knight in shining armor anymore. Jubal had always been the one she cried to and raged at when things went wrong. Sometimes he wished she would seek him out for the simple pleasure of his company, like when they were kids, not because she needed something from him.

His reverie was interrupted by a knock on the wagon's wooden body near the door flap. Otto poked his head in. He was puffing on a big cigar. "The boss told me to tell you to relieve Petey. He wants him rested for the new trick in tonight's show."

They'd already done three shows today. Crowds had been good, the gates impressive. The Phantasmagoria was as popular as ever, and all of LaVoie's magic tricks had gone off without a hitch. He'd even sold several bottles of his liniment, although his pitches seemed less enthusiastic than they had in the past. Manfred/Ophelia, with his big beard and even bigger breasts, continued to delight and scandalize.

André's slithery contortions revolted the audience to the point of fascination, or vice versa. The harpy was a sensation, easily rivaling Barnum's mermaid. And Cuff sang like an angel, doing her usual standards like "Yankee Doodle" and other "white folk" songs, as she called them.

All of the acts got to relax between their appearances on stage and again between shows. But while Jubal lay on his bed, Otto smoked his cigar, and the others did whatever they did in their wagons, poor Petey was kept busy with a constant flow of children who wanted to ride Chelsea. Jubal had never understood why the pony had such appeal. It wasn't like she was some exotic animal like a camel or elephant. She had no horn sprouting from the middle of her forehead. Everyone had seen horses before. Perhaps her diminutive size was the attraction for tots too small to mount her full-sized cousins. Whatever it was, she was always in demand, which meant she had spent hours patiently carving a circular rut in the grass, with Petey at her side holding the reins. He probably hadn't had time to eat or piss, let alone rest.

"LaVoie wants me to play nursemaid to children?" Jubal said.

Otto shrugged. "Just passing along his orders."

"All right," Jubal said. Petey deserved a break. As Jubal headed toward the boy, he noticed Otto climb into the driver's seat of the wagon and stretch out to enjoy the sun.

Jubal squeezed through the crowd and tugged on Petey's shirt to get his attention. He tried to hide the resentment in his voice as he whispered LaVoie's message in the boy's ear. It wasn't Petey's fault, but that didn't stop Jubal's anger from smoldering. To be relegated to opening a trap door for the disappearing act was one thing, but to then be expected to walk with Chelsea was humiliating.

What had he done to incur LaVoie's disfavor?

"Thanks, Mr. Lawson," Petey said. "My bladder was gonna bust if I had to stay here one more minute."

"Where you going?" one woman cried after Petey. "Stinking Injun, my halfpenny ain't good enough for you?"

"I'm here," Jubal said.

"What in tarnation are you?" the woman said. She was with two children, a boy about Petey's age and a girl several years younger.

"I'm a man," he said calmly.

His assertion was repeated from the front of the crowd to the back, raising a gale of laughter.

Jubal was used to it, but it still hurt. Every time. *Every time.* "Do I need to show you the hair on my chest to prove it?" he said to the woman.

Her mouth fell open in indignation. "How *dare* you talk like that in front of children? I don't care if you are some kind of freakshow monster, there's such a thing as common decency."

As he listened to her, Jubal imagined stuffing her into a big jar of preserving fluid, like LaVoie's new harpy.

"Come on, Auntie Sarah," the boy said. He was lean almost to the point of emaciation, with blonde hair and skin white as an albino's. "This ain't any fun anyway."

"I wanna ride the pony," the little girl said. She was as fair and thin as the boy.

"No, Isabella, I don't think we will. And you," the woman said, jabbing her finger at Jubal. "I ought to have the law on you."

"Maybe they'll lock him up in a chicken coop," the boy said. "That'd be big enough for him."

They stormed away.

Jubal sighed. He didn't curse often, but goddammit. To hell with it. LaVoie was going to be short a few halfpennies today. "Sorry, folks, the pony needs food, rest, and shade. She'll be back for tonight's show."

"We've been waiting in line for an hour," a man said, and dozens of others shouted their agreement. They swarmed around him and Chelsea, refusing to let them pass.

"She's been walking in circles for seven," Jubal said. "Come back tonight. Or don't. I don't care. Get out of my way."

"I don't think so, dwarf," another man said.

Otto was still on the wagon smoking his cigar. "See that big fellow back there?" Jubal said. "The one with the muscles? I need only call his name and he'll come pound your pointed head into the ground like a tent stake. Do I make myself understood, sir?"

He did. The crowd parted, and as Jubal guided Chelsea through the sea of people he felt like Moses leading the Israelites out of Egypt.

He took her to the lean-to Zug had provided, which was a series of large wooden panels propped up at an angle with poles to provide shade when the sun was in the west. The other horses were in the pen the crew had built for them. Chelsea's flanks heaved. She immediately went to the trough and inhaled gouts of water. Poor thing was exhausted. Jubal patted her rump. When she had sated her thirst, he hung a bag of oats over her mouth. Hay was stacked high against one end of the panel. There was a short round stool that normal-sized folks stood on to throw down bales from the top. Jubal fetched it and sat at the edge of light and shade, watching the shadows' slow stretch as the sun sank behind the panel.

He put his elbows on his knees and his face in his hands.

What was he going to do?

Everything was falling apart, and he didn't know why.

After an undetermined time feeling sorry for himself, he heard the clop of hooves and a small whinny of protest. A moment later Cuff led Rosie's little foal into the lean-to on a harness. The little fellow didn't like the bit, and halfheartedly bucked his back legs.

"Oh, you hush," Cuff scolded the animal. "You got to start drinking water and eating real food. Your momma ain't gonna put up with you gnawing her teats much longer." When she noticed Jubal she said, "What you looking all sad for?"

She led the colt to the trough and gently pushed his head down to the water. He snorted and tried to resist, but eventually took a few swallows.

"You know how I feel about you," Jubal said, still resting his chin on his palms. It wasn't a question.

"Good boy," Cuff said to the foal before turning her attention to Jubal. "Ain't nowhere to go with that, little man, so you best just let it be."

"Am I that hideous, or do you find me *cute*, too?"

"Stop talking nonsense. I like you fine, and I don't care if you're four feet tall or ten. But last thing I need right now is a man hitching his stars to me. I got too much to do."

Jubal lifted his head from his hands. "Let's talk about that. You and Marc have been spending a lot of time together since we left Jeffersonville. I know it's got something to do with Cyrus and Destiny, so don't deny it."

"Cyrus and Destiny're gone, Jubal. They went over the river to Canada this morning."

"Just up and left?"

"You think they'd be happy cramped inside that wagon the rest of their lives?"

"So we brought them to Michigan, and now they're gone. If that was the point of this trip, why are we still here? What's going on?"

"Change is what's going on. Marc's come to a new understanding."

Jubal didn't fail to notice she was calling him Marc now, rather than Mr. Major LaVoie. "What's that supposed to mean?"

"The show's joining up with the Underground Railroad."

"Like hell. Maybe you convinced Marc to bring Cyrus and Destiny along this time, but that's as far as it goes. He puffs himself up like he's somebody important—"

"If he wasn't somebody before, he is now."

"He's too much of a coward to keep risking his life, all of our lives, for something like that."

"'Something like that' seem like a bad idea to you?"

Rosie's foal stamped his foot and backed away from the trough. Cuff scooped a handful of oats from Chelsea's bag and tried to get him to eat.

"You know what I mean," Jubal said.

"Do I?"

"I hate slavery as much as you—"

"I don't think you do."

"—but one little medicine show can't save the world."

"Who can, then? Looky here, you don't wanna come, don't. Go on back to Boston, or to your momma's plantation in Georgia, for all I care. You told me they didn't have slaves, but that ain't true, is it?"

Jubal looked away. "Doesn't mean anything. I wasn't born yet."

"Ow," Cuff cried, snatching her hand away from the foal. "Little shit bit me."

Jubal smiled. "Well, it's a learning process."

Cuff examined her palm, but the foal's small teeth hadn't broken the skin. She wiped both hands together to brush the remaining oats off. "I think that's enough learning for this young fella today. But you," she said, jabbing a finger at Jubal, "you still got plenty learning to do, Mr. Jubal Lawson. Plenty. Now, you can be as small as your size, or you can be bigger than President Polk himself. But whatever you're gon be, you gon have to find another gal to be it with, 'cause there's you and there's me, but there ain't never gon be a you and me."

CHAPTER 47: MARIEL
"God has given you one face, and you make yourselves another"

The powder Doctor Finch gave her tasted awful but worked like magic. On the evening of the second day in Mrs. Winslow's home, Mariel felt better than she had since watching the base-ball match with her father in Ohio. Her chest still hurt, and the muscles in her sides ached from all the coughing, but her appetite was back and her nose wasn't as runny.

However, she was still too weak to raise herself out of bed.

"Do you need to empty your bladder, child?" Mrs. Jensen said. She'd been sitting in the same rocking chair since they arrived, leaving Mariel only to perform the necessities.

"I'm hungry," Mariel said.

"That's good."

"Where's Daddy?"

"He had some business to attend to in town." Mrs. Jensen's voice sounded funny. Was she worried? "I'll go fetch something for you to eat."

When she left the room Mariel tried again to sit up. This time she was successful. She lifted her bottom onto the pillows and propped herself against the headboard. It felt so good not to be lying down.

Seemed like half her life since she'd been in any position but flat on her back. She must have a thousand bed sores.

Mrs. Jensen and Mrs. Winslow came in together, Mrs. Winslow with a bowl and Mrs. Jensen with clenched fists. Their eyes were narrow and their mouths small. Whenever Mariel's teacher Miss Krause made that expression, she was angry and somebody was about to have their knuckles rapped.

"She should have fruit and bread," Mrs. Winslow insisted. "Gentler on her stomach."

"Meat and eggs will give her strength," Mrs. Jensen said, "if you'd let me cook for her."

"This is my house, Mrs. Jensen. I know how to care for an ailing child. I raised three boys."

Mariel liked Mrs. Jensen very much, but she agreed with the other woman. Peaches with sugar and milk or sliced apples with cinnamon sounded more appealing.

Mrs. Jensen didn't argue. Her chin began to quiver and then she wept. Covering her face with her hands, she fled the room.

Mrs. Winslow looked perplexed. "Did it mean so much to her?"

Mariel didn't answer, but she knew. It wasn't the food. Harm and Mrs. Jensen had raised no children, and had very much wanted to.

Mrs. Winslow was a large woman, and when she sat on the bed, the mattress nearly propelled Mariel into the air. The bowl she brought didn't have peaches or apples, but it did have grapes, raspberries, and strawberries, which she liked almost as well. Mariel gazed at them longingly, but didn't take any until she was invited.

"Oh, good heavens, girl, eat. My oldest son grows all of these himself and sends them to me fresh twice a week."

Mariel chose strawberries first. The berries were small but sweet. She had a bad taste in her mouth. Her breath must be horrid. She loved the way the sweetness spread across her tongue.

"Thank you," she said, remembering her manners.

Mrs. Winslow rose from the bed and crossed the room to the rocking chair Mrs. Jensen had been using since they arrived. "Who is Mrs. Jensen?"

Mariel wasn't sure what she meant. "Her name is Kristin. She's married to Harm."

"I mean, why is she here instead of your mother?"

Mariel stopped chewing. "Momma died. Fell down in the snow and hit her head."

"It's sad to go before one's time. I lost my husband to a cancer these several years past, and my middle boy at Veracruz in March. That's in Mexico."

Mariel had heard about the war with Mexico, but she didn't know much about it. She popped a handful of raspberries into her mouth. Their flavor was tangier than the strawberries, and made her scrunch up her face.

She heard a door open and close in the next room, followed by a man's voice. Her father was back!

A moment later he rushed into her room. "Look at you, sweet girl," he said with a big grin. "You're sitting up."

He raced to the bed and swept her into his arms, kissing her forehead.

"Don't break her," Mrs. Winslow said.

Her father put her down. "I'm just so happy to see her getting well."

"Give it time, Mr. Hinman."

Mrs. Jensen poked her head in the door. She shot a quick glare at Mrs. Winslow and said, "Carl, may I have a word?"

"Sure, Kristin." He winked at Mariel. "I'll be back quicker than you can blink, darling."

As he left the room Mrs. Jensen said, "Close the door."

"That's a peculiar woman," Mrs. Winslow said.

"She's my daddy's friend," Mariel said. She could hear the voices in the next room, but not what was being said.

"Friendship between males and females is just asking for trouble."

Mariel didn't know what to say to that, so she ate a grape. It had fine flavor but too many seeds. Since it would be rude to spit them out, she swallowed them, wondering if they'd really sprout in her stomach like people said. She went back to the strawberries.

"Alvin, my youngest, he went courting this girl, Rebecca Beckham. Oh, I'll never forget her! He sang her name as 'Becky Beck' with this sappy voice. You could almost hear the violins. She fluttered her pretty lashes at him and let him sweet-talk her like he was the handsomest prince in the land. Him being so young, his heart went all a-flutter, and he got these big puppy dog eyes that youths get around girls. You probably ain't seen that yet, but you will soon enough, I reckon. So my boy declared, 'I love this gal and I'm a-gonna marry her.' But what does little Becky Beck do? She sends him a letter saying, 'My dearest Alvin, I am engaged to another, but you and I can remain jolly friends.' Nothing can come of a friendship after all that."

Mariel cocked her head at Mrs. Winslow. Had she had taken a breath during that entire story?

"Mrs. Jensen says Daddy should marry again. I don't want a new Momma."

As Mrs. Winslow rocked in the chair, the wood creaked under her weight. "All men need a wife. Poor things can't care for themselves without one."

My daddy can, she thought but didn't say it. Instead, she ate the last strawberry.

"Now Roy, my oldest, he farms—"

Suddenly Mrs. Jensen's voice boomed through the closed door from the other room. She sounded furious or horrified, or maybe both. "You did *what*, Carl?"

Mariel strained to hear her father's answer, but Mrs. Winslow started talking again. "They sure act like they're married," she said with a smile. "You should've heard some of the donnybrooks my Gerard and I used to get into. Lord, I wanted to kill that man, until, of course, cancer actually did. Now I'd give anything to be able to quarrel with him again. But I was telling you about my son Roy...."

Mariel ate the rest of the raspberries and the grapes, seeds and all, as she tried to drown out Mrs. Winslow and listen to her father's conversation with Mrs. Jensen. It was useless. Mrs. Winslow just kept babbling on, from Roy to ungrateful relatives to something about a cow falling over a fence, and all Mariel could think was, *Please be quiet, please be quiet.*

"I'm finished eating now," she said.

"Thank you, dear, just set the bowl on the floor. I'll wash it later." And then she was off on another story, and *another*, on and on. Mariel thought she might scream.

"Kristin, listen," she heard her father say. He didn't raise his voice often.

"No, Carl Hinman, you listen to me."

Mrs. Winslow pushed herself out of the rocking chair and opened the door. "Shhh," she hissed. "I have other boarders. Some of them retire early. Whatever your dispute, speak civilly or take it outside."

"It's all right, Mrs. Winslow," her father said. "We're done."

As soon as he entered the room Mariel could see he'd been crying. Mrs. Jensen, too.

Her father sat on the bed next to her and took her hands in his. He was trembling so, and she was frightened for him. "You ate everything," he said. "I'm proud of you, honey. Kristin and I were talking...."

His voice cracked, and he couldn't go on.

"If you improve as much tomorrow as you did today," Mrs. Jensen said, "we've decided to take you home. We'll stop at your mother's grave, then there's a fireworks display in Belgrade your father thinks you'll enjoy. I saw a sign there for some kind of show, too."

"A circus?"

"Something like that."

"Do they have elephants? I want to be right up front."

"We'll just have to see."

Then Mrs. Jensen brushed past Mrs. Winslow and came to stand close to her father. She leaned over to whisper in his ear, but Mariel heard her. "You have placed a burden on me too terrible to bear. For your own soul, you *must* talk to someone with more forgiveness in his heart than I have."

"What's she mean, Daddy?"

"Nothing, sweet girl. It's grownup talk, is all."

"Carl," Mrs. Jensen said.

"I know someone," her father said.

CHAPTER 48: BILL
"I will a round unvarnish'd tale deliver"

Bill drifted in and out of sleep, having been awakened several times by Reverend Smith rattling around in the large room. His boots were leather, but sounded as if he'd been shoed like a horse. The sun was just now rising, but Smith obviously wasn't concerned that his guests weren't up yet, for he made no effort to be quiet. He muttered questions, which wouldn't have been so alarming if he didn't also answer himself.

Noah, of course, slept through it all, as he did most things.

But then, his friend was bone-weary. His natural melancholy had been made worse by everything that had happened since receiving the letter in Portsmouth. Visiting Claire's grave had been the final blow. Her headstone had reminded him again of the cruel, irredeemable years of neglect he'd shown her, of the gulf between them that no amount of repentance could bridge.

When Noah had returned with Smith last night, he seemed to have lost his reason. He insisted that Bill journey back to the *Titus* without him. "We've only enough money for one passage," he'd said, which was true. "The sea is your life."

Which was also true. "And yours, mate," Bill had replied.

"I never intend to set eyes on the sea again. I'll stay here with Claire."

"To what end? She's *dead*."

For an instant Noah's eyes had flared, but his anger then quickly faded. "You have been the truest of friends, Short Bill. You've done more for me than coin or affection can repay. You need to return to what you love."

"And you?"

"Darkness has swallowed me whole, mate. I despair of seeing light again."

"Is there no longer light upon the sea?"

"Not for me."

"Is it here, then, in this church?"

"I don't know. I don't know. Reverend Smith believes he can secure employment for me in Detroit. Perhaps if I settle down, stay in one place, I may find some measure of peace in working."

"I'll not leave without you."

"Then you'll not leave. But we both know you must."

With that Noah had stretched out on his blanket and turned his back to Bill. In moments he was snoring. Despite all the turmoil in his friend's mind, he could still find a way to sleep, and Bill took comfort in that.

***

Life on a whaling ship required being up before the sun, but in the short while since they'd begun their journey, Bill found himself growing lazy, sleeping later and later into the morning. He'd no sooner drifted off again when he was awakened by voices in the next room. This time Smith wasn't talking to himself. He had a visitor, a man, and both sounded as if they were under duress. Bill could tell something was wrong because he heard Smith say, "Lower your voice, we're not alone."

Curious, he crept to the door and opened it a crack. The minister was sitting in a pew a third of the way back, talking to a younger fellow across the aisle from him. The stranger appeared to be around thirty, with the tanned skin of a laborer or farmer. His hair was dark and full, save for a small bald spot on the crown. He looked as if he hadn't shaved in a week.

"What are you *doing* here, Carl?" Smith whispered rather forcefully.

Carl?

Carl?

Good God, not Carl Hinman?

"I had to come, Reverend. There's something I gotta talk to you about."

Bill backed away and closed the door silently. What should he do? Other than participating in the occasional pub fight, Noah had never been a violent person, but that was Carl Hinman out there, the source of Noah's distress.

Wake him, or no?

The decision wasn't difficult. Come what may, this was his friend's path to salvation. Or damnation. It was why they'd come to Detroit. He had to wake him.

He knelt and shook his shoulder. "Up with you, mate."

Noah was still lying on his side, the same position he'd fallen asleep in. He shoved Bill's hand away and grumbled, "Leave me alone."

"You need to see this."

Noah rolled to his back and cocked open one eye. "What do I need to see?"

"When I tell you, you must remain calm."

Noah rose to an elbow. He gazed at Bill with suspicion. "Why?"

Bill drew in a long breath. "The Reverend has a visitor. Promise me you'll behave civilly when I tell you."

"Dammit, Short Bill, who is it?"

"Carl Hinman."

Noah's mouth fell open. His face contorted in rage. Then, without a word, he reached into his rucksack and withdrew his dagger. In that moment his expression changed again, to one of grim determination. Hatred, vengeance, despair, regret…. Whatever torment he was feeling, he would have his resolution now: years of self-condemnation reduced to the point of a knife in another man's heart, at the cost of that other man's life.

"Mate, you can't be certain of his guilt. Didn't you hear what the minister said?"

"He took her from me," Noah said, "and he will pay."

Bill didn't know if by 'took' he meant killing Claire or marrying her. "You promised to be civil."

"I made no such promise."

Noah rose and advanced toward the door. He wasn't in a hurry. Now that the endgame was upon him, he advanced with the inevitability of a gathering storm. Bill knew he needed a scapegoat for his own failures, and Hinman was that scapegoat. But that was not the kind of man he was. Whether or not Hinman was a murderer, Noah was not.

Bill tried to restrain him. "How will you live with yourself?"

Noah shook him off. "I can't live with myself now."

Bill interposed himself between Noah and the door. "What can I do, mate?"

Noah pushed him aside. "Stay out of the way."

Desperate, Bill rushed through the door ahead of him, yelling, "Hinman, run."

Both Reverend Smith and Hinman looked up in surprise.

Noah followed Bill onto the dais and, brandishing the dagger, said in a low, ominous voice, "Go ahead, run, coward. If you don't, I'm going to carve you up like a whale."

Reverend Smith jumped to his feet. "Mr. Blackbourne, this is the house of the Lord! You will *not* blaspheme His name with violence in this place. Put that knife down."

"Noah Blackbourne?" Hinman said.

"I told you we weren't alone," Smith said.

"You didn't say it was *him*."

Bill was surprised by the power and vehemence of Smith's anger. Apparently Noah was, too, because he stopped short of Hinman. "He killed my daughter," he said, "and he will answer for it."

"I didn't," Hinman said.

"He didn't," Smith said. "Whoever did answers to God, not man."

"He'll answer to *me*," Noah said. "I mean you no offense or harm, Reverend, but—"

"You draw a weapon in God's house and you 'mean no offense?' Sin feeds sin, it does not destroy it."

"I'll give you an answer, Mr. Blackbourne," Hinman said. "I didn't kill her, but that don't mean I ain't guilty. Will you hear me out?"

"Your father took my wife, and you took my daughter. Why should I listen to anything a Hinman has to say?"

"Because," Smith said, "I'm asking you to. Tell him what you told me, Carl."

Hinman stood up and walked to within inches of Noah, touching his chest to the point of the blade. "You can do what you will if you ain't satisfied by what I say."

"Give me the knife," Smith said.

"You're a good man, mate," Bill said. "Don't do this. He's unarmed. Listen to him."

Noah backed away from Hinman and threw the dagger down in disgust. It stuck in the wood floor, its handle vibrating menacingly. "Talk."

Hinman sat back down in his pew. Bill led Noah to the bench behind Smith.

"When we lived in Detroit," Hinman said, "Claire used to sugar-talk me into going to Shakespeare plays with her. I didn't want to, 'cause I couldn't make head or tail out of them. But I'd've done anything for your daughter, so I went.

"One night we met a woman at the theatre. Her and Claire struck up a friendship. She was smart as Claire, and pretty soon we worked it out so that she'd go to the plays with her instead of me. That was better for both of us. Claire always wanted to talk about how the poetry and actors made her feel, and hell, I didn't know what to say. I didn't even understand what I just saw."

"What's that got to do with killing her?" Noah said.

Hinman folded his hands together and looked down at his feet. "I did an evil thing, Mr. Blackbourne, but not what you think. Claire wasn't the only person the woman got friendly with. She was so pretty, and…."

He looked in utter despair at Reverend Smith, who nodded and said, "Go on."

"…And I'm a weak, stupid man."

Hinman started to weep and needed a few moments to compose himself.

"He broke the sixth commandment," Smith said.

"You fornicated with another woman?" Noah said. He started to rise from his pew, but Bill put a hand on his arm. He could feel the rage vibrating in his friend's bones.

"Patience, mate."

Hinman sniffled. "I got no excuse. I knew it was a sin against God and Claire, and another sin to lie about it, but I was too caught up in my lustful ways. I was so *ashamed*. I still am. No pleasure of the flesh is worth that."

"'But whoso committeth adultery with a woman,'" Smith said, "'lacketh understanding: he that doeth it destroyeth his own soul. A wound and dishonor shall he get; and his reproach shall not be wiped away.' *Proverbs Six*."

Hinman nodded. "Well, the Bible got that part right. Every minute I was with that woman, all I could see was Claire's face and think how she'd cry if she ever learned what I done. No hell God could make for me could be worse than the one I made for myself." Hinman gazed up at Noah, tears and snot running down his face. "Mr. Blackbourne, I *loved* Claire more than my own life. I don't know why I did it."

"Yet you kept going back to the woman."

"Three times. Only three times, then I couldn't bear it no more. When I told her I couldn't be with her on account of I loved my wife, she acted relieved, like she was just waiting for me to be the one to say it. She said she was also fond of Claire and felt just as bad as me about it."

"But?"

"She didn't feel a thing, sir. Not one thing. Her daddy left her money, and she lived in a big house with servants. She was used to getting everything she wanted."

"And she still wanted you?"

Hinman glanced at the minister. "I wasn't no more to her than a sack of manure, a *nothing*. But I was the nothing who dared to tell her no. She couldn't abide that."

"Does this woman have a name?" Noah said.

"Satan," Hinman said.

"What happened next?" Bill said.

Hinman wiped his eyes and nose on his sleeve. "She surprised me. I mean, what the *hell*, she asked if she could still go to plays with Claire. She promised not to tell about us, and anyway, she said, Claire would be suspicious if they suddenly stopped going. I ain't an educated man, Mr. Blackbourne, and I didn't know what to do. All I knew is I couldn't let Claire find out. So I pretended it was all right.

"And for a while it was. I was scared every time they left for the theatre together that Claire might come home that night hating me. The woman always gave me a cold look when her carriage came for Claire, but that was the only sign she was still mad at me. I figured something bad was gonna happen, but when nothing did and nothing did, I put it out of my mind. Until a constable come to my door a year ago last February."

"Are you saying *she* murdered Claire?" Noah said. "What manner of man accuses a woman?"

"She wouldn't've got her own hands dirty. I don't know who done the actual deed, but I know this: She planned it. I told you she was smart."

"*You're* the one who sinned. *You're* the one who left her. Claire didn't do anything wrong. Why would the woman go after her?"

"'Cause I wouldn't suffer enough if she killed me. She knew I'd think I deserved it. Instead, she wanted to *hurt* me, and she knew the worst thing she could do was take my Claire away..." Hinman was crying again. "She tore the heart right out of me, but even that wasn't enough. No, goddamn her—sorry, Reverend—but God *damn* her. She had someone put a knife in Claire and then made it look like I done it.

"Mr. Blackbourne, she went to the undertaker pretending to be my sister Joanna. She made a down payment on the funeral, saying I would pay the balance. She produced a bank draft with my name on it. I didn't sign it, someone else did. Probably the man who killed Claire."

Bill was moved by the man's story, but Noah was still skeptical. "If you're innocent, why did you run?"

"Because Claire was already dead, and I didn't want to make an orphan of Mariel. A constable came around accusing me of murder."

"Wait! Mariel?"

"Our daughter."

Noah appeared as if he'd been struck in the gut. His face went white, then red, then white again. He swallowed hard several times as if trying to catch his breath. "Claire had a daughter? I have a granddaughter?"

"You didn't know?" Hinman said. For the first time, Bill saw the young man smile. "Would you like to meet her? She's just outside in the wagon."

Bill saw a sea change come over his friend. All the rage disappeared, all the murderous intent, all the long years of anguish and guilt. His body shook with the letting go, and it was as if heaven itself sighed. "I have a granddaughter," he said. "I have a granddaughter."

Hinman moved across the aisle and knelt before Noah. "Mr. Blackbourne," he said, clasping Noah's hands, "I swear in this house of the Lord that I didn't kill Claire, but she's dead because of my foolishness. God knows I deserve your hate. But Mariel don't."

"I want to see her," Noah said.

Hinman rose. "She favors Claire so much it'll break your heart. I'll go fetch her in."

As Hinman left the meetinghouse, Noah looked at Bill. "Don't let me weep in front of the child."

"And how am I to arrange that?" he said with a chuckle.

Reverend Smith smiled kindly and rose to pluck the knife from the floor. He offered it to Noah, who shook his head. The minister placed it behind him on the pew when he sat back down. "Mr. Blackbourne, there is blessedness in tears. Tears of grief, and tears of joy. No one will think the less of you."

Moments later the front door of the meetinghouse opened, and a small silhouette stood in its frame, backlit by the sun. As the girl walked down the aisle, Bill could see her brown hair brushing the shoulders of her blue calico dress. She was thin, but not overly so. She appeared to be about ten. Even with her face in shadow her eyes sparkled.

Hinman and a stout woman came in behind her.

Noah turned slowly and drew in a long, sharp breath. "Oh, my God," he whispered.

The girl stopped in front of the three men. She looked first at Reverend Smith, who nodded toward Noah. She faced him.

"Are you Mr. Blackbourne, Momma's father?" she said with a curtsy. "I am pleased to meet you. My name is Mariel."

Noah, great blubbering fool that he was, burst into tears.

Bill dabbed at his own eyes with his thumb.

"Why are you sad?" Mariel said, her tiny voice quivering.

Noah spread his arms and gazed helplessly at Bill, then at the minister. Hinman and the woman, who had been standing back a few feet, stepped forward. "It's all right, Mr. Blackbourne," Hinman said.

Noah swept Mariel into his arms and buried his face in her shoulder. "I am not sad, child," he said. "I have never been happier."

"Careful with her," the woman said. "She's been ill."

"I'm better now," Mariel said, but she coughed when Noah squeezed her too hard.

"Give your granddad a kiss, sweet darling," Hinman said.

Mariel pecked Noah's cheek. He lifted his head and looked into her eyes. "You're Claire reborn," he said.

"I read poems to Daddy, just like she did."

Bill stood up. Feeling something more than joyous, and something less, he walked past Noah and his granddaughter. "Back in a minute, mate," he said.

He paused to put his hand on Hinman's shoulder and nod *Thank you* to him, then headed toward the open door. Sunlight spilled in, igniting the whitewashed benches in a fierce glow.

Bill exited the meetinghouse. Heat beat down on him from above and radiated up from the brick steps below. A small wagon with a two-horse team was parked outside. He wondered briefly who the woman with Hinman was. She was too old to be a new wife. Perhaps a nursemaid? She'd said Mariel had been sick.

Bill scratched one of the horses on the nose, then went around behind the meetinghouse, where he entered the back door into the small room.

He was delighted for his friend, he truly was, but this unexpected development put him at loose ends. Noah had been too emotionally frail to have made the journey inland on his own. He had needed Bill to accompany him, whether he admitted it or not.

He didn't need him anymore. Whatever dark and brutal answer Noah had expected to find had been turned upside down by the redemptive power of a little girl's kiss.

Bella's sailor cap poked out the top of Noah's rucksack. Bill smiled and pinched the fabric of its crown between his fingers, feeling its texture: two children lost, one child found. A fair trade?

That was a question for someone wiser than he.

Noah was right about one thing, the sea was calling Bill home. Rummaging through his own rucksack, he located a pencil and a scrap of paper, then scribbled a hasty note and left it next to Bella's cap.

Write me at the Anchor & Dolphin if you've a mind to, mate.

Godspeed.

Bill slung the sack over his shoulder, took one final look around the room, and slipped out through the back door.

CHAPTER 49: MARCUS
"Apply a moral medicine to a mortifying mischief"

The evening crowd filled the tent early and spilled out into the field, lining up several hundred deep all around. Jubal, Otto, and Leopold had rolled open the front flaps to try to accommodate the overflow, but it was useless. There were just too many. From his vantage point across the fairway, LaVoie could see their eagerness as the people jostled each other for position. He'd never experienced this many human beings in such close proximity, not even in Detroit proper.

Although he would like to believe they'd all come to see his show, he knew the main attraction was the fireworks display to follow. No matter. His crew would put on the most dazzling performance of their lives, and maybe some of the audience would walk away more awed by his Phantasmagoria or the new disappearing act than by the exploding lights in the sky.

The lanterns Zug had strung up around the grounds provided excellent illumination. The two mirrors were in position. Colorful bunting and advertisements hung from each side of the stage. Because the mirrors were tilted slightly downward, from the audience's point of view they didn't reflect anything but grass. The illusion of open space was flawless. Someone could drop through the trap door behind the mirrors and nobody would be the wiser.

The night had already been different than any other. Earlier LaVoie had delivered his usual patter, trying to tempt passersby with bottles of his elixir. Despite decent sales, however, he quit after a few minutes. His heart was no longer in it. Something didn't feel right. Most folks probably knew his nostrum was a sham, and bought the stuff expecting to get roaring drunk, a use for which it proved efficient. But what about those unfortunate souls who were truly sick or had ailing loved ones, the fathers and mothers told by their doctors the only hope for their dying children now was prayer? They came to him out of desperation, seeking a miracle from a man who sold illusions.

Now he had committed to important work.

Damn you, Cuff, you've given me a conscience, and a conscience is bad for business.

Zug had provided trumpeters for the final show of the night. They were stationed at the tent's entrance and at the back of the crowd, where LaVoie stood. He nodded to the fellow nearest to him. The man lifted his instrument to his lips and blew a rousing tune. This melody was answered by the musician at the tent.

The crowd hushed.

All right, then, LaVoie thought. Let the show begin. Dressed in his Tennessee finest, complete with Grandee hat, he followed behind his trumpeter and advanced toward the tent. The people parted and let him pass as if he were a king ascending his throne. What a glorious evening this would be.

Inside the tent Jubal met him at the foot of the stage.

"All set?" LaVoie whispered.

Jubal didn't answer.

"Is something the matter? I need you in top form. Are your numbers in the right pockets?"

"Why wouldn't they be?"

LaVoie scanned the audience as he climbed the steps to the stage. Smiling, he bowed theatrically to accept their applause.

"Ladies and gentleman," he called, removing his hat. "Good evening and welcome to the grandest spectacle this side of the mighty

Mississippi River. Tonight you'll see wonders, the likes of which you have never before witnessed. You'll be mystified, you'll be horrified, you'll be shocked. But most of all, you will be *entertained*. You will see freaks of nature, magical marvels, and feats of daring. You'll hear music lovelier than the songs the Sirens sang in times of old. And so, ladies and gentlemen, I present to you, the Ten Wonders of the Universe."

They cheered and clapped. Soaking in their adulation, LaVoie put his hat back on and raised his arms as if to embrace them. He noticed one face in the front row that looked familiar, but couldn't recall where he'd seen the man before. Then it dawned on him: Tom Villisca, the slave hunter. When they made eye contact, Villisca folded his arms across his chest and gave him a defiant scowl. The scoundrel said something LaVoie couldn't hear, but he read lips well enough to get the gist.

I'll have that nigga gal tonight.

We'll see about that, LaVoie thought. He saluted with a tap of the hat's bill and gave Villisca a wink.

Jubal, who'd followed him up the stairs, nudged LaVoie's thigh with his elbow. "Come on, Billy Powell, get on with it," he hissed.

LaVoie had rarely seen him with such a mood upon him. "Yes, sir," he whispered from the corner of his mouth. He introduced the number-guessing trick to the audience and asked for a volunteer. On the other end of the first row he saw a group of four genial-looking people, two men, a woman, and a little girl. The age of the older of the two gentlemen was hard to gauge. He had gray hair, but an impressive girth filled in whatever wrinkles he might have had, giving him a nondescript face of undetermined years. The woman was also middle-aged and stout, but not as large as the older man. The younger fellow was balding and about thirty, the child about ten. She was waving her arms and yelling, "I will! I will!"

LaVoie called on the younger man. After the usual reticence and urging from the crowd, he stepped forward, but didn't come up on stage. "What's your name, sir?"

"Carl Hinman," the man said.

As soon as he spoke, LaVoie heard Jubal gasp, and then try to cover the gasp with a cough. It was all LaVoie could do to avoid breaking character and glaring at him. His behavior was peculiar, very peculiar indeed.

When LaVoie explained the trick, Hinman changed his mind. That probably meant the man couldn't read, and so wouldn't be able to confirm what number Jubal pulled from his vest. LaVoie had seen it many times before. "How about my girl?" Hinman said. "She wants to come up, and she goes to school, so she's real good with numbers."

Children were fine when things went well, and audiences loved them, but they were also harder to fool than adults. Their minds hadn't been cluttered with nonsense and conventions yet, so they didn't always look away when he wanted them to. "What do you think, little lady?"

Hinman motioned her onto the stage, but she was hesitant, holding her hands primly in front of her and gazing at her feet. LaVoie thought she looked wan, a little worse for wear. A week ago he would have offered to sell Hinman some liniment. Now, though, he simply called to her, "Do you really know your numbers?"

"Passably well, sir," she replied in a gentle voice he could scarcely hear.

"Will you join us on stage?"

The girl looked at Hinman, who nodded.

The audience hooted and applauded their approval as she climbed the steps. LaVoie met her at the top and escorted her to Jubal. Jubal's eyes rounded into something like terror and his face turned positively green. "Are you Carl Hinman's daughter?" he rasped to the child.

"Yes, and that's my grandfather Noah and my daddy's friend Mrs. Jensen."

LaVoie frowned at Jubal and said to the girl, "What's your name, child?"

"Mariel."

"Pleased to meet you, Mariel. My name is Major LaVoie."

She curtsied, which LaVoie found adorable. Despite Jubal's agitation, once they got started, the trick went off flawlessly. When they finished, Mariel returned to her family to yet more cheers. Jubal clapped his hand over his mouth and rushed offstage.

What in the hell?

LaVoie introduced the next act, Otto the World's Strongest Man, and hurried after Jubal.

He located him behind the main tent, bending over and retching.

"You should have told me you were ill," LaVoie said.

"You have no idea," Jubal said, clutching his sides. He was sucking for air, like that poor catfish LaVoie had found in a mudhole in southern Indiana.

"Will you be able to continue?"

"Dammit, Marc, do I *look* like I can continue?"

"Who'll run the slides for the Phantasmagoria?"

"Get Petey. You've got him doing everything else."

"Is that what this is all about?"

Jubal looked at him as if he were an ignoramus. "And André can work the trap door as well as I could. I've had enough."

With that he stumbled off into the darkness. LaVoie felt as if he'd been gored by an ox. He wanted to run him down and shake some sense into him, but Otto's act was a short one, and LaVoie would need to be on stage momentarily to introduce Ophelia, then Leopold, Herman, Giovanni, André, and "Guinevere Brewer"—or maybe not, with Villisca prowling about—before setting up for the Phantasmagoria and tonight's big finale, the disappearing act.

What in the hell, he thought again, and returned to the stage.

***

Peering around one of the tent's flaps during Giovanni's routine, LaVoie pointed out Villisca to Cuff.

"Don't know if I ever seen that one before," she said, "but he's got the look, all right."

On stage, Giovanni tilted his head back and effortlessly pushed the sword blade down his gullet. If Villisca was impressed, he didn't show it. He yawned and picked his nose.

"Are you sure you want to go on?" LaVoie said to Cuff. "We can skip you tonight. The disappearing act gives us enough to fill the show."

"What can he do in front of all these people?" she said. "Otto and the boys'll watch over me."

"He has a gun."

"Well, if he shoots me, you can shoot him."

LaVoie smiled at the notion. "That wouldn't be entirely unpleasant."

"Anyhow, I can't just run away and hide every time a slaver comes by. That ain't no way to live."

"Maybe you can," LaVoie said, snapping his fingers. "I have an idea."

***

The show continued smoothly. The Phantasmagoria, always a favorite, played out in its usual grand and macabre style. Petey timed the slides as well as Jubal ever had. In spite of the audience's delight, LaVoie paced back and forth behind the back curtain. He'd explained his new plan to André, Otto, and Petey, but this was all make-it-up-as-you-go. There was no time to rehearse. If anything went wrong, it would go disastrously wrong.

Cuff insisted on singing and playing her banjo. As she finished her encore tune, Villisca still hadn't made his move.

In a few seconds LaVoie would join her on stage. He tapped his boots three times on the stage to make sure André was ready with the trap door and received three knocks in response. Parting the curtain, he confirmed that Petey had taken his position on the side of the stage. Just as the applause began to fade, he made his entrance.

"Isn't she marvelous, ladies and gentlemen? Another hand for Miss Guinevere Brewer." As the applause rose again, he nodded to Petey, who stepped onto the stage carrying a blanket.

As Cuff turned to exit, LaVoie took hold of her arm and pointed her back toward the audience. "Such a performance deserves a more dramatic exit, don't you agree, Petey?"

Petey nodded enthusiastically. "Yes, sir, Major."

The crowd went silent.

"Tonight, friends, you will witness the daring, the magical, the impossible. A stupendous feat that will strike you dumb with amazement. For our final demonstration of legerdemain this evening, the young gentleman and I will make our lovely Guinevere disappear into thin air."

LaVoie glanced at Villisca, who didn't look pleased.

Neither did Cuff. "What d'you think you're doing, Marc?" she hissed under her breath.

"The little lady wants to know what I'm doing." LaVoie said to the audience. To Cuff he said in a loud, theatrical voice, "Making you disappear, my dear."

"I don't *want* to disappear."

The crowd laughed, undoubtedly thinking this was part of the act.

LaVoie whispered softly to her, "Don't, Cuff. I told you I had an idea. You said you'd do the trick if I wanted you to. Just play along. When we drop the blanket, André will open the trap door. Jump. He'll explain everything. I'll meet you in back of the tent afterward. Trust me."

"Can I take my banjo with me into the unknown?" she said loud enough for the audience to hear. They chuckled.

"Of course, my dear." Under his breath LaVoie said, "Deaden the strings as you jump."

He pulled Cuff into position behind the trap door. Petey handed him one end of the blanket. They stretched it out in front of her and raised it over her head. "Sing, Guinevere, sing," he cried.

Cuff gave him a dubious look, but nodded that she understood. She began an energetic verse of "Yankee Doodle."

"Are you ready, young sir?" he said to Petey.

"Yes, Major."

In a single, graceful motion, they snapped the blanket and let it float down over Cuff. Then he stomped his foot, startling the front row of spectators. The blanket settled flat on the stage floor. Cuff's voice and her banjo cut off abruptly, just before revealing where Yankee Doodle had stuck that feather, and poof, she was gone.

The audience gasped their astonishment. To their eyes, nobody had dropped beneath the stage. The mirrors had done their job.

Villisca rushed the stage during the applause, drawing his Colt Paterson. He pushed Petey aside and pointed the weapon at LaVoie's face. This reaction was what LaVoie had counted on.

"I've had enough of this horseshit," Villisca said.

"I see you found more bullets."

"I keep a supply. Now, Mr. Beddow wants his nigga back, and I'll have her. Or should I blow your head off and take her anyway? Where'd she go?"

Many in the audience were enthralled, hooting and guffawing as if this, too, were part of the act. This time, though, there was enough tension in their voices to indicate some had doubts.

LaVoie saw that the gun's trigger was still tucked, so the hammer wasn't cocked yet. That gave him part of one second to react. He turned to the spectators with an expression of innocence. "Whatsoever do you mean, sir?"

"Hand her over." He jabbed the barrel into LaVoie's chin.

Still part of the plan, but planning for the gun and experiencing it were different things. LaVoie could smell the turpentine Villisca had used to clean the barrel, even the gunpowder in the bullets. He was sweating under his clothes. He just hoped moisture didn't pop out on his face, as that would put the lie to his bravado. "I'm sorry, sir, but Guinevere has vanished into the ether, never to return."

"This ain't nothing but hornswoggle, LaVoie, and you know it. You're hiding her somewheres. Give her up." He cocked the Colt. "Do we understand one another?"

The crowd hushed. *Was* this part of the trick?

Raising a hand, LaVoie said, "I cannot. However, I can send you to her."

"What?" said Villisca, looking confused. Although dangerous, he was quite untroubled by intelligence. He eased his grip on the pistol.

"Ladies and gentlemen, a rare treat for your amusement. My assistant and I shall now make it possible for this most persistent fellow, Mr. Tom Villisca, to pursue our dear Guinevere into the depths of the Great Beyond." He turned and whispered to Villisca, "She's backstage behind the tent. Have André show you the way."

Before Villisca could react, LaVoie nodded to Petey.

As the blanket snapped over his head, Villisca said, "Now wait just a minute—"

LaVoie tapped his foot as the blanket fell over him. Villisca struggled underneath it, tangling his pistol in the folds. LaVoie heard André under the stage, desperately trying to pull the latch on the trap door again. He may have shoved it back into place too hard after Cuff came through.

LaVoie tapped a second time, more insistently. Be calm, André, he thought. Don't rush, just slide it nice and easy.

This time the door fell away. LaVoie and Petey held onto the blanket as Villisca fell through, giving it a little shake to allow it to settle peacefully onto the stage floor, the same as the first time.

Villisca started to cry out in alarm, but his voice was cut off in mid-scream. André was supposed to clasp his hand over the man's mouth and tell him to be quiet if he wanted to claim Cuff.

The audience, seeing the slave hunter's shape in the blanket dematerialize, apparently decided it was part of the act after all. They showed their appreciation with the wildest applause yet.

LaVoie and Petey bowed and made a quick exit through the back curtain. Most of the other acts were waiting there for the curtain call.

LaVoie nodded at them and told Petey to wait with them, then hurried down the stairs and out the back flap of the tent.

A just-past-full moon reflected enough light that the area directly behind the tent was in deep shadow. Cuff, however, was sitting in plain sight in the grass beyond the darkness, banjo on her lap, her form illuminated by the lunar glow. It would be impossible not to see her.

She smiled and nodded to LaVoie, as if to say: *I see what you're doing now*.

Villisca hadn't appeared yet. Good. He and André, on hands and knees, moved slowly enough for LaVoie to witness the festivities. He stepped to the side and ducked behind a stack of wooden crates used to transport their costumes.

Moments later Villisca emerged from the flaps.

Smiling demurely, Cuff gave him a "come hither" wiggle of the finger.

"No more running for you, Cuff Beddow. You're going straight back to your master."

"I guess you done fixed my flint good, mister," she said. "But thing is, my name ain't Beddow, he ain't my master, and I sure as hell ain't going nowhere with you."

Otto's meaty hand reached out from the shadows in a fold of the tent next to the flaps. He was clutching a long tent stake. LaVoie was standing right next to him and hadn't noticed him.

Neither did Villisca.

Otto lifted the stake and slammed it down hard on the back of the man's head. Villisca's cry of surprise and pain was masked by the continuing applause out front.

He crumpled to the ground, making no effort to break his fall. His face hit with a thud. Hopefully he was simply unconscious, but if it was more permanent, well, the world had too many slave hunters anyway.

LaVoie came out from behind the crates.

"Thank you, Otto," said LaVoie. "Did you hire the boat?"

Otto pointed to the river bank. "The Irish ferryman's gonna give him a little push. He'll be drifting down the Detroit and into Lake Erie by morning."

"Preferably on the Canadian side," said LaVoie. They all chuckled.

"Good plan you cooked up there," Cuff said. "You might've told me about it first."

"Didn't André explain?"

"Yeah, in what? The two seconds we had under there?"

LaVoie smiled and motioned to Otto. "Drag Mr. Villisca in and stuff him under the stage for now. Tie him up and gag him in case he comes to. We'll set him a-sail later. It's time to take our final bows."

They returned to the tent. The troupe, André and Petey now among them, gathered on either side of the stage, ready to parade out for the curtain call. As they stepped onto stage one at a time, LaVoie thought about the future of the show. If Jubal was truly done, Petey could take over his duties in the acts but not the finances. The rest would have to decide for themselves whether or not they'd stay on once he told them about the Underground Railroad. He was confident Otto would, probably Manfred, Giovanni, and Leopold, maybe Herman, and maybe not André.

But one way or the other, the show would continue. LaVoie would give the people the theatre they, and he, craved. Until this slavery business was settled, he'd be fooling people both on stage and off.

He wasn't a brave man, and he'd been frightened every moment Cyrus and Destiny had traveled with them. Cuff, too, if he were being honest with himself. On the other hand, he had to admit that the danger was exhilarating when confronted in the service of a worthwhile cause. Rather ironic, he thought with a mixture of anticipation and misgiving, that a former Canadian farmer would entangle himself in America's peculiar institution.

But in his dotage, when he was telling his stories, there'd no longer be a need for Osceola and the Seminole wars in Florida. No more Billy Powell. He could declare to the next generation, truthfully, *Yes, I was there. I did my part.*

For an old trickster, that wasn't such a bad legacy.

LaVoie, Petey, and Cuff walked out together. The audience, seeing Cuff, rose as one in spirited ovation. If they were disappointed that Villisca hadn't returned for his bows, too, they didn't show it.

As the three of them bathed in the glow of the crowd's adoration, Cuff tapped LaVoie on the shoulder. He leaned his head toward her.

"Ain't no turning back now," she whispered.

CHAPTER 50: JUBAL
"Hell is empty, and all the devils are here"

It was Tuesday, February 10, 1846, a cold night with huge flakes of snow drifting to the ground and coating the winter's previous crust in a glittery patina of white. At least there was no wind. Mrs. Claire Hinman had been invited to dine at the house before going to the theatre. *Much Ado About Nothing* was on the bill tonight. As per the plan, the driver who'd brought her here had been sent on another errand, and Jubal had taken his place. Shivering inside the coach, he waited for them to emerge from the house.

He fidgeted with the knife, moving it from hand to hand. Yes, he'd opened the account, he'd signed the bank draft, but he didn't have to do *this*. There was still time to back out. Simply refuse to go through with it and drive them to the playhouse. Another night, another performance, and everybody goes home.

But Annalee could be very persuasive. "Ah, *mon petit chou*," she'd said, "would I ask this of you if I were not truly in danger? She plays sweet, but she's just biding her time. 'Oh, that one may smile and smile and be a villain.' I confess to having had a dalliance with her husband, but that ended some time ago. I am fonder of her than I ever was of him. I regret the betrayal, and have been trying to make amends by cultivating her love of theatre. I halted the *tête-à-têtes* with Carl, and have paid for her admission to the playhouse ever since. She must have learned of the affair. It's in the things she lets slip, the little biting comments, the veiled threats. She means to do me harm."

"Just stop seeing her," Jubal had said. "Don't let her near you."

"And spend the rest of my life looking over my shoulder? How would you feel if something happened to me? Something you could have prevented?"

They'd been alone in the house when the plot was hatched. Annalee had been wearing only her robe, which she'd casually let fall open as she spoke. "Please, cousin? If you do this for me, I believe I can persuade Mr. Kürten to release you from your contract, and you'll be free to leave with that French fellow's whatever-you-call-it. You'll only have to don those ridiculous shoes one more time."

Those gigantic shoes were on the carriage seat now. Jubal placed the knife next to them, checked his pocket watch, then sat on his hands for warmth. He could see his breath. She'd promised they'd be finished dining by six. The play started promptly at seven-thirty.

You don't have to do this, he told himself.

You don't have to do this.

But if Mrs. Hinman really meant to hurt Annalee.…

He took off his boots and put on the hated shoes Kürten made him wear. One more time.

The front door to the house opened, and yellow lamp light spilled out onto the lane. Annalee and Mrs. Hinman appeared in the doorway. Jubal couldn't hear what was being said, but they were laughing. Annalee lightly touched Mrs. Hinman's arm the way ladies did sometimes. As they approached the carriage, Jubal slid the knife up his sleeve, still uncertain he could muster the courage and anger he'd need to use it. He climbed out and held the door open. Despite the cold, he was sweating. No matter how hard he breathed he couldn't seem to take in enough air.

The women stopped before him. There was a lamppost on either side of the lane. Their light illuminated Mrs. Hinman's face and gleamed in her eyes. She was radiant, almost as beautiful as Annalee.

She cocked her head at him in exactly the same manner as a dog does when it hears a strange sound.

"Mrs. Hinman," Annalee said, "allow me to introduce you to my cousin Jubal Lawson. Our other driver was called away, so Jubal will be taking us to the play tonight."

Mrs. Hinman smiled and patted his cheek. "Well, aren't you cute?" she said.

Cute.

God damn it.

Annalee entered the coach first. Jubal offered Mrs. Hinman his left hand. He glanced at Annalee, who nodded. He let the knife slip down his sleeve and into his right hand. Its metal handle felt cold in his grip.

Well, aren't you cute.

He drew his arm back and plunged the blade between the ribs in the middle of her back, then withdrew it quickly, as if the length of time it spent in her body would somehow minimize his guilt. "Oh!" she gasped as she slumped forward into Annalee's lap.

She managed to turn her head up to Annalee, who was smiling triumphantly.

"Why?" Mrs. Hinman said, the last word she would ever speak.

Jubal felt sick. He leaned back against the wheel of the carriage and wept.

"Stop that nonsense," Annalee said. "Lift her legs inside and close the door. You know where to go."

Jubal couldn't stop crying. He wiped his eyes, but it was useless. After slipping the knife into his coat pocket and pushing Mrs. Hinman into the carriage, he climbed onto the driver's seat, tears channeling down his face. His hands shook as he took up the reins, which had nothing to do with the cold. When he clicked his tongue at the horse, the carriage lurched forward. It wasn't far, an open field just beyond Annalee's property line. They were there in minutes.

Jubal hopped down and opened the door. He glared at Annalee.

She laughed, a flippant little giggle like she might have made if he'd told an indecent joke. "You carry on so," she said.

Mrs. Hinman's winter coat had soaked up much of the blood. Jubal pulled her from the carriage and held her in his arms. She wasn't heavy, but then he'd always been stronger than he appeared.

"Come along," Annalee said. "It's almost over."

The shoes he hated so much were only big when he wore them. They'd fit a normal-sized man perfectly. A man like Carl Hinman.

Annalee walked beside him into the field. She held her dress up to avoid soiling it in the snow. Though they brought no light and the clouds obscured the moon, it never got truly dark in the winter. Snow seemed to provide its own luminescence.

When they were sufficiently far off the road she said, "Well, drop her."

Instead, Jubal laid her down gently. Mrs. Hinman moaned.

"She's still alive," Annalee observed.

"I won't stab her again."

"Do you want the poor thing to suffer?"

Jubal knelt beside her. All color had drained from her face, and blood trickled from her mouth. The blade must have pierced a lung. Her eyes were open and fluttering, but she wasn't seeing anything. He took the knife from his pocket. His hand was tiny, and its handle extended several inches beyond his grip. He turned it around, using the guard to protect his fingers from the blade. "Forgive me," Jubal said, brushing her cheek with his fingers. He turned her face away and, with all his strength, clubbed her in the back of the head with the butt end of the knife.

She exhaled one more time. Jubal watched her final breath rise like white mist and dissipate in the cold winter air.

It was done.

He looked up at Annalee. She smiled coquettishly.

"Now what?" he said.

"Carry me back to the carriage like we discussed."

Her plan was brilliant. It was diabolical: Two sets of footprints leading into the field, one set leading out. One male, one female. Only the male came out.

"I should plant this knife between your pretty bosoms," he said.

"But you won't," she said, opening her arms to allow him to pick her up.

He thrust the knife toward her. "I believe this is yours."

She examined Mrs. Hinman's blood on the blade. "'Out, damned spot,'" she said, chuckling at her own cleverness, then tucked the weapon inside her coat.

Jubal placed one hand around her waist and the other beneath her knees and bore her from the field to the coach.

When they arrived at her house she presented him with an envelope. "Take this letter to Constable Nortman. Then," she added with an angelic smile, "this matter will be behind us and Carl Hinman will spend the rest of his life in prison."

"I will never speak to you again," Jubal said.

"Yes, you will," she said, placing his hands on her breasts.

And he did.

✳✳✳✳

Within the week Annalee had followed through on her promise to free him from Kürten's clutches, deploying her usual method of persuasion. Furious, Kürten later rightly claimed he'd been duped, believing Annalee's seduction was LaVoie's doing. He and the Major had still been negotiating the price of Jubal's release when Annalee showed up.

Before Jubal had departed with the medicine show, he and Annalee were on friendly terms again, much to his initial chagrin. He'd been amazed and appalled at how quickly even the most revolting crime could be rationalized, self-forgiven, and nearly forgotten. Either he was a monster who'd taken the life of an innocent woman, or he was a hero, saving his cousin from certain death.

Jubal had chosen the latter. If he told himself the lie often enough, he would come to believe it. He *had* to believe it.

Belief didn't take long. By the time he'd left Detroit, a few weeks later, he and Annalee were laughing together and behaving as if nothing had happened, much as they'd always done in their youth following a misadventure. As he'd walked out her door that last day, she stooped to kiss his cheek. "Write to me?" she'd said.

***

He made it through the number trick, no fumbles, no pulling out the wrong paper, no shouts of fraud like in Jeffersonville. He bowed to the Belgrade audience's applause, favoring them with the broadest false smile he could muster. Then he bolted from the stage.

LaVoie followed him behind the tent. They spoke briefly, and then his final night with the medicine show was over.

After parting with LaVoie, Jubal returned to his wagon and packed a small suitcase. Petey was preparing for the disappearing act, so Jubal knew Chelsea was no longer in use tonight. He made his way to the lean-to, saddled her, and climbed up. Without a look back, he rode into the darkness, taking the main road through Belgrade. He found lodging in an inn north of town just as fireworks lit up the sky. Chelsea didn't much care for the explosions, but he'd brought a bag of oats, and that seemed to mollify her after he stabled her behind the inn.

Sleep was impossible. His stomach was still unsettled, and the Independence Day celebration lasted well past midnight. He could hear the fireworks bursting and, even at this distance, the crowd applauding for particularly spectacular displays. In the quiet following the festivities, he alternated between pacing and lying on the bed to stare at the ceiling. He kept the chamber pot at the ready, but didn't vomit again. Sometime after sunrise he gave up any notion of rest, settled with the innkeeper, and retrieved Chelsea.

His destination was not far, two or three hours, depending upon how hard he chose to push the pony. He wasn't sure what he meant to do, so he was in no hurry to do it. Around nine a.m. he turned up a familiar lane. At the house he dismounted, tethered Chelsea to the post, and knocked on the front door.

It was Sunday morning, 4 July, so perhaps the servants hadn't arrived yet, or possibly they'd been given the holiday off. Whatever the reason, Annalee herself answered, already dressed for the day in a modest blue dress. Though passably pious when it suited her purposes, she attended church only when one of her Lotharios insisted on it. Since that rarely happened, Jubal had been confident she'd be home.

And here she was.

Her face lit up when she saw him. "Cousin Jubal," she beamed, and cradled his head to her stomach. "A courier just delivered your latest letter a few days ago. I had hoped you would visit, but I didn't expect it to be so soon."

"Am I interrupting anything?"

"No, of course not."

"May I come in?"

"Please. Join me in the pantry."

The house was exactly as it had been when he was last here over a year ago: the Georgian furniture, the latticed mahogany woodwork, the silk cushions, the magnificent pendulum clock, everything. Indeed, the place was no different than when he'd arrived here from Boston in 1826, except that with the death of her parents Annalee was now the mistress of the estate.

The pantry was dark and smelled of kerosene. A small lamp occupied its usual place in the center of the table where they'd often sipped tea together. Its wick barely glowed. Annalee turned the knob to bring up the flame, filling the room with a harsh yellow light. Jubal climbed into the seat. Annelee sat next to him.

"How have you been, Cousin?" he asked.

"I have a troublesome beau," she laughed, "but then, I'm used to that, aren't I? I'm so happy to see you."

Jubal pulled the lamp closer and watched the flame. Despite the luxury displayed throughout the house, the lamp was an inexpensive one, with a thin and brittle glass bowl holding the kerosene. "May I ask you something?" he said.

"We have no secrets between us."

Jubal looked her in the eyes. "Did you know Claire Hinman had a daughter?"

Annalee appeared taken aback by the question. "We have no secrets, but I thought we agreed never to speak of that again."

Without changing his inflection, Jubal said again, "Did you know Claire Hinman had a daughter?"

Annalee paused, then shrugged. "Well, how could I not, silly? Carl babbled on about her incessantly. Mariel, Mariel, Mariel. It became quite tedious."

"So I took a little girl's mother away from her. You know how fond I am of children."

"This little girl, who you never met, is more important to you than my *life*?"

"I did meet her. Last night."

Annalee's face showed surprise and perhaps a tinge of alarm. "Claire would have killed me. You know she would."

"The only harm Mrs. Hinman ever did you was to your pride, and she didn't intend that. I'll wager you didn't leave Hinman, he left you. You didn't even care about him, only that he chose his wife over you."

"Do you think so little of me? That I would have a woman killed out of spite for her husband?"

"I knew you were vain, but I never realized the extent of it."

"Jubal. Cousin. Every family is plagued by misfortune. My own parents died, yet I survived. Thrived, actually. These are the things that make us strong." She looked genuinely confused. "Isn't it a bit late for remorse?"

"You know how fond I am of children," he repeated.

Jubal removed the glass globe from the top of the lamp and set it on the table. Without warning he flung the bowl at Annalee's head, the force of the blow knocking her backward onto the floor. The glass shattered on contact, cutting her in several places and sending kerosene cascading down her face and chest. Her hair, skin, and dress ignited in a fireball of heat and agony.

Annalee shrieked and beat at her face with her bare hands.

Jubal watched her writhe and scream. He let her burn for a few moments before retrieving a pillow from the sofa and using it to smother the flames.

She didn't die. He didn't want her to die.

Her lovely countenance, her sensuous lips, her manipulative tongue, and her perfect, perfect breasts were now a mass of blood, blisters, and blackened, shriveled skin.

"Now," Jubal said, "the world will see you as you really are."

***

Annalee was mistaken about one thing: the night Jubal killed Claire Hinman was not the last time he would wear the oversized shoes. He had them on now, along with the silken blouse with lace cuffs, the waistcoat, the round cap, and the funny pantaloons.

He stepped out onto the stage. Unlike the medicine show, Kürten had a permanent location. The crowd was sparse. Those few were already guffawing before he started his routine.

Their ridicule was fine. Their scorn, their contempt, their thoughtless arrogance, Jubal welcomed it all. Let them throw eggs and rotting vegetables if that's what they wanted.

Claire Hinman had had a daughter. If Jubal spent the rest of his life juggling and dancing like a trained monkey, it would be so much better than he deserved.

LETTER TO A FRIEND
1849

CHAPTER 51: BILL, 1849
"Cut him out in little stars,
and he will make the face of heaven"

Bill and his friend Samuels, the bosun of the *Titus*, entered the *Anchor & Dolphin* late on a warm night in October. The inn was dark, as always, and, as always, crowded with sailors trying to go broke indulging their chosen vice, be it spirits, women, cards, or dice. Or each of them in their turn.

The latest voyage on the *Titus* had been a success. Bill bragged to the barkeep Lowe that they'd brought back enough whale blubber to light every lamp in Portsmouth for a year. Lowe shrugged. His gnarled nose seemed to have grown redder and more grotesque since Bill last saw him. "More money for you, more money for me. What'll you have?"

"Whisky," Samuels said.

"Beer for me," Bill said. He wasn't averse to getting drunk, but tonight hard liquor didn't appeal to him. Drinks in hand, he and Samuels had just started toward their comrades at a back table when Lowe called, "Hey, Short Bill, I just remembered. Before you sit down, a letter came for you some months back. Let me see, where did I put it?"

"Go on, mate," Bill said to Samuels, "I'll join you in a moment."

As he returned to the bar, Lowe pulled a stack of mildewed papers and other trash from beneath the counter. It contained envelopes, bills, receipts, a log book, crumpled notes, stained rags, labels from bottles, a small burlap bag, and what appeared to be a woman's corset, all covered with layers of cobwebs, oil, and filth.

"Wondered where that went," Lowe said, holding up the corset. "Lord, was she spitting mad at me when she left that night."

"How do you stay in business?" Bill said.

"My good looks and congenial nature," he said. He picked at a scab on the top of his head, then coughed up some phlegm and spit it into a cuspidor beside him. "Now shut your pan and help me look. Has your name on it."

They dug through the mess for several minutes before Bill found it. "Who's it from?"

"How in hell would I know? Do you think I read other people's mail? You're lucky it was in the first pile."

Bill smiled and examined the envelope. *William Short, Anchor & Dolphin, Portsmouth, New Hampshire.* It bore a postage stamp, the government's fancy idea from two years ago. "Thanks," he said, and started back toward his table.

"Think nothing of it," Lowe said with a twinkle in his eye. "It's from Blackbourne."

Noah. Bill's heart fluttered. Noah.

Samuels and their friends at the table could wait. Good news or bad, this letter was a private matter, so he headed for the door, waggling a finger at Lowe on the way out: *Shame on you.*

The barkeep waved him off. "Bah. Have your mail sent somewhere else, then."

Outside, lamps illuminated either side of the door to the inn. Bill leaned against the wall. His hands trembled as he opened the envelope and held the letter under the lamp's flame.

As he read and reread Noah's scribbled handwriting, tears filled his eyes and he broke into a big grin.

First mate of my heart, it ended, *I am becalmed in a place of peace. I wish you fair winds and fallowing seas.*

When he had memorized every word, he folded the paper and tucked it inside his vest pocket. The music of swooping gulls and lapping waves washed over the harbor on this autumn evening. Bill walked to the end of the peer and sat down. Noah had carved Claire's name here two years ago. He traced the weathered grooves with his fingers.

Rows of boats bobbed against their moorings. The sky was clear and the stars ablaze with distant fire.

Bill looked up. If he watched long enough, he would see their slow migration across the heavens. He didn't know if it was the stars or the earth that moved, but night after night the majestic panorama wheeled around to inspire his sense of mystery and wonder.

END

ACKNOWLEDGMENTS

Many people have helped make this book possible. For being beta readers, special thanks to Betty Adams, the late Maggie Elliot, Katherine Gannett, Terry Hertges, Carol Kean, Carole Kern, Nora Meierotto, Karen Nortman, Bob Schott, and Diana Weiss-Hoffman.

And of course, a big thanks to Reagan Rothe and the editors at Black Rose Writing for all their expertise in bringing *Shun the Heaven* to fruition.

We used the names of friends and acquaintances for many of the characters. All of these names are used fictitiously and do not reflect the authors' opinions of the actual people. It's just our way of winking and saying hi. We extend our gratitude to the following people: Cindy Bancroft, Alonzo Beckham, the late Julie Ann Beddow, Kristin Beermann, Seth Bemis, Kelly Brumm, Paige Buns, Destiny Cyrus, Whitney DeVilbiss, Jessica Slade Dunagan, Kendra Finch, the late Clarence Paul Finch, Joanna Freking-Smith, Zach Freking-Smith, Katherine Gannett, Pam Garrett, the late Ed Gorman, Jovan Hampton, Lu Hileman, the late Estella Hinman Hoing, Annalee Hollingsworth, Chuck Hosier, Mallory Hymes, Janeen Jensen, the late Beryl Kelley, Kenzie Koerselman, Julie Krause, Ciara Lewis, Alison Leytem, Zach Lowe, the late Jane Mangin, Chelsea McNamee, the late Alvin Miller, Karen Nortman, Sue Olive, Dave Ralston, Nurse Rebecca, Marykaye Barnes Roberts, Evelyn Russell, Vicki St. James, and Bob Spielbauer.

The names of historical personages pop up occasionally. Sharp-eyed readers might even catch a glimpse of a very young George Armstrong Custer. However, the most important of the real-life figures in our story is Samuel Zug, who was a wealthy furniture maker in Detroit in the mid-nineteenth century. Although Zug was an abolitionist as portrayed, his role in bringing a medicine show to Belgrade, Michigan, is entirely the product of the authors' imagination.

ABOUT THE AUTHORS

Dave Hoing is retired from the Rod Library at the University of Northern Iowa, where he was a Library Associate in the Special Collections and Archives unit. His tenure there could be measured on a geologic time scale, and he was often mistaken for one of the artifacts.

In his other life, from which he has not retired, he is a member of Science Fiction and Fantasy Writers of America, although he now concentrates primarily on literary and historical fiction. In addition to writing, he pokes his fingers into a lot of other creative pies, dabbling in composing, drawing, painting, and sculpting. Music is his first love, but he concedes that he's better at stringing words together than notes, so there are times when he must tear himself away from one kind of keyboard to work at another. He also enjoys traveling and collecting books printed before 1800.

Dave lives in Hudson, Iowa, with his wife Joni and two cats, Squeakers and Wiggle. His adult stepchildren, Jon and Jovan, have emigrated to the fantasy land known as California.

Roger Hileman is (mostly) retired from the University of Iowa College of Public Health, and now divides his time between his two passions, writing and music. He gigs around Iowa with jazz bands and brass groups, directs a brass choir, sings in his church's chorus, and writes musical arrangements for all of the above. He began his writing career as a playwright and screenwriter, but turned to prose when writing with Dave. Roger also enjoys history, especially the family kind, so his ancestors frequently become fodder for his fiction.

In addition to his published works with Dave Hoing, Roger has edited and published *A Biographical Sketch of Michael Hileman, Jr.*, his great-great uncle who lived from 1820-1915.

Roger lives with his wife Lu in Iowa City, near most of their three daughters and four grandchildren. He claims to have no pets, but he plays a bass trombone he calls Eddie.

NOTE FROM
DAVE HOING & ROGER HILEMAN

Word-of-mouth is crucial for any author to succeed. If you enjoyed *Shun the Heaven*, please leave a review online—anywhere you are able. Even if it's just a sentence or two. It would make all the difference and would be very much appreciated.

Thanks!
DAVE HOING & ROGER HILEMAN

We hope you enjoyed reading this title from:

www.blackrosewriting.com

Subscribe to our mailing list – *The Rosevine* – and receive **FREE** books, daily
deals, and stay current with news about upcoming
releases and our hottest authors.
Scan the QR code below to sign up.

Already a subscriber? Please accept a sincere thank you for being a fan of
Black Rose Writing authors.

View other Black Rose Writing titles at
www.blackrosewriting.com/books and use promo code
PRINT to receive a **20% discount** when purchasing.